A
HANDFUL
OF ASHES

Also by Rob McCarthy

The Hollow Men

A
HANDFUL
OF ASHES

ROB McCARTHY

PEGASUS CRIME

NEW YORK LONDON

A Handful of Ashes

Pegasus Books Ltd
148 West 37th Street, 13th Floor
New York, NY 10018

First Pegasus Books hardcover edition May 2018

ISBN: 978-1-68177-771-9

10 9 8 7 6 5 4 3 2 1

Printed in the United States of America
Distributed by W. W. Norton & Company, Inc.

'The fool, fixed in his folly, may think
He can turn the wheel on which he turns.'

T.S. Eliot

ONE

Sunday, 24 August
Early Morning

The woman who'd tried to kill her husband stank of aniseed and alcohol. The stench hung off the walls, the mattress, every strand of hair. She was lying on the flat mattress against one wall of the cell, dressed in the standard white zip-up jumpsuit, her clothes long since taken into evidence. But the sterile clothing didn't cover the scratches on her arms, hands and face, which were starting to heal, though no scabs had yet formed.

These observations told Harry Kent two things about his patient. It was likely that her wounds weren't healing because her liver wasn't making the clotting factors that process required. And liver dysfunction in an otherwise healthy thirty-four-year-old woman was more than likely related to the stench of Sambuca that had struck him as he'd opened the door to the cell.

'Who the fuckin' hell are you?'

Her accent straight off the television, not unlike his own before medical school had blunted it. Harry noted the Millwall FC tattoo on her wrist as she stood up. All eighteen stone of Keziah Barnes, the custody sergeant, followed him in. The patient sat down again.

'Morning, Mrs Wright,' Harry said. 'I'm a doctor.'

At about five o'clock the previous evening, Pauline Wright had smashed a bottle of extra-value Morrison's sambuca into the face of her husband of twelve years. The husband was now at the John Ruskin University Hospital, where Harry usually worked, being monitored for the seizure he'd suffered after the impact. Thirty-eight-year-old men didn't often have seizures, but thirty-eight-year-old alcoholics who'd killed off a decent proportion of their brain cells did. He'd pull through. At the time, Harry had been told, the seventy-centilitre bottle was almost empty, having been drunk by Mrs Wright's husband. That had been the cause of the argument, it appeared. One drunk stealing the other one's liquor. By all accounts, Pauline Wright had not had a drink in what was fast approaching twelve hours. It showed.

'Jesus, you've got to put me under. These bastards have been treating me like shit.'

Barnes had told a different story, along the lines of requiring four officers to drag Mrs Wright from the police van into A&E for a quick check over, then back into the van, and then finally into the custody suite. It had taken the threat of sedation at the hospital to calm her down.

'I'm sorry to hear that,' Harry said, crouching down and putting his bag on the floor. 'I'd like to examine you, if that's ok?'

'Be my guest,' said Wright. 'Does that bitch have to be here?'

Barnes was behind him, but Harry could feel the custody sergeant's sarcastic smile burning into the back of his head.

'I'm afraid so,' said Harry. 'That's to protect you as much as it is to protect me.'

'Fuckin' pigs.'

Wright scratched at her neck, and Harry watched her hand as it rested back on her lap. The tremor was noticeable, one that he had seen thousands of times before. It confirmed the diagnosis that he'd suspected the moment he'd walked in the door.

'How are you feeling at the moment?' Harry said.

'Shit. I've been throwing up all night. Haven't slept a fuckin' wink thanks to these cunts, and I woke up in my own crap.'

Harry nodded.

'Are you in any pain?'

'Got the worst fuckin' headache in the world, and the bastards won't even give me a fuckin' paracetamol.'

'Well, I'll try and sort that out for you,' Harry said. 'But I need to assess you first to make sure there's nothing serious going on.'

'You go right ahead, mate.'

Harry reached into his bag and pulled his stethoscope around his neck, picking up a blood-pressure cuff, and fastening it around his patient's arm.

'Have you got any medical conditions?'

'No.'

'Are you on any medication?'

She had a good, strong pulse in her elbow. A little fast, but that wasn't unusual in someone undergoing alcohol withdrawal.

'Citalopram. For depression. But I ain't took none in ages.'

'Any other drug usage?'

'You what?'

4

Harry sighed. 'Anything you say to me is covered by doctor-patient confidentiality. They can't use it against you in court.'

Maybe the two-thousandth time he'd said that in almost two years as a Force Medical Examiner. It was necessary, though. Even if their life depended on it, patients would keep quiet about important but incriminating details if there was anyone in uniform present.

'Bollocks,' said Pauline Wright.

'Sue me if I'm lying,' said Harry. 'I promise you, you'll win, and you'll get at least fifty grand.'

That line usually produced a laugh, but Wright just stared at him, her eyes and teeth yellow, her hair grey before its time. He pressed ahead with the question nonetheless, as he started to inflate the blood pressure cuff.

'Do you take any recreational drugs?'

'No.'

'Have you ever?'

'Done a bit of everything when I was a kid. Nothing really did it for me.'

Harry took the blood pressure, which was normal. The doctor at the A&E had done a basic assessment of her injuries, which were numerous but superficial, and had deemed her not to require hospital admission. At the time, she had noted that Wright had been agitated and intoxicated – she had also taken blood at the police's request for toxicology testing. Now Wright had sobered up, she was rapidly going cold turkey, and Harry's job was to decide whether she was safe to remain in the cells and await interview from the detectives who'd arrive in the morning. An attack as serious as the one her husband had sustained could go down as attempted murder if the duty prosecutor was feeling particularly confident.

'How much did you have to drink yesterday?'

'Few in the pub before the game, few cans in the park afterwards,' said Wright. 'Came home and the bastard's had me fuckin' sambuca.'

The second home game of the season had seen the Lions defeated to Rotherham, sending the Den's diehards into their infamous belligerence with the expected consequences for the emergency services. It had been a hectic evening in A&E at the

5

Ruskin, so he'd heard, and he was glad to be spending his night shift on-call for the police instead of working there.

'How many's a few, Mrs Wright?' Harry said. 'I need to know.'

'Might've been five. Might've been twelve. Fuck off.'

'And how have you been feeling tonight?'

'I fuckin' told you. Shit. Shat myself, and puked me guts up.'

'And when was that?'

'I dunno,' said Wright. 'I don't know what fuckin' time it is.'

She scratched at her arms and snapped her head up at Barnes, who was shaking her head and muttering something. It was only a minor gesture, but it triggered an explosion from the woman in the cell.

'Dunno what the bloody hell you're shakin' yer head at, you slag!' Wright shouted. 'This place is a fuckin' mess. Covered in shit, all these fuckin' maggots, it's a health risk!'

'Ha!' Barnes said, turning to Harry. 'Don't listen to her, Doc. Maggots, eh? That's a new one, love.'

Harry knew there weren't any maggots in the cell, but he was fairly sure that Wright wasn't making it up. She was seeing them, and probably feeling them too, crawling up her skin. If her hallucinations were similar to the ones he'd known patients experience before, this could be an entirely new presentation of something more sinister. But Wright had no history of mental illness aside from her alcoholism.

'Tell me about the maggots, Pauline,' Harry said, trying to stay calm.

'They're all over me,' Wright said, scratching at her arms again, 'I can't get 'em off. I can't get no sleep.'

'I see,' said Harry. 'Mrs Wright, I'm going to take some blood to take back to the hospital for a few tests, if that's ok. Then I'm going to give you some pills and an injection to calm you down.'

'You do whatever the fuck you like, mate. Don't give a fuck.'

The first few weeks he'd worked with the police, Harry had insisted on proper, informed consent before every injection, every blood test. But the woman in front of him had withdrawal so extreme that she was hallucinating after just eleven hours without a tipple, and barely had the capacity to consent to a haircut, let alone a medical treatment.

Wright stayed mercifully still as Harry found a vein, took three tubes of blood for tests, and drew up the haloperidol into a syringe from the drugs packet in his bag. He injected it into her thigh, pushing the syringe in slowly. He could have given her tablets, but she'd just have vomited them back up.

'There you go,' he said.

'Cheers, doc.'

Harry picked up the bag, and shuffled towards the door. He never turned his back on them, even if they were beaten-looking women with visions of maggots crawling up their skin. Barnes shut the door, Pauline Wright yelling after her.

'Yeah, you lock it, you cunt-licking bitch.'

Barnes locked the door with the ever-present smile, shaking her head.

'Lovely customer,' she said.

Harry was about to reply when they were interrupted by a detective he recognised striding into the corridor. DS Moses Wilson's loose, crumpled shirt, coffee-stained jeans and three days' worth of stubble combined with the bags under his eyes to tell Harry that he was the CID sergeant on overnight duty, and was probably working the whole weekend. He would have caught the case, and he'd want nothing more than to wrap it up with a quick confession, so whoever was coming in later in the morning could have her charged by Monday.

'Nice to see you, Harry,' Wilson said, shaking his hand. 'Homicide & Serious should be here by eight, tell me we're good to go.'

'Sorry, Mo,' Harry said. 'She's cold turkey. I had to give her a shot to calm her down.'

'Ah, come on!'

Wilson stamped his foot on the floor.

'No way we could speak to the duty solicitor? Ok it with her?'

Harry shook his head. It was a conversation he'd had many times, usually like this. Tired detectives wanting to wrap up the preliminary work on a case before they went off-rota. But whenever a suspect had mental health issues or had been under the influence, a doctor had to declare them fit to be interviewed before CID could sit down with them.

'Look, Mo, even if you get the lawyers on-side, if it gets to court then you'd be screwed. You know I'd have no choice but to testify that I thought she wasn't fit to be interviewed.'

'Sorry, Harry, I come back on tonight at six, and I don't want to have this shit waiting on my desk.'

'I get it,' said Harry. 'I'm—'

A shrill ringing in a descending modal scale cut him off, the sound of his work phone. He nodded an apology to a pissed-off Wilson, and took the call.

'Harry Kent.'

'Are you the on-call FME?'

'Speaking,' said Harry.

The voice, female and distinctly Geordie, sounded far too happy for the early hour of the morning. 'Requesting your services on Calais Street, Myatt's Fields, if it's not too much trouble. We've got a certification for you to do.'

He had never heard of the road before, but he knew Myatt's Fields, sandwiched within a concrete triangle of Camberwell to the east, Stockwell to the west, and Brixton to the south, a mix of tall Edwardian terraces, leafy green streets, and two brutalist housing estates, not too far from the hospital where he worked. A few of his colleagues lived in the area.

'Right,' said Harry, 'What does it look like?'

He usually tried to find out a little more when he was asked to certify death at potential crime scenes. If the act had occurred within the past half hour, or the circumstances were at all ambiguous, it might be worth dispatching an ambulance and starting resuscitation efforts. It had never happened to Harry, arriving to find a body potentially alive, but there had been a highly publicised case recently in Scotland. A man dragged from the River Ness, hypothermic and half-drowned, and assumed dead by both the local cops and the on-call Force Medical Examiner, only to show signs of life in the mortuary.

'I'm DS McGovern, with the Homicide Assessment Team. We have a female in her forties who's slashed her wrists. Looks like a suicide, but we're keeping an open mind.'

'No signs of life?' Harry confirmed. At the question, Wilson got up off the wall he'd been leaning against, his interest piqued.

'She's cold,' the detective said. 'Dead as Elvis. Paramedics took one look and got the hell out of there. Girlfriend came home from a bender and found her, the poor thing. There's blood all over the place, like.'

'Ok, then,' said Harry.

'How long do you reckon you'll be?'

'I'm at Walworth nick,' said Harry. 'I've just seen a patient here, so I can't leave for a few minutes, I need to write it up.' He checked his watch. 'Should be there by five, though.'

'No bother,' said McGovern. 'The DCI just wanted to know, that's all.'

Harry rang off, stabbing his phone's screen with a finger and shaking his head. Wilson gave a weary laugh, the laugh of a man at the very edge of his sleep cycle.

'Anything fun?' he said.

'Cert waiting for me down in Myatt's Fields. Suicide, apparently.'

'Good timing,' he said. 'Bet you they're a night-shifter.'

Just like Harry, and presumably the detective who'd just called him, Wilson was working a twelve-hour overnight shift, and had been for the whole weekend. Unless it was an emergency, a job two hours from finishing a night shift, just like this one, was the perfect opportunity to string things out a bit, meaning that he'd finish up and become available at about six twenty-nine, when he could usually avoid another job in the minute before he clocked off.

Harry slipped the tubes of Pauline Wright's blood into a zip-lock bag, and handed it to Wilson.

'Give those to the custody nurse,' he said. 'I've written the orders for which tests to send for.'

'And the interview?'

'I've given her a decent dose of haloperidol, and there's a prescription with the nurse for some chlordiazepoxide if she needs some. She'll be knocked out until about lunchtime. Get the guy who's on tomorrow to assess her. Sorry I couldn't have been more help.'

Wilson was pissed off, and Harry sympathised. After arresting a suspect, the police only had twenty-four hours, and then it was charge and release. By the time she was sober and in a state to be interviewed, Pauline Wright's time would almost be up. CID could apply to a judge for an extension, but Harry suspected they wouldn't bother. The case would be open-and-shut – Wright would be charged nonetheless, and she'd do the rest of her detox in the infirmary at Holloway Women's Prison awaiting trial.

'Not your fault,' said Wilson, yawning. 'It was good to see you anyway. When are you on the telly?'

'Monday night.'

A month ago, Harry had recorded a segment for *Crimewatch*, along with some detectives from the Specialist Case Investigation team. The subject was a patient he'd treated back in August 2011, a young woman brutally attacked in the midst of the worst riots London had seen that side of the millennium. She was still in hospital in a minimally conscious state, and despite the police's efforts she still had no name, no identity, and any chance of discovering who had beaten her into a three-year coma appeared slim at best. In the absence of clues to her real name, they called her Zara, based on a clothing label. Monday would mark just over three years since she had been left for dead in an alleyway off Eccles Road, and Harry had managed to persuade a cold-case team from the Met to put out an appeal. He'd been the first doctor to see her in A&E, so he and the neurologist who oversaw her care had recorded soundbites.

'Well I hope you get something good,' Wilson said. 'I'll be watching.'

Harry thanked him and turned to leave. As he did, a thought emerged from behind the clouds in his mind, the final words of the Geordie detective on the phone still ringing in his ears.

'Mo?'

Wilson turned around. 'Yeah?'

'How normal is it for the DCI on the Homicide Assessment Team to attend the scene?'

'It's completely routine if it's obviously a murder,' Wilson said. 'They tend to be too busy otherwise. Send the grunts in and let them make the call.'

'Hmm,' said Harry. He often encountered the HAT at the sudden deaths he was called to, detectives from whatever Homicide

& Serious team were on the rota for new cases that week. In the vast majority of cases, they concurred with the opinion of everyone present that the death was non-suspicious, signed off and left the investigation to the coroner. Harry checked his watch again. 4:35 a.m. He'd done police work getting on for two years now, and he'd never seen a DCI at a suicide, let alone in the middle of the night.

'Who called you?' Wilson said.

'McGovern,' said Harry. 'Geordie girl.'

'Ah,' said Wilson. 'She's new, with Southwark. Looks like you're in for an awkward night.'

The expression on Wilson's face was sheepish, a token attempt at sincerity whilst the smirk broke free at the corners of his mouth. Harry didn't laugh. Wilson's former boss, Frankie Noble, had been Harry's girlfriend for nine months and had moved to Homicide & Serious shortly after they'd broken up. If the Southwark team were on the rota for this week, Noble would be attending.

'Well,' said Harry. 'I'd better get down there, hadn't I?'

Harry yawned and turned and headed for the exit, fumbling in his jacket pocket for his car keys. He stepped out of the station, into the car park, and broke into a run, anything to wake him up. The sky was full of storm clouds, black against the blue of the lightening sky. There was a big one expected in the morning, the tail end of some hurricane making its way over from the Caribbean.

He tried to banish all thoughts of Frankie Noble and think instead about the dead woman he was driving over to certify. Unlocked his car and threw his bag onto the passenger seat. Set the SatNav for Calais Street, and headed south.

Something a bit like dread had started brewing on the drive, arriving in his stomach near Kennington. Harry wasn't quite sure what it was, but the Subway sandwich he'd wolfed down at midnight was sitting uneasily. He parked the car, took his bag from the passenger seat and headed over.

The feeling didn't ease with the morning air. Walking up to the scene of a death always made his mind wander, thoughts about mortality, his and other people's. Not with regards to time, but to place – he had long since accepted that life was something fragile that whatever force drove the universe had no respect for. He saw death all the time, but on the hospital wards, where people succumbed despite the tubes and wires anchoring them to their beds, death was sanitary, awful but understandable. Death belonged in a hospital. It was part of the furniture. There was something about encountering death in a kitchen or a bedroom or a garden that always irked him. That feeling had faded with experience, but it never went away completely.

The police had cordoned off a section of road that formed one side of a square of five-storey red-brick terraces that looked out onto the park. The park itself wouldn't have been out of place in an Oxfordshire village, with a tennis court, an old bandstand and a pond, above which a mist rose, tendrils of dawn poking into the summer night. Here, though, the park and its genteel apartments were sandwiched between Camberwell and the estates of Akerman Road. That was South London for you, Harry thought, as he approached the line of tape marked by a solitary uniformed officer under a streetlight. There were nice parts and rough parts of every city, but few places where the demographic could vary so drastically from one street to the next.

The whole street was quiet but for the various police vehicles, only two of which had their blue strobes on. In a few hours, the residents would wake up to find their houses behind a police cordon. Harry counted two unmarked police cars inside the tape, a forensics van, ambulance and two patrol vehicles.

'Can I help you, sir?'

Harry showed his ID. 'Force Medical Examiner.'

'Right you are,' the officer said, leaning into his radio. 'Shona, the doctor's here.'

Harry looked across the street as he waited. Fiat 500s and Minis parked on the road, old-fashioned wrought-iron grilles guarding the bottom of the wide windows on every floor, the odd house with a name as well as a number. He allowed himself a few moments' distraction to ease the nerves, wondering if celebrity was the reason for the DCI's presence, if it was a politician or a pop star waiting for him with slashed wrists. If it was a case like that, one where every detail was set upon by the media like vultures to carrion, then he wanted nothing to do with it.

DS McGovern came down from a communal hallway, heading towards the cordon, frizzy hair down to her shoulders and a trenchcoat down to her knees.

'We spoke on the phone,' she said. 'Good to meet you.'

She held up the police tape and signed him in. The address had a communal courtyard accessed by a dark archway, through which Harry caught glimpses of activity. Two uniform coppers held a foil blanket over a silhouette, despite the summer heat. A forensic photographer set up equipment. No glimpse yet of Noble. Harry made to move towards the arch, but McGovern blocked his way.

'Before we head in, Dr Kent, I need to ask you something,' she said, her voice quiet. 'The victim's a thirty-four-year-old female. Our provisional ID is that she's a doctor. I just wanted to check it's not someone you know before you go inside.'

'Christ,' said Harry. His brain started listing his colleagues and friends who he knew lived around here, matching it with the age and the gender. No obvious candidates. He looked up at the dark morning sky, now dreading the grim task that faced him even more.

'What's her name?'

'Susan Bayliss.'

Harry knew it, but couldn't remember where from. She was around the same age as him, so maybe she was an old medical school classmate, or they'd rotated together as juniors. Every doctor had colleagues who'd killed themselves, so the sadness he felt was not a new one.

'I don't know her,' said Harry. 'Thanks for checking.'

'I'll take you through, then.'

The local uniforms were milling around in the courtyard and Harry nodded to the faces he recognised. McGovern let him into a wide stairwell, where two detectives stood with their back to the wall, arms folded. The younger one, male and Asian, stepped forward to greet them. The other detective stayed with her back to the wall, arms folded, in the half-light.

'This is Dr Kent,' McGovern said. 'Dr Kent, DC Bhalla and Acting DCI Noble. She's the boss.'

As Harry stepped further into the hallway Noble came into the light, and he got a good look at her. More than that, he got to watch her react as she recognised him. The leather jacket, dark jeans and Doc Martens that had once been her calling card were gone, as was the short fringe, replaced by a white collared shirt, smart trousers, flat shoes and a conservative bob. The face was different, too, but he couldn't work out how, though the expression hadn't changed. Her face moved little.

Harry shook Bhalla's hand, looked at Noble and nodded. The weight had moved from his stomach to his chest, and he found himself using all of his willpower to look at the stairs, the ceiling, anywhere but at her. The two of them had met two Januarys ago when she'd investigated the events leading up to the shooting of a local teenager, and then the cruel slaughter of one of Harry's closest friends. In those two weeks he'd lost an immeasurable amount, but the case had built an emotional connection that had evolved into an intense and complex relationship. She'd moved in in September, and Harry had kicked her out for the final time, drunk and screaming, on New Year's Day. Since then they'd managed to avoid one another, even on the few occasions they'd been in the same building. Harry hadn't expected the first rendezvous to be in the middle of the night with a dead woman lying upstairs, though on reflection he probably should have.

'Right, Harry,' said Noble. 'Thanks for coming.'

Harry noticed Bhalla and McGovern share a raised eyebrow at her use of his first name. They wouldn't know the story, he reasoned. Christ, if he was in Noble's shoes, he'd keep it secret. It would take up so much time at the water-cooler no murder case would be solved in South London for weeks.

'The victim's a thirty-four-year-old female, lives in Flat 5b with her girlfriend,' Noble continued. 'The girlfriend came back from a night out about four and found the victim sat in a chair, incised wounds to the wrists and upper arms. There's an empty packet of pills on the dining-room table.'

They started up the wide staircase to the fourth floor, where the door to Flat 5b was open but covered with an 'X' of crime-scene tape. It reminded him of plague houses, how they'd been marked with the same shape.

'Who's been inside?' Harry said.

'Paramedics, the first pair of responding officers, me and Gurpreet, and the girlfriend. We were waiting on you to certify before Forensics go in.'

Christ, Harry thought. On the stairs above him, a uniformed officer, a woman of no more than twenty-five, was in conversation with a forensics tech. The uniform had a dark red smear of blood across the collar of her white shirt. It was fairly difficult to commit suicide by slashing your wrists, though many tried. You had to cut painfully deep in order to hit an artery. In fact, in the time he'd now been working with the police, he'd not certified a single cutter out of all the suicides he could recall. Plenty of hangings, and jumpers – bridges, tower blocks, underground trains. Four or five overdoses. A solitary carbon monoxide job, stuck in a stuffy garage in Dulwich with taped-up doors, once the hazmat team had cleared it. But not yet someone who'd bled themselves to death. They tended to show up in A&E, surrounded by confused friends or terrified parents.

'Is there a pathologist on the way?' Harry said.

Noble shook her head.

'Not yet. I'm waiting to see what Forensics make of it. It looks like a suicide for sure, but there are a few things that seem a little strange . . . It's pretty brutal. I dunno, call it gut instinct. I'm open-minded, but I need a bit more before I kick off a murder inquiry at this hour. Don't want to seem too eager, that's all . . .'

'Right . . .' said Harry.

'You'll see what I mean.'

'Ok.'

They arrived at the top of the stairs and a forensic tech handed each of them a white paper zip-up, overshoes and a facemask. They got dressed in silence. Susan Bayliss's name was an itch in the back of Harry's brain. He still couldn't place it and the fear began to rise. Fear that he'd step through the cross of tape into the flat and see the face of a friend or a colleague, fear that Noble would be able to notice his reaction. But as Harry pulled the white paper suit over his arms, he tried not to think about that. He'd encountered plenty of bodies before, and that's just what this was, he told himself. Another life shortened prematurely, and one subject to the procedures and protocols and paperwork of the police doctor, just like any other.

He finished suiting up and realised Noble, the detectives and the forensic techs had all done so before him, the benefit of frequent practice. One of the techs gestured towards the cross of tape barring the door.

'After you, Doc,' he said. 'After all, whoever she is, she's not dead until you say so.'

There was so much blood on the floor Harry could actually smell it, bitter and metallic, catching in his throat. He stood in the kitchen holding the dictaphone to his mouth, his skin clammy beneath the forensic jumpsuit.

'05:12, Sunday, 24 August,' he said, holding down the record button, 'I am examining the body of a female believed to be Susan Bayliss at the request of the Metropolitan Police Service.'

There were seven of them in the flat: Harry, Noble, Bhalla and McGovern, the crime scene manager, a forensic technician and a videographer, who was still in the hallway. Susan Bayliss, limp in a chair a few metres away, with a dead face that gave Harry no clues as to why he remembered her name. On opening the front door, they'd been met by a macabre trail of red-black footprints, all of them upside-down, as if leaving the house. In a zip-locked evidence bag on the welcome mat were the shoes that had left them, the faux-leather sandals of Teodora Guzman, Susan Bayliss's partner, who'd smeared blood along the hallway as she'd run to let the paramedics in.

The apartment was open-plan, not unlike Harry's own, with the kitchen facing out into a spacious living room, black leather sofas, a wall-mounted plasma screen, another wall covered in at least twenty picture frames, many of them of the Bayliss couple in various exotic locations. Coffee table, a bowl of pistachio nuts, a smaller bowl of shells. A bookshelf, mostly travel, a library of CDs, classical and country and western. Lots of titles in Spanish or Portuguese, too. The living room itself opened up onto a balcony, and Harry suspected that the apartments on this side of the building commanded a better price than those whose balconies faced into the inner courtyard, as the view from this one was excellent. From this far south, all the monoliths of the City and the South Bank morphed into a single beacon of light and glass, the rest of the city sprawled out underneath it. The doors were still open and warm air swept through the apartment, heavy with the humidity of the approaching storm.

Had that been the last thing Susan Bayliss had ever felt? Harry wondered. Warm early-morning summer air blowing in through the window? Her life had ended in a wicker chair turned to face out of the balcony doors. Harry followed her dead eyes out and took in the view again. It was probably better at night than in the daytime, and she hadn't enjoyed the sunrise. The proof of that was the thick lake of blood that the chair stood in, a rich black scarlet against the varnished wooden flooring.

Harry put the dictaphone down and went through the motions. Calling Bayliss's name into each ear in turn, flicking his hand in front of her face. Next he shone a pen-torch into each eye. Both pupils were paralysed wide, black and reflective like the dark blood beneath the chair. He opened two buttons on Bayliss's blouse, just enough to place his stethoscope over her heart. Good practice said he ought to listen for three minutes, whilst simultaneously checking for pulses. But in a situation like this one, he didn't want to touch anything he didn't absolutely have to, and there was no doubt at all that she was dead.

He found this moment unsettling. He always had. It had been a bread-and-butter duty when he'd been a junior doctor, being called to one of the geriatric wards at two in the morning to confirm the death of an inpatient. For two minutes, he would sit there, pressed up against a stranger, usually someone whom he had never encountered in life, the thoughts going through his head often existential in nature. The earpieces of his stethoscope acted like plugs and blocked out all the ambient noise, so there was only the transmitted sounds of his own breathing. The heart and lungs of this woman were silent.

Done with his ritual, Harry looked across at the woman in the chair, at her face, trying to imagine how she may have appeared in life. Bayliss's life was long since extinct, but Harry had to raise his dictaphone to his mouth in order to legally depart her.

'No response to verbal stimuli or pain, pupils fixed and dilated, no heart or breath sounds heard for two minutes. Fact of death confirmed, 05:16.'

Behind him, Noble exhaled loudly. The crime scene manager had crouched down between Bayliss's body and the balcony, examining something. A short knife, almost entirely enveloped by the blood on the floor, lying just below Bayliss's right hand.

'Cause of death would be haemorrhage, would it?' Noble said.

'Looks like it,' said Harry, taking a step back, trying to see the big picture. Bayliss had cut into her brachial arteries on both sides, two hesitant slices into the crook of her right elbow, and then the wound which had killed her, a deep gash running longitudinally on the left-hand side. Here, the pale fabric of her blouse was sodden with blood, which was speckled across the other side. It was all over the walls too, spurts decorating the dining table next to her, on which stood a bottle of wine the dark colour of the blood on the floor, three empty blister packets and a packet with a prescription label. Spatter up the right-sided balcony doors, too, from when she'd first cut into the artery, and the pressure had launched her blood across the room.

'I've not seen that before,' Noble said, pointing. 'Cutting at the elbows. They usually go for the wrists, don't they?'

'The brachial artery's bigger,' Harry said. 'But it's deeper. You'd have to know what you were doing.'

'And she would have, I take it?'

'Any doctor would know that,' said Harry. 'What specialty was she, do you know?'

Not that it would make a difference, not really. Basic anatomy was covered in undergraduate teaching the world over. He was asking out of curiosity. DC Bhalla disappeared and returned holding a zip-lock evidence bag, inside which was an NHS hospital ID badge not dissimilar to Harry's own.

'There you go, Doc.'

Harry stood up from his crouch and leant forward to make out the writing.

BELGRAVE HOSPITAL FOR SICK CHILDREN
SUSAN BAYLISS
SPECIALIST REGISTRAR
CARDIOTHORACIC SURGERY

The face on the ID card was younger by a good few years, or at the very least looked younger. In death, Bayliss looked far older than thirty-four, hair by her shoulders, her blood coagulating on the floor. But it was from reading the position and specialty that the itch in his brain finally sprang into a connection, and he knew where he'd seen that name before. And the memories returned. A small boy, dead on a hospital trolley, an A&E nurse performing CPR with two fingers. Placing a tube narrower than a drinking straw between his vocal cords, whilst paediatricians and cardiologists threw out any ideas to get this boy's heart pumping again.

'She was a heart surgeon,' said Noble. 'So I guess she'd know where to find an artery.'

Harry said nothing. A deep sadness had passed over him, and as hard as he tried to hide his emotion, Noble took a glance at his face and knew he was hiding something. A part of him became angry that she could so easily read him, but deep down he knew that she'd have picked it up even if she'd only met him that morning.

'What is it?' she said. 'Did you know her?'

'Knew of her,' said Harry. 'You haven't googled her name yet, I take it?'

Any trace of concern on Noble's face vanished as she shot a venomous look at Bhalla and McGovern, who both went pale and looked at each other.

'Tell me, Harry,' she said.

'She was in the news recently,' he said. 'Belgrave was under investigation. They suspended heart surgery there for a while and transferred all the kids over to Great Ormond Street or the Evelina. She was the one who blew the whistle. I don't know the details, you'll have to check them yourself. But she lost her job, I remember that.'

And now she was dead, he thought.

'I read about that!' the crime scene manager volunteered. 'Them kids who died after heart surgery!'

'Thank you, Oscar,' Noble snapped. Harry turned. DC Bhalla was already on his smartphone, tapping furiously at the screen.

'Here,' he said, presenting the phone to Noble. Harry took a few steps towards her so he could look at the screen, then instantly regretted his curiosity. He was far too physically close. He could even smell her, the unmistakeable scent of menthol cigarettes covered up by perfume. Or was it perfume covered up by menthols?

The page Bhalla had found had a few paragraphs of text:

Heart surgeon who leaked death report suspended

A trainee surgeon at a top London hospital has been
suspended following an investigation into the leaking of an
internal report into the deaths of several children.
Susan Bayliss, 34, a registrar at the Belgrave Hospital for
Sick Children, was identified as the source of a leaked report
which was sent to NHS officials in May. The report, which
identified four children who died shortly after undergoing
surgery for congenital heart problems at Belgrave, led to the
postponing of all children's heart operations at the hospital
for two weeks whilst Department of Health officials
conducted an emergency investigation. The investigation
reported that there was 'no concern whatsoever' about the
internationally renowned hospital and operations have since
resumed.

'Unprofessional conduct'

A spokesperson for the hospital, which is administered by the
South London University Hospitals NHS Trust, said, 'A
member of the congenital heart surgery team has been
suspended following an internal disciplinary hearing which
substantiated allegations of unprofessional conduct. We
would stress that whilst this decision is related to the inquiry
into the cardiac services provided at the Belgrave, the

suspension of this staff member is not in relation to any clinical incidents. The hospital is fully cooperating with the Department of Health and looks forwards to being able to continue to provide world-class care to the sick children of South London.'

The spokesperson also confirmed that Miss Bayliss had been referred to the General Medical Council.

The article was dated two weeks ago, on 10 August. Harry had read the article, or a different one on the same topic, before. Last week perhaps. Brief memories of conversations with the A&E nurses on a quiet afternoon shift, those who remembered the boy who had died, who had been one of the patients the inquiry had mentioned. Bhalla went to scroll down, but Noble just shook her head and said, 'Fucking hell, why are we only finding this out now?'

'I'm sorry, guv, we—'

Noble cut him off. 'Not good enough. Shona, get your arse back to the station, I want everything about this investigation in a report in an hour. Wake up everyone you have to. For God's sake!'

'I'm on it, guv.'

With that, McGovern was out of the door, and the silence that was hanging over them was thick in the air. Harry took another look around, appreciating the brutality of the scene, all the more poignant now the story was coming to light. Bayliss had committed the doctor's cardinal sin, blowing the whistle on her colleagues, and she'd paid for it with her job, and now perhaps her life. Harry pictured her girlfriend coming in and finding her, sat in a chair, facing outwards, her life in a pool around her. Ruining the floor, the walls, the table. The bottle of wine on the table was a nice-looking one, gold webbing around the label.

'Right,' said Noble. Harry looked up and saw she was looking straight at him. 'Forget that stuff. If this one's going to get media interest we've got to make sure we don't mess up this crime scene, ok?'

As a motivational speech it was weak, but it worked. Harry was imagining the headlines already. *NHS whistleblower driven to suicide. Suspended heart surgeon found dead in flat.* More ammunitions for the tabloids' reliably vitriolic salvoes against the health service, more material for the broadsheet editorials to tut and judge over. Noble stepped forward to the body, where the videographer was filming.

'The wound on the left arm looks deeper than the right,' she observed.

'She's probably right-handed,' Harry said. 'Did the ones with her left hand first, but they were only hesitation wounds. Then she switched to her dominant hand to finish the job.'

As he said the words, he felt a chill go through him, despite the hot, sticky air coming in through the balcony doors. There was something very cold about the way Susan Bayliss had apparently elected to die, a deliberate indignity about it, and that bothered him. Noble walked around the body again, shaking her head.

'How long would it have taken?'

Harry leant over, took another look at the wound in the left elbow. The serious arterial bleeds he'd previously seen had been in Afghanistan, gunshot wounds or amputations from IEDs, or gang-related violence coming into the Ruskin's A&E, young men stabbed and shot. Those injuries were far uglier, far cruder than the neat cut in Susan Bayliss's left arm.

'Hard to say. Could've been five minutes, could've been ten,' Harry said. 'A pathologist would have a better idea.'

'How long until she lost consciousness?'

'She'd have gone into shock almost immediately,' Harry said. 'You need to lose maybe a third of your blood volume before you pass out. I can't say how long that would have taken, but not long. A few minutes, perhaps.'

'And during that time, before she lost that much blood, she'd have been able to save herself?'

Harry looked around the body again. There were no indications at all that this act had been a cry for help. No note, no smears of blood around the fabric where she had tried to staunch the bleeding. From the location of the blood pool, she'd not moved from the chair since the cuts had been made. If this was a choice she had made, she'd done it properly. Cut herself in the right place, with the wine perhaps to ease the pain, and the pills just in case it didn't go to plan . . .

'The pills,' Harry said. 'What are they?'

Noble turned her head over to the kitchen side, where the videographer was leaning next to the wine and the pill packet.

'What does it say on that label?' she said.

The videographer couldn't resist.

'Casillero del Diablo, Winemaker's Red Blend, Chile . . .'

She trailed off when nobody laughed. Noble fixed him with the look of a drill sergeant, and she meekly read out the prescription.

'Sertraline, fifty milligrams twice daily.'

Noble turned to Harry.

'It's an antidepressant,' Harry said. 'And a fairly hefty dose at that.'

'She was being prescribed them. Makes sense to take an overdose, too, yeah? Belt and braces.'

Harry shuffled onto his front foot.

'Maybe,' he said. He tried to think quickly in his head, knowing that soon he would have to do so out loud. But it was something that didn't tally, that added weight to the lump in his stomach. Again, it was sensed before he could verbalise it himself.

'What is it?' Noble said.

'If it was a suicide, it doesn't really make sense,' he said. 'There'd be no point. Sertraline takes hours to work, and it'd probably take a few days to kill her, even if she took a massive overdose. She would have known that. It'd be a waste of time.'

The faint shouts of a distant argument entered the apartment from outside, a resident wanting access to his car. Somewhere to go early on a Sunday morning. It was pretty much light now.

'A fail-safe?' Noble suggested. 'In case the cuts didn't work?'

Harry mulled this option over, too. He'd encountered the myth that doctors have high suicide rates several times. The truth, perhaps more macabre, was that doctors attempted suicide as often as the normal population, they were just better at succeeding. Because they knew which drugs would do the job, and which would more than likely earn you a few days in a high-dependency unit and a Section 3 to sort your head out. Sertraline, like most antidepressants, was firmly in the latter category.

23

'Doesn't make sense,' said Harry. 'If that was her plan, why leave the packet out? To be found? If it was a fail-safe, she'd want to disguise the drug, wouldn't she?'

'She obviously wasn't in her right mind,' Bhalla said.

Harry disagreed, but he said nothing. Everything about the scene looked like it was planned, from the open windows, the cut along the elbow, opening the artery right up, not like the horizontal slashes often seen in self-harmers. Contrary to popular belief, you didn't have to be insane to take your own life. This appeared to him as rational a suicide as any he'd seen, yet there were one or two things out of place. He knew exactly what Noble had meant when she'd said it didn't feel entirely right, even without the pills. It felt wrong that a person would choose to die like that, in the middle of a room, their girlfriend on the way home from a night out.

One of the forensics technicians was crouching by the pale chinos Bayliss had died in, touching her pockets with gloved fingers.

'Her phone's still in the front pocket,' the tech said. 'No blood on the inside.'

Harry followed the logic. She hadn't tried to call for help, nor had she sent any final messages. He walked around the body, looking at the knife lying in the blood on the floor, serrated teeth on clean metal, a black carbon handle. In the kitchen, there was a magnetic knife rack above one of the worktops. Cookery books on the shelves.

Footsteps in the hallway and everybody turned. It was McGovern, her forensic jumpsuit half-undone, but her lower half and shoes still covered.

'Guv,' she said. 'You should see this.'

She had her phone out too, and thrust it towards them. Again, Harry craned his neck to see. McGovern had a Twitter page open, the profile photo one of Susan Bayliss on a white beach with palm trees in the background. The top tweet was addressed to @BelgraveHospital and read simply, '*You did this to me.*'

Noble swore under her breath, as did Harry. He had sympathy. Given Bayliss's very public admonishment of the hospital, when the media found out there would be a true feeding frenzy. Harry was glad for one thing: that his involvement with the case would cease the moment he stepped under the plastic tape and past the outer cordon. This was the kind of landmine that could wreck careers. Not that Harry had one to wreck.

'When was that sent?' Noble demanded.

'12:45, guv.'

'Harry, I need a time of death.'

All seven pairs of eyes staring at him, Harry trying to contain his anger.

'I'm not a pathologist,' he said.

'Yeah, and I'm not a jury. Have a guess for me, would you?'

Harry stepped forward. Noble was smiling without smiling, the way a poker player did when they knew they had the winning hand.

'Who's CSM?' he said.

The crime scene manager, a bearded man whom Harry vaguely recognised, raised a hand.

'Am I ok to touch the eyes again?'

The CSM checked with the videographer then nodded. Harry leant in again, taking care that the front of his suit didn't brush against the body. If there was rigor mortis, the oculomotor muscles around the eyes would be affected first. His fingers touched Bayliss's eyelids and swept down over the blank, lifeless corneas, the skin moving without resistance. No rigor. He crouched, moving his eyeline to where Bayliss's blouse had ridden up out of the chair, exposing a line of pale skin around her waistline.

'No hypostasis, either,' he said. 'Or none that I can see, anyway. Which means, I don't know. Four or five hours, maybe. A pathologist would give you a better idea.'

'Between midnight and one,' Noble said. 'Fits with the tweet. The girlfriend was out for drinks with work friends. She'd told Susan that she'd be back on the last Tube, but they decided to go clubbing instead.'

A worried look passed between Noble and McGovern, and Harry knew why. If Bayliss had truly wanted to die, and not be discovered in time to be helped, then she wouldn't have chosen to do it so soon before she expected Guzman to come home. Or maybe she'd planned it so that she'd find her, barely dead. That was a hell of a statement, one final fuck-you. The whole thing was a statement, much more so than all of the suicides Harry had yet seen. In the middle of their house, windows open, staring out at the city. He leant away and began looking around the saddle of her back, anywhere else that the livor mortis might have formed, but there wasn't anything. Instead his eyes were drawn upwards, to the backs of her shoulders.

'Can I get some light, please?' he said. 'There's something on her back.'

The CSM and the forensic tech were on Harry immediately, helping him tilt Bayliss forward and pull back her blouse, further indignity and humiliation in death to what she'd experienced in life. When they were done, Noble leant over so Harry could show her what he'd found. A line of yellowish-red bruising on the ridges of her shoulder blades, where they'd been touching the chair.

'Shit,' said Noble, 'That's livor, is it? You think she died on the floor and someone put her in the chair?'

At the word 'someone', a visible rush went through McGovern and Bhalla, both of whom started pacing around the room. To Harry, it felt like the blood-spattered ceiling and walls were encroaching inwards, building up the pressure in the apartment.

'I don't think so,' he said. 'Livor's usually darker. And if she died on her back, we'd see it in the lower back as well.'

Livor, the mottling produced by the post-mortem settling of blood within the body, would grow darker with time, and moved with gravity. Harry came around to Bayliss's front and looked at her chest in the light, noticing something he'd seen before but not realised the implication of. There was more bruising, paler than that on her shoulder blades, across the top of both collarbones, darker on the underside. Subtle, not fully developed, which suggested it had been inflicted either shortly before or after death. On closer inspection, the bruises were in two distinct lines, symmetrical on either side, and he thought he could make out small patches of similar discolouration either side of the sternum. When the inescapable conclusion came to him, he spoke quietly, but still managed to strike silence into the rest of the room.

'I think someone might have held her down.'

★   ★   ★

Ten minutes later felt like an hour.

The CSM had concurred with Harry's opinion of the likely cause of the bruising to Bayliss's chest and back, and though he'd stopped shy of saying it was murder, he'd said it needed to be ruled out. Photos had been taken and emailed to the on-call Home Office pathologist, who was requested to attend the scene as soon as possible. More people had been woken up and instructed to set up an Incident Room at Peckham, and the other twenty-two detectives who made up Noble's Major Investigation Team were in the process of being woken up and called in. Harry had remained in the apartment, waiting patiently to be told his services were no longer needed.

He ran his tired eyes over Susan Bayliss's shoulders, watching the CSM taking more photos, the tip of his plastic covershoe dipping into the blood pool. Bayliss was still staring out into the window, and involuntarily Harry pictured the scene. Her terror as she watched her killer open the artery, knowing that she would bleed to death, trying to fight her way out of the hands pressing her firmer into the chair as she kicked and thrashed.

The blood would cover all of the chaos, the signs of a struggle, or the killer might have cleared them up. And added the hesitation marks, the bottle of wine and the pills. And then reached into her pocket and sent the tweet from her phone.

If he was right, and Harry totally, absolutely wished that he wasn't, the implications were even more horrific than if she'd committed suicide. That story – a young, successful doctor who tried to do the right thing, got thrown out by the establishment and was driven to take her own life – was tragic enough without the spectre of murder.

Noble came back into the room, transformed from a sleep-deprived woman on the edge of losing it to an effective coxswain for her team. When she spoke, it was low so only Harry could hear.

'Trust you to make things difficult,' she said.

'I try my best,' Harry said, then regretted it. It had been her fault their relationship had ended, but he didn't have sufficient grievance against her to be that narky.

'We've got all we need from you here,' she said. 'But I need a favour.'

She indicated out of the flat with a nod of her head, and Harry followed her. As they got onto the landing, past the cross of tape, he began to take off his forensic suit and Noble's phone rang.

'It's the super. I'll see you downstairs.'

He found her in the courtyard, trying to shelter from the growing rainfall. More vehicles were arriving, both patrol cars and unmarked detective units, the word having spread that this was now a murder inquiry until proven otherwise. From the serious tone of the voices around him, it appeared no-one was under any illusions about the amount of scrutiny the case would be subject to.

'Sorry,' Noble said, done with her phone call. 'I need you to do an examination. We've taken the girlfriend over to Brixton, just for clearing. She's not under arrest, but I'll need forensic samples and a fitness-to-be-interviewed statement. I think she was on something when she came home, and I'm not having a defence lawyer come at me with that if this goes to trial.'

'Sure,' said Harry, looking at his watch. Assuming that Teodora Guzman was cooperative, the examination shouldn't take more than half an hour. It would still have him home before seven.

'Thanks,' said Noble. 'And thanks for showing my detectives how to do their job.'

'It's the rumour-mill,' Harry said. 'If it had been a sacked copper, you'd have known about it.'

'I meant more the bruising,' said Noble. 'Anyway, that wasn't the favour.'

They'd slipped effortlessly into professional civility, but now the nervousness returned.

'Oh?' was all he could manage.

'I need to get over there to direct interviews on Guzman,' she said. 'Any chance of a lift?'

Harry didn't answer. He was sure she was making some kind of play, that Acting DCIs had gophers to drive them places and that this was some way of asserting her authority, but he was too tired to decipher it. So he gave up the armchair psychology, nodded and grunted, and headed towards the car.

They got in and stayed silent until Harry started the engine and moved away. Then Noble said, 'How are you?'

On average, Harry slept between fifteen and twenty hours per week. He kept a bottle of amphetamines in his flat, car and locker to keep him going. He spent four or five twelve-hour stints per week at the hospital, working in the A&E department, and despite that his career was going nowhere. He was meant to be a consultant by now, but that hadn't happened. He'd failed his fellowship exam, flunked out of the training programme, failed to demonstrate adequate progress in his latest year of training. Compared to his contemporaries, his portfolio was a mess. He lived alone and had a girlfriend that he barely saw. Spent a considerable amount of his free time wandering around Clapham Junction showing people photos of a girl he'd first met just over three years ago now, the woman in a coma whose identity had vanished along with almost all of her higher brain function. Noble, of course, knew most of this already. She also knew that Harry would not have changed in the eight months since they had last spoken, not without outside pressure.

'Yeah, fine,' Harry said. 'You?'

Noble shrugged her shoulders.

'Alright.'

Harry drove through the back streets of Myatt's Fields, towards Brixton, for the most part the only moving car on the road, until they stopped. A red light at an empty crossroads. The air in the car grew thick with tension, and finally Harry had to lower a window or he felt like he might suffocate. Eventually Noble relented, and started talking.

'How's work?'

'Much the same,' said Harry. 'Kinirons is trying to persuade me to apply for the air ambulance rotation next time it comes up. Bit of a challenge.'

'Might do you good,' said Noble.

'McGovern introduced you as Acting DCI,' Harry said. 'Congratulations.'

'It's not to be congratulated,' she said. 'I don't think I'm ready for a DCI job just yet.'

It was a frank admission and one Harry was sure she wouldn't have made to her colleagues within the force. But it added depth to the picture – given Noble's relative inexperience, it made more

sense for the divisional detective superintendent, the man responsible for all murder investigations south of the river, to be sniffing
around. The light went green and Harry drove off.

'Why'd you take it then?'

Noble pulled an e-cigarette from the inside pocket of her blazer
and puffed on it, the orange glow lighting up her face. That was
new, too.

'Ian's got lung cancer,' she said. 'They say it'll be weeks, a
couple of months if he's lucky.'

'Christ,' said Harry. He'd met DCI Bruce, her old boss, once or
twice, and found him blasé and irritating, but nobody deserved to
end their career like that. But that was how life worked out, and
thanks to a few million errant cells in another man's chest, the
woman next to him was responsible for one of the busiest murder
investigation teams in the country.

'What can you tell me about Susan Bayliss?' Noble said after a
while. She'd timed the conversation opener well, Harry thought,
as they were just up the road from the station. It put a limit on the
extent they could discuss the case.

'I can tell you she's dead. That's about it.'

'You know I didn't mean that. I mean about the report, those
kids.'

Harry looked across at her. It was like looking at a student's
copy of an old master's painting, the change in her appearance, a
different impression of the same subject. A lot cleaner, a lot more
righteous in her work than he remembered. Perhaps it came with
the responsibility of investigating murders.

'Not much,' he said, 'and nothing you won't get from the news
reports. She was a reg over at Belgrave, reported that they'd had
four children die a while after heart operations, all of them operated on by the same surgeon, her supervising consultant.
Apparently the hospital didn't take it seriously enough, so she
went to the Department of Health.'

'Which surgeon?'

'I can't remember,' said Harry. 'I don't think the papers named
him. There are rumours going round, I think, but it's not my
department. I've never done paeds.'

'Him?' said Noble, her look accusatory.

'Balance of probabilities,' Harry said. 'Some of our specialties are still stuck in the dark ages. I don't think I've ever met a female heart surgeon. Certainly not a consultant, anyway.'

'Right,' said Noble. 'So Bayliss blew the whistle on this guy, and she's the one who gets suspended?'

'The investigation didn't find anything wrong at Belgrave, no evidence of negligence or malpractice. You remember the report?' Harry said. 'She wasn't suspended for negligence.'

He looked over as he headed up Akerman Road. She had the news website open on her phone, flicking through it with a finger.

'Unprofessional conduct,' Noble read.

'Yeah,' said Harry. 'Which between you and me, and entirely outside my official position as an FME, sounds like a complete load of bollocks.'

'What do you mean?'

Harry kept his voice low, though it was for no reason. 'It sounds like exactly the kind of thing a hospital trust would come up with to get rid of a troublemaker. Someone who'd already gone to the press, for instance.'

'Really?'

'Some of these hospitals, you piss them off, they'll do anything to shut you up. I had a friend who ended up looking after eighty patients by himself as an SHO, when he was just two years out of medical school. He tried to flag it with the trust, that the hospital needed to hire another SHO, and all they did was force him to go on a time management course, then threatened to fail his ARCP appraisal if he didn't pipe down. I think he ended up moving to Australia.'

By now, they'd arrived at the station and were sitting in the car with the windows down, the sunrise resplendent around them in summer rain, the city not yet awake apart from a steel band packing their instruments into a van in the courtyard of a church opposite them, ready for an early start on the road.

'You sure you can't remember the name of the consultant she reported?'

'Frankie, if I knew, I'd tell you!' Harry said, palms up. If they'd been in a room he'd have backed away. Instead he placed one hand on the door handle and clicked it open. 'I've never met her. I've never done paeds, I've never worked at Belgrave. All I did was read the papers, like you.'

It was only a small lie, of course. He had seen children, in his job at A&E, and he'd seen one child who had been operated on at Belgrave and then died months later. In front of his eyes. He recalled the empty face of one of his colleagues, in tears at the prospect of being unable to save the child. The name came back to him now, too.

'Sorry,' Noble said, running hands through her hair. 'I'm tired.'

Harry looked across. His morning was getting worse by the minute, and the last thing he needed was another attempt at reconciliation. Statistically, they'd only need to encounter one another a couple of times a year, and they could manage it better than this. He opened the door and went round to the boot to get his bag out, frustration building up inside him. He knew he was overreacting and found himself physically biting his tongue to stop himself talking.

'You're not involved with any of this, are you?' she called from across the car.

Harry took one look at her and knew that she'd twigged he'd held something back. Harry was fairly sure that Noble would have spotted that even if they hadn't been a couple for the best part of a year. There was a reason she'd been transferred to Homicide & Serious.

'One of the boys who was part of the report was brought into the Ruskin just before he died. I was working in A&E that day. It was a paeds case, so I wasn't in charge, but I helped out a little. A lot of the staff took it pretty badly . . . he was very young. I think some of them might have helped out with the inquiry, but I didn't.'

Noble looked at him, maybe suspicious, maybe angry.

'Ok,' she said.

They walked up into the police station and Noble signed him in to the custody suite.

'Be careful in there,' she said as they descended old stairs with ripped vinyl flooring.

'Why?' said Harry. 'She got a history?'

'Not that we know,' said Noble. 'But she lashed out at one of the uniforms at the scene, clawed him in the face. Maybe it was just shock, y'know. But watch yourself.'

Her eyes were sorrowful, as if they were saying goodbye at an airport or a railway station. Harry looked away and headed towards the cells. The feeling in his stomach hadn't gone away.

The custody officer who opened the cell door was a civilian, though his uniform was indistinguishable from the real coppers unless you scrutinised the epaulettes and badges, which bore the logo of the corporation who employed him. He'd looked unbelievably pissed off when Noble had woken him up to tell him the doctor was coming for the woman in F-4, and he struggled with the keys, taking half a minute or so to find the right one. Noble was going upstairs, to sort out the Incident Room, to sleep for an hour perhaps, and then start briefing her team and taking a formal statement from Guzman, so she'd left him with DC Bhalla, who'd been designated as exhibits officer. It was an unenviable job. Bhalla was responsible for tracking every piece of evidence gathered during the investigation, which meant signing for the samples once Harry took them, and delivering them to the forensics lab personally. Chain-of-evidence was a good principle, but it was dull as hell, and Harry couldn't help wondering if it had been assigned in anger after Noble's earlier embarrassment.

Forensics had already taken Teodora Guzman's clothes for analysis, so when the custody officer finally got the cell door open it revealed a hunched-over figure in a white forensic jumpsuit, her face pale, her eyes bloodshot. Guzman looked a good few years younger than Bayliss. Her hair was cut to a half-inch, the same jet black colour as her eyes, and her face was adorned with multiple piercings, a loop and a bar in each ear, studs and stones in her nose, tongue and lips.

'Good morning, Miss Guzman,' he said, setting his bag down on the floor, 'My name is Harry Kent. I'm a doctor.'

Guzman looked up slowly.

'What kind of doctor?'

Both her hands were shrouded in white fabric mittens to preserve the bloodstains beneath, sealed at the wrists. Harry noted a smell, and spotted the pile of vomit in one corner of the cell.

'I work with the police to ensure the welfare of people like you, who've been detained. If it's ok with you, I'd like to check you over and take some samples. It's entirely routine.'

Guzman quivered slightly. She was staring down at the mittens, as if she could see through them to her girlfriend's blood on her skin.

'I'd like to wash my hands, please,' she said.

'Of course,' said Harry. 'The sooner I examine you, the sooner we can let you do that.'

He stepped aside, letting Bhalla enter the cell.

'This is Gurpreet,' he said. 'He's a detective, but he's not here to question you. He's just here to take care of the paperwork.'

Guzman nodded and offered up her hands gingerly. Harry opened his bag and got his kit ready. He'd need to do a physical examination, but only a brief one. Forensics had taken the necessary photographs when they'd removed Guzman's clothes for blood-pattern analysis. So Harry would swab the cheeks for DNA elimination, take samples for toxicology analysis and then examine the hands. As he put his gloves on, he noticed that Guzman was already crying, muttering incoherently between sobs in a different language, Portuguese, not Spanish, he reckoned.

'I'm sorry for your loss,' Harry said. Guzman didn't reply, but looked up at him. He knelt down opposite the mattress she was sitting on, coming to eye level.

'Are you injured at all?'

Guzman shook her head.

'Are you feeling unwell?'

'I feel like I'm gonna throw up, but there's nothing left.'

'That's to be expected,' said Harry. 'Are you in any pain at all?'

'My chest hurts.'

'Is it alright if I call you Teodora?'

Guzman nodded.

'Where does it hurt?'

'All over.'

Harry reached into his bag for a stethoscope. It wasn't uncommon for relatives of those suddenly deceased to have heart attacks minutes or hours after hearing the news. It had happened to another FME, who'd ended up having to run a man suspected of killing his daughter to the local coronary care unit. But Teodora Guzman was thirty, tops, and appeared to be in good physical condition.

'Do you have any medical conditions?' Harry said.

'No,' said Guzman. 'I'd like to wash my hands, please.'

'As soon as I can let you do that, I will. Let's get you checked over first. Is that pain spreading anywhere?'

Guzman shook her head. Harry picked up a smell from her breath, something like rum or cocktails. She didn't seem drunk to him, but the sight of your girlfriend, sprawled in a wicker chair with her arteries carved open was enough to sober anyone up, he reasoned.

'How much have you had to drink tonight?'

Guzman looked over Harry's shoulder at DC Bhalla, who was standing by the cell door, arms folded, eyelids flittering shut.

'Gurpreet, if you wouldn't mind,' Harry said.

Bhalla grunted and stepped outside, pulling the cell door ajar.

'Nothing you tell me in confidence can be used against you in court,' Harry said. 'I'm here to make sure you're safe. That's my first job, ok.'

'Three or four cocktails and a couple of beers,' Guzman said, beginning to shake, the tears flowing now. 'Oh, fuck. This can't be happening.'

'I'm sorry I have to ask this question,' Harry said. 'Have you taken anything else tonight?'

'Just some MD,' Guzman said. 'Nothing major.'

'Ok,' said Harry. When he was asking those questions in A&E, treating revellers who'd over-indulged, fallen down stairs or got into nightclub fights, he often built rapport with something along the lines of *Good party then, was it?* but that hardly seemed appropriate now.

'The detectives have asked if I can take blood and urine samples from you,' Harry said. 'That's likely to show up, but that won't get you into trouble.'

'What if I don't want to give a sample?'

'They can arrest you and then you have to give one,' said Harry. 'Hopefully that won't be necessary. If I were you, I'd just tell them.'

Guzman nodded. Harry watched her try and follow his words, and then she offered up her arm. Just like Pauline Wright with the sedative injection, it was unlikely that she had any idea what she was agreeing to, but that was the nature of the greyness in which the police operated. Harry found a good vein in her elbow, took a sample and called Bhalla back in, who diligently signed for it while Harry held a gauze pad over the oozing wound. It was hard not to look Guzman in the eye and he tried just to stare at the floor.

'It's all my fault,' Guzman said.

Harry looked up.

'It's probably best if you wait until you're being interviewed before you say anything,' he said. 'And after you've been offered legal advice.'

'I can't believe it. I wasn't there when she needed me.'

Harry said nothing, just nodded forlornly.

'She'd tried it before, you know.'

Harry looked across at Bhalla who had his head down, filling out the exhibits paperwork. Guzman was looking up at him with desperate eyes. He knew how she felt. Two Januarys ago, he'd sat in a hotel room in Old Street on the night his best friend had been killed. Something would distract you, a welcome unrelated thought, and then you were hit by the reality of the situation once again. She'd just remembered that her girlfriend was dead, and she was naked in a paper suit in a police cell with two strangers. Harry lifted up the gauze pad – the wound had stopped bleeding, so he stuck on a plaster and went back to change his gloves.

'She tried it before,' Guzman repeated. 'A long time ago, at uni. I think it was when her parents divorced, she was going through a shit time, but she got over it. It was why she didn't want to go on the medication again. Only reason she was depressed in the first place was because of the way they stitched her up. She promised me she'd never . . .'

'I'm sorry,' Harry repeated. He could see where this was going. Bhalla was paying attention now, looking up from his forms at the crying woman in front of him.

'What happened?' Bhalla said. 'The last time?'

'She took some pills,' Guzman said. 'Then she regretted it, called me and I took her to A&E. She spent some time in hospital.

A psych hospital. But that was ten years ago. She's never cut herself before. The bastards! They drove her to it, the fucking bastards!'

As Guzman spoke, she sped up until words merged with tears, the whole process interrupted as she staggered forward, dry retching. Harry couldn't help thinking of the tweet Bayliss's account had posted that morning. *They drove me to this.* He looked at Bhalla, wondering if he'd spotted the resemblance, too.

'Who did?' said Bhalla.

Harry was beginning to feel uncomfortable about the whole situation. Guzman didn't have a solicitor present and she had no obligation to answer any questions, and Bhalla didn't have the mandate to be asking them. Technically she was free to leave at any time, though if she tried she'd likely be arrested. As with the samples, it was the ultimate catch-22. Spouses and partners of murder victims almost always had to endure the indignity of being treated as a suspect, usually not too long after being informed of their loved one's violent death. The statistics said that was how it had to be.

'The hospital,' Guzman said. 'Belgrave. They found out about all that shit somehow. And they made sure everybody knew about it, even though it was all in the past. Turned it into a "history of mental illness". All she was doing was trying to keep the children safe. Those fuckers treated her like she'd tried to burn the place down. You can't imagine the kinds of things they said, the way they treated her.'

Harry said nothing. Some people thought doctors were in some way incapable of the sort of abuse and violence that other human beings engaged in. In his experience, the opposite was true. If Susan Bayliss had indeed been victimised for trying to do the right thing, it wouldn't be the first time, a fact which made Harry ashamed of the profession he belonged to. But then he thought about the symmetrical bruises underneath Bayliss's collarbones and felt cold again.

On the mattress, Guzman retched.

'Of course, it turned into a self-fulfilling prophecy, didn't it?' she said, pleading now. 'She went to see a shrink, she got a prescription. She told me to go enjoy myself, not to stay in all the time. I thought she was better, and now . . . We'd been together ten years this month. She wanted to get married. Oh, God. Oh, God oh God oh God . . .'

Teodora Guzman let out a long wail that seemed to dissolve into the walls around them, looking up at Harry with begging eyes, as if he could offer her absolution for the fact that, as the woman she loved had perhaps taken her own life, she'd been out at a bar in Vauxhall, drinking mojitos and popping pills, dancing the night away as the last spots of blood fell onto her living room floor. Harry looked back at her, unable to disguise his pity. He knew that whatever had happened to Bayliss, this woman would revisit the decisions she'd made tonight every day, for the rest of her life. In that moment, he almost wished that it was murder, so that Guzman's grief might abate even a fraction.

When she was done crying, Harry stepped forward with a fresh pair of gloves and removed the forensic covers over Guzman's hands. They had already photographed the distribution of her girlfriend's blood, mostly smears as she had shaken her face and tried to wake her up, then held her close to hear if she was breathing. Forensic analysis of the blood patterns would confirm whether or not they matched her account. Harry took swabs of the blood from each hand, scrapings from under the fingernails, and passed them all to Bhalla. He then examined the hands closer for bruises, cuts, grazes, other signs of defensive injury. Then he did the same with the forearms, the shoulders, the throat, neck and face – the places where Bayliss would have hit her if there had been a struggle – and he found nothing. No evidence at all that Teodora Guzman had been involved in a fight that evening.

Once Harry was finished, he said, 'You can wash your hands now, if you'd like.'

'This can't be happening,' Guzman said. Then she fell from her mattress onto her knees, and before either Harry or Bhalla could stop her, curled a finger around the largest of her facial piercings, a studded ring in her right nostril, and yanked it onto the floor, a spurt of fresh blood gushing onto the white paper.

It took five of them to restrain her: Harry and Bhalla, the custody sergeant and two of the civilian staff. She'd calmed down without

Harry needing to do anything. Indeed, the custody sergeant, a matronly woman with touches of creole in her voice, had done most of the work, holding Guzman close as she wailed and cried, telling her everything was alright. Harry had gone back in to clean and dress the wound to her nose, and now the sergeant and the duty custody nurse practitioner were sitting with her, patiently helping her remove all of her facial piercings. The incident would have to be recorded as deliberate self-harm in police custody, which meant an additional form for Harry as a witness, and five-minute checks on Guzman for the rest of her stay, to the delight of the custody officer with the corporate epaulettes.

He met Noble in the main link corridor of the police station when he was done. She was heading outside, looking for a smoking spot. He gathered his bags and followed her, matching her steps as she scrolled through various text messages.

'What did you find?' she asked, continuing to read. Harry knew where they were heading – the nearest place Noble could smoke.

'Nothing,' said Harry. 'Zero defensive injuries, no signs of trauma at all.'

'Right,' Noble said. 'But it's possible she could have held her down without incurring any resistance, isn't it? Susan Bayliss wasn't a large woman and Guzman looks like she works out.'

They came out into the August morning around the back of Brixton police station, looking out onto a hexagonal housing estate which was all but dead at half past six. The rain had stopped, but the streets were damp with moisture, the air humid. Harry pictured Bayliss in the wicker chair she'd died in, the dark lake of blood at her feet, the balcony doors open, London spread out in front of her.

'It's possible,' Harry said. 'But surely she'd have ended up covered in blood, not just her hands? Assuming she held her down from in front, not behind.'

She would have screamed too, he thought, unless the killer had stopped her doing that as well.

'You a blood spatter expert now?' Noble said, retrieving her e-cigarette, putting it back and then pulling a real cigarette from a pack of Benson & Hedges. The effect of her superior's terminal diagnosis had obviously been short-lived.

She lit up and held the phone up to Harry. 'Her alibi's bullshit. She told DS McGovern that she'd gone to this club and been there until four, but we've rustled some of her mates already and they said that she left with a friend around half-one, two max. That's a two-hour window.'

Harry said nothing and thought nothing. Noble finished her cigarette and lit another one, furiously bashing out a text with her other hand. At the back entrance to the station, a police van arrived, the sound of its prisoner screaming and bashing on their metal cage audible from outside the vehicle, the chilling howls of withdrawal.

'Guzman said that the hospital tried to make it look like Bayliss was mentally ill,' Harry said. 'To discredit her after her claims.'

'What?'

'She told us about it when I was examining her. Apparently Bayliss took an overdose once when she was at university, a long time ago. The hospital found out about it somehow and leaked it to the press.'

'Shit,' said Noble.

'DC Bhalla was there,' said Harry. 'He'll know more. But it's something you might want to look at.'

'Thanks,' Noble muttered. She didn't seem to mean it.

'There's something else,' said Harry. 'She used the same phrase that Bayliss did in her tweet. Assuming that she sent it herself. *They drove her to this.*'

Noble said nothing, just raised an eyebrow and nodded slowly.

'Anyway, I'd best be going,' Harry said. 'I'll need to write up my report before the morning.'

He went to walk past Noble but she stopped him, looking up, looking lost.

'I need your help,' she said.

Though Frankie Noble appeared hard, the concrete exterior was deliberate, cleverly crafted. Seeing her lift it, show some fault-lines when she was still at work and not in a pub with a beer in one hand, or lying on his bed with a quarter of a bottle of vodka spilt on the sheets and the other three swilling around her atonic stomach, seemed out of place, and it made him afraid. The conversation on the drive over might well have been civil, but that didn't mean she wasn't trying to play him now.

40

'With what?'

'This is my first murder case as SIO. I didn't expect to be in charge and I'm out of my depth. That's why I've got the super buzzing around my ears.'

'You don't know it's a murder yet,' Harry said, immediately regretting it. 'I really ought to be going, Frankie.'

She grabbed his arm and pulled him close.

'Answer three questions for me and I'll let you go.'

Maybe it was because he hadn't slept in twenty-two hours, or because of what he'd just seen in the flat on Calais Street, but Harry was suddenly furious.

'Who the hell do you think you are?' he seethed. 'You wouldn't treat any of your other professional colleagues like this, would you?'

'If Bayliss was murdered and it's something to do with the investigation that happened at Belgrave, then I'm going to need someone who knows that world.'

Harry took a deep breath, trying to calm himself down but instead he inhaled a large gulp of Noble's cigarette smoke and coughed, exhausted.

'For fuck's sake, get that out of my face,' he said, waving a hand between them. '*I don't know that world.* You'll be able to find an expert in paediatrics, probably even in congenital heart surgery. They can help you out.'

'My arse,' said Noble. 'They'll just sit on the fence, won't tell me anything useful. Especially if it turns out Bayliss was murdered because of something that happened at that hospital. I need someone I can trust.'

'And you can trust me?' Harry asked, aware of how ridiculous what Noble had said sounded. Doctors were investigated all the time, some of them even struck off. It wasn't that uncommon for it to make the news, and far too often a GMC investigation would provoke a doctor to suicide, another situation Harry found desperately sad. But the possibility that it could compel somebody to murder was hardly credible. Yet here they were, standing directly opposite each other now, hands on hips, another couple having an argument in public.

'Look, I'm asking you as a one-off favour,' Noble said. 'You can invoice for the time it takes you. All I want to know is that you'll pick up if I call.'

Harry took a deep breath and tried a different angle.

'There'll be another FME on-call during the daytime. Several, I'd expect. Find out who's on the rota and ask them.'

'Oh, come off it, Harry,' Noble said. 'They'll be way too busy and something like this is too sensitive for whichever G4S plonker they've got on for tomorrow.'

'I don't have access to any more details than what's in public. The DoH will have the report, it'll probably be in the public domain, in plain English, and like I said you can call the duty FME if anything gets lost in translation. I can't get involved, I've got too much going on at the moment to get wound up in something like this.'

'Harry, I'm just asking a favour!'

He barged past her, going in with his shoulder first.

'Harry, please!'

He kept going, trying to block out the sounds of her swearing and cursing his name, hating the echo of his own words, how self-important it sounded. But she was asking him to go above the call of duty in a case that appeared so politically toxic he wanted to be nowhere near it, and despite her protestations he possessed no skills or knowledge that could help her, only the fact that he was a pushover, that she knew he could be guilt-tripped into almost anything. He was still enraged, coughing up her cigarette smoke, when he reached his car, slamming shut the door.

In the car Harry reached for the pill-bottle he kept in the glove compartment, shook two into his open hand and swallowed them without any water because he didn't have any to hand. The kick didn't come in until he was about ten metres away from Brixton police station, past the two smoking coppers who'd watched him take a Class B substance metres from them. He felt swelled by the amphetamine, though he knew that it was chemical trickery, dopamine and noradrenaline flooding his brain, deluding him into thinking that he had more energy than he actually did.

Harry didn't self-prescribe. The doctors who did, and there were many, were usually caught before too long. He bought the drugs online in bulk, every three months. They were delivered to

42

an Amazon locker in a shopping centre near St Paul's, and he picked them up and transferred them to the three pill-bottles labelled as aspirin, one in his house, one in his car, one in his locker at work. Of course, it looked like a habit and yes, it was, but it was a necessary one. He knew it could kill him if he wasn't careful, so he was. He had three rules: no more than seven pills a day, never fall asleep at work, never fall asleep whilst driving.

He got into trouble with the definition of a day, though. That night, he'd come straight into the shift on the back of a day's work in A&E. He'd been awake and functioning for twenty-two hours, and he hadn't really slept the night before, either. He'd been out until four in the morning, first in the pubs around Lavender Hill and then at a homeless shelter up towards the common, holding a picture of the girl with pink hair. The one they called Zara, the girl the *Crimewatch* appeal was about to go out on, the girl lying on Tennyson Ward at the Ruskin, being turned every other hour to stop the pressure sores building up on her skin.

Harry picked the homeless shelters for a few reasons. She'd been severely malnourished when she'd been attacked, and it would go some way to explain why nobody had reported her missing or come forward to claim her as a relative. That said, apart from a piece last year in the *Sunday Express*, the case had garnered little attention. It had taken Harry months of emails and calling in favours to get the Met to launch an appeal. The detective who'd organised it was a high-flying DS with the unfortunate name of David Cameron, part of a small unit based at the Yard who reviewed open cases, usually violent crimes. Even to him it had been a tough sell. Frankie Noble had introduced them – Cameron had been trained by her late husband, who'd been a DCI before he went under the front wheel of an articulated lorry on his way to work. Now, Harry hoped more than anything that the appeal would draw something, that he could add a method to his strategies. At the moment all he had was a list of the shelters in the area. So far he'd visited almost all of them, at least those which had been open on 8 August, 2011. And, as he'd now been told several times, the guest turnover was such that even a young girl was unlikely to be remembered from three years ago. He'd urged them to watch the *Crimewatch* episode on Monday, and get all their colleagues to as well, and had been met with patronising nods and hollow promises.

After the staff at the shelter had got tired of him, he'd driven home half-asleep and fallen fully asleep in the car park underneath his block of flats. Waking up three hours later, he'd cycled to the hospital and changed, eaten and showered there. Then twelve hours in A&E and straight back home to get in the car and start his police shift. He'd managed an hour's sleep during the night, between two-thirty and three-thirty, when he'd got the call to come and take a look at Pauline Wright, but now, as he waited in traffic on the Elephant & Castle roundabout, he found himself fighting just to stay awake behind the wheel.

That was the problem. Sleep to Harry was like catching smoke. It threatened when he didn't need it, when he needed to be alert, when other people's lives depended on the functioning of his brain. But on the rare occasions he got between two sheets it eluded him, his body too restless, his mind too full. Sex helped, as did alcohol.

So exhausted as he was, Harry didn't go to bed when he got home. He drank a glass of water, then sat in his living room looking over at the view, waiting for his laptop to load so he could write his crime-scene report. His view was north-facing, like Susan Bayliss's had been. He sat in the chair, imagining hands on his shoulders, forcing him down as a blade sliced open an artery in his arm, his life spilling out onto the floor.

The sound of his phone brought him back.

'Hey.'

'Hey babe. How was your shift?'

Harry yawned. He'd met Beth Prideaux in March, when she'd been working in A&E at the Ruskin. She was a GP trainee, rotating through the specialties, and now she was down at Bethlem, doing psychiatry.

'It was ok,' he said. 'You're ringing early.'

'I'm walking up to work from the station now. Thought I'd try and catch you before you went to sleep. You see anything interesting?'

'Maybe,' said Harry. 'A suicide that might be a murder.'

He gathered that she hadn't yet heard about Bayliss. When she did, she'd immediately figure out that Harry would have been called to certify. Beth had worked in paediatrics at Belgrave, though two years before the scandal and in general paediatric medicine, not cardiac surgery. Still, she would have a million theories.

'Cool,' she said.

'You on-call today?'

'No, just ward cover. The mad and the bad of Bromley. Shame I can't see you tonight.'

She said it unloaded, without blame, frustrated only at the inevitable nature of a relationship between two junior doctors. She being on day shifts, he on nights meant that it could be weeks without seeing one another, but that was life.

'Remind me when you're off?' Harry asked.

'Tomorrow and Wednesday. Then ward cover Tuesday, Thursday and Friday, on-call Saturday night.'

Harry nodded in his chair, yawning. He'd taken Monday to Thursday off as annual leave. The *Crimewatch* appeal aired tomorrow night and Cameron had assured him that he would be in touch that same evening if there was any news, particularly an ID. But he expected that the phone calls would need searching through, following up on, and as Cameron didn't have any official assistance Harry had volunteered to spend Tuesday and Wednesday making phone calls. It had taken long enough to persuade the police to reopen the investigation, and an opportunity like this one was unlikely to come again.

'We still good for lunch tomorrow?' Beth said. Harry realised he'd been ignoring her, his thoughts away with the appeal.

'Sure,' said Harry, 'We can do something in the afternoon if you wanted, too. Come back and—'

'Sweet!' Beth said. 'The weather's meant to be gorgeous, hottest day of the year according to the *Metro*. We can go up to Hyde Park and take a boat out on the lake?'

Harry had been about to suggest coming back to his flat and sticking on a box set. She liked political dramas, and they were halfway through the first season of *House of Cards*. He scolded himself for wanting that, for wanting her with him just because it made it easier to sleep.

'That'd be nice,' he said, clicking the bones in his neck together. A blank word document on his computer stared out at him. Harry yawned, too loud for her to have missed it. He braced himself for the question.

'You get any sleep last night?'

'Millwall lost,' said Harry. 'Never bodes well.'

'And you're sure I can't join you at Peter's tomorrow? I'd love it if we were together for your big moment . . .'

Harry had arranged to watch the *Crimewatch* episode with his old superior from the RAMC, Peter Tammas, who lived in a care home down in Kingston. Tammas had taken a bullet in the neck out in Afghanistan and was paralysed from the shoulders down, on a ventilator, and he was the closest thing Harry had to a parent. Beth had met him a month or so back and they'd immediately hit it off. Beth was like that – she had an overwhelming capacity for pity. It was the only reason Harry could come up with as to why she was still interested in him, given that he hardly had the optimum lifestyle for a relationship.

'It'd be nice just to catch up,' said Harry. 'Boys night. But we'll do something in the afternoon, I promise.'

'Ok then. Borough Market, oneish?'

'Sounds good.'

'I'll find somewhere,' said Beth, the excitement bouncing in her voice. 'Right, I'd better go.'

'Have a nice day.'

'Have a good sleep. Love you, Harry.'

Harry never knew what to say. She'd been saying it for a couple of weeks, the first few times after a bit too much wine, something that just slipped out, but now more deliberately, saying goodbye, waiting on the doorstep, daring him to challenge her, look her in the eyes.

'Take care, babe. Bye.'

He put the phone down on the table and massaged his temples. Beth was fantastic, the best thing that had happened to his life in a long, long time. She'd asked him out, not the other way round, in a well-constructed ruse involving arranging some after-work drinks with the other SHOs, inviting Harry along, and arranging for the others to drop out one-by-one. She took no prisoners and loved him despite his obsessions, which he'd told her about in an attempt to scare her off after she'd suggested a proper, grown-up, exclusive relationship. She'd even come with him, once or twice, to hand out photographs of the girl with pink hair, outside Clapham Junction.

But he wasn't sure he loved her. He might, in time, but not yet.

He thought a little bit more about that before his mind was back with Susan Bayliss and Teodora Guzman, crying and shaking in the police cell in Brixton, alone and grieving. He imagined the horror of coming into this house, seeing the chair facing the window and Beth there, touching her, finding her cold.

He stopped that thought, crushed it like an autumn leaf underfoot, and started typing.

TWO

Sunday, 24 August
Afternoon

Harry slept for four-and-a-half hours that morning, though it was a case of quantity over quality. Twice he half-woke, pulling the sheet off him to fight the heat, the humidity. He couldn't open the window because of the train line that ran past his apartment block, and the two fans he owned were on full power already. He had snapshots of dreams, one with a helicopter and a field of lavender, another where he was on a boat, feeling hot liquid on his skin, then sinking into cold, dirty water. Another with him and Beth in a police cell, her crying as she ripped a piercing she didn't have from her face. The first two were familiar pseudomemories, one from Afghanistan, the other from the January before last when he'd lost his friend. They didn't bother him, but the one with Beth made him feel cold.

He woke to the noise of someone knocking on his door. He pulled the sheets off his body, rolled out of bed, muscles stiff, and grabbed a T-shirt from a chair in the corner of his bedroom. The front door to his apartment block had a code, so unless someone else had let them in there was no way a visitor could get up to his sixth-floor flat.

'Hang on!' he shouted. His throat was raw, as if he'd been smoking, and he was aware of his own smell as he wandered into his hallway, his need for a long shower. He grabbed a look at the time. One-thirty. He still felt tired. Might even get to sleep again before his shift started. The person outside knocked again and Harry wondered if it was the postman, or some kind of trader who'd managed to get in the front. Usually they left post in the boxes in the foyer and he didn't remember ordering anything that would need a signature.

Harry opened the door, ready to apologise for the appearance and odour, until he saw who it was.

'Did I wake you?' said Noble. 'I'm sorry.'

'How the fuck did you get in here?' Harry said. He opened the door wider and checked the hallway. She was alone.

'Nine four six eight,' she said, trying not to grin. 'Copper's memory. And you should email the landlord and get that changed, it's a security risk.'

'What the fuck do you think you're doing?' Harry said. 'Aren't you meant to be running a murder investigation?'

'Can I come in?' Noble said quietly.

'No you fucking can't! I mean who the hell do you think you are? If a bloke treated an ex like this they'd be done for harassment. Leave me alone.'

He was speaking through clenched teeth rather than shouting, not wanting another scene with the neighbours. Of the other two flats on the sixth floor, one was owned by a Saudi businessman who only used it a few weeks a year and the other was rented by a married couple who'd twice asked Harry over for a candid chat after Noble had moved in. The first time it had been the day after three consecutive five-in-the-morning rows, the second a month later when she'd vomited on the landing outside their door. Seeing Noble back in his home made all those moments flood back, like the dream he'd had, snapshots of negative experiences, all combining into one another. It made him furious. He'd given her chance after chance, but in the end he could never compete. If he really thought about it, it would be more than hypocritical to blame her for an addiction. A phrase that he'd been told in medical school by a goatee-sporting psychiatrist long since retired spun in his head.

Nobody ever chooses to be an alcoholic.

Nobody ever chooses to fall in love with one, either, Harry thought. Here she was, back in the doorway to his flat, and he faced the choice to let her back in. He'd been in this exact situation at least ten times in the three months she'd shared the apartment with him. The last time he'd stood facing her in that doorway was the first time he'd turned her away.

Harry said nothing, just turned and headed back into his apartment, going into the kitchen, almost on autopilot. He heard Noble close the door behind him and realised he was only in a T-shirt and the boxer shorts he'd slept in. It felt like he was back in his first year at uni, in his halls of residence down on Champion Hill, caught out by a fire drill while he was showering. He filled the kettle and switched it on, for a distraction.

'I'm putting on the kettle,' he called. 'Make us both a coffee, I'm gonna get dressed.'

With that Harry darted from the kitchen into his room, shutting the door behind him. He'd shower when she was gone. It seemed unlikely he'd get a chance to go back to sleep now. He went through his cupboard, found a shirt and buttoned it, his fingers trembling. Either from the fact Frankie Noble was making herself coffee a few metres away or the withdrawal he got whenever he woke up and didn't take one of his pills within ten minutes. Or both. Fucking hell, he told himself as he ran clammy hands through sticky, unwashed hair. You had no good reason to let her in. Should have told her to come back when she had a warrant, that would have pissed her off.

He got some trousers on eventually and pulled a belt through the loops, trying to cut through all the noise in his head. As he headed back into his living room, Noble was standing looking out of the window, and in that moment Harry saw into her mind. Again he thought of Susan Bayliss, staring out of the open window as someone opened up her brachial artery and held her against the chair.

'I told you, Harry,' she said, not turning around. 'I need your help.'

Steam rose from a mug she'd left on the kitchen side. Harry took it and sat at the breakfast bar, shuffling awkwardly on the stool.

'I told you to ring the duty FME,' he said, burning his lips on the coffee. She'd made it with two teaspoons of instant and filled only three-quarters full, the way he liked it. It pissed him off.

'I did,' said Noble, 'He was a useless wanker who gave me some bollocks about being outside the limits of his malpractice insurance. At least that's what I think he said, he could barely speak fucking English.'

As reluctant as he was to engage, Harry could believe it. There were relatively few independent Force Medical Examiners around anymore, especially in London – the vast majority of police surgeons were polo-shirted agency doctors provided by the same contractors who staffed the custody suites, harbingers of the tide of privatisation that was washing over every public service since the election of the last government. There'd even been a couple of occasions where he'd witnessed one of his agency-employed colleagues at work and become concerned to the point he'd had to intervene. Though many were competent, some were the kind of bottom-feeding doctors who'd fallen out of the training system at some point, the types who found jobs on cruise ships.

She turned around and her eyes were wet.

'I really need your help. You know I wouldn't ask unless it was true.'

This time he was fairly sure the emotion was genuine. He'd been all too eager to dismiss her that morning. Maybe it was the fact he'd been awake something like twenty-two hours, or that he'd been so stirred up by having to interact with her all of a sudden. A lot of Harry's life was in boxes in his head, because the things he had done and the choices he had made necessitated it, and Frankie Noble was bursting out of hers now.

'This is fucked up, Frankie,' he said. 'I've moved on. We can't just click our fingers and go back to being . . . friends, or whatever.'

'I don't want us to be friends,' Noble said. 'But I know you're the best person for what I need and I am really in the fucking shit here.'

Harry took a sip of coffee, spilling some as he did. It made him jump back, trying to get his shirt clear, which just made him spill more. As he wiped his hands, he went into the kitchen cupboard, took the pill-bottle with the aspirin label on it, shook two into his cupped hands and washed them down with the coffee. Noble didn't know about his habit. She'd asked him about the aspirin once, because she'd never seen it in a bottle before, only in blister packs, but he'd spun her some bullshit about cluster headaches and a mate who worked in neurology prescribing it. A few times when she'd seen him pacing the living room in the wee hours, the result of his fucked circadian cycle, she'd asked him if his head-aches were bad again.

'I'm out of my depth. I was lucky to get the transfer to Homicide & Serious when the DI's post came up, if I'm honest. And now Ian's gone and got fucking cancer, and it's me calling up the super in the middle of the fucking night. I'm not ready for this shit, but I don't have a choice, do I?'

'Put in for a transfer, then,' Harry said. The hit had gone straight to his heart, like it always did, and then to his skin, the buzz up the hairs on the back of his neck.

'As if,' said Noble. 'You know I've been trying to get back into SCD-1 since they fucked me over the Finsbury case. Anyway, transfer or not, I'm here now. It's my murder.'

'If it's your murder, why are you here making me coffee instead of out there working it?'

Noble had a satchel slung over her shoulder, and she reached down and unclipped it, walking over to the breakfast bar and laying down a plastic document wallet. Inside was a quarter-inch dossier, photocopied going by the stains and lines on the front page. The title was all in capitals, printed and large.

SERIES OF POSTOPERATIVE DEATHS AMONGST CONGENITAL CARDIAC SURGERY PATIENTS AT BELGRAVE HOSPITAL FOR SICK CHILDREN.
SUSAN K. BAYLISS BSc. MB BS MRCS
23 MAY 2014

'Where'd you find this?' asked Harry, lifting the document out of its wallet and placing it on the table.

'In a hiding place underneath the floorboards in her bedroom,' said Noble. 'She'd also left a copy with her solicitors. Can you believe that?'

'Christ,' said Harry. He knew he should ask her to leave again, but in his mind he went back to Bayliss's flat, saw the symmetrical bruising about the collarbone, the whole discordance of the scene. Then he looked back at Noble, there in his kitchen, across the bar from him, the two of them talking over one of her cases as they'd done many times before. Work chat in the evenings, the patients he'd seen, the wife-beaters and drug pushers she'd charged. It had only taken seconds to go back to normal, curiosity getting the better of him.

'Why do you need my help?' he asked.

'Open it,' said Noble.

Harry did so. The first page was entitled 'Case 1: Patient A'. There followed two pages of text, which seemed to be a summary of a patient history and subsequent operation, written in prose, an almost journalistic style. Phrases jumped out as Harry skim-read . . . *placed on ECMO – a type of specialised life support* . . . *operation conducted by Mr Elyas Mohamed, Consultant Cardiac Surgeon* . . .

nineteen days old ... discussions with Great Ormond Street ... now too sick to survive a transplant ... died of cardiac failure.

'The next page,' Noble said. 'We can deal with that.'

Harry flipped over, recognising the orange paper of an intra-operative surgical note – the logo at the top was that of the Belgrave, but it was otherwise identical to the one the surgeons at the Ruskin used. Part of the notes had been censored, gone over with a black highlighter in an attempt to protect the patient's confidentiality, so the name wasn't present, but the rest of the records were clear. Date: 06/12/13. Surgeon: MOHAMED, E. Assistants: PADMORE, T., BAYLISS, S. Anaesthetist: REED-CARROLL, J. The name Elyas Mohamed rang a bell, the rumours he'd heard.

Harry skimmed the notes outlining the surgical procedure, the fuzzy photocopy of handwritten cursive, before flicking through to further pages. These were daily notes from the Cardiac ICU, discussions with specialists, and the family members, another operative note from a second operation – Surgeon: GILMARTIN, H. H. Assistants: MOHAMED, E., PADMORE, T. – more and more print-outs of ICU notes. The final page was the grimmest of medical bureaucracy. A death certificate, listing Cause 1a) acute cardiac failure 1b) rupture of grafted aortic valve following Ross procedure 1c) congenital aortic atresia.

This would be one hell of a ground for unprofessional conduct, Harry thought. Photocopying medical notes and taking them home was bad enough, but putting them into some kind of dossier to give to the press was career suicide. He reread the title. This was her manifesto. It was like she'd read *Whistleblowing for Dummies*, going through every chapter. The suspension, the mental breakdown and the grand exposé.

'Was this what she leaked to the DoH?' Harry said.

'Looks like it. But she kept copies.'

'You really think that her death had something to do with this?'

'That tweet,' said Noble. 'We can't ignore this.'

'We?'

'My team,' said Noble. 'The investigation. Look, I need some-one with a medical eye to look over this, see if it's legit, see if there's anything suspicious that could give someone a motive. I've been in touch with the people at the Department of Health who are doing the inquiry, and they say they're cooperating, but none of them are in London today. You know how fast this shit moves.'

Harry breathed deeply and closed his eyes, perhaps hoping that she'd be gone when he reopened them.

'Do you know what's going on tomorrow?' he said.

She looked at her watch.

'25 August,' she said. 'Your birthday's not until September.'

Harry didn't laugh.

'Zara's TV appeal is going out,' he said. 'Nine o'clock, BBC One. I've taken some annual leave so I can help DS Cameron with following up the calls. I've been working towards this for months, Frankie.'

'And I won't get in your way,' Noble said. 'I promise. I know how much this means to you.'

Not enough to agree to work the case when we were together, Harry stopped himself from saying. Sure, she'd been in CID, so it hadn't been her remit, but she could have helped him on the side. Instead she'd just asked around her colleagues, which was effectively what he'd been doing since he started his police work.

Finally, Harry said, 'What do you need?'

'A summary of what happened with the kids who died at Belgrave,' Noble said. 'The inquiry. Susan Bayliss's role in it. Just the relevant details.'

'How do I know what's relevant?'

'Use your judgement. I trust you. How long do you reckon it'll take?'

'How long's this thing?' Harry said, picking up the document and taking another slug of coffee.

'A hundred or so pages.'

Harry winced. 'Ok,' he said. 'I guess you want this ASAP?'

Noble nodded.

'We're trying to locate Mr Mohamed, Bayliss's supervisor, as we speak, bring him in for questioning. We're also trying to liaise with the Department of Health investigation, see if we can get access to their material. There's a lot going on. So it'd be nice, yeah.'

'Get your team to send me everything you've got so far. Newspapers and that stuff. The DoH report. I can't be arsed trawling through Google for you.'

'I'll get it done,' Noble said, walking past him, already heading for the door. 'Are you working tonight?'

'Night shift, A&E.'

'You starting at eight?'

'Yep.'

'The Bayliss post-mortem's at two, so it should be done by then. I'll buy you dinner at seven?'

Harry tried to tell himself that his rage was disproportionate, that he needed to calm himself down.

'You owe me more than dinner for this, Frankie.'

'I know,' said Noble, turning around. There was still something wrong, with the suit, with the hair, with the energy in her step. 'But I know you're not doing it for me, are you?'

She left him on that, thinking about the woman he'd certified dead eight hours ago. Guzman's voice again: *Those fuckers treated her like she'd tried to burn the place down.*

Harry finished the coffee with a single gulp. His laptop was still on the table by the window where he'd left it after doing his notes that morning. He opened it up, sat down and looked out at the summer sky. Heard his front door close and the sound of the arriving elevator.

The first child to die was Emmanuel Abẹdiji, who'd been six months old when his parents had taken him to the GP, concerned he wasn't quite growing as fast as he ought to be. The GP, who'd heard a heart murmur at the six-week check but had assumed all was relatively fine as the child was growing well, had referred them to their local hospital, the Ruskin, where the diagnosis of congenital heart disease had been made.

As he'd developed, Emmanuel's aortic valve, the one between the left ventricle and the aorta, the main blood vessel that supplied the entire body with blood, had failed to develop correctly. The result was that the aorta was too narrow to allow enough blood to pump out of the heart, and much of what did escape flowed back into the ventricle. The paediatricians at the Ruskin had said that the only treatment was open-heart surgery, and Mr and Mrs Abediji, an ordinary young couple who lived in a flat above the dry-cleaner's that they owned and operated with two brothers in Nunhead, had feared the worst.

Mr Mohamed received the Abediji family in his clinic at the Belgrave within a week, and listed out the options. In his opinion, the best way to proceed was a Ross procedure, a complex operation in which the pulmonary valve, which had developed healthily, would be removed and used to replace the failed aortic valve; the pulmonary valve would then itself be replaced by a transplanted valve from an organ donor. The procedure was commonplace among older children at Belgrave, but done rarely on an infant as young as Emmanuel. Nevertheless, Mohamed was confident that it was the boy's best chance at a normal life. Emmanuel was admitted, and a suitable donor valve arrived on a cold November morning. Mohamed took Emmanuel to the operating theatre with both his registrars, Susan Bayliss and Theo Padmore, assisting. The operation was a total success, and after a week in the intensive care unit and another two recuperating on the Belgrave's cardiac ward, Abediji was discharged home just in time to spend Christmas with his family. Indeed, the *Metro* had run a story on eight-month-old Emmanuel, including a photo of him smiling in his hospital bed, a feeding tube in his nose. BABY EMMANUEL GETS A CHRISTMAS MIRACLE.

The follow-up scans and appointments were all fine, and Emmanuel's heart gave him no trouble until a Sunday morning in March, when his mother had trouble rousing him to get up in time for church. They called up the out-of-hours GP who said she'd be around to see him, but when his lips turned blue they began to panic and called an ambulance, who brought him straight into the Ruskin.

The skeleton of a memory Harry had recalled in Bayliss's flat now had flesh. He had been in Resus when the patient had been brought in and had helped the paediatricians stabilise him before the consultants arrived and took over. He recalled watching them from the back of A&E, after the specialists had taken over. They'd run test after test to work out what was wrong, but after a few minutes Emmanuel's failing heart had stopped completely. They'd worked on him for at least an hour, and Harry remembered trying vainly to pretend he was focusing on the paperwork in front of him as the consultant was saying the final words:

'I think we've reached a point where we should stop. Does everyone agree?'

There had been silence, Harry remembered. Absolute silence, apart from the grating sound of CPR on an infant's chest. That sound had stopped as the consultant took her young colleague's hands and held them at her side.

Abdul Mubarak had been born with congenital aortic valve stenosis, the same problem as Emmanuel Abediji but much, much worse. Often such severe disease was picked up during the pregnancy, but Abdul's mother – a refugee from Somalia who spoke no English and survived off benefits in a damned flat on an Abbey Wood housing estate – hadn't attended her more recent antenatal scans, being too busy looking after her other two children while their father worked double shifts. The doctors on the neonatal unit at Woolwich Hospital had told them Abdul's only hope was to transfer him immediately to the specialist unit at the Belgrave, where he went, rushed across London in a specialised neonatal ambulance. Barely hours after he was born, Mr Mohamed placed cannulas into his great vessels and attached Abdul to a heart-lung machine in their intensive care unit.

That bought them a few days, but it was only life support, not a cure. So Mr Mohamed had told the Mubarak family that Abdul was a candidate for the same procedure he had performed the previous week on Emmanuel Abediji, with great success.

And so, on only his sixth day of life, Abdul had been put to sleep, and Elyas Mohamed had opened up his miniscule chest, switched around the valves in a heart the size of a golf ball, and transplanted one donated from a child who had died of a brain abnormality two floors below. The operation took seven hours, and when Abdul was returned to the intensive care unit, his heart was pumping poorly, and he took a while to come off the heart-lung machine, but was doing ok. He woke up and even took a little feed.

A week after the operation, the replacement valve ruptured. Mr Mohamed took Abdul back to theatre, this time with Professor Gilmartin, the head of the heart surgery department, but they could only limit the damage. Soon Abdul's heart had failed completely and he was back on the heart-lung machine. They talked about a complete heart transplant, and the deeply religious Mubarak family had kept a vigil at his side in the ICU around the clock, praying for a miracle, but Abdul died before they could get him on the waiting list.

He was twenty-three days old.

The third child to be operated on was Jayden Capp, though he was actually the second to die. The family were from Eastbourne, three hours' drive away from Belgrave, and Jayden had spent most of his two years of life in hospital. He'd been born with severe learning disabilities, neuromuscular disease and deafness, the product of a chromosomal abnormality called DiGeorge syndrome. In addition, his aorta had failed to develop in the womb. He'd been transferred to Belgrave shortly after he'd been born, when Mohamed had repaired the blood vessel, widening the outflow tract and inserting a Gore-Tex graft. When Jayden had been discharged, Mr Mohamed had been sure to inform them that the graft was only a temporary repair and he would likely need a Ross procedure in the years to come.

When he was approaching three, that moment arrived. William and Sonja Capp had waved their son goodbye as he'd been wheeled into theatre holding his favourite toy, a stuffed version of the main character from the film *Cars*. The operation was performed by Mr Mohamed, the expert in valve repairs, with Gilmartin ready to assist given the complexity of Jayden's case. The Capp family had been told that the operation would take about four hours, so when Jayden hadn't emerged from the operating theatre after seven and a half they feared the worst. When they saw Professor Gilmartin running into the operating theatre, those fears were all but confirmed.

A part of the wall of Jayden's heart had come away, causing uncontrollable haemorrhage and a massive heart attack. They tried and tried to take him off the bypass machine, cooled him right down again and warmed him up again, tried to buy the surgeons time, but it took them hours to get the bleeding under control. Sonja Capp had refused to leave the corridor outside the operating theatre until two o'clock the following morning, when she watched the team wheel Jayden towards the PICU, their faces grave. They sat the Capps down and told them that, whilst there was always hope, children who'd needed as long as Jayden had on the bypass machine almost never woke up.

They'd been right. Over the next few days, it became obvious that the brain damage Jayden had suffered after the haemorrhage was irreversible.

They switched the machines off a week before his third birthday.

Olivia Roberts had been up all night sweating and shaking, and had a fever that wouldn't go away, so her mother took her to their GP in Blackheath to be told it was probably the flu – it being winter – but to be on the safe side she should probably take Olivia to A&E for a check over. Half an hour after they arrived at her local hospital in Lewisham, the diagnosis of endocarditis, a bacterial infection of the heart valves, had been made, and she was accepted for transfer to the Belgrave. Despite strong antibiotics, and a ventilator, Olivia got worse, not better. Further scans revealed the culprit, an abscess the size of a grape on her tricuspid valve, and the only chance of rescue was to take it out and put a new one in. Mohamed and Bayliss took her to theatre as an emergency case on a Monday night, taking out the pus-filled, infected valve and putting a prosthetic one in place. Olivia was out of the ICU a week later, home two weeks after that, and back at nursery inside a month. It was about as simple as open-heart surgery could get.

The following month, Olivia fell ill at nursery, drowsy and breathless, so they called her mother to take her to A&E. When they got her to Lewisham General, she was barely alive, and she went blue, and collapsed in the waiting room. They did CPR, rushed her into the Resus room, gave her every drug they could think of, but there was nothing to be done.

And so it goes.

After he finished reading the document, Harry took a fifteen-minute shower, spending half of it sitting down, before popping another pill and sitting down in front of the computer. Assuming that none of the information he'd just read was false, he could see how Susan Bayliss had come to the conclusion she had, that something was awry at Belgrave Hospital for Sick Children. Indeed, in a letter at the back of the dossier, filled with the typos and rambling sentences of someone writing drunk, despairing, or both, she had outlined the people she'd reported her concerns to. First to Mr Mohamed himself, then to Professor Gilmartin, then to the manager responsible for heart surgery, Alison Price. According to Bayliss, all of them had promised an internal investigation, and done nothing.

The children had all undergone surgery at the Belgrave between November 2013 and January 2014, four of the nine children Mr Mohamed had operated on in that time period, but Bayliss hadn't noticed the link until months later. Whilst Abdul and Jayden had died in hospital, Emmanuel and Olivia had died months after their operations, in March and April respectively. Only when Mohamed had asked Bayliss to deputise for him at a follow-up clinic in early May – and half the patients she had expected had failed to turn up – did she make the connection. The mortality statistics compiled by the Department of Health covered only deaths in the first thirty days after surgery, Bayliss argued, and therefore Mohamed had thought he could get away with it.

No bloody wonder she'd blown the whistle, then, Harry thought. All hospitals that did heart surgery on children had to publish mortality rates for each procedure, and the national average for all operations combined – Harry had checked – was two and a half per cent. For the three-month period comprising November to January, forty-four per cent of Elyas Mohamed's patients hadn't lived past six months. You didn't need to be a statistician to know that the numbers were different enough to be worth investigating.

Now he spent his time going through the news websites. After the story had broken, the interest had briefly exploded. The hospital had quickly announced that a 'thorough internal review is already ongoing into these sad deaths, but as individual adverse incidents and not part of any trend', but it had been too little, too late. The Department of Health was soon involved, quietly suspending all children's cardiac operations at the Belgrave at the start of June whilst it conducted an emergency review of the service headed by Dame Sheila Anderson, the Deputy Chief Medical Officer. All attempts to contact Mr Mohamed or Miss Bayliss appeared to have been met with blank silence. The parents, on the other hand, had been vocal – it didn't take long to find interviews with both Olivia Roberts's and Emmanuel Abediji's parents, lambasting the hospital for its lack of communication, firm in their belief that there was some cover-up of their children's deaths, thankful to Bayliss for finally speaking up for them.

The Department of Health report came out amid much less media attention than the start of the investigation, which was no surprise to Harry. Good news was no news when it came to the NHS, and nobody was interested in the fact that the cardiac surgery service had been deemed safe, the four dead children merely a 'tragic coincidence', reduced in a twelve-page report to a quirk of statistics. Both Abdul and Jayden had been incredibly sick children who would have inevitably died without their operations, and almost certainly even if they'd been operated on elsewhere. As for Olivia and Emmanuel, who'd died suddenly months after leaving hospital, the investigation was inconclusive, but stated that there was 'nothing to suggest that their surgeries were anything other than correct and satisfactory, and no evidence that the operation had contributed to death in either case.'

And then came the darker side. Harry read the news reports naming Bayliss as the whistleblower and announcing her suspension from Belgrave, including the BBC article they'd skimmed that morning on DC Bhalla's phone, paper suits sticking to their clothes, craned necks around the screen. Some of the articles had a dignified tone, but in the tabloids, the campaign Teodora Guzman had alleged was obvious. *Children's hospital whistleblower had 'serious mental health issues'* read one. Another led with *Anonymous hospital source decries 'wild' accusations made by 'deranged' trainee surgeon.* Both quoted unnamed sources from within Belgrave confirming that Susan Bayliss had a history of psychological illness and in one case asserted that her instability was 'widely known' by hospital staff.

The story announcing Bayliss's suspension was dated 12th July. Going back to the very start of the document, Harry went through it again in detail, creating a timeline on his laptop.

27/11/13 – Emmanuel operated on
6/12/13 – Abdul operated on (1st time)
1312/13 – Abdul operated on (2nd time)
23/12/13 – Abdul dies
3/1/14 – Jayden operated on

6/1/14 – Jayden's life support switched off
20/1/14 – Olivia operated on
16/3/14 – Emmanuel dies
8/4/14 – Olivia dies
6/5/14 – SB takes clinic, discovers deaths of Olivia + Emmanuel
Last week May?? – SB leaks report
1/6/14 – DoH suspends surgery @ Belgrave
19/6/14 – DoH announces findings, surgery resumes
12/7/14 – SB suspended
24/8/14 – SB killed

It read sparsely for an account of the deaths of five people, and Harry looked at his glowing screen and the thick report by its side, and thought of Susan compiling something similar, but over how long? Weeks of internal wrestling to decide whether or not to blow the whistle. The Belgrave was internationally renowned, not just for congenital heart disease but for paediatric neurosurgery, cystic fibrosis, all manner of things. It was the oldest children's hospital in Europe, and took referrals from all over the world. To suggest that it was killing its patients, that one of its top surgeons was incompetent, was sacrilege.

But he couldn't stop the feeling of anger that was building up in him, which was almost equal to what he'd felt when he thought Bayliss had died by her own hand. For two hours he had been immersed in the words of this stranger, whom he felt he now knew. She had a tenacity, not just in her actions, but in the language with which she described them. He tried to remind himself that he was drawing conclusions based on one side of a story, that he knew next to nothing about this woman. Perhaps she had been depressed, perhaps she did have some vendetta against the hospital. But even if it was more subtle, if Bayliss had been one of the hundreds of doctors who succumbed to burnout, to the pressure of doing more with less, to see her humiliated like this in the national press made Harry more furious than he'd felt in a while. And to think that it might have led to her death, either at her hand or someone else's, intensified that by an order of magnitude.

Whether she had been wrong or right, surely it had been the right thing to do to raise the issue, so it was investigated at least.

He had no reason to doubt the Department of Health inquiry, but as far as he could see, Bayliss had done nothing but flag up a worrying statistic. He knew that many doctors, himself included, were witness to much more obvious deficiencies in treatment and care and said nothing, just kept their heads down and waited until they moved on to their next rotation, when it would be someone else's problem. Because, as every good doctor knew, this was what happened if you stood up for what you thought was right. First the ridicule from your colleagues, then the loss of your employment, then the smear campaign . . . If he really thought about it, suicide made more sense than murder.

Harry finished typing, emailed his summary to Noble, and got up, his thighs and calves numb from the length of time he'd been sitting down, his eyes sore from the screen of his laptop, his brain tumbling with thoughts of small hearts stopping their beats and women being held down in wicker chairs as they bled to death.

His phone buzzed. Two texts from Beth.

Omg have you seen news?

Was that your 'suicide' last night? Bet you couldn't tell me even if it was . . .

He flicked straight to a news app on his phone, already knowing what the headline would be. The article was a stub, just a few lines of text. *Metropolitan Police confirm that 34-year-old woman found dead at an address in South London is Susan Bayliss, a surgeon recently suspended from Belgrave Hospital for Sick Children in London. This is a Breaking News story and will be updated shortly.* He tried to lift his hand to reply to Beth, but he found it paralysed. Sometimes he got like this, unaware of where he was, even whether he was awake or asleep. He stole a brief thought about Noble, and how much harder her job had just become.

Harry snapped out of it after too long and glanced at his watch. His shift started in three hours. He should head to the gym and swim or something, something easy, where all he had to do was push instead of thinking. Instead he pulled the blinds in his bedroom shut, set his alarm for two hours' time, stripped down to his boxers, and got between the cool sheets. Closed his eyes, for all the good it would do.

★   ★   ★

The mortuary at the John Ruskin University Hospital bore no resemblance to the chrome steel and floor-to-ceiling glass of pathology departments in TV shows. The subterranean room dated from the nineteenth century, a fact reflected in the chipped, off-white tiles and the lack of anything resembling ventilation, something Acting Detective Chief Inspector Frances Noble was all too aware of as she paced around, the August warmth oppressive. The mask, gloves and apron she wore to protect her from fluids only trapped more heat, and she wiped the sleeve of her blouse on her forehead again, the salty reek of sweat in her nose mixing with the liquorice taste of the lozenge she was rolling around her mouth. Fisherman's Friends at a post-mortem was one of those gems of police work picked up from a former mentor, a tiny detail that made an immeasurable difference.

There was no-one left to disseminate such advice now, Noble had realised. Hearing her own voice introduce herself as Acting DCI was still foreign enough, but the real fear had come when the mortuary technician had started the recording and she'd been asked to identify herself as Senior Investigating Officer. That was it, the line crossed. This was her investigation now – yes, Detective Superintendent Grenaghan was around, but he was over in the divisional headquarters at Sutton to talk about media strategy and resource allocation and other grown-up stuff. She was the one in the trench.

The other people in the room knew nothing of the inner turmoil she was going through, arms folded in one corner of the autopsy room. Not Professor Jain, at the table in a white gown, wellington boots and elbow-length rubber gloves, nor Williams, the forensics tech, nor DC Bhalla standing behind him, ready to receive whichever cavity swab or sectioned sample needed to be signed for. Nor Susan Bayliss, who was lying with her head on a block, naked and dissected in the name of evidence. This was Frankie Noble's tenth post-mortem as a detective, and she had no qualm with the sight of internal organs or the sound of a bonesaw on a human skull. The indignity of it all affected her every time, though. It was horrific enough to be murdered, but the violations which followed were worse still. Swabs of the genitalia, a stranger's hands delving through your heart and lungs, a thermometer placed into the anus.

For a woman who, in life, had reached her downfall by being vocal, by speaking out, Susan Bayliss hadn't made a sound when Jain had cut her open. The traditional Y-shaped incision had been avoided in order not to disturb the patches of bruising which Harry, appearing as he had out of the ether, had found on Bayliss's shoulders, so instead Jain had sliced through the midline and then laterally underneath her ribcage, dividing the skin into four flaps. Removing the internal organs en bloc, placing them with his assistant's help onto one of the long chrome tables for further analysis.

So far, he'd told them nothing they hadn't known already. He'd started with the wounds to the wrists and elbow, confirming that they were consistent with the short kitchen knife that had been recovered from the scene. He reiterated that the wound to the left brachial artery was serious enough to cause exsanguinating haemorrhage, wasn't so sure on the wrists, which appeared to be superficial, so he'd taken slides from all three and was now onto the top-to-toe examination. He'd also referred to the bruising on the shoulders and upper back, and agreed that it had been inflicted shortly before death. It also appeared to be diffuse, he'd said. More like the result of continued pressure over the area in question than a single blow.

Harry's voice burst into Noble's head again. *I think somebody held her down.*

'Could they have been caused by someone holding her?' Noble had asked Jain, as he'd examined the shoulders. When the professor leant over to inspect something, he always clasped his gloved, bloodied fingers behind his back, becoming his own stereotype. Every time he stood back up, his bones clicked.

'They could have been caused by lots of things.'

Noble stepped forward, up to the body. Jain was over at the side table, separating Bayliss's internal organs from one another. A creaking door from one side of the mortuary made all their heads turn, a young woman entering the viewing gallery. The gallery contained three rows of seats, so medical students would watch demonstrations, but today's was closed off from the scholars. The new arrival was DC Emily Acquah. As of a month ago, Acquah was Noble's aide, tasked to follow her around, note down everything she ordered and actioned, and even drive her places. Noble had refused that last part.

'This isn't open to—' Jain began.

'She's with me.'

Noble headed over to the glass partition, her plastic covershoes squeaking on the tiles.

'How's it going, Emily?'

'Door-to-door's just being wrapped up, guv. DC Simpson should have a report for you soon. I've been trying to call you, ma'am, but I don't think you've got any signal down here.'

The word *ma'am* unnerved her. It tended to precede bad news.

'What is it?' she said.

'It's leaked, I'm afraid,' Acquah said. 'About half an hour ago. Don't know where it came from, probably one of the uniforms, or Guzman, but it's out there. Twitter, online, all the major news websites. The super sent a message, said he had no choice but to officially confirm. It'll hit the six o'clock news as well, we think.'

'Shit,' Noble seethed. It had always been a question of when, not if, Bayliss's death would become public knowledge, but she had hoped for more than fourteen hours.

'I'm sorry.'

'It's not your fault.'

'Grenaghan told me to tell you he'll handle the media side, and anything on the budget.'

The budget wouldn't be a problem anymore, Noble thought, not now the case was about to catapult onto the front pages. The Met would pay for anything necessary to get it solved.

'Thanks. How are the guys? Are they doing alright?'

Before Acquah could answer, Jain called over in his booming, room-filling professor's voice.

'Inspector? I think you might be interested in this.'

Noble nodded a goodbye to Acquah and headed over to the dissecting table, where Jain had removed the upper part of Bayliss's digestive tract and sectioned it longitudinally, the contents poured out into a dish. Noble pulled another Fisherman's Friend from her pocket and slid it into her mouth.

'Her stomach and oesophagus,' Jain said, indicating the organs with a tweezer tip. 'That's the food-pipe.'

'Is it?' said Noble. 'I thought that was her gallbladder.'

Jain looked up at her sternly. She had never seen the pathologist smile, and she wouldn't be surprised if he never had in his life.

'The stomach contents, as you may be able to smell, consist of a large quantity of red wine,' Jain went on, pointing at the dark liquid rolling around one of the dishes on the table. 'It is remarkably undigested, so I suspect that a great deal of it was consumed immediately before death.'

Noble pictured Susan Bayliss in her chair, balcony doors open, summer night breeze on her face, drinking glass after glass, the knife hovering in her hand. Dutch courage was something she had enough experience of, though not to muster the intent to take her own life. In her case it had been simpler things she'd needed help with, like getting out of bed, or going to work.

'We also found remnants of white tablets in the stomach,' said Jain, 'and then this, lodged in the lower part of the oesophagus.'

Between his tweezers, Jain held one of the pills Noble recognised from the packet on Bayliss's kitchen table. Jain had attended the apartment after Harry had left, and had been shown the wine bottle and the antidepressants. He'd performed all the invasive tests to determine time of death via visceral temperature, and had arrived at a window of one to two in the morning.

'Sertraline,' said Noble.

'We'll need to test them to be sure, but it would appear so. However, it's rather odd to find a tablet of this size in the oesophagus, undigested. So I dissected the entire tract.'

Jain pulled open the cut surfaces of the gullet on the table, and Noble peered over to see. She'd stopped sucking the lozenge now, but the smells of bile and sick and death didn't bother her. What she was seeing was enough to block out all other senses. Nine or ten circular pills, some lodged in clumps of two or three, dispersed along the cut surface of Bayliss's oesophagus. The thoughts in Noble's head were beginning to combine, like streams forming a river, when Jain paced over to Susan Bayliss's empty, organless body.

'Naturally, my next step was to examine the oral cavity,' Jain said, leaning to look into Bayliss's mouth. 'I found five more tablets in the oropharynx. Again, entirely undissolved.'

The light was poor, but if Noble stooped over then she could see them too. Either way, there was no doubt. Jain had no reason to make this up. The professor stepped over to another table now, where Bayliss's heart and lungs sat, held upright by his assistant.

'And another one at the level of the carina, the bifurcation of the trachea,' said Jain, looking at Noble with the final word. She wondered whether the medical terminology was a dig at her for her earlier insubordination, but she didn't care right now. She was looking at a pill in Bayliss's windpipe.

'There is no conceivable way that those pills could have ended up there, undissolved, if the deceased had swallowed them whilst she was still alive,' Jain said, now standing between the tables, hands behind his back as if giving evidence in court. 'So I can say with certainty that they were placed there by an unknown party, when this woman was dead, or at the very least profoundly unconscious.'

Noble closed her eyes, trying to block out one sense at least, let herself focus. The public knew Susan Bayliss was dead, but they didn't yet know she'd been murdered. Much of the day had been built on hunch and suspicion, but now they had something concrete. Jain's voice saying the word *certainty* echoed in her head.

When she opened her eyes, all in the room were looking at her.

'How much force would it take to get the pills down that far?' she said.

'A considerable amount,' said Jain. 'The attacker would have had to tip her head back, hold her mouth open, and push them down the back of her throat.'

'Right,' said Noble, turning to Bryn Williams, the forensics tech: 'I'd like you to examine the face and neck for fingerprints, and swab everywhere you haven't already that we might get DNA off. And let's get those pills off to the lab, just so we know what we're dealing with.'

Routine cheek, nasal and oral swabs had been taken at the scene, and there were few in the business as thorough as Arif Jain, but if they had any opportunity at all to nail their killer – who now, undoubtedly, existed – then it had to be seized. They'd already failed to lift prints off Bayliss's bruised collarbones. The blister packets, Noble thought, and the wine. If the scene had been staged, everything was a potential giveaway, but even as those things excited her, her natural defeatism set in. If a killer had been careful once, they'd likely been careful the whole time.

'I'll let your man work,' said Jain.

'Sure,' said Noble. 'Emily, can you ring Maurice at Forensics and double-check if they've taken prints off the blister packets yet? Tell them to prioritise it if not.'

Immediately DC Acquah was heading out of the door. When she'd left the Incident Room that morning, there had still been a team at the flat in Myatt's Fields, so they wouldn't take long getting back to her.

'The cut, is it consistent with the knife we found?' Noble said.

'Very much so,' said Jain.

'But not self-inflicted?' said Noble.

Jain paced around the body, crouching at Bayliss's left-hand side. At her head, Williams took RTX powder from his work case and began dusting the face and mouth. They had to take extra care taking prints off cadaver skin, because the lawyers liked to pretend it was in some way a less reliable technique than lifting them from glass or doorknobs.

'The incision was made lateral to medial,' Jain went on, pointing to the wound in Bayliss's elbow, 'Inside to outside. The way that a right-handed person would most naturally do it. But with the knife held from the lateral side, with the knife blade at an obtuse angle, rather than an acute one which you'd would expect for a self-inflicted wound. It's possible she could have done it herself, but it hardly feels natural.'

Jain took several steps back and picked up a scalpel blade, with the sharp not attached, and mimed slashing right-to-left with it held in his right hand, exaggerating the difficulty. Noble ignored the posturing.

'You'd testify to that effect in court?'

'Of course.'

'This is murder, isn't it? One hundred per cent?' said Noble, though it was self-affirmatory. She already knew the answer.

Jain clicked his fingers behind his back again.

'Unless she slashed her elbow cack-handedly and got lucky hitting that artery, then someone else turned up and shoved those pills down her throat,' he said. 'I suspect the wrist wounds may have been post-mortem as well. You'll have to wait for the histology to be completely sure, but based on the scant amount of bleeding, that's my impression.'

That image flashed into Noble's mind, her internal cinema her best asset and worst enemy, and it was all the worse when she realised that given their current version of events, it had indeed happened. The pool of blood around the chair hadn't appeared disturbed. The killer must have climbed on top of Bayliss to get the pills that far down her gullet, she reasoned – she was glad as hell that they'd taken the time and resources to document the scene properly and call Jain out. Thanks in no small part to Harry, a voice told her, but she ignored it.

'I'm not seeing much,' said Williams. Acquah headed back inside, slamming the door and mouthing an apology to Noble.

'Right, you'll be ok for ten minutes here, will you? I need to make a phone call.'

Noble left Acquah to hold the fort and took off out of the mortuary into the scrub room, one hand clawing at her own covershoes, the other pulling off the white plastic apron. She rolled the plastic covers into a bin and spat the lozenge in it while it was open, its taste cloying at the sides of her mouth, dry from the heat. Not for the first time that day she pined for a drink, and not just to rehydrate. Then it was up the stairs and into the main corridor of the Ruskin, sweat sticking her biceps to the fabric of her blouse. It still took a lot of getting used to, wearing shirts and jackets, but that was the territory that she was into now. Finally some bars of signal arrived and she placed the call.

Detective Superintendent Grenaghan answered after two rings.

'One second,' he said, the Ulster accent almost impenetrable. She could hear the thwack of tennis balls in the background and suspected that he was at his club in Hampstead. It was a hard life, senior rank.

'Afternoon, boss,' she said once he was done. 'Thanks for helping out with the media side.'

'Not a problem, Frankie.'

'I thought I'd let you know, PM confirmed it's murder. Without doubt.'

73

'Ok. Let me know if there's anything you need done for tomorrow. I've no intention of leaving you high and dry on this one, not with you filling in for Ian and everything. The moment you feel your head slipping below the waterline, you call me, ok?'

Noble nodded, picking up a pace towards the exit. Grenaghan was relatively new, a transfer from the PSNI, and a high-flyer at that, at just a touch over forty despite his senior rank. Being an outsider, especially a young one, was not a recipe for success in the Met, but he'd fast formed a good relationship with the eight DCIs who worked for him. She liked what she'd seen of the man, but she didn't see the compassion as anything other than the veiled threat it was. He'd waste absolutely no time either taking over the investigation himself or transferring it to another team if they put a foot wrong.

'Absolutely, sir. You'll be sick of the sound of my voice by the end of the week.'

'I'm sure that won't be true,' Grenaghan said. 'And stop calling me sir. Stephen's fine. Good luck. And you call me, day or night.'

He hung up before she could reassure him that probably wouldn't be necessary, and she briefly swore in the middle of the hospital corridor, attracting a disapproving look from an elderly woman. She moved towards the exit at a jog, moving along a memorised path to the small cage between this building and the neuroscience institute that functioned as a smoker's refuge. If she was quick, she could get a quick one in and be back in the mortuary before anyone noticed.

Harry wasn't sure if he'd managed to sleep or not, but he felt somewhat refreshed as he cycled over to work. There was little better on a good day in London: the adrenaline of weaving through the bus lanes on Walworth Road, the chaos of Camberwell Green, the final push up the hill to the hospital. He could take it easy as he wasn't late for work, only for a meeting which he had no real desire to attend. As he secured his bike to the racks in the hospital car park – with two ultra-heavy D-locks, of course – he checked his email and saw a missed call from Noble. Christ, he'd only got around to deleting her number from his favourites at Easter.

'I was on my bike, sorry.'

'It's fine. Are you at the hospital?'

'Yeah.'

'I'm in AMT.'

Harry looked at his watch, wishing that it would wind forward so he'd be due on-duty and he'd have an excuse not to see her. But even handover wasn't for another forty-five minutes. As the overnight registrar, Harry would be running the A&E department after midnight, and there was no guarantee that he'd get a break at all, so lining his stomach beforehand was essential.

'Come to the hospital canteen,' he said.

'I'll be there.'

And so Harry found himself opposite Frankie Noble for the third time that day. She was nursing a massive Frappuccino in a plastic cup, sucking thick brown liquid through a straw. The coffee-shop in the hospital atrium was well liked by the local police, because it did them a discount and it was open twenty-four hours a day, making it just about the only place in Camberwell you could get a coffee at four a.m. On nights, uniform coppers were often to be found in the queue among the doctors, nurses and porters.

'You were right,' she opened with. 'She was murdered.'

'You sure?'

'The prof said he'll go to court on it,' Noble said. 'When he opened her up, there were undigested tablets inside her oesophagus and mouth. And one in her trachea.'

'Shit,' said Harry. He'd had no appetite earlier, either from the amphetamines or from reading about the dead kids and their families. Luckily, the canteen did a decent Sunday roast, and the plate in front of him was piled high with chicken slices, potatoes and gravy. Noble had brought him a coffee as well, an Americano with an extra shot in it, his usual order. The gesture, whilst appreciated, grated, pissed him off.

'And you were right about the bruises, too. Jain reckons they were caused by the killer's arm, holding her into the chair, that he was kneeling on top of her as she died. That's why we delayed, we had Forensics take more swabs for DNA. We're getting it sent through on a fast-track so they can compare to the national database first thing Monday morning.'

It took Harry a few seconds to put that together in his mind, go back to the scene. The wine and the blister packet on the side in the kitchen, the blood on the wooden floor. She'd looked so peaceful, he thought. Looking out of her open window. But Susan Bayliss had not decided to depart this world of her own volition, she'd been forced out. Overpowered, held down whilst somebody opened up her artery. Maybe she'd thrashed in the chair, maybe she hadn't. Maybe she'd screamed, maybe she'd been too shocked, or maybe the killer stopped her. Then she'd gone still, and the person who'd killed her had shoved those pills down her throat, maybe poured the wine in too. Whatever the motive, the act itself was brutal in the extreme.

Then he reminded himself that he didn't need to know all this, that his involvement with the murder of Susan Bayliss had finished when he'd emailed his report to Noble a few hours before.

'I got your report. It's fantastic, Harry. Exactly what we needed.'

Harry said nothing, just chewed down on a slightly raw potato.

'The death certificates,' Noble continued, 'on the two that died in hospital. Is there anything in them that implicated Mr Mohamed?'

'Not obviously.'

'Harry, if I was only interested in obvious things, I wouldn't have got you to read it.'

He couldn't stop himself smiling there.

'The second child, Abdul,' he said. 'He received a transplanted aortic valve.'

It wasn't strictly true. In actuality, one of his own heart valves had replaced his absent aortic valve, and the transplant had replaced it in turn, but Harry guessed that kind of medical detail was what Noble wanted him to filter out.

'The graft failed after a week,' he continued. 'That's a recognised complication of the procedure that he had, and from what I gather it's fairly unusual to do such a massive operation on a six-day-old baby.'

'So?'

'So the operation didn't work,' said Harry. 'But I can't tell you if that was Mr Mohamed's fault. Bayliss put the graft rupture on the cause of death, but the DoH review said that there was no evidence that anything they did on the operating table contributed to that.'

'But the operation killed Abdul?' said Noble.

Harry winced. He'd seen enough of that kind of tabloid simplicity in his afternoon reading to let it infect someone as intelligent as her.

'It's not that simple. What killed him was the fact that he was born without an aortic valve. Twenty, even ten years ago that would probably have been a death sentence. I'm not an expert but if they'd done nothing he'd likely have died within a week, maybe less. Lots of these situations, people think there's one right decision and one wrong one.'

'So what is there?'

'Lots of right ones, and in most cases, lots of wrong ones. And even then only with hindsight.'

'What about the other kids?'

'Jayden bled to death during his operation,' said Harry. 'It's a recognised complication of any heart surgery which involves cardiopulmonary bypass, but if I'm thinking about it, if any of the cases would implicate Mr Mohamed, it would be that one.'

Noble wrote that down.

'And the other two? The ones who died after they left hospital?'

'There wasn't that much information on them,' said Harry. 'Again, Emmanuel was very young to have a major procedure, but maybe that's not so unusual at the Belgrave. Olivia's seemed bread-and-butter. According to the operation and the ICU notes, both their operations seemed to go swimmingly. The next thing we see is a letter from their GPs informing Mr Mohamed that they died, both apparently after some kind of sudden cardiac event.'

'Post-mortems?' said Noble.

'Yes, in both cases inconclusive,' Harry said. 'There's a standard procedure for an unexpected child death. A designated paediatrician leads a full inquiry. Bayliss didn't have the full reports though, just letters from the designated paediatrician to one of the surgeons at the Belgrave. But the DoH inquiry did, and they mentioned that nothing suspicious was found.'

'And that's why they've restarted the operations at Belgrave?' asked Noble.

'Yep,' said Harry. 'There's only one thing that seems suspicious.'

'Do tell.'

'Susan references the operation notes in her dossier, but the inquiry didn't have access to any of the notes made during the operation,' Harry said. 'They had the medical records from outpatients, and from the time the kids were on the ward, but the notes from the surgery itself were lost when the Belgrave moved to a new computerised system.'

'Allegedly,' said Noble.

'Allegedly. You've got a copy of the inquiry?'

Noble didn't, but she had her iPad, which had one downloaded. She passed it over and he scrolled through until he remembered which section he was looking for. He'd only skimmed it earlier, but the inquiry had investigated the fact the notes had been lost, too. The phrase they used went something like, *We have no evidence that this was anything other than an unfortunate coincidence.* Which Harry translated as *We know you bastards got rid of the notes, but we can't prove it.*

'Here we go,' said Harry, reading off the screen, pointing with his finger. Noble shuffled her chair around the table a few degrees, so she could read, and Harry smelled her. Benson & Hedges and Radox shower gel. Fuck that, he thought, and kept reading. *The main obstacle to our investigations was the inability to access contemporaneous operative notes, as only anaesthetic handovers were available from the computerised ICU systems. However, we believe we derived satisfactory information through interviews with all surgical, anaesthetic and theatre staff present during all five operations.*

'So they didn't have these,' Harry said, tapping the operative notes. 'They didn't bloody have them, and neither did the pathologists who did the post-mortems on the two kids who died later in the New Year.'

He looked up and Noble had a determined look, though Harry was sure she was concealing a grin. He'd taken the bait. She'd known it'd be irresistible to him, damn her.

'Why the hell would she blow the whistle, hand them this dossier, but not include the notes from the operations?' she said.

'The dossier only included her recollections. Having the actual notes, unanonymised, in her house is a one-way ticket to the GMC. If she was worried about repercussions from the hospital or the other surgeons, then she wasn't going to hand them any rope to hang her with.'

'Harry, I need complete discretion on what you've just seen,' Noble said.

'Of course. I'm not telling anyone. Christ, do you really think that what happened to Bayliss is connected to all this?'

'Not necessarily. We have a natural prime suspect.'

Harry dug his fork into another potato, this one so raw it bounced off the plate and splattered gravy onto the formica table.

'Guzman?'

He pictured her in the white paper suit, the flash of red against it as she pulled out her nose-ring.

Noble nodded. 'She's got the means and opportunity, and her alibi's shoddy. She could easily have killed Bayliss, staged that crime scene and then called it in, and her guilt routine is just an act.'

Harry knew that methodologically that was the right way to think. As cerebrally satisfying as it was to theorise about motives and all those who might have wanted Susan Bayliss dead, he'd picked up enough over his experience to know that the police tended to get better results when they started with the person who'd been found in a pool of the victim's blood and worked outwards from there.

'The tweet is the main thing,' Noble continued. 'Of course, Guzman could've sent it to lead us up the garden path. But it fits. You've seen this, I presume?'

She passed over her phone, which displayed the front page of a blog called *Broken Hearts*. The sub-title said 'Justice for our Children', and the top photograph was of four smiling faces Harry took to belong to the children he had just been reading about. He scrolled through the blog posts.

'It looks like the parents formed some group to take on the hospital,' Noble said. 'And that Bayliss was in touch with them.'

'She's not mentioned on here,' said Harry.

'Yeah, but her phone history has plenty of communications between her and Michelle Roberts, the mother of one of the children in that report. She set up this site.'

'Have you spoken to her?'

'Briefly. She was the last person Bayliss called, but it was at five in the afternoon and it only lasted four minutes, so we were only following it up. Apparently they were discussing when to meet with their lawyers on Monday.'

'Lawyers?' said Harry, 'Were they going to sue the hospital?'

'God knows,' said Noble. 'We'll find out, though.'

Harry thought about that as he doused cold chicken with cold gravy and shoved it into his mouth. Of course, it was possible that none of this was relevant to Bayliss's death, or it was only relevant in the context of being planted as a red herring by the killer. But Noble didn't sound convinced, and neither was Harry. The disgust with which Guzman had described how the hospital managers had treated Bayliss, and the horror she felt at having abandoned her girlfriend in what she'd thought had been her hour of greatest need, felt uncomfortably real to him.

'Four children in a row, though. All dead down to bad luck. And the one doctor in that whole hospital who flagged something up winds up first persecuted, and now dead. Lots of reputations wrecked, lots of people who might feel bitter towards Susan Bayliss. Elyas Mohamed especially.'

Harry said nothing. Even though both the inquiry and the newspapers hadn't reported his name, he could envision how Mohamed might blame Bayliss for the fact that the deaths had come to light, that his reputation had been dragged through the mud. Weak men often did that – blame others for their own mistakes. Two years or so ago, Harry would have included himself in that category. He arranged his cutlery on his plate and stood to leave.

'Well, good luck with it all,' he said. 'I'm sure you'll make a lot of waves.'

He stood up again. He was hearing his own voice as he'd read off that screen, excited like a kid trying to pester a parent with a foolhardy plan to get rich.

'Sit down,' said Noble.

'I'm sorry?'

'You're not going anywhere, Harry. I've got a plan. Tomorrow morning we've got interviews at the Belgrave with Elyas Mohamed and the rest of the hospital staff. I've seconded Mo from CID, but I need some more help. Someone with medical nouse.' She tapped the dossier. 'Once I'm done, you and I are going through this thing and if anything doesn't match up between what they say and what it says here, then we've got them.'

'No way,' said Harry. 'I'm not getting involved.'

'You already are,' said Noble. 'I need someone I can trust.'

'Get an expert, then,' said Harry. 'One of the designated paediatricians from social services, or a cardiac surgeon.'

'I don't need an expert, I need someone who can sniff out BS and knows a cover-up when he sees one.'

'I meant what I said earlier. I've got too much on my plate right now to get involved in something like this.'

He turned and walked towards the tray rack, and told himself over and over that no matter what she said, he'd keep going, walk away, maybe turn his phone off for the first few hours of his shift.

'Cameron's leaving.'

He turned around.

'What?'

'Dave Cameron? From Special Projects, right? He's the one that's been helping you out with Zara, isn't he?'

Harry threw his dirty tray back onto the table and leant over the seat. Despite the fact it was a Sunday, there were at least ten or twenty faces in the canteen who he knew, and he was determined not to make a scene.

'You better start making sense pretty fucking soon, Frankie.'

Noble stood now too, arms folded.

'He's got a bit of a reputation. Ambitious. He's being seconded to the National Crime Agency as of September 1st.'

'Next Friday,' said Harry. The anger was only just starting to build up.

'He's pulling a fast one,' Noble said bluntly. 'They reckon it's a no-hope case to give the guy who's off to pastures new in a week. A nice easy TV appeal to sort out that's a cushty job for his last few days, bugger all prospect of anything useful coming through from it.'

'Why are you telling me this?'

Noble came around the table, moved to touch his arm. He swatted her hand away.

'Because I know how much it means to you,' she said. 'You deserve to know.'

81

'The bastard!' Harry said. Cameron knew how much the girl with the pink hair meant to Harry, too, and although the detective owed him no personal loyalty, to treat her with such contempt filled him with frustration. Yes, it was a case with a minimal chance of actually being solved. No, it wasn't in the newspapers that often, or at all, but somebody in London had to know who the girl was, and what had happened to her. And somebody had bashed her head against the tarmac and squeezed her neck until her hyoid bone shattered.

'I'm aware that I'm asking you to go way beyond a favour,' Noble said, quietly now, 'even for a friend, ok? So I'll go equal with you. You help me out with this, and I'll take up the case after Cameron is gone. I promise. I'll get it assigned to Homicide & Serious South. If we get anything at all from the appeal I can spin it as an active case, and I'll do it as soon as this is done. You have my word.'

A length of time that could have been a breath or could have been a few minutes went past, Harry seething and looking at the floor, heart heavy in his chest. Noble looking up at him, thumbs in the loops of her belt.

'You've got some bloody nerve,' he said.

'You'll be there tomorrow morning?'

'I've got plans at lunchtime. I come off shift at eight in the morning, if I finish on time. I'd been hoping to get some sleep.'

'You might sleep tonight?'

Harry said nothing. In his old job, upstairs on the ICU, if he was lucky he'd manage three or even four hours of sleep on a night shift. Since he'd moved to A&E that seemed luxurious.

'I could move the interviews to lunchtime. What are your plans?'

'I'm seeing my girlfriend,' said Harry.

'Oh.'

A look of offence or surprise or both flashed across her face, but Harry ignored it.

'Make the interviews at eleven and I'll be there,' he said. 'You've got me for three hours, I'm out of there by two at the latest. And you wouldn't mind clearing my tray, would you? I'm late for work.'

★   ★   ★

A quarter to midnight in A&E, Harry Kent looking down at the man in Resus One with grey skin and blue lips.

He was probably dead, but they were trying anyway, because you had to. He was forty-four but looked older, the result of living in a boarded-up old factory in Norwood, an address the paramedics and the local police knew well as a citadel for the dispossessed and the desperate. Two of his mates had called the ambulance after finding him collapsed on the floor and not breathing, and one of them had even managed to attempt CPR despite having put away at least two caps of GHB and some smack, too. There was a lot to say for London's public CPR education programme when even the junkies were having a crack. When the paramedics had arrived, the combination of pin-prick pupils and the needle-marks along his arms had led them to a diagnosis of heroin overdose. Two minutes or so of chest compression and two shots of naloxone, the antidote, had restored his pulse, and they'd intubated him, cannulated, and made it to the Ruskin in twelve minutes on blue lights. He'd arrested again about two minutes from the door, and they'd been trying since then.

Harry gripped the ultrasound probe, aiming it underneath the ribcage, the view awful because Josh Geddes, the charge nurse, was doing chest compressions, pumping what he could of the patient's blood up to his brain. They wanted to look at the heart, confirm the diagnosis. The electrical waveform on the ECG trace that had been present was so fine now it might be a flatline.

'Right, stop compressions,' Harry said. Geddes moved aside, another nurse stepping in to replace him. There were lots of people in the room: three doctors, two nurses, the resuscitation officer, the paramedics who'd brought the man in, without whom he would be long dead. Harry dug the probe into the jelly over the man's skin, a chalky yellow-white, watching the grey and black dance on the monitor. Every second he took to get a view was a second without oxygen for the man's brain. He was only allowed ten.

'Good motion,' Harry said. 'Heart looks empty. Continue compressions, and let's have another dose of naloxone, squeeze in 500 of cold Hartmann's and some adrenaline, please.'

The nurse, Charlotte Osugu, went back to CPR, and Harry lifted the probe off and swung the ultrasound monitor back to the side of the bay. The dead man was in PEA, which meant that the electrical wiring in his heart was still working but it wasn't pumping anything. Harry looked at his watch. Including the time in the ambulance, they'd been resuscitating for ten minutes, had delivered three shots of naloxone and one of adrenaline, as well as some fluids. Based on the shaky history given to the paramedics by two fellow squatters off their heads on whatever they could find, they had no way of knowing how long this man had been down before he'd been found. Harry put all that together and prepared to run for ten more minutes or so, give him as fair a chance as anyone, and then call it. He decided to announce it.

'We'll run it for another four cycles,' he said. 'Anyone disagree?'

No-one did.

'What's that smell?' one of the nurses said. She was a student and it was her first week in A&E, and from the way she was acting Harry was fairly certain that this was the first cardiac arrest she'd experienced. It wasn't like TV. Patients who arrested died with twelve broken ribs, vomit and blood spurting out of their mouths, lying in their own shit on a hard hospital trolley. Geddes was already arranging the incontinence pads underneath the man, a true nurse, trying to maintain whatever scraps of dignity he could. All of them were wearing masks and eye protection, just in case any of the fluids they were splashed with contained HIV or hepatitis.

Harry headed to the back of the cubicle, where the paramedics were standing. He felt for them, the adrenaline rush of being first on-scene, performing CPR, making a diagnosis, administering treatment and getting the heart restarted, and now it looked like all that work might be for nothing.

'Do we have a name?' he said quietly.

'Vincent. That's all we know at the moment.'

Harry nodded. He hated it when patients were nameless, but in the chaos of the dead man coming through the doors of the Ruskin, one of the paramedics leaning over him on the trolley, doing compressions, he'd not heard that, if they'd said it.

'Coming up to two minutes,' the resus officer said.

Harry stepped forward.

'Ok. Pulse check.'

Osugu grunting with exhaustion as she lifted her hands off the chest. The junior doctor leaning in to take the pulse at the neck, the resus officer ready to go for another round of compressions.

'I've got an output.'

It was the junior doctor, looking up at the monitor, almost in disbelief. The heart trace was on, eighty beats per minute, sinus rhythm. Geddes felt for a pulse in the patient's groin, nodding as he found one, too. Harry darted in with the ultrasound probe, finding a view, watching the atria and ventricles contract, the rhythm irregular, beats skipped, but pulsing, alive. The front wall appeared flappy, unmoving, but that could be fixed now he wasn't dead.

'Let's get a twelve-lead, please,' Harry called. 'I reckon those ST-changes are global ischaemia, not an infarct, but let's double-check.'

One of the nurses headed to organise the ECG, and Harry kept talking.

'And let ICU know that they've got one coming to them.'

The next five minutes was full of quiet graft, like a pit-stop crew. The ECG was printed out and handed to Harry, who confirmed that Vincent's battered heart was still in working order. The anaesthetist established him on a portable ventilator and set up a central line for monitoring. The junior doctors took blood and sent it for a battery of tests, and an arterial gas, which showed that Vincent's blood was extremely acidic and that he had plenty of carbon dioxide swimming around in there as well, neither of which were good signs.

Josh Geddes came back from a phone call: 'ICU say bring him up when you're ready.'

Harry looked over at Sujan, the anaesthetist, who was fiddling with the ventilator settings.

'You hear that?'

'Yeah.'

'You given him any sedation?' said Harry. He'd been caught out in cases like this before, heroin ODs. Naloxone, the reversal agent, did a great job of waking people up, but sometimes it could be too effective, and the patient would wake up too quickly, aggressive and fighting, pulling out tubes and lines. Given everything that had happened, Harry was fairly sure that young Vincent wouldn't be waking up any time soon, but one thing Harry tried to make sure of was that every patient received pain relief and sedation, even if they probably wouldn't need or appreciate it.

'Yeah,' said Sujan, 'A bit of propofol. Want to watch his blood pressure, mind you.'

'Great,' said Harry. 'Ready when you are. You happy to transfer with Josh?'

Geddes appeared once they'd done the checks, pulling with him a bag of emergency kit for the short journey to the ICU upstairs.

'Who's on today?' said Harry.

'It's Tammy. I'll say hi for—'

They were interrupted by Vincent, who arched his back and flexed his elbows inward, drawing his fists up to his face, his knees bent in an attempt at the foetal position. The student nurse, who was closest to him, panicked and jumped back. Osugu – who recognised the contortion for what it was, the beginning of a myoclonic seizure – calmly reached into the nearby drugs trolley for an aliquot of lorazepam, and had it drawn up before Harry had even given the order.

'Four of IV loraz, please.'

'Already there.'

Harry grinned. 'I might as well go home.'

The seizure stopped a few seconds after the injection, and once they were sure the patient was stable Sujan bid them farewell. Harry had done his bit, led the team, preserved life. He watched as Vincent was wheeled out towards the lift, Sujan suctioning vomit from his mouth. The smell of shit and sweat was all left behind. The resus officer stood in the corner filling out the necessary paperwork.

'Are there any family?' Harry asked.

The paramedic said, 'Police are working on that now, apparently.'

'Ok, someone let me know if they arrive.'

He pulled off his gloves and his apron, throwing them into a foot-pedal bin, hearing it clang shut. The nurses were cleaning up, bringing in a new trolley. Harry cleared his throat and tried to address what was left of the team.

'Good job everyone,' he said. 'Everyone did well. If anyone wants to talk about something, I'm here all night.'

'Do you think he'll make it?' the student nurse asked, her face full of excitement or horror or both.

'Maybe,' said Harry. Almost definitely not, he thought. They might have got his heart pumping again, but the seizure they'd witnessed combined with the acidosis on his blood gas both conveyed a dismal prognosis. Harry would be surprised if the poor bloke lasted the night, and if he was being brutally honest then slipping away in the wee hours of the morning would probably be better than waking up to a severe catalogue of neurological disabilities.

He thanked the paramedics, and then he headed to the other end of Resus where Jay Sinha, the evening's consultant, had been occupied leading a trauma call, the patient airlifted to the Ruskin from the A21, and the reason Harry had led the cardiac arrest call by himself. Sinha was writing up notes, reviewing an X-ray, a right femur broken cleanly through the shaft, the patient on her way to theatre to have it fixated. Harry's money was on a driver-side impact, at least fifty miles an hour to cause that damage. Dr Sinha was a balding man approaching fifty, with a thick Australian accent and an uncanny ability to know who was behind him without looking.

'Wouldn't have bet on him making it upstairs,' he said. 'Nicely done, Harry.'

Dr Sinha finished filling out his notes and turned around.

'How long was he down?'

'Don't know,' said Harry. 'Sounds like his mates all shot up together, they woke up and he didn't. His arrest in the ambulance was witnessed, mind.'

'Must have been going a while?'

'Half an hour or so. First pH post-ROSC was 6.95.'

Sinha nodded solemnly, and Harry knew what he was thinking. There were many magic machines on the ICU upstairs, but none which could resurrect dead brain cells.

'Right. Let's do a quick stock-take then.'

It was past midnight, and thus Sinha was late for his meeting with the plush double-bed of his on-call room, leaving the A&E

department in Harry's hands pending a major trauma call or a really tricky case. It was common for the consultant to do a quick walk-over of all the unstable patients with the registrar before leaving and deal with any potentially thorny issues. It was mostly, of course, to reduce the likelihood of the consultant needing to be woken up.

'Sure.'

It took them about ten minutes to go through the list of patients – five in Resus, sixteen in Majors, twenty-one in Minors, and ten in the waiting room. Then Sinha wished Harry goodnight, shaking his hand. Harry nodded and headed out of the department, grabbing a coffee en route and dissolving an amphetamine into it, stirring it with his pen. There was only one seriously ill patient Harry had missed in all the excitement of the cardiac arrest and the trauma call: an eleven-year-old girl suffering from a sickle-cell crisis. She'd been triaged straight to the A&E's dedicated children's section, staffed by paediatricians and children's nurses. Harry went over, sipping his coffee, feeling fresh as the morning as Sunday turned to Monday, passing through a play-area, two noisy siblings of a feverish toddler paying no heed to the hour.

Nearing midnight, one of those summer evening nights that never really gets dark, and Frankie Noble sat in an uncomfortable plastic garden chair, looking at the weeds coming through the gaps between the concrete slabs in her patio. A cool breeze on her face, which was illuminated only by the lit end of the thirty-fifth cigarette of that day. She still needed to decide what to do with the garden. The place in Deptford had only been hers two months, just after she'd got the Acting DCI appointment. Rented, of course. Thirty-eight and still she couldn't settle. The move was a final acceptance that work wouldn't be taking her back to West London any time soon. Although, she reflected, it would difficult to tell Brixton or Peckham from South Kensington within a few years. Stick a Waitrose in a shithole and watch the rest happen. Soon enough, even Lewisham's schoolchildren would be queuing up outside organic tofu bars instead of kebab shops.

A train rumbled past, and Noble finished her cigarette, sat back in her chair and got her phone out, placing the call she'd spent the day veering between putting off and counting the minutes to.

Susan Everscott picked up on the second ring.

'Frankie,' she said in her estuary grumble.

'Sorry to call so late, Sue.'

'That's alright, Franks, I was expecting you. I've been following the news, couldn't quite work out the geography, but is it safe to say you've been busy today?'

'Yeah. Only just got home.'

'Are you SIO?'

'I am indeed.'

'Well, good luck to you. And don't worry, I'm not gonna be asking you about work. How are you feeling?'

'About a seven if I'm honest with you.'

Everscott had a simple system for talking about Noble's feelings, about her risk. A simple scale, from zero meaning that nothing on this earth would ever make her go near a drink again, which in reality she knew was almost unattainable, to a ten, where she was on the way to the 24-hour offy at the end of the street for two bottles of Glen's and a one-way ticket to Sodom and Gomorrah. Seven was bad for her, the worst in about a month. There'd been a scattering of eights and a single nine since Everscott had started sponsoring her.

'Oh no, Franks. Do you want me to come over?'

'Don't be silly. I'll be fine.'

Everscott lived in St John's Wood, at least half an hour's drive from Noble's place. Three times now she'd spent the night there, plenty of times on the other uncomfortable plastic garden chair, watching the planes go over and talking about life and the things they'd done and the things they'd wished they'd done.

'Really?' said Everscott. 'What are you doing right now?'

'I'm in the garden. Smoking.'

'Real ones?'

'Yeah, real ones.'

'I'm jealous,' Everscott said, and laughed. Susan Everscott had been a sergeant in Hertfordshire Constabulary for twenty years and an alcoholic for most of them, which had come to the fore when she'd crashed a patrol car into a road sign in Watford town centre and broken the breathalyser. The disciplinary had led to even more drinking, to divorce, and then to a liver transplant ten years ago, which meant she'd had to quit the fags as well as the drink. Everscott now helped to run the three London-based AA groups that were exclusively for emergency services personnel, serving and retired, one of which Frankie Noble had joined in March.

'So you want a drink, don't you?' Everscott said after a while. She always did this – make Noble admit it. It wasn't humiliation, it wasn't shame, Noble told herself. It was about accepting that there were things beyond her control, and that this was one of them.

'Yeah.'

'Why?'

'Because I had a shit day, Sue, and I just want to feel better.'

'What was so shit about it?'

'I saw Harry. Not on purpose, he turned up to certify this morning. I needed his advice with all this medical shit. Obviously he didn't want anything to do with me, so I went to his place. I just wanted to talk him round.'

She didn't need to explain. Everscott knew everything about her. Knew about the dead husband that had started her on the road to oblivion, the nights when she'd put away two or three bottles in the hope that she'd get to that nirvana of intoxication where she was drunk enough to hear his voice again but sufficiently sober to remember it. She knew about the case she'd fucked up that had almost got a colleague killed and was the reason there was a loaded Glock pistol on the table by her front door. And she knew about Harry Kent. The murder investigation that had brought them together and the long nights of vodka-fuelled rows that had driven them apart.

Silence on the other end, and Noble pictured Everscott on her sofa, in her pyjamas, the TV muted, a cup of tea going cold on the side. She kept talking.

'When I was there, back in that flat, I just kept remembering all the things I'd done. That time I was sick on the neighbour's door, the time I split his lip on mine and Jack's anniversary. I just felt awful, I wanted to stay, start apologising for all of it. Y'know, make a list of all the ways I fucked him over and tell him I was sorry for every single one. That I've changed, that . . .'

Eventually Everscott filled the silence.

'From what you've told me, Franks, he was hardly an angel himself.'

'No-one deserves to be treated the way I treated him. I didn't realise how much I fucking missed him until he turned up today,' she said. There was no point explaining the minutiae of the Bayliss case to Everscott, but she was thinking of him in the paper suit that morning, spotting the bruising on her chest, pointing out that the pills on the side didn't fit with the rest of the scene. He'd been proved right on both accounts, of course, one of his most insufferable characteristics.

'I had to stop myself telling him that I was sober. And then I felt ashamed at how proud I was feeling, all the fucking self-pity. And then I missed him some more. And this case is slipping away from me already. I'm losing the fight, there are just too many variables.'

And all I want is oblivion, she didn't say. Everscott would know. She'd been there a thousand times, she'd fought it and she'd won. She was an undefeated heavyweight, Frankie Noble a newcomer in the ring, wondering if she'd last this fight, even this round.

'Franks, I'll come over if you want. Honestly. I've got nothing on tomorrow.'

'Honestly, Sue, don't.'

'Alright. Listen to me, love, cause what I'm going to say now is really important.'

Noble sat back in the garden chair, flicking the lid on her Zippo back and forth between her fingers. The air was hot, heavy with the weight of coming rain.

'You wanted to tell Harry you'd stopped drinking, because you felt proud. You shouldn't feel proud because you haven't had a drink in six months, Frankie.'

Noble stopped mid-breath, her chest aching.

'You should feel proud because you haven't had a drink *today*.'

There it was, the mantra again. Every day a victory, whether it was day eighty-seven or four thousand. She'd been sceptical at the first meeting, but all the spiritual bullshit aside, the principles were ones she'd always known. That there were things in life that were outside of people's control. Like the fact that she was an alcoholic, or that sometimes lorry drivers didn't check their mirrors before turning left, or that four kids might die after undergoing surgery by the same man. Noble smoked another cigarette, Everscott talked to her for a while longer, and made her swear that if she wasn't in bed asleep in another hour she'd give her another call.

Inside she booted up her laptop and brought up a spreadsheet which had the names of everyone assigned to South Major Investigation Team 3, as well as the officers who'd been seconded to her from Lambeth and Southwark CID. Grenaghan had pulled some strings for her, thank God. She typed a new column for tomorrow's date and began assigning each actions. Officers to chase up CCTV, house-to-house and forensics. Shona McGovern and a couple of DCs ruling Teodora Guzman in or out. She and Wilson over at Belgrave to conduct interviews there.

After that last one, she clicked the box next to that action and added '+ Harry Kent' and her chest ached again. She knew what would make it go away, but she also knew she'd won the battle for today. She saved the file, emailed it to the area office manager and cc'd Grenaghan, and shut her laptop, heading through to the cross-trainer in her living room. It had been Everscott's suggestion: she'd discovered in the first weeks of sobriety, after the withdrawal had passed, that exercise helped her urges, but going for a run took her past off-licences, pubs and supermarkets, an unacceptable risk when she was at a low. Many times she'd asked Everscott how she'd ever repay her for the things she'd done, and her answer had been simple: you do what I'm doing now, for someone else.

Frankie Noble thought about that as she stretched and clicked her neck, got onto the trainer and started to run.

The little girl, Imogen, was pretty quiet, which was never a good sign in kids. She was sitting upright on the bed, an oversized oxygen mask strapped to her face, the hiss of the high-flow gas coming out of the sides, audible from the end of the bed. Two drips ran through miniature lines into her hand and elbow, one a blood transfusion, the other a course of antibiotics. Harry smiled at her from the end of her bed, and though she didn't respond in kind, she looked up, her eyes vacant. Harry knew that'd be the effect of the morphine. Imogen's mother, asleep in the chair next to her daughter, didn't notice him, either.

Amy Floyd, the overnight paediatrics registrar, had been at university with Harry and was filling him in on the girl's history. It was her third visit to A&E this year, although this one was by far the most serious. Effective and prompt intervention by Dr Floyd and her team had likely saved Imogen from needing an ICU admission, and she would be seen by the specialist sickle team in the morning. Harry was there not to oversee Floyd's management but to check that everything was going to plan, that a bed had been found for Imogen on one of the children's wards, that no tests or blood products needed chasing. The paediatrics department at the Ruskin was small, especially compared to somewhere like the Belgrave, only forty beds or so, but they saw more children with sickle-cell than any other hospital in Europe, given the high proportion of South-East London residents who were of African descent.

'I think we've got it all sorted out,' Floyd said, smiling at Harry. She was one of those people who still managed to both look fresh and sound enthusiastic whatever the time of day or night.

'Glad to hear it,' said Harry. 'Sorry none of us were around to help with the resus. We had a trauma call and a cardiac arrest come in within ten minutes of each other.'

'Aye, I heard the helicopter come in. It's grand, we never expect you lot to be around anyway.'

Harry laughed, but she had a point. It was now the norm rather than the exception that the A&E department was understaffed. It was a picture seen all over the country, though he had benefited from it indirectly. He'd fucked up the exam required to make the final stage of his training in intensive care, and then there'd been other candidates filling his old job. His bosses had suggested he find a post in ICU at another hospital, one in the North or in Wales, but he'd wanted to stay in London, and given the staffing shortage he'd walked into a locum job in A&E.

'Can I help you with anything else, or are you just admiring my new scrubs?' Floyd said. Harry realised he'd been looking at her the whole time he'd been thinking. Then she lowered her voice: 'And how're you getting on with that junior of yours? Hope the GMC don't find out you've been shagging your SHOs?'

Harry laughed.

'Piss off, she wasn't *my* SHO. And while you're here, you can help me, actually.'

The thought had occurred to him as he'd been carrying his coffee through to the paediatrics department, when he'd heard it was Floyd who was on tonight. He hadn't thought through what he was about to say, but he decided to say it anyway.

'Anything for you, Harry,' she said. 'As long as it's not anything I don't want to do.'

'You spent a couple of years at the Belgrave, didn't you?'

'Aye, I did my core training there.'

'Does the name Susan Bayliss mean anything to you?'

Immediately, Floyd's smile vanished. She pulled the curtain across Imogen's cubicle and came close to Harry, her voice low.

'Why are you interested? Just cause she's gone and topped herself?'

So news spread quickly, then. He'd heard Bayliss's name come up on the six o'clock news, but late on, fighting for airtime with Israel, Ebola and a small American town called Ferguson, but that was all he'd heard. He saw no point in lying.

'No, it's not like that. It's my side-job with the Met,' Harry said. 'One of the investigators has asked for my help in reviewing some of the medical details around the children who were treated at the Belgrave. I just want to get some different perspectives. You don't have to talk about it if you don't want to.'

'I don't mind,' said Floyd. 'But maybe it's best to take a walk first, eh?'

Harry understood the subtext, and they waved at Imogen, Floyd smiled at the nurse, and they made their way towards one of the cubby-holes in A&E where staff could dine on whatever the vending machine had to offer that night, and enjoy caffeinated drinks of hot, tepid or chilled varieties.

'Why are you asking me?' she said. 'Because of that wee lad back in March?'

'No, mostly because you worked with her. But I guess, now you mention it. You led that, didn't you?'

Floyd nodded. Harry's own role in that resuscitation had been on the sidelines – making sure the right equipment was there, that the correct personnel were involved, that all the blood tests were done immediately. By the time Emmanuel Abediji had died, there had been so many doctors around his bed trying to salvage him, Harry had lost track of who was in charge.

'He was one of the kids in the investigation, so he was,' Floyd said. 'And I followed all the developments on that inquiry. We all did. Weren't surprised when they turfed Bayliss out, mind you.'

'Weren't you?'

'No. But I didn't think she'd do herself in.'

She didn't, Harry thought but didn't say. He didn't need to.

'I didn't know her all that well,' Floyd went on, 'but after the whole inquiry thing happened, everyone was asking me about her, over in paeds. Still sad, though, when it's a doc you worked with. Another one of us bites the dust, and all that.'

'Why weren't you surprised they turfed her out?'

'She never really fitted in with the surgeons. Something of a black sheep.'

'In what way?'

'Come on, Harry,' Floyd said, laughing now. 'You've seen her, haven't you? For a start, she's a woman, and that's unusual enough at that place. And she had tattoos! She used to walk into work with those big headphones around her neck, over her scrubs. Must've given some of the consultants hernias.'

'That bad, was it?'

'Oh, aye,' said Floyd. 'Belgrave might have cutting-edge technology, but the consultants' attitudes are stuck in the 1970s.'

Harry laughed hoarsely.

'The paediatricians weren't as bad as the surgeons, but . . . I learnt a lot, but I was glad to leave. This place is much more down to earth.'

'Did you get interviewed by the inquiry?'

'No,' said Floyd. 'Dr Jaffry did, mind you.'

Harry's face asked the question without him needing to speak. Dr Jaffry was one of the Ruskin's senior consultant paediatricians, a specialist in children's bowel diseases, and had been at the hospital for decades. Harry could think of no reason for her to be caught up in the events surrounding Susan Bayliss's whistleblowing.

'She led the resus on Emmanuel,' Floyd said.

She leant over and touched a wooden desktop, and Harry nodded solemnly. There was an aphorism that doctors only remembered the names of the patients they'd lost. It didn't quite hold true in the ICU, where a fifth of the punters who came in the door left only in blue boxes, or in A&E, where interactions were so numerous and quick that he struggled to remember the patients he'd seen that shift, let alone in his career, but he could well imagine that for paediatricians, who saw the vast majority of their patients get better and grow old, the deaths could haunt.

'Must have been pretty awful.'

'Yeah. About the worst resus I've ever done, if I'm honest.'

She stared at the floor. Children rarely died in such sudden circumstances, and Harry thought back to Vincent, to the resuscitation, the assault on all of his senses. He had never had to do that to a child, and couldn't bear imagining it.

'I'm sorry.'

Floyd eyed him briefly, then shrugged.

'It's fine, it was just a shit thing to happen. One of those arrests where you spend the rest of the week working out whether you could've done something different.'

He'd had plenty of days like that.

'That's why I followed the inquiry, to try and see if there was something that'd be changed because of it. But hey, everyone got cleared, and Susan lost her job, and now . . .'

Harry put a hand on her shoulder and said, 'Fresh cuppa?'

Floyd smiled. Harry was about to console her again when his bleep went off, the two-tone alarm of an emergency alert. He raised it to his ear.

'Adult trauma call ETA five minutes. Trauma team please attend A&E Resus.'

'That's saved me the rest of the interrogation, yeah?'

'Sorry,' said Harry. 'You've been helpful.'

'Are the police really looking into this? They don't go this deeply into suicides, do they?'

If only you knew.

'Yeah.'

'What've they got you doing, when you say you're helping them out?'

'They're doing interviews at the Belgrave tomorrow,' said Harry. 'I'm sitting in. But that's confidential, ok?'

'Jesus,' said Floyd. 'Well, you just be careful. That department's got more egos in it than a Premiership football team.'

'I will,' said Harry. 'Can I ask you one more favour?'

'Only if you leave me alone all night.'

Harry crossed his thumb and pinky and raised three fingers. 'Scout's honour.'

Floyd laughed now, properly.

'Bollocks were you ever a scout.'

'You got me there. Anyway, let's say they do keep looking into this, and let's say it becomes interesting. Would you meet with me and walk me through exactly what happened with Emmanuel?'

'Only if you buy me lunch.'

'You got a deal.'

Josh Geddes had the red phone in one hand when Harry got back to Resus.

'It's a good one,' he said. 'Twenty-one-year-old woman, fell down the escalators at London Bridge running for the last train. Suspected head injury, reduced GCS, ETA five minutes.'

'Neurosurgery aware?'

'Doubt they're even awake,' said Geddes.

Harry nodded. There was no point going to see another patient in the five minutes until their new one arrived. There was something he was going to do though, while it was still fresh in his mind.

It still felt weird seeing her name under the heading 'recent calls'. It went to voicemail.

'Hi Frankie, it's me. I know you'll be asleep but hopefully you'll get this in the morning. I'm just saying you might want to ring Belgrave and ask for the full post-mortems of the four kids who died. It'd be useful to take a look. They've probably got copies lying about after the inquiry. And for Emmanuel and Olivia, the hospitals they were taken to on the days they died, the A&E notes there, too. Emmanuel came here, to the Ruskin. Dunno about Olivia. It might be an idea. Anyway, I'll see you tomorrow.'

He hung up, greeted by the sound of the double doors at the other end of Resus flapping open. It was Jay Sinha, eyes still half-closed, hand rubbing his bald forehead.

'Bloody oath,' he said. 'Just as I close my eyes. Literally, just as I close them. What is it?'

'Female, early twenties, PFO on an escalator,' said Geddes.

Sinha laughed. The acronym was well known, one of those banned from patients' notes but still used between those in the trenches. It stood for Pissed, Fell Over.

Sinha came over to Harry and gripped his bicep, grinning.

'We'll put her in three,' he said. 'It's gonna be one of those nights, I can already tell.'

In the end Dr Sinha was right. Harry ended up intubating the twenty-one-year-old woman who was pissed and fell over, and she went to theatre, where a team of neurosurgeons set about evacuating the blood clot that was building up on her brain. She'd managed to fracture her skull in two places in her attempt to make the 00:23 to Brighton. An hour later, a car full of teenagers ploughed into a shop front in Bexleyheath. One was dead at the scene, and of the three the fire brigade managed to pull from the wreckage two had come to the Ruskin. Harry spent an hour working on one in Resus before he was stable enough to go to interventional radiology to fix his torn blood vessels. After attending an urgent stroke call in a ninety-four-year-old lady, who died not long after arrival, Harry had spent the rest of the night in Majors, ringing the various specialty registrars in a vain attempt to get every patient in the department some kind of plan before the day shift arrived.

He took a risk cycling back with no amphetamine, but he wanted to sleep when he got home. Made it back to his apartment in one piece, so it worked alright. Before he got into his bed, fully clothed, he set the alarm on his phone for ten. It would allow him ninety-five minutes.

But he dreamt about his girlfriend in the wicker chair again and the lake of blood, and couldn't wait to be awake.

THREE

Monday, 25 August
Mid-Morning

Harry always thought children's hospitals were strange places – the way they outwardly tried to portray a happy, fun exterior – and that feeling returned as he stood in the atrium, watching a boy with a nasogastric tube duelling a girl with Down's syndrome on a Wii tennis court. Belgrave Hospital for Sick Children, the oldest dedicated children's hospital in London – some claimed Europe – had undergone a significant refit last year, and this was the result. Though the red-brick Victorian façade remained, making the exterior look like an old university, the atrium had been redone, with new windows and natural light, bean-bags, games consoles, and giant foam obstacles for the waiting area, interactive exhibits brought in from the Science Museum, a concave TV screen playing *Finding Nemo* to a captive audience sitting on animal-shaped benches or their own electric wheel-chairs. All set up to put the kids at ease, Harry thought, or perhaps con them into thinking this was a place where good things happened.

Noble met him at reception, DS Wilson by her side.

'Thanks for coming,'

'No problem.'

She handed him a coffee, another Americano, which he thanked her for. She offered him a croissant, too, but he declined. Breakfast had been two amphetamines, and they tended to obliterate his appetite. It was what made them so popular with anorexics. He wasn't regretting it though – he'd walked to the hospital, and though it had taken him the best part of an hour, the glorious summer weather had made him almost euphoric. He felt good. Noble looked like she was doing well, too, that same brightness he'd noticed yesterday, the cause of which he still couldn't figure.

Their first appointment was in the consultants' offices on the second floor. It wasn't hard to navigate – the building had a cruci-form design, each arm of the cross containing one of the four departments: cardiology and cardiac surgery in the North Wing, respiratory medicine and the cystic fibrosis unit in the East, neurology and neurosurgery in the West Wing, and the operating theatres and PICU in the South. They waited for a lift, and Harry continued to look around.

'It's changed since I was last here,' Wilson said.

'When were you last here?' said Noble. Harry looked at him, trying to remember whether Wilson had ever mentioned children.

'Our school did a fund-raiser for this place when I was in Year 10,' Wilson said. 'We picked it cause some girl in our class had a brain tumour and she was treated here. Apparently I came here when I was born, too, cause I was premature.'

Harry laughed as the lift arrived and Wilson stooped to get his six-foot-seven frame inside. His bulk probably meant he counted for two people for the elevator's weight rating.

'You were premature, were you?' Harry said.

Wilson started laughing too and said, 'Course I bloody wasn't.'

They both looked at Noble, who was stony-faced, scrolling through windows on her phone, and rode the rest of the lift in silence. Harry arched his neck and took a glance, and saw that she was looking at news stories. One news website had managed to pick up on Bayliss's last communication and run the headline *Mystery of Dead Doctor's Final Tweet*. Mysterious wasn't the word he'd have used, Harry thought. If the Met had a team of PR people running around managing the media, then the frenzy that would be going on behind closed doors at Belgrave was even greater.

Wilson broke the silence as they headed out onto the second floor, turning into a corridor with a view of Kennington Park.

'Who have we got first, then?'

'Dr Mohamed,' said Noble. 'Thought we'd get it from the horse's mouth before we start with the collateral.'

Wilson nodded.

'It's Mr Mohamed, if I'm being pedantic,' Harry said. 'He's a surgeon.'

Noble stopped mid-stride and turned around.

'Ok,' she said. 'Does that mean it'll piss him off if I call him doctor?'

Harry tried his best not to smile.

'It might.'

Noble shrugged and kept on walking.

'Probably worth a try.'

They got to a pair of double doors requiring a swipe card to access: one leading to Elephant, the cardiac unit – all the wards were named after animals – and the other to the consultants' offices. Noble pushed the buzzer and Harry read off the list. There were ten cardiologists, five cardiac surgeons. Mr E. Mohamed was second from the top, bested only by Professor H. H. Gilmartin. They had wanted to speak to the professor, but he was on two weeks' annual leave, and was trekking somewhere in the Andes.

As they waited for the secretary to answer, Noble came closer to Harry and Wilson and spoke in a hushed tone, 'Right, Harry, I'm going to lead this one, and Mo's going to scribe for me, ok? I want you to hang on every word he says. I'm not going to let him know that you're a doctor, alright, just in case he tries to pull one on us. Anything he says that doesn't sound right, you make a note of it, ok? Anything that's obvious BS, you get an email and you have to go outside to make a phone call. Is that clear?'

Harry nodded, gracefully accepting the notepad that Wilson handed over. He wasn't quite sure how he felt about being in the room without proper introduction, but as Noble had made clear with the entire enterprise, it was on her head.

'Crystal,' he said.

'Great.'

The double doors buzzed and they were met by a secretary. The pink lanyard around her neck read 'Congenital Heart Disease Unit, Belgrave Hospital for Sick Children – Mending Broken Hearts for 40 Years'.

'Morning, officers,' she said. 'Mr Mohamed is just reviewing a patient in the unit. He asked if I could take you through.'

Wilson looked over at Noble who shrugged, and they navigated through the corridors of consultants' and their secretaries' offices, and came out into a clinical-looking area with big cartoon animals painted on the walls. The secretary opened the door to the main thoroughfare and the three of them followed her through the ritual of rolling up sleeves and scrubbing hands with alcohol gel. Perhaps because she was out of her comfort zone and he was in his, Noble stepped aside and let Harry lead the way.

Standing by the central console, speaking to a nurse, was Elyas Mohamed.

He looked different in the flesh. Harry had put him through Google on the walk over and seen his charming profile, a headshot of a man with a strong, clean-shaven jaw, olive skin and a jet-black quiff, not far off Roger Federer in a pair of hospital scrubs. Yet the man who stooped forward to shake their hands was a far cry from that chiselled look: Mohamed's hair had grown down to his shoulders and a carpet of salt-and-pepper stubble covered his face and neck, but the most striking difference was the amount of weight he'd lost. Gone were the full jowls and rotund consultant's waistline, replaced by prominent cheekbones and spindly surgeon's fingers.

Lots of things could do that to a man, Harry thought. Frustration. A conscience.

'Thanks for seeing us, Dr Mohamed,' Noble opened with. 'I'm Frankie, we spoke briefly on the phone. This is Mo, and Harry, my colleagues.'

'No problem,' said Mohamed. 'I'm still shocked by the news. Susan was a very valued colleague of mine. It's just terrible.'

'Indeed,' said Noble.

'We ought to talk in my office, where we can have some privacy,' said Mohamed. 'While you're here, shall I show you around?'

'If you insist,' said Noble.

The unit, he explained, was a purpose-built ward which included twenty inpatient beds, all with their private rooms, a ten-bed ICU, an MRI scanner and two catheterisation and electrophysiology labs. Mohamed led them through the central corridor, one arm swept behind him, narrating his guided tour of his kingdom.

'We're a tertiary referral centre for paediatric heart surgery from across the South of England,' he said, 'and further afield for highly specialist conditions. Professor Gilmartin basically wrote the book on hypoplastic left heart syndrome, and I run a national service for complex valve surgery.'

'That was what the patients from the inquiry were under, wasn't it?' said Harry.

A scowl crossed Mohamed's face, as if he'd said a taboo word or brought up God at a dinner party. In all fairness, he probably had. He had merely wanted to make Noble and Wilson aware of the fact.

'Yes, it was,' said Mohamed. 'Anyway, this is the catheterisation lab. We have the capability of performing a full range of catheterisation procedures in theatre, too, which allows us to do hybrid operations working with our cardiology colleagues. We're one of only two hospitals in the country with that capability.'

Noble and Wilson followed behind, she wearing an expression Harry had come to know as feigned interest. They came to another corridor, near a nurses' station, where two of the nurses sat making tea with one of the junior doctors, who quickly returned to scrolling through computer records and filling out forms once they spotted Mohamed. The windows off the corridor revealed the ICU, a selection of children of different sizes hooked up to extracorporeal life support, transparent tubes draining their blood into heart-lung machines, returning it full of oxygen and nourishment. The closest bed to them contained an infant no larger than a rugby ball, dwarfed by the cannulas keeping it alive.

'These are some of the sickest children in London you're looking at,' Mohamed said.

'Well, it's something, that's for sure,' said Noble. 'And I'm sorry to curtail this, but I have a number of interviews to conduct, so if we could get started . . .'

'Very well,' said Mohamed. 'Let's get on with it, then.'

They filed into Mohamed's office, which looked out onto a communal garden the other side of Clapham Road, Harry taking a seat in the corner of the room, Noble in the chair opposite his desk and Wilson off to one side, a skewed V formation. The secretary who had let them in to the unit entered holding a pot of coffee, which she set down on Mohamed's table. They were about to start in earnest when someone knocked on the door.

'Oh, for pity's sake,' said Mohamed. 'Come in.'

A woman entered, middle-aged, in business dress and vastly overweight. She too wore one of the pink Belgrave lanyards. Harry watched Noble squint and try to make out what was written on her ID badge.

'Seems I didn't get your text telling me this was going on, Elyas,' she said.

Harry returned his gaze to Mohamed, who was gritting his teeth and rolling his eyes. The woman pulled up a chair next to Mohamed and crossed her legs. Wilson looked across at him, also none the wiser.

'My apologies,' said Mohamed. 'This is Alison Price, the senior service manager for the department. Hospital management seems to insist on sitting in on all interviews. I would rather she wasn't here, I don't think it sends across the right message, but what can you do?'

'I see,' said Noble, shuffling on her chair, sitting forward. Wilson did the same, standard police peacocking. Harry smiled inwardly, realising Noble's legal predicament. As Mohamed was under neither arrest nor caution, he had the right to leave at any time, or indeed insist on hospital management being present. But Harry made the same snap judgement that he was sure she was also doing, the same way she'd judge the husband of a missing wife who turned up at the station already having hired a lawyer.

As if to cement her authority further, Price smiled and said, 'It's standard trust policy.'

Calmly, Noble explained how the interview was going to work: the police appreciated his cooperation, and he was free at any time to end the interview or ask for legal advice. Wilson and Harry would be taking notes and, just for convenience, Noble would be recording the conversation, which he could ask to stop at any time. By this time, Harry had finished watching Mohamed, and was instead watching Noble. The body language, open, friendly. Her voice, tired and over-formal, as if this interview was just a hoop that had to be jumped through by everyone present. Which, no doubt, was exactly what she wanted Mohamed to think.

'How long had you known Susan Bayliss?'

'She started working here July of last year,' Mohamed said. 'I'd never met her before that.'

'And how would you describe your relationship?'

'Up until a few months ago, we had a very good working relationship. She was a good registrar, incredibly hardworking, with a good attitude and a lovely patient manner. The parents loved her. She was a decent surgeon, too.'

Everyone waited for him to add a second half to the sentence, but he didn't. Every time Mohamed spoke, Price looked at him, then back at Noble, and Harry began counting down the seconds they had left in the room. He wondered how long they'd spent rehearsing the interview that morning, or perhaps the night before.

'And what happened a few months ago?' Noble said.

Mohamed pulled his glasses off and rubbed the bridge of his nose. 'It was a Tuesday afternoon, the day I normally conduct my monthly follow-up clinic, but I was going to Brussels that evening to talk at the European Society of Cardiac Surgery the next day. I'd asked Miss Bayliss to cover my clinic, which is not an unortho-dox practice for consultants.'

Mohamed replaced his glasses and sipped his coffee and Noble subtly looked at Harry, who nodded. It wasn't at all unusual for registrars to cover their consultant's clinic, and often it was for reasons nowhere near as good as international conferences. One of the benefits of working in A&E was never having to spend the afternoon in a windowless clinic room.

'I got a phone call at St Pancras from her. Two of our patients who were meant to be coming into the clinic had sadly died. I'd known this for some time – in both cases I had received a letter from the coroner requesting information. I had neglected to tell Miss Bayliss, who I have to say was quite upset. Really quite upset. She was concerned that we should report it, but I reas-sured her that we would discuss both cases at the upcoming M&M.'

'M&M?'

Noble shuffled on her seat. It was the first attempt at the use of hospital jargon to throw the detectives off balance, and Harry tried to stay impassive.

'Morbidity and Mortality,' Mohamed explained. 'Basically, all the consultants get together in a room and discuss our cases over the last month. Any with poor outcomes get discussed in full, so we can learn from any errors or change our set-up to deal with new eventualities.'

'She didn't accept that?' said Noble.

'No, she didn't. And she used some pretty dramatic language, I seem to recall. Went on about children being in danger. I told her she was emotional, she should take the rest of the day off, and we could discuss it when I was back.'

'Didn't you feel that children were in danger, Dr Mohamed?'

Any semblance of civility had disappeared, and the air in the office hung as thick as the humid August morning outside. Mohamed took a long pause, switching his eyes between Noble, Wilson, and Harry. Behind him, Price inhaled deeply, frowning at Noble. Harry held his breath and waited for the response, studying the framed certificates hung on the wall. MB ChB, University of Cambridge. Fellow of the Royal College of Surgeons, London. PhD, Columbia University, New York. A photograph of a younger Mohamed with an older man in academic dress, possibly a family member from the look of him.

'I did not,' said Mohamed. 'I have operated on twenty-nine children in the past six months. Eighteen before the hiatus, and eleven since. All are recovering excellently. My mortality data is published online and ratified by the British Association of Cardiothoracic Surgeons. No child at this hospital, in this department, is in any more danger than at any other hospital in the country.'

'Thank—' Noble began, but Mohamed kept on going.

'I would not operate on a child if I thought there was any possibility of them coming to harm, or if I doubted my ability to achieve the best possible surgical outcome. In my opinion, doubt has no place in an operating theatre.'

The silence hung in the room after that response. Noble made a show of checking her phone and placing it back in her pocket, and Wilson made a show of writing down notes, and Harry sat cross-legged wondering what the hell he was doing in a surgeon's office with his ex-girlfriend on his day off, conducting what was rapidly becoming an interrogation. He was also wondering why Mohamed hadn't doubted himself after two of his operations had ended in the death of the patient.

'What did Miss Bayliss do next?' Noble asked.

'She sent an email to our head of department, Professor Gilmartin. She cc'd myself and Alison. She said that she wished to officially raise concerns over the deaths of four patients in the valve surgery service under my care, and asked for an internal investigation to begin immediately. The Prof rang me that evening when I landed in Brussels. He said he needed me back on the Thursday morning for an emergency M&M meeting. And that's what we did. We reviewed the cases, the entire department – all five consultant surgeons, four of our consultant cardiologists, and both of our specialist cardiac anaesthetists.'

'You were present at these meetings, were you?'

Mohamed nodded.

'We don't operate a blame culture here at Belgrave,' Price said. 'We're a team, and in a team one should feel entirely comfortable discussing instances where things didn't go quite to plan.'

Harry thought about Jayden Capp, bleeding to death on the operating table, his little chest filling with blood faster than the suction catheters could drain it out. It made the understatement even worse.

'Thank you, Ms Price,' Noble said. 'I am quite pressed for time, so if you would allow Dr Mohamed to answer the questions himself, please.' She turned towards Mohamed, 'I assume that he is fully capable of doing so. What exactly happened at this meeting, then?'

Mohamed seemed to fluster for the first time, an actor going off-script. 'Well, as I said, we all got together and reviewed all four cases, and then we, umm, as a team, came to the decision—'

'How did you review the cases? From the notes?'

It was out of Harry's mouth before he remembered that he was only here to observe, and note things down, and to her credit Noble managed to stop herself reacting, her face not even moving. Her shoulders tensed though, the back of her hair quivering. Mohamed and Price looked up briefly, their eyes focusing on Harry at the rear of the room.

'We, umm, talked through what happened with each case. Myself, Miss Bayliss, Prof, the theatre nurses, the anaesthetists, management. And yes, we did look over the notes.'

This time, Noble spoke before the sentence was even finished, more a message to Harry than the man she was interrogating.

'Which notes?'

'What do you mean, which notes?' said Mohamed.

'Which notes did you look over?'

Mohamed's mouth contorted, and Harry was reminded of medical school, the faces of dismayed consultants after a poor attempt at answering a question.

'The patient notes,' he said slowly. 'For the four patients who sadly died.'

Wilson shuffled on the chair, sitting up straight.

'Let's cut that out, ok, Doctor,' said Noble. 'You might think that you're being clever, but you're not. Which notes did you have access to in that meeting, and which didn't you?'

'I don't know what you mean,' said Mohamed.

'You know exactly what I mean.' She turned her chair slightly and looked across at Harry, and kept quiet, and Harry realised she was cueing him. He became aware of his heartbeat, and sweat on his brow. This is what you fucking get into when you don't keep your mouth shut, he thought.

'The DoH inquiry only had access to the anaesthetic and ICU notes, from the electronic system,' he said. 'And the clinic records. The operation notes were lost, weren't they?'

'Ah,' said Mohamed, waving a hand, adjusting his glasses, forcing a smile, 'I didn't realise that was what you meant. We did not have the operation notes, no.'

'Why not?'

Mohamed was silent for a while. Then he looked over at Price, who answered.

'Mr Mohamed is not at liberty to answer that question, I'm afraid,' she said.

'I beg your pardon?' said Noble.

Mohamed cleared his throat and repeated, looking scathingly at Price, 'I was told earlier that I am unable to answer questions on that subject. I'm very sorry.'

'Are you aware that withholding information from a police investigation is a criminal offence, Dr Mohamed?' Noble said.

'I know this seems a bit—'

Price interjected again.

'The whereabouts of the operation notes for a number of patients is currently subject to an internal trust investigation,' she said. 'Hospital policy states that staff members do not comment on internal matters.'

It was that particular hospital policy which Susan Bayliss had fallen foul of, Harry thought. Or at least that was the one they had used to show her the door. He could see a vein beginning to bulge on Noble's right temple, a sight he was all-too familiar with, and in that moment he knew, reassuringly, that if either Elyas Mohamed or Alison Price had had anything to do with Susan Bayliss's death then she would show them no mercy whatsoever. That venom was apparent with the next question, delivered at Mohamed's throat.

'How did Miss Bayliss act during the meeting?'

'Cooperatively, at first. But when it became clear that our colleagues didn't feel there was anything amiss with the cases – other than what we'd already spoken about at a previous M&M with regard to Abdul and Jayden – it was like a switch flipped on her or something. She told us bluntly that she was going to the Department of Health, to that whistleblowing service they've set up. I have no idea why she wouldn't just do it anonymously, but well, I mean –' he adjusted his glasses again. 'I didn't see her in person again after that.

'At first, I wondered whether this was just a bit of maladjustment. Often, trainees come to us having only really worked in adult hospitals before, on older people, and they can find poor outcomes difficult to deal with. Miss Bayliss was experienced, though. That was when the facts about her mental health began to emerge, and by that point it didn't come as much of a surprise.'

He took a deep breath in and stood up like a spring and said, 'And here we are. Very sad. Is there anything else I can assist you with, detectives?'

'Yes,' said Noble. 'Where were you on Saturday night between eleven and two?'

Silence. Harry held his breath again. He hadn't been expecting that one. Evidently, neither had Mohamed who, flustered, looked around the room, as if help might appear from somewhere. He even looked across at Price, who just stared at the floor. When the answer came, it was measured, as if Mohamed had rehearsed the entire thing in his head before saying it out loud. Maybe he had.

'On Saturday evening, I had dinner with my brother, Hasan, at the Athenaeum Hotel. He's visiting from Los Angeles. I called a taxi about eleven and got the 11:24 train from Charing Cross to Sevenoaks, then I took another taxi home from the station. The taxi driver in Sevenoaks is called Stefan, he runs the cab company and he often picks me up. I'm sure he'll remember me. He dropped me off at about ten past twelve. Then I went to bed.'

Harry looked across at Noble, who smiled, and Wilson, who was taking all of that down.

'When was the next time you saw someone, Dr Mohamed?' Noble asked.

Mohamed looked briefly irritated, though he didn't bite.

'I played tennis at nine. Tonbridge and Weald Tennis Club. I can give you the name of my partner and my opponents, if you want.'

Harry was trying to work out if it was an alibi or not. Bayliss had died some time between one and half-one, Noble had said. Ten past twelve to that time from Kent to South London wasn't out of the question. Harry had noted how Noble had said *suspicious death* but stopped short of *murder*. That revelation could wait until later, although the line of questioning hardly gave the impression it was a definite suicide. For the first time in the interview, Wilson spoke, his question indicating he was thinking along the same lines as Harry was.

'What type of car do you own, Dr Mohamed?'

'I've got two. A BMW X5 and an '83 Alfa Romeo Spider.'

Wilson nodded and wrote those down, too.

'Thank you, Doctor,' Noble said.

For their next interview, Alison Price had kindly volunteered the use of her office, arranging the chairs around a table, with her at one end and the three of them at the other. Theo Padmore, registrar to Mr Mohamed, had technically been a year junior to Bayliss, but as senior registrars their workload would have been roughly the same. He cut a very different figure to Mohamed: roughly unshaven, dressed in a corduroy shirt, trousers and smart suedes and a Mickey Mouse watch. He was probably Harry's age, or a touch younger. He sat down nervously, tapping his feet on the floor.

'Good morning, Dr Padmore,' Noble said.

'Good morning,' Padmore said. 'It's Mister, if you wouldn't mind.'

'Sure,' said Noble, flashing a glance at Harry.

'Sounds arrogant, I know. I'm sorry,' said Padmore. 'I took my membership of the Royal College of Surgeons exam four times before I passed. So I'm a bit proud of it. Sod it. Just call me Theo.'

Noble smiled.

'Ok, Theo. You know we're here about what happened to Susan.'

'Yes. I'm still in shock, really. Can't quite, err, believe it.'

'Did you know her well?'

'Yes. We'd been regs together for almost a year now. She was great to work with . . . I liked working with her. She was . . .' he trailed off. 'Yeah.'

Every three or four words, Harry noticed, Padmore would look across at Alison Price, and Harry looked at Padmore's ID badge in more detail. He was a clinical fellow in the department, placed there for a limited time to gain experience of a specialist field, unlike Bayliss, who was on a training contract. It meant his job was far less protected than Bayliss's had been, and everyone had seen what had happened to Bayliss. Harry got the distinct impression that Padmore was shit scared, and not of the detective inspector who was interviewing him.

'How about outside work?'

'I mean, yeah. We had the odd drink. She and her girlfriend had me and my wife over for dinner a few times. She was a very good cook, she enjoyed cooking a lot. God, it feels strange talking about her in the past tense. I can't believe she's gone.'

'Had you been talking to her recently?'

He looked out of the window, then at Price, who was scrolling through emails on her phone.

'Umm, well. Not since she was suspended. I sent her a text, to ask if she was ok. She didn't reply.'

'Why do you think that was?'

That question brought some soul-searching, until he eventually said, 'I think Susan thought I'd taken Mr Mohamed's side.'

'Side in what?' said Noble.

'The whole dispute, about the deaths on the valve operations. Her whistleblowing thing. She wanted me to sign the letters too, to say I thought Mr Mohamed was dangerous.'

'And you refused?'

'I did. I didn't agree with her.'

'You were involved in most of the cases, weren't you?'

'Yes,' said Padmore. 'I was in theatre with Jayden, Emmanuel and Abdul, and I looked after Olivia in intensive care.'

'And you didn't think that there was anything unusual about four consecutive patient deaths?'

At that, Price looked up, first at Noble, then at Padmore, which caused him to cough a little.

'Of course it was unusual,' said Padmore. 'But unusual means just that, doesn't it? Unusual. It doesn't mean you should just jump straight to conclusions.'

'What should you do?' said Noble.

'As they did. To my mind, it was handled rather well. Professor Gilmartin called an emergency M&M and insisted that the whole department be present, as well as the anaesthetists, the cardiologists, the management. And all of Susan's scaremongering about the fact that Mr Mohamed and Prof were covering it up was an exaggeration, too. We publish one-year data as well as thirty days, so we would have published the outcomes, just next year, rather than this month. So, eventually, someone would have seen it.'

'What, Susan just wanted it brought to attention sooner?' said Noble.

'Yes. Immediately.'

'What's wrong with that?'

'What's wrong with it is that it creates a climate of suspicion and fear,' Padmore said. 'You're police officers, you must know what the media is like. The moment there's an official inquiry, there's newspaper headlines about death rates being higher at this hospital or the like. And of course the *Sun* never points out that it's sicker children being operated on, no, just that the death rates are higher. And that does damage. I lost count of the number of families I had to persuade still to bring their children in for life-saving operations after the inquiry, even with other surgeons, nothing to do with valve surgery. Once something like that happens, it's toxic. So that's what's wrong with it.'

Harry had to concede it was a fair enough point. If getting hauled over the coals had been damaging for Mohamed, it must have been even worse for the rest of the department, seeing their reputation tarnished.

'Is that why the hospital let her go?'

Padmore held his breath and looked over again at Alison Price, who gave him no help. Christ, he really was a lamb to the slaughter, Harry thought.

'I believe that Susan was alleged to have made some comments to parents of children who had died, potentially suggesting that their deaths may have been avoidable. Or that's what I was told, anyway.'

Price looked up at him again.

'What about Mr Mohamed? How did he feel about it all?'

'He wasn't best pleased, as you can imagine.'

'Because he felt threatened? Undermined?'

'I don't think he was undermined,' said Padmore. 'In fact, he said he was quite proud of her for having the guts to raise it to him. But after the M&M, when she still wouldn't let it go . . . I mean, this is a man who's set up the valve surgery service here almost single-handedly. He's an absolute genius. I applied for the fellowship here partly so I could work with him, learn from him. And her bloody-mindedness damn near ruined his reputation. You know, he was lined up to give the keynote at the world's top congenital heart disease conference, and they got someone else instead. On a week's notice, because they'd seen the press reports and they thought it'd send out the wrong message.'

Padmore must have realised he'd been ranting, but shook his head and turned back to Noble. He seemed insightful for a junior doctor, even a senior one. Maybe that was just the type of person it took to get to where he was. Cardiothoracic surgery was one of the most competitive specialties, and in London it was only for the very best.

'That was what Susan was like, though,' he went on. 'Once she got the bit between her teeth, she'd never let it go.'

They let Padmore leave and Noble took a phone call. Harry said he needed the toilet, and Alison Price gave him directions before getting up to leave herself. Once he was sure Price had disappeared, Harry doubled back on himself and ran down the linking corridor towards the heart unit, hoping that he'd catch Padmore before he went through a locked door.

Harry caught him just as he was swiping clear.

'I'm sorry, is there something you forgot?'

'Mr Padmore, I'm not a police officer. I'm a doctor. They brought me along to advise on the case.'

'I see.'

'What I'm saying is, I know what it's like. With management hanging over your neck, and a boss who you rely on for your whole training. Do you get what I'm asking you?'

'Perhaps you should spell it out.'

Harry leant in and lowered his voice.

'I understand it's not black and white, and I'm not here to judge you in the slightest. I'd say the same thing in your position. But did you really think Bayliss was barking up the wrong tree with those kids?'

Padmore looked around, then back at Harry.

'I think that Mr Mohamed's a very good surgeon. Now, I really must go.'

He went through the door, and though it was obvious that he knew more than he was letting on, Harry couldn't think of anything else to say. He made his way back to the main atrium and joined Noble and Wilson in the queue for the lift.

In the lift down Harry said, 'You should have told him that she was murdered.'

'What, and throw away the only cards we hold?' said Noble. 'Those bastards control the flow of information right now. Or they're trying to. The only thing we know they don't is that Bayliss didn't kill herself. Who the bloody hell is that Price woman anyway?'

The lift stopped and a parent wheeled in a young boy with muscular dystrophy, smiling at Harry, who smiled back, and at Noble, who stared out of the glass onto the traffic of the A3, kids on their summer holidays in Kennington Park. The rest of the descent was silent, and the conversation didn't restart as they walked through the atrium, filled with parents and children. They got out onto the Oval junction and Wilson left to find the car and bring it around. They walked until they were far enough from the hospital that Noble could light up, and they could be assured of some privacy.

'Arseholes,' she said, pinching her thumb and forefinger. Harry felt similarly frustrated and he wondered when he'd made the conscious decision to allow this to happen, to allow himself into this world again, and then remembered his contribution, his blurting accusation of Mohamed. As he thought about that he realised that what was bothering him about the morning wasn't how out-of-place or awkward it was, but instead how normal it all felt. Bursting into a stranger's office with Frankie at his side.

Noble stubbed her cigarette out and lit up another.

'Mohamed tried to pull the wool over our eyes with the notes, didn't he?'

Harry nodded.

'And Padmore was full of shit, too, wasn't he?'

'Yeah,' said Harry. 'He was doing his best though. Scared for his job, after what happened to Bayliss, and given who was in the room.'

'The manager.'

Harry nodded.

'I'll see if I've got the resources to call in and see her face-to-face later today,' Noble said, exhaling into Harry's face. The nine months they'd spent together must have taken at least a year off his life expectancy from the passive smoke alone, maybe a year more from the exertion. 'Maybe down at the nick, put a bit of pressure on. I mean who the hell does that bitch think she is?'

They came around the corner to the ramp which led behind the hospital to the car park, and she leant against the door to finish smoking.

'Do you really think what happened to Bayliss was linked to all this?'

'It's got to be,' Noble said. 'Either Bayliss sent that tweet under duress or it was sent from her phone by her killer. So either it's linked to what happened here or somebody wants us to think it is.'

'So what now?'

'I'll let you know when I'm meeting the doctors who conducted the inquiry. I'll want you for that. And if we get the PMs through or the hospital notes, I'll give you a ring.'

'I can't wait,' said Harry.

A police-issue Volvo swung around and parked up, Wilson at the wheel. Noble got into the car and, as she closed the door, said, 'Don't pretend you don't love it, Harry. I'll be watching tonight.'

Tonight, he thought. In the hospital, as he'd sat opposite Mohamed and Padmore, he'd almost forgotten that tonight was the appeal, a date he'd been waiting for for months. Then the familiar feelings of haze and fatigue descended, his body yearning for more drug, the brand of fear only an addict can feel, memory of past withdrawals and the horrors of the stages to come coupled with an irrational terror of some external cataclysm if he didn't find himself a pill soon. He reached into his bag and found the bottle without the need to look, clicking off the lid and flicking it between his fingers like a poker chip whilst his other hand brought two of the tablets straight into his mouth.

Then he set off, towards the Tube, and the sun felt warmer and the breeze felt cooler and the world was right again.

When Harry arrived, Beth was already waiting at the restaurant, a Mediterranean café sandwiched on the thin strip of concrete between Southwark Cathedral and the railway lines that covered Borough Market, oversized dishes of Catalan stew and paella teasing the queues of South Bank creatives, tourists and the recently arrived corporate executives waiting for their lunches. She rose and kissed him on the mouth, tasting of Pimm's and lemonade.

'You're starting early,' he said, grinning.

'It's my day off, isn't it?'

There was a jug on the table.

'You want one?'

'I'm driving to Tammas's later, aren't I?'

'Your loss,' she said, and poured herself another. The waiter came. Harry ordered a Coke and the house sandwich, a ciabatta stuffed with chorizo, chicken and halloumi and heaps of tzatziki. If the Spanish economy going under meant more food like this in London, he didn't mind a bit.

'Why are you dressed so smart?' Beth said.

'I was helping out the police this morning.'

'What with? You were working all last night!'

'It was only a few hours,' Harry said, his previous hunger having been wiped out by the pills. 'Some interviews that needed a medical opinion.'

'If you keep up this work rate we'll be able to afford that safari,' Beth said. 'Although with my rota I think you need to give a decade's notice if you want time off.'

Harry smiled. It had been a pipe dream they'd cooked up after a nice meal and two six-packs one night, scrolling the late-night channels and eventually settling upon David Attenborough narrating lions chasing antelope across the Serengeti, and Harry pointing out that he'd never been to Africa. Beth had spent part of her gap year volunteering at a hospital in Mozambique, and then travelled all the way up to Cairo. So they'd spent the rest of the evening browsing travel agency websites, even though neither thought it would ever come to anything.

'How was your shift?' Harry said.

'Ok,' said Beth, 'C Team had a patient abscond on their leave, a stable Type 2 bipolar – well, stable assuming he takes his pills. Apart from that it was pretty run of the mill. Nowhere near as fun as attending high-profile suicides.'

Harry waved a hand in front of his face, but Beth carried on undeterred.

'That might be murders, eh?'

He briefly wondered how the hell she knew that, and then remembered telling her on the phone, exhausted and sleep-deprived.

'Shush!' Harry said, leaning in, his voice low, 'I shouldn't have said that. It's not public information.'

Beth grinned and tapped her nose.

'Come on, it's a hell of a lot more interesting than my work. Deciding who gets the privilege of a walk to the shop and who doesn't, and then it's downhill from there.'

'I don't want to talk about it,' said Harry. 'What do you fancy doing later? Still fancy Hyde Park?'

'Maybe one of the cruises along the Thames. I still haven't done one,' Beth said. 'Or the amphibious things, the ones that look like ducks.'

Beth was from Norfolk, had gone to medical school in Newcastle and then spent her foundation years in deepest, darkest Yorkshire, so the novelty of London still held strong for her. For Harry, who'd been born in the same hospital he worked in and grown up on a council estate in New Cross, the tourist activities they often did together were less comfortable, and not just because he couldn't stand the crowds in Leicester Square or Oxford Circus. They reminded him of things his mother had done with him when he was younger – trips to the aquarium or the theatre, always the last weekend of the month, nurses' pay day – in that blissful window of memory and ignorance, ten or eleven years old, old enough to know his mother loved him, young enough not to realise the significance of the brandy bottle that was always half empty, or the old cuts on her arms she covered with foundation because the hospital wouldn't let her wear long-sleeved tabards anymore.

'Not the duck boats,' he said. 'One of them caught fire and capsized not so long ago.'

'That could be cute. It'd be like *Titanic*.'

'The guy drowns in *Titanic*, Beth.'

'You little shit!' she said, laughing, 'I haven't seen it. You've spoiled the ending now.'

The food arrived and they tucked in, Harry dripping oil down his front. Another couple arrived and sat down on the other end of the table, and it took Harry a few seconds before he placed where he had seen them. They'd been waiting in the atrium at Belgrave, and he and Noble had walked straight past them as they exited. A bit of a coincidence that they'd decided on the same restaurant.

'How's your sandwich?' Beth said, ripping the head off a prawn.

Harry made a ring with his thumb and forefinger and ate another large mouthful. Beside them, the couple from the hospital were silent, and Harry tried to work out why a man in his twenties and a woman ten or fifteen years older would be eating out. Stop it, he told himself, you're being paranoid. It's a coincidence.

'It's good.'

'You excited about tonight?'

Harry shifted on his chair, so the couple were no longer in his peripheral vision. There was a band of pain spreading across his head, a throbbing right behind his eyeball. It usually came after at least a day without sleep, so its appearance now was premature.

'Excited's the wrong word,' he said. 'If anything, I'm nervous.'

'How come? You've already recorded your segment.'

'It's not about that,' said Harry. 'I'm not looking forward to talking to Dave again.'

His head was still throbbing, the couple to his right still silent.

'Frankie told me he's got a new job,' he went on. 'The bastard never said. He's strung me along like he's really taking this to heart, like he's the one bloody copper in that place who gives a shit, and all this time he's been taking me for a bloody ride.'

'God, really?'

'Yes, really.'

'But there'll still be someone investigating, won't there?'

'Officially, maybe. Lambeth Homicide & Serious had the case for a year and did bugger-all with it. It's a non-starter in their heads, and it'll go right back onto the bottom of the pile when they get it back.'

Harry scratched at his head and mopped up the bits of food left on the greaseproof paper the sandwiches had been served in and thought back to his conversation with Noble, the one she'd referenced that morning. *We had a deal.* We had a lot of deals, Harry thought. That you'd stop drinking. That we'd go on holiday. And then, the self-pity, his worst enemy, returning to his thoughts. The deal you made with yourself to stop the pills. The shrinks called it co-dependency – how Noble's addiction, though a separate beast, somehow validated his own.

'Frankie might take it back,' he said eventually.

'What?' said Beth. A look of anger crossed her face, and Harry realised he'd really gone and put his foot in it now. She didn't know much about his ex, just that she had been a detective who he'd met during the investigation he'd been involved with last year, she'd been a drinker, and it had ended badly.

'This case I was helping on this morning,' he said. 'She told me about Dave. She says if I help her out, she'll take up Zara's investigation.'

'And you believed her?' Beth said. The only time he'd previously seen her this angry was during particularly testy episodes of *The Great British Bake Off*.

'Why would she lie?'

'To manipulate you? To guilt-trip you into helping her out? To insert herself back into your life? You name it, Harry!'

He wanted to rise to her defence, to tell Beth that a woman had been murdered, the case looked like it was getting more complicated by the minute, and Noble genuinely needed assistance from a medical perspective. But he'd already told her too much, especially if the police party line was that Susan Bayliss had most likely committed suicide. Not to mention that defending her would only incense Beth more.

And, on second thoughts, he wasn't sure who he was trying hardest to convince. Beth or himself.

'I wasn't thinking. I thought she wouldn't call me unless she really had to. And I'm not letting her into my life in anything other than a professional capacity.'

Beth leant forward, taking one of Harry's hands in both of hers, her voice hushed, her eyes pleading.

'You don't have such a thing as a professional capacity, Harry. Just look at Zara. That's not professional, that's personal. Everything you do is personal. You agree to help her with this case now and it'll be personal by tomorrow.'

Harry gave a grim laugh.

'You know me too well,' he said.

'I need the toilet,' Beth announced, shaking her head as she got up and headed away. Harry's appetite had vanished, so he sucked his Coke through a straw and arranged the debris on his plate, thinking about how lucky he was to have found a woman who was normal, and sane, to replace the other two in his life: Noble, the tempest, and Zara, in a coma, both with needs he couldn't meet. Yes, he'd been an idiot, and as always his desire to do the right thing had proved foolhardy instead of heroic. He began thinking of something to do with Beth to mend things, acquiesce to the duck-boat tour at the very least. Maybe a shopping trip to Bond Street, his treat.

He didn't know how long Beth had been gone when he first noticed that the couple next to him were leaning in close and speaking in quiet whispers. But it did nothing to help his paranoia when the woman leant over and said, 'Excuse me, Detective, I'd like a word.'

'I'm not a detective,' Harry spluttered, his heart pounding as the implications played out in his head. Whoever these people were, they'd been waiting in the atrium for the police, and they'd followed him from the hospital. They looked at each other, and Harry shuffled away and got to his feet.

'You were with the police at the hospital,' she said.

'Who are you?' Harry demanded.

'I'm sorry,' the woman said, now standing too and extending her hand.

'I'm Michelle Roberts. My daughter Ollie died in April. I'd like to have a word.'

It didn't take Harry long to realise that Michelle and the man she was with – surely not her husband, he was far too young – had followed Harry from the hospital simply because he'd left on foot and taken the Tube, rather than through any chauvinistic assumption that he was senior to Acting DCI Noble. They'd waited for the police to arrive, she said, before following them after they returned from the cardiac unit.

At least he'd been vindicated in his paranoia, he thought – he wasn't yet totally descending into madness. Now he looked at her more closely he saw the resemblance between her face and that of Olivia's, the innocent four-year-old whose face had been featured on the news stories he'd spent yesterday reading.

'I'm so sorry for your loss,' Harry said, still standing. 'But I'm afraid I can't discuss any aspects of the investigation with you, Mrs Roberts. I'm sorry.'

He moved to leave – he could wait for Beth by the toilets – but she blocked his path.

'I don't want you to discuss the investigation with me,' Roberts said, 'I just need you to hear my story. Our story.'

Harry sat down again, looking between Roberts and the man she was with. Her eyes were misted over with loss, and as he recalled what he knew of Olivia's story he felt a pain growing behind his sternum. Beth returned from the toilet and came to stand behind Harry, looking between him and the woman with the wet eyes and tangled hair.

'Like I said,' Harry said. 'I'm not a detective, I'm a Force Medical Examiner. A doctor. I was only at Belgrave this morning to help the detectives conducting interviews with hospital staff.'

'So they're investigating the hospital?'

The hope in her voice was palpable.

'I can't comment,' Harry said, silently cursing Noble for ever dumping him into this affair. 'Interviews were conducted with staff members.'

'Mr Mohamed?'

Harry said nothing and consciously willed none of the muscles in his face to move. But Roberts stared him down, eyes pleading. Eventually Beth saved him.

'You said you didn't want him to discuss the investigation with you,' she said. 'So don't ask, then.'

Roberts looked over at her, then shook her head.

'Have you not spoken to the police already?' said Harry.

'Somebody called yesterday,' said Roberts. 'But they just wanted to know when I'd last seen her, if she'd said anything about her plans for Saturday evening. I tried to tell them the whole story but they wouldn't listen, they said they were in a rush.'

'I see,' said Harry.

'I'm sorry for ambushing you like this,' she said. 'I just . . . We went there this morning in the hope that now, with Susan dead, the police would finally take this seriously. That I could get justice for Ollie, that someone would stop that man from killing more children.'

Harry winced as she said those words and thought back to sitting in Mohamed's office with Alison Price standing guard, censoring everything he said. Could a man truly be blind enough to his own incompetence, so unwilling to accept the consequences of his mistakes, that he would go on harming children purely to save face? Of course he could. It had happened before, at hospitals across the world. Behind the surgical mask lay a human mind with the same human flaws as bin men or bartenders. Harry could believe that. What he couldn't quite comprehend was that anyone would make the leap from covering up negligence to murdering a colleague and leaving her body to bask in its own blood.

'I'm so sorry that you lost your daughter,' Beth said.

'Thank you,' said Roberts. The man she was with reached into the inside pocket of his jacket, which he was wearing despite the twenty-five degree heat, and passed her a tissue. Harry looked between them, and though a voice somewhere in his head told him that the path he was about to embark on was a poor decision, he spoke.

'What makes you say that? That you need justice for her?'

'They said she recovered well after her operation, but that's a lie,' Michelle said. 'She wasn't the same as before, even with her infections. I'd taken Ollie to seven different hospitals. She was under two immunologists, one at the Evelina, one at Lewisham, and no-one was ever able to tell me why she kept getting infections. She kept getting them, they even accused me of not washing her properly, called me a bad mother. Then she got one really bad and it spread to her heart, and they moved her to the Belgrave and told me they had to replace her valve or she'd die in a few months' time. I asked about the side effects, and Mr Mohamed told me that this wasn't a decision that could be debated. It was the operation or certain death, that's what he said. And I bloody believed him.'

She blew her nose into the tissue, and Beth squeezed Harry's hand again. From the notes, it seemed that the endocarditis had left Roberts with very severe tricuspid insufficiency, and that based on what he'd read, Mohamed's assessment of Olivia Roberts's situation had been nothing but accurate, but he bit his tongue.

'Even after she was out of hospital, I was sure she was never the same. The doctors said she'd recovered fully, but she was slower. She used to be able to read like a six-year-old, even though she'd been in and out of nursery with her infections. She couldn't get through a page after that operation. She couldn't sleep more than an hour. Some days she didn't even recognise her little brother. I kept saying she wasn't right, but all they cared about was that her new valve was working ok. I told them, my daughter's more than a heart valve, but they wouldn't listen. The only person who listened to me was Susan . . .

'I took Ollie in to see her a few more times, not officially, but just at the end of the day when she wasn't busy. She tried to get Mr Mohamed to come down and see her, but he wasn't interested. Always made up an excuse. I tried to get her referred to Great Ormond Street instead, but before they wrote back . . .'

She trailed off. Harry wanted to look anywhere but her face, but couldn't. The man she was with leant forward and grasped her forearm, rubbing it.

'It was a Tuesday,' Roberts said. 'I dropped Ollie off at her Montessori and I went to the gym, and they called me about eleven. They said that Ollie had collapsed and they'd called an ambulance, and the paramedics were taking her to Lewisham, and by the time I got there she was surrounded by all these doctors, there were all these tubes and wires in her, it was just like when she was in the ICU, but they were doing CPR on her, and I just knew then that she wasn't going to make it, that I'd lost her.'

She broke down in tears, and her companion brushed her arm with his hand and passed her another tissue. Around them, the workers and students and tourists enjoyed their lunches, with no apparent notice of the grieving mother beside them. Harry felt nothing but sympathy. Whilst losing a child in any circumstance was horrendous, there was something exquisitely painful about Olivia Roberts surviving two weeks in intensive care and then a major operation and seemingly recovering, only to go to nursery one day and die halfway through the morning. His discomfort was exacerbated by the strange man sitting holding Michelle Roberts's arm.

'I'm so sorry,' Harry said, 'it must be awful for you both.'

'Oh,' said Roberts, 'this isn't my husband.'

Harry tried to suppress his pride at the veiled question, and looked over at the man, whose face had turned red.

'Noah Skelton,' he said in a high-pitched Mancunian accent. 'I'm a solicitor assisting Michelle, and the other families.'

'Other families?' said Beth.

'At the moment I'm representing the families of Olivia Roberts, Emmanuel Abediji, Jayden Capp and Abdul Mubarak.'

Harry held his breath.

'Pro bono, of course,' Skelton added.

'You're suing the hospital?' said Harry.

'We haven't ruled that out,' said Skelton. 'But we're not after money. We want a judicial review and a full police investigation into the deaths of these children under Mr Mohamed's care. That's our main objective.'

Beth looked over at Harry, who knew he shouldn't be here, that he should never have entertained Roberts, or listened to her story. But the images of the last few days that were flashing in the slide-show of his memory refused to allow a retreat. The tweet Bayliss's attacker had sent from her phone, or the one she'd sent before she'd been killed. Mohamed's feeble attempts to deceive them earlier. The cheek of the hospital manager. Maybe the itch inside him was only due to professional sympathy, to wish that Bayliss was right in her thoughts of a conspiracy simply so that the destruction of her career was for some noble objective.

'Was Susan Bayliss helping you?'

Roberts and Skelton looked at each other, before Skelton began to nod slowly.

'We have a support group,' Roberts said. 'It started with all families of kids having heart surgery at the Belgrave, but after the deaths we sort of split up. Susan came to meet with us a few times, said she thought she was being followed. She said that the hospital was refusing to allow an independent investigation. So she went to the Department of Health, and the last time we spoke she . . .'

More tears, Skelton passing her another tissue. A train thunder-ing over the overhead tracks.

'She was absolutely devastated the DoH had let Mohamed off. Said she was sure there'd been even more of a cover-up. She didn't know what to do with herself. And now she's gone and bloody killed herself.'

Harry let the silence roll in, and tried to work out what he'd learnt from the sad story. The four sets of parents were meeting with Bayliss in secret, with a solicitor. Planning action against the hospital from within, their woman on the inside. In the final weeks of her life, Bayliss had thought she was being followed. Paranoia, or the truth? He looked across and saw Beth biting her lip but thought, fuck it, what did he have to lose?

'What did she say was the cover-up?'

'She said Mohamed was a good surgeon, not a great one, and he was obsessed with breaking records. Doing dangerous opera-tions just for the thrill of it. Like Emmanuel and Abdul. She said they were both far too young for such a major procedure, but Mohamed wanted to show off.'

Harry tried to process that thought. If that was the case, why hadn't the experts brought in by the Department of Health said anything about the decisions to operate?

'I'm sorry,' said Harry. 'This is all a bit too much. I'm going to call the police officer conducting the investigation. You need to speak directly to them.'

Beth looked at him again, relieved. That he'd finally decided he was out of his depth, perhaps, or just that the torture of this conversation was coming to an end. Harry was trying to make sense of it all, fully aware that the prophecy his girlfriend had made just a few minutes ago was already half-formed.

'You do believe me, though, don't you?'

Harry had been asked this question so many times, by patients in A&E or a police cell, that he could answer it regardless without so much as blinking.

'Of course.'

'Oh, thank you,' Roberts said, her hand shooting across the table and grasping Harry's, 'thank you, thank you, thank you.'

'Do you have contact details?' said Harry. 'In case I want to be in touch.'

She ripped off a corner of a napkin, took a pen from her purse and scrawled a number on it. Harry picked it up and met Beth's scowling eyes, left some money on the table, and moved to leave.

Noble was just finishing her own lunch when the phone rang, a tray of Marks & Spencer's finest sushi washed down with a bottle of juice with beetroot and kale and a few other things which had no place in a drink. That was the downside when the gopher who went to get you lunch was a health freak who ran marathons for fun, not just for charity. The screen displayed Harry's name. She had expected he might call, but perhaps not quite so soon.

'Hello?' Noble said. She was in her own office in the Incident Room at Peckham, which was just beginning to take shape, the Actions board that took up the entirety of the far wall covered by a growing mass of post-it notes, calls she needed to make.

'Can you talk?' said Harry.

'If I couldn't, do you think I would've picked up?'

'You won't believe who I've just spoken to. Michelle Roberts. Olivia Roberts's mum. She's with some solicitor. They followed me from the hospital, thought I was a detective. Wanted to give me their side of the story.'

'You're fucking kidding,' Noble said, walking to her office door and pulling it closed. 'What was she doing at the hospital?'

'She said they'd expected police to come to the hospital after Bayliss died. They were waiting for us.'

'Bloody hell.' Noble said. 'What did she say?'

He told her, and she began to scratch at her neck, frustrated. She'd just come out of an hour-long meeting with Grenaghan in which they'd discussed the politically sensitive nature of investi-gating members of staff at an NHS hospital, particularly one which had just emerged unscathed from a government inquiry. And the fact that murders were most often committed by the victim's nearest and dearest, for the simplest of motives. With that in mind, a team of six detectives had just been devoted to pulling apart Teodora Guzman's life, with the intention of finding any possible motive for faking her partner's suicide. Harry Kent had rarely brought her good news with his phone calls, and so this was no change.

'Right. Email me an address and a contact number. I'll have them interviewed fully tomorrow.'

'Can you not do it this afternoon?' asked Harry.

Noble crunched on a California roll, thinking about the words she'd said last night, trying to convince him to help her out, that she needed his clarity of thought, his instinct which she knew to be often correct.

'You think she's legit?'

'I think she and Bayliss had quite a close relationship, and if this is all related to the Belgrave, she may be able to give you some pointers.'

'Ok. Thanks, Harry.'

He was silent for a while, then just hung up the phone. Ok, Noble thought. She didn't need him to like her – she just needed his mind in an easy place for her to pick it. The afternoon looked like hell, meetings with the various forensics teams about the scene-of-crime and decisions for which tests to prioritise, the sub-teams who'd been running down CCTV and the rest of the minutiae of Bayliss's life: finances, exes, the boring stuff they couldn't afford to overlook. And then a whole-team meeting that afternoon, which the super had kindly informed her he'd be attending. It was approaching thirty-six hours since Susan Bayliss had been murdered, and despite a bunch of doctors whose careers she'd almost ruined, a girlfriend with a made-up alibi, and a confusing history of mental illness, no obvious prime suspect.

She ate another roll and heard her phone buzz with an arriving email. Pulling the door open, she yelled to DC Bhalla and thrust the phone at him.

'Call her,' she said. 'Get Michelle Roberts in for interview this evening. Make sure the solicitor she's with is the same one she was with at lunchtime. I'll brief you in half an hour.'

'Yes ma'am.'

Harry hadn't hung up. In fact he'd dropped the phone and remained as he stooped, bent double, the pain in his skull too much. He caught it with his foot, and as he bent to pick it up the pain slightly abated, and when he rose Beth was there, holding him in her arms.

'I don't like this,' she said. 'You shouldn't be this involved. I don't want people following us around.'

'I'm sorry,' Harry said. He didn't want people following him around, either. He thought about his derision of Beth for her earlier statement that Noble had been manipulating him. But he'd let Michelle Roberts sit down and pour her heart out, and Noble hadn't forced him to shoot his mouth off with Elyas Mohamed. Beth's earlier words rang even truer now: *You agree to help her with this case now and it'll be personal by tomorrow.*

'Let's go back to yours,' she said. 'We can go out tomorrow.'

'No, let's go out,' said Harry. He knew if he went back to his flat he'd fall asleep the moment he hit the bed or the sofa, and that would just upset Beth even more.

'Let's not let that spoil our day,' he said.

He took a breath in, looked between her and the hubbub of the market. All he could think about was sleep. Sleep, to banish the thoughts of Bayliss and the chair and the blood on the walls and ceilings, and Noble with her unnaturally fresh face, and Zara and her unthinking eyes.

'We're ok, aren't we?'

'Of course we are,' Harry said, kissing Beth on the mouth. 'Now, what do you want to do?'

'Let's walk along the South Bank and see what takes our fancy.'

Harry sucked in warm air, tried as best he could to smile, and took her arm.

It was surprisingly fun fighting through the crowds of school groups, tourist families, buskers playing 'Wonderwall', and living statues dressed as Yoda, Shrek and Freddie Mercury. They stopped for an ice-cream, and when the path came out by the riverside and the blasted stone dome of St Paul's with the high noon sun hitting the glass of the City and shining down onto the water, Beth insisted on finding a kosher-looking passer-by to take a photo of them.

'Jesus,' said Beth, swiping through the six snaps on her phone, 'You could have at least smiled. Or looked at the camera.'

'Sorry.'

'You didn't deliberately thwart it because you don't want me putting it on Instagram?'

'As if I'd do such a thing . . .'

They kept walking until they arrived at the Tate Modern, its big coal-stack chimney rising like a middle finger to the cathedral and the corporate offices on the other side of the river.

'Let's go in!' Beth said.

'Really?' said Harry.

'Oh c'mon,' said Beth, 'I know you've probably been a hundred times, but I haven't done it yet. And I'm sure they bring in new stuff from time to time.'

Harry laughed and they started walking up to the entrance, shaking his head.

'I've never been in,' he said, trying to hide his embarrassment.

'What? Seriously?'

He laughed again.

'National Gallery? Tate Britain?'

He shook his head, unsure quite why he found it so funny.

'You've had so much culture on your doorstep your whole life, you've made use of absolutely none of it!'

Harry put his hands out as if she was to handcuff him, and she slapped them, now also grinning and shaking her head.

'I'd have killed for an art gallery growing up in King's Lynn!'

'Would any of you have been able to paint, y'know, with six fingers?'

'Oh, shut up.'

They took the escalator up to the main galleries, and after about fifteen minutes or so of Beth bombarding him with questions – *What do you think she was trying to say? Does that look like a city to you? Christ, that must have taken him ages!* – his mind began to wander. She looked at paintings and saw things – impressions, shapes, emotions – and all he saw was a blank slate, onto which he projected his thoughts. Michelle Roberts's face, in a particularly grotesque wrinkle of pain, and the limp, grey form of Emmanuel Abediji on the resus trolley at the Ruskin. He knew of examples of hospitals covering up incompetent surgeons for months, even years, but at a place like the Belgrave, such a conspiracy would have to involve tens of people – cardiologists, anaesthetists, surgeons, nurse specialists, senior managers. He couldn't imagine it . . .

'Let's go upstairs,' said Beth.

'Sure,' said Harry.

'You ok?'

'Yeah, this stuff's good. A little weird . . . I like the ones where you can tell what it's meant to be, y'know?'

'Philistine.'

'Snob.'

She kissed him and he kissed her back. Not for the first time, he wondered what exactly it was that she saw in him. Unstable rota, unstable lifestyle. He'd been selective about just what he'd told her of his history. She knew he'd been to Afghanistan and he didn't like talking about it, and that something big had happened that gave him scars on his back and had put Tammas on a ventilator. She knew that last year, he'd been involved in the police investigation into the shooting of a local teenager, which he didn't like talking about either, partly because it involved Frankie, but mostly because his best friend, James Lahiri, had ended up getting killed.

He brought all that baggage to the table, and she brought stability, normality and laughter. For sure, she was what he needed. Harry just hoped that the converse was true.

On the fourth floor there was a special feature, a big room playing a silent film on a projector where some children wearing old-fashioned gas masks were exploring a deserted beach on a grey, stormy day, and trying to build some kind of frame out of detritus washed up on the sand. It played and replayed, each time changing subtle details like the colour contrast or the position of the tide.

Harry gave it his best, but after five minutes his hand wandered to his phone, where he googled Michelle Roberts's name and found her blog without much effort. There was a post from that morning, linking to the news stories about Bayliss's death. *Stunned to hear about Susan's death. She was a true ally. I can't believe it.* He scrolled down, finding another link to a petition calling for an official public inquiry into the deaths at the Belgrave. He clicked the menu, finding sections for Blog, Contact, Donate, and Olivia's Story.

The blog posts contained many of the same themes as Susan's manifesto, and Harry wondered whether Bayliss had had a role in writing it. He recalled Roberts's self-belief, and it matched the picture of Bayliss he was beginning to build in his head. Again, he recalled the politics of the official inquiry. *No evidence to challenge the individual clinical decisions or the overall care provided at the unit.* If it was a whitewash, it was one which went straight to the top, and would require a conspiracy of astonishing numbers to keep it quiet. All this logic and more hung like cirrus clouds in Harry's brain, but he couldn't convince himself. By all accounts Susan Bayliss had been a logical, sensible person too, and she had sacrificed her entire livelihood to bring this to the public's attention.

A quick Google search found him the inquiry report again. Looking up at Beth to ensure her attention was fixed closely on the film, he clicked on it.

Noble massaged her temples as she listened to the whirrs of the coffee machine in the small cupboard that functioned as a canteen for the twenty-four detectives assigned to the Bayliss case, trying to summon one of the mindfulness exercises Everscott was so keen on, but failing. If she was brutally honest, she didn't really see how imagining the sand between her toes on a deserted white beach was supposed to improve her mood, instead of reminding her where she actually was, with the feeling that the truth she sought was slipping away from her.

The coffee clicked and poured, and someone gave two short knocks on the door.

'Come in.'

It was DC Bhalla.

'They're all ready for you downstairs, guv.'

'Right,' said Noble, picking up her coffee mug and following Bhalla through the back-to-back desks and workstations which formed the Incident Room, waving to those team members who were still in the office. Most were out, assigned on actions, chasing forensics, completing the house-to-house around Calais Street, interviewing known associates. Others were delving through Susan Bayliss's social media and email accounts, others still on background. Full profiles of everyone connected to the case so far were required, particularly the emerging suspects: Elyas Mohamed, maybe Padmore or anyone else involved with the hospital, Professor Gilmartin, the head of department, and the woman Noble was on her way to interview, Teodora Guzman. As the team nodded back to her, one question ruled her mind. Who has less confidence in me as a leader – them, or me?

Noble waited for a while outside the interview room, puffing on her e-cigarette, eyeballing the lineup. Guzman had replaced her facial piercings with a masking plaster covering her right nostril. The solicitor next to her was a gaunt-looking man despite his young age, and as Noble entered the room she briefly considered whether he shared the same habit she did. Or rather, had.

'Morning,' she said. 'I'm Acting DCI Noble. We met on Sunday, but you may not remember. I'm sorry.'

Guzman nodded. Noble went to shake hands with the solicitor, glancing subtly as she could at the CD recorder to check if it was switched off.

'Noah Skelton.'

'You were with Michelle Roberts when she approached one of my colleagues this morning, weren't you?'

Skelton said nothing. DS McGovern, who was seconding on the interview, looked across, puzzled. It wasn't her fault she hadn't connected the dots – they weren't bringing in Michelle Roberts for her interview until that evening. As soon as she'd had time to consider her question, she decided against asking him anything about the encounter they had had with Harry Kent that morning. The purpose of this interview was to eliminate Teodora Guzman as a suspect, and it was best kept that way.

'Unless there's two solicitors with your name in this city?' Noble went on. 'Which would be pretty crap advertising.'

'Mrs Roberts is a client of ours,' Skelton said. 'My firm represents many clients. Though I fail to see what this has to do with the arrangement to interview Ms Guzman under caution.'

'Susan Bayliss?' Noble said.

Skelton nodded. 'Miss Bayliss and Ms Guzman have been a cohabiting couple for ten years. Their having the same legal arrangements is hardly a stretch of the imagination. Or at least it shouldn't be, for a DCI.'

He punctuated each initial with a scoop of saliva. Noble placed both hands on the table and leant forward, hissing her rebuke into Skelton's ear.

'Just you watch it, you smarmy cunt.'

Before Skelton's face could even change, she slammed on the CD recorder and announced herself. 'Acting Detective Chief Inspector Frances Noble present for the interview of Teodora Guzman in relation to the sudden unexpected death of Susan Bayliss. Interview is being conducted at Peckham Police Station on Monday, 25 August, 2014. Also present are Detective Sergeant Shona McGovern and Noah Skelton, legal representative for Ms Guzman. The time now is 15:06.'

Noble sat down as the others identified themselves, Skelton through gritted teeth. With the formalities complete, McGovern took two documents from her folder, the statement Guzman had given last night and the report they had recovered from the crime scene, the one Bayliss had leaked to the Department of Health. It was this she passed over to Guzman.

'For the tape, I have just presented the document entitled, *Series of Postoperative Deaths amongst Congenital Cardiac Surgery Patients at*

Belgrave Hospital for Sick Children, recovered from Flat 5b, Victoria House, Calais Street, on Sunday 24 August,' McGovern said.

'Do you recognise this?' asked Noble.

'Yes,' said Guzman. She was forlorn, depressed. It had sunk in now that her partner was dead, but Noble thought the dead eyes might also be from medication. Perhaps the same kind of antidepressants that had been forced down Bayliss's throat.

'What is it?'

'It's the report Susan compiled into the children who died at Belgrave. The ones they covered up,' Guzman said.

'I see,' said Noble. 'Susan involved you in all of this, did she?'

'Yes. I remember her the night she found out Olivia and Emmanuel had died. She was in pieces, completely. And then the night she came out of the meeting they'd had all day, and said that Professor Gilmartin wasn't going to have an investigation.'

'I can understand how difficult that must have been, losing the two patients,' said Noble, 'but why was she so upset about the investigation?'

'Because she knew she was going to have to choose between her job and doing the right thing. Those bastards already hated her guts, and she knew that to go above Gilmartin's head meant going outside of the trust, and they'd destroy her for that. Suse had worked so hard to get that job, it was a dream come true when she got it. Working with kids, the cardiac stuff, it was all she'd ever wanted to do.' She wiped away a tear, Skelton on hand with the tissues. 'And even after Mohamed started making her life hell, she loved working there. Every day. So she knew she was going to have to sacrifice that, in order to stop him. Mohamed.'

In her sincerity, her fortitude, Noble saw an unshakeable belief, or at least a very good act. There was a video camera high in the left-hand corner of the room, carefully placed to capture an excellent view of the interviewee's face. Some detectives liked to go over their interrogations, replaying them frame-by-frame to judge the suspect's expressions, but Noble eschewed that. She worked in the room, with what was in front of her, and that instinct told her that Guzman wasn't lying. But then again, just because Teodora Guzman genuinely believed that the hospital was perpetrating a cover-up didn't mean that she hadn't used it as a smokescreen to disguise the murder of her girlfriend.

'What do you mean, Mohamed started making her life hell?'

'Elyas Mohamed is a dangerous man,' Guzman said. 'When Susan started working at Belgrave, he was very helpful. He offered her the chance to help on a research project. She said she thought he might have been hitting on her a bit, but she was used to that.

'Before they decide to do surgery on a kid, they have something called an MDM – multidisciplinary meeting – to decide what the best option is. Suse said usually the registrars wouldn't say anything, just sit there and watch, even if they disagreed. She'd spent some time down in Southampton, and at the Evelina, and she said compared to them Mohamed and the surgeons were just gung-ho. All they wanted to do was the most complex operation possible, whether or not it was best for the child. So then at one of the meetings, the one for Emmanuel, she spoke up. In a quiet way. All she did was ask Mohamed why a less invasive procedure, something involving a balloon, wouldn't work just as well.'

Noble made a note of that, thinking that she hoped Harry wasn't asleep, as she'd need him to translate some bits. From the sound of it, it didn't really matter, but it would be good to know.

'Apparently, no-one had ever questioned him before. The next day the whole hospital knew about it,' Guzman went on. 'And from then on, Theo was the favourite. Every time he was in thea-tre, he got Theo to be his first assistant, do the majority of the work, even though he was Suse's junior. He took her name off the research paper, even though she'd done most of the work. And then we know what happened to Emmanuel. After she raised the issues with the dead kids it went nuclear. He did everything he could to get her out, reported her to management if she was five minutes late for a ward round. He'd told her she would never make consultant, that she might as well start preparing for a staff grade job or switch specialty. That kind of puerile, misogynistic bullshit.'

'Would you say she hated him, then? Would you go that far?'

Guzman's eyes went hard, and for a moment Noble tensed involuntarily, preparing for another outburst like the one on Sunday morning.

'Did she hate him?' Guzman repeated. 'Yes, she did. Because he was putting kids' lives at risk to make himself famous. If you're suggesting that she hated him enough to get rid of him by concocting some kind of—'

Before she could finish her sentence, Skelton had reached across and gripped her wrist, squeezing it, a hard look on his face. It wasn't quite quick enough, of course.

'I'm sure if the DCI was suggesting anything of that kind, she would put it to my client in a direct question,' he said.

Noble stared at Guzman slightly, determined not to give Skelton the satisfaction of eye contact.

'Did anyone else from the hospital support her?'

Guzman shook her head.

'They all knew their precious cardiothoracic department was at risk if they spoke out. No-one blows the whistle. That's just how it is.'

'She told you about it, yeah?'

'She told me everything,' Guzman said, wiping away tears.

Genuine ones perhaps, thought Noble. But the information they had in front of them cast a different shadow, one that Noble had to exclude. No alibi between midnight, when her friends last recalled being with her in the club, and four, when she walked in to find her girlfriend dead in the living room. And so, in the room, she ignored all of the bullshit Harry and her detectives were spinning about Belgrave, and thought about that. In fact, she wondered if she was being a little sexist. If Bayliss's partner had been a man, without an alibi for her murder, they'd probably have arrested him by now.

'Did you have access to her Twitter account?'

Guzman said, 'No.' Skelton's face contorted.

'Can you account for your movements on Saturday night, between nine and four a.m. the next morning?'

'My client has already answered that question,' Skelton interjected. 'This is harassment.'

'Indeed,' said Noble. 'But we spoke to your friends, Ms Guzman, and none of them saw you after about twelve. We asked them where you'd gone, and none of them could tell us. You didn't say goodbye. They assumed you'd gone home.'

Guzman began to cry a little more, and Skelton started to look nervous. A tingle of excitation spread across Noble's skin, the exact same feeling caused by the vodka fumes hitting the roof of her mouth as the drink was on its way in, and she took a breath before her next move. With all the distraction of Harry and the hospital, she'd not really considered Guzman as a suspect outside of simple due diligence. But now she thought she could even be on the brink of a confession. It would all have been so easy, Noble thought. Send the tweet from Bayliss's phone, plant the dossier somewhere they'd find it, and send them on a wild goose chase.

Despite the humid August day outside, it was freezing in the interview room.

'Listen to me, Ms Guzman,' Noble said. 'We will find out where you were, whether you tell us or not. We have CCTV from all entrances of the club. Vauxhall's covered in cameras. We'll go through every single one of them if we need to. And we'll get all your friends in here and tell them they'll go down as conspiracy to murder if they don't grass you up. Do you get that, Teodora? We *will* find out.'

The word had the desired effect. Guzman cried more and said, 'Murder?'

'This is a murder investigation now,' said Noble. As you may well know, she thought. All the blood had drained from Guzman's olive skin, and she was now as pale as the ceiling.

'Where were you, Teodora?'

Skelton, cutting across, 'You don't have to answer that.'

Guzman broke down and cried and said something so quiet none of them could hear it. Even Skelton leant in, hanging on her every word.

'What was that?' McGovern said.

Speak louder, Noble thought. Nice and loud for the tape.

'I was with another woman!'

McGovern looked across, mouth open. Noble's eyes were fixed on Guzman.

'We met in the club,' Guzman said, 'and we, erm, went back to her place. In Dalston. We messed around for a bit, but nothing happened. Nothing really, anyway. I got cold feet and I came back home and . . .'

As she trailed off, Noble switched her view to Skelton, who was trying to conceal his frustration. He evidently hadn't known that nugget of information before. As far as Noble was concerned, she had to tease this out, try and fit it into a motive.

'Had you ever met this woman before?'

Guzman shook her head. McGovern said, 'For the tape, Ms Guzman is shaking her head to indicate no.' It wasn't that necessary with the interview being simultaneously video-recorded, but old habits died hard.

'Is this something you've done previously?' Noble said.

'Susan was being so miserable with this work stuff,' Guzman said. 'She was obsessed. It was like she was a different person.'

Always the excuses, Noble thought. And the devastating guilt that came with the knowledge that she would never have the opportunity to make right her wrong.

'How'd you get to her place?' said Noble.

'Uber. It'll be on her phone.'

Noble stood up, reached into the folder and flipped open a notepad, slid it in front of Guzman and clicked a pen and laid it on the pad.

'Her name and address, please,' she said, and left the room.

'Dammit,' McGovern said as they headed back upstairs, 'I thought we were heading for a confession there.'

'So did I for a moment,' said Noble. 'Christ, that would've been nice, wouldn't it?'

McGovern held the notepad up, rereading the name. Guzman hadn't given an exact address, but had identified a street and a block of flats, so it wouldn't require the most advanced police work to pin it down. They headed into the Incident Room and heads turned, conversations halted, phones were covered.

'She pulled at the club,' McGovern announced. 'We'd better run the alibi.'

'Shit,' said one of the detectives. Noble made her way towards her office, hoping there'd be nothing urgent waiting and she could sneak out the back for a real cigarette rather than vaping. She was fairly certain that Guzman's alibi, now they had a real one, would pan out, and the elegant solution, that of her killing her girlfriend and attempting to distract police with the hospital conspiracy, was beginning to appear increasingly improbable.

So she thought about what she'd said about the operations. Her expression of hope to McGovern had been loaded with much more than wanting to wrap up the investigation in the quickest time possible. If it turned out that Bayliss's death was indeed related to what had happened at the hospital, the investigation into that process would be the most complex one Noble had participated in, let alone run.

'Guv?'

It was DC Acquah, her personal assistant.

'There's a woman who's been trying to raise you on the phone, she's tried a few times. Alison Price, from the Belgrave.'

Noble instantly recalled the hospital manager.

'She's on now, is she?'

Acquah nodded, and Noble told her to connect the call, shut the door to her office and waited for the phone to ring.

'Hello?'

'Good morning, Chief Inspector,' Price said. Noble pictured her in her office, looking out at Kennington Park. 'I understand that you are currently interviewing Teodora Guzman.'

Noble sat up straight at her desk.

'I can't comment on the police investigation. But I must say I find your—'

Price cut her off.

'Are you aware that Ms Guzman is a member of hospital staff? That she works as an interpreter for the Belgrave NHS Foundation Trust?'

'So she is. What of it?'

'I'm reminding you that, in line with the agreement between the Metropolitan Police and the Belgrave Hospital for Sick Children, you are obliged to interview any staff members alongside either a member of the trust's legal team or hospital management.'

'Are you kidding me?' said Noble. 'Just who the hell do you think you are?'

'The cooperation of hospital staff is dependent on—'

'You listen here,' Noble said. 'I will interview whoever I like, wherever I like. Because I'm a police officer, and you're not.'

Price began to speak, but Noble cut her off.

'This is a formal warning. We have an agreement with your NHS Trust. My superiors have a direct line to your Chief Executive. You do not interfere in this investigation any further, or there will be consequences. Goodbye.'

She slammed the phone down, stood up, got her cigarettes out of her coat pocket and headed for the door. On the way, she grabbed her mobile, found Harry Kent's number in her contacts, and dialled.

FOUR

Monday, 25 August
Evening

After leaving Beth at London Bridge, Harry had wandered back home barely awake, and sunk into bed fully clothed. He didn't bother to shower – Tammas wouldn't mind – but he doused himself with deodorant, put on a fresh T-shirt, a hoodie and clean jeans, downed a pint of Diet Coke and an amphetamine and made himself a chicken sandwich with stale bread which he gobbled down whilst rushing down the stairs towards the underground car park.

In his car he checked his phone. Two missed calls from Noble, at four and four-ten. It was worrying when he was sleeping so deeply that he didn't hear his phone ring, but so lightly he barely felt as if he'd slept.

He called her back on the hands-free.

'Evening.'

'You rang?' said Harry.

'I wanted to let you know a few things. We've pretty much eliminated Guzman as a suspect. So that leaves us with someone at the hospital, unless there's another angle.'

'Is there another angle?'

'Not at the moment.'

He drove up the ramp into the outside world, which was bright enough to hurt his eyes.

'I brought Michelle Roberts in,' she said. 'Two of my guys interviewed her. I haven't debriefed them fully yet, but it sounds like she was saying the same as she did to you, and what Guzman said. Bayliss was worried that Mohamed was doing big operations on very young babies when there were other options, and that's what she raised concerns about.'

'Right.'

'Apparently, Michelle said she wanted us to meet with the rest of the families. I think we'll need to speak to them anyway, so it would make sense to do it all at once. I've asked her to arrange it for tomorrow evening.'

Harry had a nasty feeling where this was going. He felt sick, and he wasn't sure if it was due to eating a sandwich in half a minute or the topic of conversation.

'I was wondering if you could come with me. It'd be good to have you there, in case medical stuff comes up, which it inevitably will. And you made the first contact with Michelle.'

Not intentionally I bloody didn't, Harry thought.

'I'm not sure,' he said.

'Why?'

He pulled up at the Elephant & Castle roundabout and its eternal roadworks.

'I'm not sure about this whole business,' he said. 'About what my role is. I feel I'm getting too involved, and I'm not sure it's entirely appropriate. The more I think about it, the more I realise that if it hadn't been you who'd approached me, I wouldn't have been involved at all.'

Noble said nothing, and Harry listened to the sound of rustling static and blaring car horns. He hoped the A3 was free of congestion. He didn't want to miss the start of *Crimewatch*.

'Funny you should say that,' said Noble.

'What?'

'Do you know what I've got in front of me? You won't guess, so I'll tell you. It's the ACPO 2011 Guidelines on Coordinating Major Investigations in Healthcare Environments.'

'Sounds thrilling,' said Harry.

'It's not, I can assure you. But one of its suggestions is that the SIO appoints one or more expert advisors to the investigation, to provide assistance with assessment of medical evidence.'

Harry said nothing. He felt like a man who'd gone fully dressed to the beach, taken off his shoes to dip his toes in the water and now found himself in a riptide.

'I'm not an expert in congenital heart disease,' he said. It was the best he could think of. He couldn't say that he didn't want to do it, because he did. That was the problem.

'No,' said Noble, 'but you are a fully accredited FME, which means you know how criminal investigations operate. And it might be good, politically, that you're not a heart surgeon. I want to be very clear that our objective is investigating the murder of Susan Bayliss, not the deaths of the children under the care of the Belgrave.'

Harry nodded, making some progress around the roundabout.

'How much time commitment do you need?'

'You'll be there tomorrow evening?'

'I will be.'

He had hoped to help out with the results of the *Crimewatch* appeal, but even in the best-case scenario things would move slowly. And he'd agreed to see Beth for dinner, but he could arrange things around that. He had the next few days off, anyway, and to him there was no worse feeling than vegetating in his apartment, bored.

'If it turns out you do link it to the deaths, you'll appoint another advisor who's a heart surgeon, alright?'

'We'll cross that bridge if we come to it. If.'

'Ok then,' he said.

'Great,' said Noble. 'I'll be in touch. See you tomorrow.'

She hung up and Harry searched through his phone library for something that fitted his mood, settling eventually on Explosions in the Sky. Just south of the Elephant, he realised that his route would take him straight past the Belgrave, something which he had noticed before but never fully appreciated. Like having never gone to the Tate despite living almost the entirety of his life in London, it had just been one of those things that was present but without really being there. Now, though, as he cruised past, its façade glowing ochre in the twilight, he thought of the report, of little Jayden's chest filling with blood, the team unable to stop it, Death marching on unrelenting despite the efforts of man to hold it at bay.

He switched the music to The Killers, something a little more upbeat, to try to remove himself from such thoughts.

To no avail.

The digital numbers on the dashboard clock flicked onto 20:30 just as Harry edged his car into the car park of Marigold House. Outside the air was heavy, the day's sunshine gone, another thunderstorm threatening. Summer in London brought little joy, Harry thought. His hayfever was worse, there were more tourists, and England always lost at football, much to the pleasure of Tammas, who had been raised in the hills of Galloway. In fact, England's impending failure at the World Cup in June had been so exciting for him that he'd decked out his room with the flags of Uruguay, Italy and Costa Rica, the three group stage opponents. It was late August, and Tammas had only just stopped taking the mick out of Harry for it. But then again, entertainment took on a new perspective when your life was largely confined to a single room in a residential care home in Kingston-upon-Thames.

Harry nodded at the receptionist and smiled at the night nurse, who he passed in the corridor on the way to Tammas's room.

'Evening, Harry,' she said. 'Peter tells me you're on TV tonight?'

'Well, he's got a big mouth, hasn't he?' Harry said, yawning as he finished the sentence. He'd fallen straight into bed the moment he'd returned to his flat, and sleep had come quickly. He'd woken with the alarm at seven, a whole, glorious three hours. The nurse smiled at him, and Harry knocked on Tammas's door.

'Enter!' Tammas barked.

Harry pushed through the door, smiling and saying, 'Evening, boss.'

'Took your. Time. I hope you've. Brought me something?' Tammas said. Due to his injury he was dependent on the ventilator which connected to the tracheostomy port in his neck, and could speak only when the ventilator wasn't pumping.

'You can't have finished that Aberlour already?' Harry said, coming closer to the bed where Tammas was lying. Tammas rolled his head so he could see Harry approach, about the largest movement he was capable of, and grinned as he saw the grey carrier bag in his hand.

'Well, it's a special occasion, isn't it?' said Harry, revealing a cask-strength Talisker.

He went over to the desk where the tumblers were kept and took one out. Tammas had decided, after his brother had given him a bottle for Christmas, that he was going to try every single malt in the book he'd ordered from the internet: *101 Whiskies to Try Before You Die*. There was a specialist shop just outside Borough Market where Harry picked them up from time to time. Tammas was on about his twentieth bottle, getting through them at a rate of about one a fortnight. Harry pulled out the cork and the smell hit his nostrils, Scottish peat and ocean spray mixed with fifty-seven per cent ethanol. He poured the whisky slowly, listening to the treble sounds of the liquid moving from the bottle to the tumbler over the bass of the cycling ventilator. A symphony of solitude, he thought.

He passed the whisky over to the table by the side of the bed Tammas was on, placed a straw inside, and watched as he tasted it.

'Man. That's good.' he said. 'Pour yourself. One. Why don't you.'

'I'm driving home,' said Harry.

'Not for a few. Hours. You're not.'

Harry acquiesced and poured a little into a second tumbler, just enough to enjoy the taste. The sip gave him instant heartburn, and he realised he was still hungry.

'How've you been?' he said.

'Shite,' said Tammas. 'Had a fever. Thirty-seven three. Yesterday. Thirty. Eight this morning. There's nitrites. In my urine. They've got me. On trimethoprim. And they. Changed my catheter. They wanted to. Give me one of. Those condom things. But I told them. Where to shove it.'

Tammas turned his head to Harry and grinned again.

'I'm far. Too young. To have a bed. That smells. Of piss.'

Harry laughed. He had long stopped pitying Tammas, although he still bore the grief for his condition. The shrinks called it 'survivor syndrome'. The bullet after the one which had entered his boss's spinal cord had passed through both of Harry's lungs and split his liver in two. The only uninjured medic, his friend James, had come to his aid first, and spent three minutes placing drains into Harry's chest, all the while Tammas lay beside them both. Over the years, he had realised how irrational that part of his guilt was – the damage to Tammas had been done the moment the bullet had hit, and no amount of medical treatment could have reversed it. But Harry still recalled his hand faltering over his pistol as the rogue policeman ran through the base, a slip that had almost cost Harry his life, and had cost Tammas all the sensation and movement from the neck down.

'When are you. On? Nine o'clock?'

'Yeah,' said Harry.

'Bet you've been. Counting down. The minutes. All day.'

Harry rubbed his temples and sipped the whisky and went over to the sink to add a little water.

'I haven't, actually. I've been busy.'

'You're. Always busy.'

'I saw Frankie again, boss. I did a certification and she was the SIO. The victim's a doctor. She blew the whistle on a children's hospital. Now she's dead.'

'Jesus. Christ. Harry. Will you never. Learn.'

Tammas twisted his head again and sucked on the whisky.

'I'm just advising. I'm not involved.'

Except mothers of dead children are following me and my girlfriend to restaurants, and I keep calling a DCI to give them my half-baked advice on leads they might want to follow, Harry thought.

'Just like. The last time. You were advising. And we all. Know how that. Turned out.'

Harry went quiet, and stared at the floor.

'I don't. Want to bury. Any more of my friends.'

'You won't,' said Harry. 'I don't want to bury any more of mine, you know.'

That was why the last case, the one which had got James Lahiri killed, had gone so badly. Because his friends had been involved, and it had clouded his judgement. He had done much thinking about that. James and he had gone to Afghanistan together and stared oblivion in the face, and he had brought Harry back from the brink, both in a literal sense in saving his life and in a figurative one. They had never been such fast friends after his return, and Harry had never been able to bridge that divide before Lahiri's murder. He had gone some way to doing so by helping bring his killer to justice, but Lahiri's memory of him had been blown onto the side of a boat in Surrey Quays along with the rest of his consciousness, so he had no way of knowing if that recompense was enough. It sure as hell didn't feel it.

This case was different, though. All were strangers here, and Harry told himself that that made all the difference.

'I've got no skin in this game,' he said. 'It's just professional.'

'Just like. This girl. You're obsessed with. Is strictly profess—' The ventilator cut him off, 'Strictly professional.'

'That's different,' said Harry.

'You're. Committing. The fallacy of. Passivity. You think that. You exist. In a vacuum. That things happen. To you. Not because. Of you.'

'That's not true!' Harry protested.

'Yes it. Is,' Tammas insisted, slurping at the whisky again. 'You don't have. A need. To see justice. Done. You need. To be the one. Who does it. It's not. About. This girl. It's about. You. Redeeming yourself.'

Harry ignored that last statement, just went over to the desk and poured another whisky for himself, only a fingerful, then went over to the table by Tammas's bedside and topped him up. Then he checked his phone, a missed call from Beth and three texts. The first two were from her, one in the afternoon saying *I'm here for you if you need me. Hope you enjoyed your sleep*, and another more recently. *Good luck with tonight, I'm watching at home with El and Resh! x*. The third message was from Noble. *Meeting Roberts + families at 5pm, Greenwich. I'll pick u up.*

'I'm sorry,' Tammas said after a while. 'That was. Harsh. I know. Your motives are. True. You just. Struggle to let. Things go.'

'Forget about it,' said Harry. 'It's five to nine.'

'Ok.' said Tammas. He twitched his cheek, which activated the voice-recognition system that controlled the entirety of his room: the electric blinds, the lighting, the TV, the computer.

'Television. On.' he barked. 'Channel. One. Volume. Up.'

They watched the last five minutes of a cooking show in the same recumbent silence, marred only by the slurp of single malt through a straw and the rotation of the ventilator.

At nine, the garish opening sequence of exploding cars, low-flying choppers, blue lights and men in masks gave way to Kirsty Young direct to camera, rows of police officers behind her pretending to answer phones and scribble down notes.

'Three years after disorder and rioting spread throughout the nation, some of the worst crimes committed during those four days remain unsolved. Tonight, police from across the country need your help to find the criminals and bring them to justice. In Manchester, a shopkeeper beaten to death trying to defend his property, the culprits never found. West Midlands Police are looking for the gunman who opened fire on riot police and even shot at a police helicopter. And Martin has dozens of CCTV images of rioters suspected of crimes as serious as arson, robbery and rape.'

'She's not bad. Is she?' said Tammas. 'Not for. Her age.'

Harry laughed for the first time in a while. Kirsty adopted a serious tone and switched to another camera.

'But first, we go to South London, where police are appealing for information regarding a brutal attack on a young girl from which she still hasn't recovered. And in this case, it's not just the perpetrator's identity that is unknown, it's also the victim's.'

The shot darkened to black and the date – Monday, 8 August, 2011 – shot across the corner of the screen accompanied by a typewriter sound effect, cuing news footage of the rioting, the iconic images of burning shops whilst hooded youths ruled the streets, arms up in Ys of victory, BlackBerrys in hand, filming, tweeting. No blue strobes, no high-vis jackets. Harry had turned up for a shift on the Sunday at eight a.m. and worked for forty-eight hours with only four hours' rest, such was the volume of walking wounded coming through the doors. As he saw the images, he remembered the chaos of the A&E, the madness of the patients coupled with the ordered calm of the doctors and nurses.

The narrator summed up the situation before cutting to a paramedic in uniform. Harry remembered her, though she'd had much shorter hair when she'd brought the girl in, almost shaved.

'Control had received a number of calls around eleven p.m. about a young female who was lying in the street near Lavender Hill, and I think one person said they'd seen her being hit around the head. We made our way towards the incident but at the time, we weren't sure if it was safe to proceed and the police advised us to wait at a rendezvous point until they could make the area safe.'

The narrator continued: 'Both ambulance and fire crews had come under attack near Clapham Junction earlier that evening, but the police were fielding over a hundred 999 calls a minute and were heavily outnumbered.'

The next interviewee was an officer from the TSG, the riot unit.

'Our serial was tasked to assist the LAS in reaching a female who was believed seriously injured in an alleyway off Eccles Road. When we arrived there was almost nobody in the area, the main centre of the disorder had moved towards the St John's Road area. We found the female, she had obviously been the victim of quite a sustained attack. In fact, I thought we might be too late. I was quite surprised when we discovered she was still breathing.'

The reconstruction showed the unit of riot police with plastic shields and batons raised running single-file down an alleyway, finding the girl lying face-down on the tarmac, waving to the ambulance. The camera shot showed her pink hair, her most distinctive feature, quite clearly.

'They should. Have sent in. The Army,' Tammas said. 'Showed those. Yobs. What a proper. Fight. Looks like.'

Harry couldn't take his eyes away. He wondered how many people were watching, whether that circle overlapped with those who'd been there that night.

The paramedic again: 'When we finally got on-scene it was obvious the young girl was in a bad way. She had injuries to both her head and neck, and our assessment revealed she had very low oxygen levels. Due to her injuries we were unable to place an airway into her mouth, so we had to put a needle into her throat so we could give adequate oxygen. Our priority then was to get her straight to hospital.'

The reconstructed footage now showed an ambulance rushing on blue lights, the night skyline backlit by orange flames, burning shops and factories. The narration continued in slow, serious timbre.

'The unidentified woman was rushed to the John Ruskin University Hospital, where Dr Harry Kent was on duty.'

As he appeared on the screen, Harry felt all the hairs on his body stand on end. The disconcerting effect of hearing his own voice different to how it ought to sound added to the feeling that he was only an observer in the world, that, whatever he did, nothing could change the forces which acted upon him.

'We had to perform an emergency procedure in A&E,' Harry watched himself say, 'which involved making a cut in her windpipe and placing a breathing tube into her throat. The CT scan revealed a skull fracture, brain contusions, fractured ribs, as well as an injury to the hyoid bone, which strongly suggests that the attacker attempted to strangle her. The other injuries are consistent with punches or kicks to the head and chest, probably whilst she was already unconscious and on the ground.'

The narrator continued, explaining how police had searched her belongings and the area where she had been found for any clues to her identity, but had found none. Then he recounted how, as they were sealing her clothing into evidence bags, the ICU nurses had found a pair of denim shorts from the high-street chain Zara, which became the temporary name for their patient.

'Or at least it was supposed to be temporary.'

And then Harry was back. Even he was taken aback by how serious he looked, how forlorn. When they'd come to the hospital to film the segments, the producers had almost seemed to be taking pleasure in his outrage.

'We knew that she'd been starved of oxygen for a significant amount of time, due to the injuries to her neck, so a degree of brain damage was expected. But the level was anyone's guess. The only way we were going to tell was to see what happened when she began to wake up. Over the next few weeks, physically she began to recover, and we were able to remove her from the ventilator. But then it started to become obvious that she wasn't waking up as we would hope.'

Harry faded to black and was replaced by Professor Niebaum, the consultant who ran the neurological rehabilitation unit at the Ruskin, which had been Zara's home for the majority of the last three years. He explained the situation, avoiding the uncomfortable word 'vegetative'. Harry yawned and looked into the glass of whisky. He knew the score. She could breathe unaided, she could move her eyes to follow medical staff, she slept, though irregularly, but she couldn't communicate with anyone. Zara was awake, Niebaum explained, but not aware.

The narrator then painted a picture of the police investigation, again employing stock footage of detectives making phone calls, forensic scientists trawling the crime scene, and police poring over CCTV footage. That pissed Harry off. In reality, the case had been bumped from unit to unit, starting with the grossly overworked and understaffed Operation Withern, more interested in quantity of convictions than quality. No more than ten detectives had ever worked her case, and even then only for a couple of weeks. It suited the mayor and the commissioner fine to be able to stand up and say they'd sent hundreds of youths down for stealing bottles of water and pairs of shoes whilst the man who'd robbed a young woman of her consciousness walked around the city. And it wasn't going to get any better, not with bastards like Cameron feeding him crap.

Cameron, who was there now, talking to Kirsty Young. Between them, on a glass board Harry had never seen in any police station, or indeed anywhere other than TV, was a blown-up photo of Zara in her hospital bed.

'Now, this was a particularly brutal attack, wasn't it?'

'This was certainly a vicious and sustained assault on a young woman,' Cameron said. 'And it's made all the more sad by the fact that she has not recovered from this assault, and we remain unable to identify her.'

'So what kind of information are you appealing for?'

'Firstly, we're asking that if you know who this girl is, or if you remember interacting with her at any point in her life or have any information that might help us to find out who she is, please get in touch in confidence. We believe this girl will have a family somewhere who will want to know what has happened to her.'

Damn fucking right, thought Harry. For three years now he'd held on to an unshakeable belief that somebody had to know who Zara was, that it was impossible to exist in a city such as London and not appear in anyone else's life. Now he prayed that whoever that was was watching and might have an attack of conscience.

'Of course,' said Kirsty.

'Secondly, we're asking for anybody who witnessed this attack or who saw this girl in the Clapham Junction area on the night in question to come forward, again in confidence. As has been mentioned repeatedly, the victim has very distinctive pink hair which hopefully will spark a memory for someone. We recognise that some of the witnesses to this horrific attack may have been involved in criminal activity, and we can assure anyone who comes forward with information that that will not be held against them.

Of course, anyone who wishes to stay anonymous can use the Crimestoppers number.'

'Thank you, DS Cameron. As you can see, the number is in front of you now, and it's worth mentioning that a reward of five thousand—'

'Is that. It?' said Tammas. 'You could. At least. Have bloody shaved.'

After the programme was finished, Tammas said he wanted a walk out into the gardens, so Harry and the night nurse transferred him into his wheelchair and they headed out into the muggy night, not yet raining, to wander among the summer flowers in the garden and stare into the black water of the fishpond.

'You be back in here before it rains,' the nurse said. 'We're not having you get pneumonia on top of your water infection.'

Tammas gave her a look of muted indifference, and they were left in peace.

'Has he. Called yet?'

'No,' said Harry. 'They're doing the update at ten thirty-five. He'll call before then.'

'Sure.'

The sound again of sucking through a straw. Tammas had enjoyed the Talisker so much he had a glass with him, bolted into one of the arms of his wheelchair. They looked at the water for a while, Tammas wincing a little. Harry placed a hand on his forehead.

'You're a little warm,' he said.

'You're not. My. Doctor,' Tammas grunted. 'Please. Spare me that.'

Harry laughed.

'Have you. At all. Considered. What might happen. If nobody calls?'

'He'll ring,' Harry said. 'He said he would.'

Although given the amount the bastard's lied to me, Harry thought, nothing would be surprising. That said, it hadn't taken him long to realise that what really infuriated him, perhaps more than the fact that Cameron had deceived him, was that he wouldn't have known if it hadn't been for Noble. That, even on a purely professional level, he still needed her. He thought about the deal they'd made and how it reflected the same uncomfortable truth. If he wanted to get true justice for Zara, he needed Frankie Noble.

'I didn't. Mean that,' Tammas said. 'I mean. What if. Nobody from the public. Watching that show. On. A Monday night. Calls in? What if. You never. Find out. Who she is. Or who. Did that to her?'

Harry looked up at the sky. It wasn't a thought he entertained. Not because of what it meant for her, but because of what it meant for him.

'What. Then. Harry?'

As if sent from God, drops of warm summer rain began to fall from the sky, one striking Harry on the head, another plopping into Tammas's whisky, accompanied by a fork of lightning somewhere over Wimbledon, the thunder following.

'We should get inside,' said Harry.

'You know, Harry,' said Tammas, 'I haven't. Been outside. In the rain. Since I was. Put into this. Damn chair. Every time. I see a storm. From the window. I want to. Go outside. And sit there. And feel it. On my skin.'

But the rain was quickening now, and the lights in the porch were already on, and the night nurse was running out towards them, a plastic folder raised above her head.

Cameron didn't call, so Harry called him after he'd wished Tammas goodnight. Tammas didn't usually sleep so early, but the water infection seemed to be making him more tired than usual. That worried Harry.

'Hello?'

'Good work,' Harry said. 'How's it going, then?'

'Busy,' Cameron said. 'Over fifty calls so far. One very promising lead in terms of an ID, and ten other strong ones we're following up.'

'What's the lead?'

'Christ, Harry, I've been up since seven,' Cameron said. 'I'll fire you an email in the morning. In any case, it'll take a few days to see if any of this amounts to anything.'

'Will you now?' Harry said, speaking through his teeth. The lobby of Marigold House was deserted at this time, no sound but the rain bouncing off the covered porch.

'Yeah,' said Cameron, 'and we're still on to meet Wednesday morning, ok?'

'Well, I hope you're hitting it hard,' Harry said. 'We're short for time.'

'Are we?' Cameron said, almost jovial, possessed of the same prejudice that had given the case the inertia it still struggled to shake. *She's been a vegetable for three years, she can wait another week or so.* 'What's the rush?'

'Well,' snapped Harry, 'we've only got so long until you get your pay rise, don't we?'

Silence.

'When were you going to tell me?'

'Jesus Christ!' Cameron said. 'Give me a break, yeah? You're not my bloody boss!'

With that, the detective hung up.

Harry's limbs were leaden as he sealed himself into the car, put the belt on, windscreen wipers on full, and drove through rapidly expanding puddles, heading north, a journey he'd done so many times he could do it on autopilot.

He awoke just as the back wheels of his car left the road. He fought for control, slamming on the brakes, and by the grace of some entity, he had reached the more suburban part of his journey, the edge of Richmond Park, so it was grass and mud the tyres were chewing up, rather than tarmac or someone else's front lawn, or worse still, the central reservation and oncoming traffic.

The rapid deceleration jolted him forward as he bounced across the field, eventually striking a wrought-iron fence, though at a speed low enough to avoid any obvious damage.

'Fuck,' Harry whispered out loud to himself. 'Fuck, fuck, fuck.'

He clicked on the hazards, opened the door and leant out to check the damage to the front bumper, which was negligible, and then arched his neck back into the rain. There were no blue lights. No lights of any kind. The thoughts shot through his head like the view of an opposite platform through a passing train. The amount of whisky he'd had with Tammas was just the start. Worse was the sheer luck of falling asleep at the wheel on an empty road next to a park. A drink-driving conviction he could explain away. Killing some child on a pavement he couldn't.

He'd never fallen asleep at the wheel before. Of course, there were times when he became suddenly aware and couldn't remember the last five or ten minutes, or he arrived at the hospital on his bike but couldn't recall having left home, or any of the journey. Those episodes had increased in frequency as the pills had done, but never resulted in anything like this.

Harry reversed back onto the road, bumping over the mud and the kerb, the hazards still on. Then he reached into the glove compartment, retrieved the plastic pill-bottle inside, and flipped off the cap.

It was empty.

'Fucking shite!' he screamed, throwing the bottle so hard against the dashboard it bounced off and hit him in the head before coming to rest in the footwell.

Harry closed his eyes, took a deep breath, and held it, as if he was weighing up the merits of taking any more.

He reached over to his phone and found the most upbeat music he had, an album by Avicii he'd bought mostly for the gym, and turned the volume up to its loudest. He lowered the windows, allowing the midnight rain to strike his face. And set off for home, his scleras burning with pain.

FIVE

Tuesday, 26 August
Morning

Harry woke up in a sweat, the summer rain pounding against the windows of his apartment. The sensation in his body was an old friend. It was sixteen hours since his last dose, and the tightness in his chest, like asthma, told them that he needed to find a pill and take it now, or he wouldn't be able to breathe. He'd slept for almost twelve hours, but as he pulled himself out of bed, his head felt like an old medicine ball, and his muscles ached as if he'd just finished a triathlon.

He pulled himself to his feet and shuffled into the bathroom. He'd only had a glass and a half of whisky the night before, but he felt like he'd been on a binge. He felt how he remembered Frankie Noble looking. And like her, he knew the cure, and as he pulled open the cabinet the sick feeling of guilt added to the mix of pain and anxiety.

The bottle was empty, just like its sister in the glove compartment of his car had been. How? He'd worked out that the bottle would last him a month at five a day, and he was a whole week from the end of August. He thought he'd been taking four. This was not good. This was not good at all.

'Shit!'

The empty bottle bounced off the porcelain sink, rebounded off his jaw, and came to rest slowly rolling on the bathroom floor.

As the team filed in to the Incident Room at Peckham, the mood was far from jubilant. Frankie Noble had been looking forward to being an SIO, the challenge of managing an investigation, but standing up and talking to the team for half an hour every day was perhaps her least favourite part. Perhaps it was because she remembered too well the tedium of sitting through briefing after briefing when she was a young DC.

And she had felt better. Unhelpfully, she was thinking of Harry again. Her afternoon would consist of meeting the doctors from the Department of Health inquiry who, if they were anything like the arseholes they'd interviewed yesterday, would only raise her blood pressure and increase her need for nicotine, and for that other demon, the unspeakable. She had spent yester-day evening at a meeting in a church hall in Shoreditch, where she repeated her creed, the one which seemed so totally at odds with her vocation. She had not spoken herself, except to thank the speakers – one a retired paramedic who had almost broken nine years' sobriety when presented with a glass of champagne at his daughter's graduation, another a young copper who missed going to watch West Ham play on a Saturday afternoon. In a strange way, they were becoming her friends. They too had dead spouses, they too heard voices in the night and had fuckups they could not exorcise.

Once the room was full, she sipped her coffee, tried to ignore the eyes on her, and began.

'Morning all,' she said. 'Welcome to the second briefing for Operation Rhodes. Thanks for coming.'

Frankie Noble had been with the Metropolitan Police for four-teen years now, and she still had no idea how the operational names were generated. Every six months there appeared a new theme, and now they seemed to be going for ancient cities, many of which had the annoying coincidence of being sunny holiday destinations, reminding everyone present that whilst the rest of the free world were enjoying themselves in Greece, Spain or Turkey, they were stuck in a stuffy room listening to her ramble on about the latest murder. Not to mention the passing associa-tion with a genocidal colonialist.

'We have three main agenda points this morning. I'm aware for operational reasons some of you were unable to make the briefing yesterday, so I'll quickly run you all through where we are so far.'

She was also aware of the smiling, suited figure of Detective Superintendent Grenaghan in the third row of seating, taking notes on an iPad.

'Susan Bayliss died at some point between midnight at one. She was at her home address, which she shared with her long-term partner, Teodora Guzman. There are no signs of forced entry, which suggests that her killer or killers were known to her. She had consumed a decent quantity of alcohol, most probably of her own volition, when she was attacked. There were minimal signs of a struggle, so it's likely she was already in the chair she was found in when she was attacked. The killer slashed her brachial artery at the elbow and held her down in the chair, then added the wrist wounds and the pills in her throat post-mortem in an attempt to stage it as a suicide. The pills were antidepressants which she had been prescribed following a period of depression after the loss of her job.

'Any questions or comments on the crime scene?'

'How big was she?' one of the detectives asked.

'Pretty small,' said Noble. 'Five-seven, maybe fifty or so kilos. Wouldn't take much to overpower her, if that's what you're asking. Pathologist suggested the killer sat on her knees and held her down, including a hand over her mouth. Forensics are going to update very shortly. Anything else?'

No-one spoke.

'Right,' said Noble. 'Forensics. Oscar?'

Oscar, a forensic scientist with a long grey beard and chequered shirt that made him look more like a church organist, took the floor. Crime scene photographs of Bayliss's flat on the projector.

'It's a very complex scene,' he said, in a heavy Glaswegian accent. 'The stairwell and the courtyard gave us absolutely nothing. Too many present, in terms of both prints and DNA. There's trace amounts of blood which we believe to have been left by both Guzman and the first officers and paramedics to respond when they exited the flat. Inside the flat's not much better, I'm afraid. The scene's been contaminated by a number of persons prior to forensic precautions being initiated, and also we've no way of knowing how many people were there beforehand.

'The scene of death being a living room, you see, often presents problems. In a bedroom, or bathroom, you tend only to have DNA profiles of the inhabitants present, but in a living room, particularly one that's not cleaned too often, you might have the profile of anyone who's visited, even if they've just sat down on a chair. We've isolated at least twelve different profiles, excluding Bayliss, Guzman, and the police officers and paramedics. At this point it becomes very difficult to isolate a separate individual and match them to the scene.'

'So if we identified a suspect, you couldn't conclusively place them at the scene?' asked McGovern.

'We could exclude them for sure. But if we tried to place them, aye, we could, but it might be shaky in court. We certainly couldn't differentiate between them being there at the time of the murder or at some other time. We could only say they had been in that flat at some point, most likely since it was last cleaned.'

Noble thought about that as he spoke. They were fairly sure that the person who killed Bayliss had probably known her, but that didn't necessarily mean they would have been to her flat. She hadn't been to the houses or flats of many of her closest colleagues or friends. She made a note to action somebody to contact Mohamed and the main players at the Belgrave if they were going down that route, and ask if they'd ever visited Bayliss at home.

'Thanks, Oscar,' said Noble. 'Anything else?'

'Aye.'

The slide advanced, showing the chair and the pool of blood.

'There were two depressions in the blood pool, where it seems it was disturbed,' Oscar continued, highlighting the area with a laser pen. To Noble it looked exactly the same, but she trusted him. 'We think this is where the killer stood up after killing her, in the blood pool.' The slide advanced again, showing ultraviolet spots in a broken line from the living room to the bathroom. Some of the younger officers in the room gasped, and Noble rolled her eyes.

'This was the blacklight analysis,' said Oscar. 'A few spots leading to the bathroom, but no footprints. So it looks like our offender slipped his feet out of his shoes, stepped outside the pool, and took them to the bathroom to clean up. Indeed we recovered a few fibres consistent with socks in the bathroom, which we could match with socks recovered from a suspect. But again, don't get your hopes up. The fibres are a commonly-used elastic material in most supermarket brands, so it probably wouldnae stand up.'

'How'd he clean up?' someone called.

'Hang on, I'm getting there!' said Oscar.

The next slide was split-screen, one half showing the floor, the other Bayliss's phone and the bathroom sink.

'Both the phone and these two taps were totally clean. No prints, no DNA, nothing.'

Noble put that together quickly enough. The only way for the phone to be in Bayliss's pocket with no forensic traces at all was if the killer had cleaned it and placed it in the pocket. Likewise with the taps.

'We found traces of her blood in the U-bend, so it looks like our killer washed his hands and the shoes in the sink and then wiped the taps and door handles, before removing the stains from the floor. The floor, her shirt, the phone and the taps had traces of chemicals commonly found in make-up remover, and an exact match to the brand of make-up wipes in the bathroom. Which again would suggest that he was improvising.'

'I think that's fair to say,' said Noble. 'To me, that's what this scene suggests. In fact, we don't even know that the killer arrived planning to murder Bayliss. Maybe it was a spur of the moment decision, but one that they had the composure to cover up to at least a reasonable degree. Even then, our offender leaves the house with bloodstained clothing, undoubtedly. That's a vital fact, so remember it when you're conducting interviews. Thank you, Oscar.'

There was nodding and note-taking.

'That brings me on to the day's other major action. Calais Street is not well covered by CCTV, but we need to be analysing cameras in an outward spiral from the flat. Look both for suspicious individuals, anyone we may recognise, or anyone getting into a taxi or private hire. Nearest Tubes are Stockwell, Oval and Brixton, we'll probably need to re-canvas those if and when we identify a person of interest.

'And as regards persons of interest, we have three major lines of enquiry,' she continued. 'The first is domestic.'

A picture of Teodora Guzman in a white paper suit, with a bloody gash on her right nostril, filled the screen. Taken as documentation after the self-harm incident. Guilty or innocent, she sure as hell looked like a murderer.

'Shona will bring you up to date on this.'

DS McGovern stood up and took the pointer from her, coffee in the other hand.

'We know that Teodora and Susan had been having problems. Susan was depressed, she was facing losing her job, her vocation.

She'd started drinking.' At that one, Noble looked at the floor, and her heart twitched a little. 'That took its toll on the relationship. Saturday night, Teodora met a woman in a club and went back to hers. We checked this out this last night, and the Uber records confirm her story. We've also got CCTV from a business opposite this woman's address in E8 showing her arrive just after midnight and leave at 3:45 or so, so on those timings she's in the clear.'

Murmurings around the room at the realisation that they'd cleared their prime suspect. Noble caught Grenaghan's eye. The superintendent had looked up from his emails and appeared somewhat interested.

'Guzman's mostly cleared, but let's just be one hundred per cent sure,' Noble said. 'It's possible she's still connected. Perhaps she was involved with this other woman, and they arranged for someone to kill Bayliss while they provided alibis for one another.'

'Wouldn't be the first time,' one of the other detectives grunted. There had been a memorable case in Wimbledon a few years ago, when a prison guard had paid a man who was about to be released to kill his wife while he was on holiday in Barcelona. Except the ex-con had blabbed about it whilst spending his payment in a pub in Mitcham, and had been promptly returned to custody, this time for life, with his former jailer joining him.

'Any questions?' Noble asked of the group.

'Run us through the timings again, would you Shona?'

'She's on CCTV leaving the club at 00:15, with the woman she identified, getting into a minicab. We traced the Uber driver, and he confirmed dropping them up in Hackney about 00:35 – Uber's fantastic for us, by the way, you get the whole route on GPS. Anyway, the other girl says that Guzman left at about 03:30. The 999 call from Guzman's mobile came at 04:12. So that would fit her story about taking the night buses back. We're still working on getting the bus CCTV to confirm it, as Guzman says she can't remember which stops she got on at or which buses she took. So it's some work.'

Nods around the table.

'It's doable then, isn't it?' the other detective said, the oldest man in the room by far. 'If this other bird is lying, if she's been covering for her, and she left the flat by a back entrance, away from the cameras. she's got plenty of time to get to Calais Street within the time of death window, doesn't she?'

'That's very true,' Noble said. 'Shona, let's cover that too. Check other CCTV in the area, we'll check on the bus routes and Overground, Dalston to Myatt's Fields, for the whole period between midnight and four.'

Shona and her sub-team nodded, feigning enthusiasm for the crowd but obviously annoyed by the grim duty of going through hour after hour of grainy footage from night bus cameras. Another luxury of being SIO was not having to do that.

'And we'll make sure to action a full go-over of all of Guzman's communications over the last two months, find out if this other woman has been in any contact with her. We've got to eliminate the possibility that they're working together.'

The reasons for ensuring that Guzman wasn't being given a false alibi went far beyond the possibility, however slight, that she was the murderer. If – no – when they did charge a suspect, the first thing a defence lawyer would do would be to try and pin the crime on an alternative, and if it emerged that the victim's partner had a shaky alibi, that could seriously damage the prosecution. She'd been in court enough times to know that defence lawyers would take any anomaly and run it to extremes.

'Due diligence aside, we can be fairly sure that Ms Guzman is not responsible for her partner's murder. And as such we're going to be shifting the focus of this enquiry.'

Noble clicked through to a slide with a photograph of the Belgrave's exterior.

'As you know, Susan Bayliss had recently been suspended from her position as a surgical registrar at the Belgrave Hospital for Sick Children. This was shortly after raising concerns about the deaths of four children operated on between November and January by this man.' The slide revealed Elyas Mohamed in a photo copied from the hospital website, in which he beamed at the camera in scrubs, the cobalt blue accenting his olive skin, tufts of chest hair protruding from the V. 'Elyas Mohamed, consultant paediatric heart surgeon and Susan's immediate boss. The hospital conducted an investigation into the deaths, but Susan wasn't satisfied and leaked a report to the Department of Health in May, which sparked a public inquiry that significantly damaged the reputation both of the hospital and of Mr Mohamed.'

More of the detectives were taking notes now, and the mood in the room had switched from early-morning token attention to one of intense concentration. This was the stuff they lived off.

'Our new main line of enquiry is that the offender is somehow connected to that hospital, to the inquiry, and that Bayliss's actions led them to murder her on Saturday night, and stage it as a suicide.

'Now, the addition of this line of enquiry means that the investigation has the potential to become seemingly more complex. I want to make it very clear that it is not within our remit to re-examine the findings of the Department of Health or the clinical practice of the hospital. Any such queries will be examined by a smaller group of officers led by the D/SIO, DS McGovern. We've appointed one of our FMEs, Dr Harry Kent, as an expert advisor, to assist them, and we may bring in other advisors as the investigation develops. If anything comes up you need advice on, you can contact him through me, Shona or Brandon.'

She rushed over those words in the hope that nobody commented on them. Yes, most of the people in the room would know about her history with Harry, and no doubt the gossip over lunch or in the pub tonight would cover that subject countless times, but her request to him yesterday had been a purely professional one. He was the best-placed man to help them.

'But for the rest of you, I want you to treat this like any other workplace killing,' said Noble. 'Half of you will be interviewing all of Bayliss's close colleagues in the cardiac department. Don't just focus on the person you're interviewing, get them to spill the beans on someone else. Who liked her? Who disliked her? Who had something to gain by her death? Who had something to lose by her staying alive? With this kind of investigation, you'll learn more by finding out what people say about their colleagues' relationship with the victim than their own accounts.'

The younger detectives were furiously making notes now, the older ones chewing pens and nodding.

'The other half, we'll need to follow up every contact Bayliss made over the last few weeks. Remember, it looks like the offender knew her well enough that she let them into her apartment late at night, and there was a confrontation. My guess is the offender didn't come to the flat planning to kill. Which suggests they would be close enough to have been in contact. Perhaps they argued in the last few days? Perhaps the offender made a threat? This is basic stuff, guys, I know, but I'm going over it because it's important, and more importantly, it's what's gonna get us an arrest.'

'Any questions?'

There were none.

The sleepiness wasn't the problem. He could happily slip into a slumber for a whole day, and stave off the inevitable withdrawal. But the suffocating feeling in his chest, the feeling that if he didn't take a pill now, something so dreadful would happen that he would just stop breathing, that was the true addiction, that had made him rip apart every drawer and cupboard in his home, even though he knew that the only other place he kept the pills was in his locker at work. He'd cycled over, the rain keeping his somnolence at bay. Wet hair, sweating, he let himself into the A&E staff room, sneaking through the back entrance, opening his locker, searching through the half-empty drink bottles, used to-do lists, and changes of clothes, retrieving the pill-bottle from the back. Harry laughed. Even though it was disguised as aspirin, he still hid it.

He opened the bottle, and stared for a while at the single pill inside. Then he swallowed it with some three-day-old Diet Coke. He changed into a fresh shirt and trousers, slung a stethoscope around his neck on top of his lanyard, and texted Beth to ask how her morning was going and apologise for what had happened at the restaurant.

It was understandably quiet when Harry arrived in A&E, it being a Tuesday lunchtime. A busier time would make this easier, but he didn't quite have that choice. He nodded and waved to the nurses, doctors and porters as he made his way towards Majors. One of the consultants, Dr Kinirons, accosted him.

'Harry, what on earth are you doing here?' she said. 'Don't tell me you've signed on for the locum – you need a few days off!'

Harry smiled, the lie rehearsed on the cycle over.

'I only went and left my logbook here, didn't I?' he said.

'You bloody idiot.'

She shook her head.

'How's that going? Have you decided if you're going to apply for that HEMS job?'

'Not quite yet,' he replied, heading to a desk and crouching, searching through the drawers. 'I'm not sure I can make the commitment with the police work, as well.'

He pretended to look through the top drawer, though he knew what he sought was in the drawer below.

'It'd be good for your CV,' Kinirons said. 'You've got the skills already.'

'I know,' said Harry, silently praying for a shout for assistance from a junior doctor, the sound of the emergency phone, an announcement on the tannoy.

He moved down to the next drawer, and Kinirons leant over the desk, and Harry looked up and saw her and shut the drawer so quickly he almost trapped his hand inside.

'I'm just saying that you're too good to wind up as a staff grade,' she said, her voice low. 'And there's an inertia that comes with these things. If you don't keep your eye on the ball, before you know it two or three years will have passed and you'll be no further along. And you deserve better than that, ok?'

She patted him on the shoulder and walked slowly away, her pumps clacking on the linoleum floor. Once she'd turned the corner into Resus, Harry silently retrieved the prescription pad from the drawer, tore off three sheets, folded them and put them into his shirt pocket.

At the hospital pharmacy he tried his best to act like he was just another patient picking up a prescription, but of course that just made him paranoid that he was acting shifty, so he tried not to think about it. He'd thought about losing the lanyard that betrayed his name and profession, but that too would probably have sparked more suspicion if a colleague happened upon him. Plenty of doctors collected prescriptions from the pharmacy, if not for them then for a relative, and most of them weren't drug addicts. Yet he felt, sandwiched in the queue between a wheezing respiratory case and an elderly woman bent double, that the guilt was somehow visible to those about him.

He'd never self-prescribed before. He'd never needed to. But his usual online order took three days, and Harry knew there was no way he could wait that long without physically and emotionally collapsing.

And technically, of course, it wasn't self-prescribing, Harry reminded himself as he slid the prescription, made out in the name of Peter Angus Tammas, over the counter. The phone in his pocket started buzzing.

'Hello?'

'Harry, it's me,' said Noble. 'How are you doing?'

'Not bad.'

The pharmacist picked up the prescription and headed back towards the shelves.

'I enjoyed your TV debut,' Noble said. 'You heard from Cameron about how it went?'

'Fifty calls. A lead, apparently. That's it.'

Noble's silence said it all. The pharmacist had disappeared now.

'I'll call him this afternoon, see if I can chase it up for you.'

Harry felt close to vomiting, like the whole corridor was beginning to spin.

'Can I help you?'

'Just calling to check you're still coming with me to see Mrs Roberts and the other families this evening. Five o'clock. You did make first contact, after all.'

He moved to correct her, remind her that it had been Roberts who'd made contact with him, not the other way round, but instead he just sighed.

'I'll be there.'

The fight was gone in him. He'd expected that when he half-woke his thoughts would be of Zara, of the TV appeal, but they hadn't been. Instead, he'd remembered Bayliss and the scene in her living room, and Elyas Mohamed saying he couldn't answer the question about the medical notes.

'There's something else I'd like to run past you, if that's ok? I'm meeting the docs who did the inquiry this afternoon. It's been a nightmare to organise. But I'll be done by four. If you can meet me at the nick, how about I drive you over? We can discuss it on the way. And I'll ring Cameron once I've got a minute, I promise.'

'Ok,' he said. 'I can do that.'

'What about this afternoon?' Noble said. 'What are you up to then?'

'I'm meeting a friend who used to work at the Belgrave.'

Noble gasped quickly, almost a laugh. He pictured her, in a smoke-filled office, husking into the receiver of an antique telephone.

'Now, Dr Kent, I'm not sure that's on my little spreadsheet of actions for my investigation team . . .'

'Piss off,' Harry said, quite seriously. The pharmacist handed over the green-and-white packet and he mouthed a thank you, turning out of the queue and making his way back towards the locker room.

'Suit yourself. I'll see you at four, then.'

'Ok.'

'And another thing. Your suggestion from the other night. The post-mortems are on their way over to us. I'll get them forwarded to you.'

Harry thanked her and wished her good luck again and hung up, thinking about all the reasons he'd forced her out of his life, and how easily he'd let her back in. Of course, Tammas was right. He had no concept of a purely professional relationship, either with dead women like Susan Bayliss, those very much alive, like Noble, or those hanging in the purgatory between.

The guilt came again as, alone in the locker room, he popped two pills from the blister pack into his desperate palm and swallowed. Not guilt, though, about addiction, or the fake prescription, but at the sick realisation that he was enjoying this. Being back with Noble, them against some unknown force, in the throes of a conspiracy. It made the days go faster and pass with less pain and self-pity, the dedication to a search for a solution to a complex problem. It was a hell of a lot more exciting than waiting in A&E for the next shattered life to reach him that none of them could fix, or being shouted at by patients with minor ailments who'd been kept waiting for a whole hour.

The pills stuck briefly in his throat, but as they partially dissolved a small piece of bliss hit his veins and he smiled.

The problem was, as always, that he enjoyed it too much. He'd already gone off-piste, a message sent to Amy Floyd, his paediatrician colleague who'd tried – and failed – to resuscitate Emmanuel Abediji when he'd been brought into A&E. She was currently taking a copy of those notes, and they were going to meet for lunch, at half-twelve. The idea had formed on the drive down to Kingston, when he'd been internally reciting phrases from Bayliss's dossier which had stuck with him. In all likelihood, she would shed nothing of light. But still, it was a symptom of the disease. He wanted something else, another puzzle to distract himself with, to avoid confronting the shambles of his own existence.

He looked at his watch – he wasn't due to meet Floyd for an hour or so. With time to kill, and already at the hospital, Harry made his way from the pharmacy towards the hospital's South Wing, which housed the general medical and surgical wards, as well as Tennyson Ward, the neurorehabilitation unit. The ward was actually split across three floors, with S5 focusing entirely on stroke rehabilitation, S6 on other acute neurological patients, and S7 on those with brain injuries from trauma. It was to the seventh floor that he headed, to the small annexe which hosted patients in minimally conscious states, one of only a few such units in the country.

Professor Niebaum, his co-star on *Crimewatch*, saw Harry from the door of his office as soon as he was buzzed into the ward.

'Harry, my friend!' Niebaum said. They shook hands and paced briskly towards Zara's room. Not much happened on a ward with stable, comatose patients, so the activity quickly brought the nurses and physios, all of whom Harry was on first-name terms with, into the corridor.

'Any news?' said Niebaum. 'How's it all been going?'

Harry saw the looks in their faces and realised that perhaps they envisioned he'd been up all night in an Incident Room, on the end of the phone. He tried to smile and hide his frustration as he parroted his phone call with Cameron.

'They've had over fifty calls so far,' he said. 'With at least one promising lead. And that was just last night.'

Two of the nurses who regularly looked after Zara grinned and high-fived, and Niebaum reached forward and squeezed Harry's shoulder. Harry had always regarded the professor as somewhat self-flagellating, specialising as he did in waking up patients who had been written off by the rest of medicine. But despite the fact he only succeeded with one patient in twenty-five, those who did wake up, to the sound of weeping family members who hadn't seen their loved one talk in a decade, were enough to sustain him. Of course, if Zara ever woke it might be to an empty room, or to some professional like Harry, and that was what they were fighting to fix.

'Thanks so much for driving this forward,' said Niebaum. 'I know we'll get a result out of this, I just know it!'

'I hope so,' said Harry. 'I really do.'

'Even if it's just an ID,' Niebaum continued, now addressing the gathered crowd, 'it'll make a massive difference. I mean, even knowing what language she speaks will be a huge step forward.'

Niebaum's clipped words brought nods from the nurses and junior doctors. When they spoke to Zara, they used English, and she appeared to understand, occasionally moving her eyes deliberately in response to questions. But her answers were inconsistent, and many of the hospital team suspected she was foreign. There were theories of Poland, based purely on statistics, and the appearance of her two fillings, which appeared slightly cruder than normal western standards. Forensically, an analysis of the chemical makeup of bones could determine where on the planet their owner had grown up, but those tests could only be done on a dead person.

'Have they told her she was on TV?'

'Yes, they showed her the programme,' a nurse said. 'And look at what a response we've had already!'

She moved out of the way for Harry to see, and his jaw dropped as at least a dozen bunches of flowers placed at one side of Zara's room came into view. The crowd dissipated into several conversations and shortly he was alone with her, her shallow breathing competing with the air-conditioning to break the silence. He stepped closer and read some of the cards, his heart stirring with the gesture. *Very best wishes for your recovery. You are in our prayers. Mr and Mrs A. S. Davies, Surbiton.* Another: *Know that somebody loves you and is waiting for you. Get well soon.* Harry shook his head at these words, and looked up through the glass at the brittle, broken young girl lying motionless on her hospital bed, her pink hair in brutal contrast to the lemon-yellow hospital pillows, who knew nothing of the efforts being undertaken on her behalf, or the love she was being shown.

A knock on the glass.

'Morning, Harry.'

The voice belonged to a social worker called Nathan Klein. Klein's uncle Samuel was in a minimally conscious state since a fall down stairs eleven months ago, and he was the only living relative. He lived on the other side of London, in Hampstead, so he didn't get much of a chance to visit, and they hadn't arranged a residential care placement, which was where most of the S7 patients were destined to go, if Niebaum had determined that their states would not improve. Samuel Klein was making steady, if unbearably slow, progress towards some kind of recovery. As the two of them often visited the unit at odd hours, Harry and Nathan had become something close to friends.

'I thought you deserved a BAFTA,' he said. 'Or at the very least a nomination.'

Harry shook his head. Klein had been on the ward when the BBC crew had come to film, and had riotously taken the piss out of both him and Niebaum.

'Day off, then?' he said.

'Yeah. Working some nights, though.'

Klein had copies of the *Times* and the *Jewish Chronicle* folded under his arm, both of which his uncle had fastidiously read, and both of which he would summarise to him cover-to-cover when he visited. He pointed down at the flowers.

'They from the public?'

Harry nodded.

'No confession letters, I take it?'

'There's a lead, apparently.'

'Ok. If it's your day off, you don't fancy getting a beer later, do you?'

Harry shook his head, thinking of the fun which awaited him this afternoon with Noble and four pairs of grieving parents.

'I've got plans, sorry,' he said. 'Some other time, though.'

He had an idea though, a seed which Klein had unknowingly sown. He said his goodbyes, to Zara, to Klein, to Niebaum and the nurses, and got his phone out as he walked outside.

DS Cameron answered with a single word, the acrimony of last night evidently unforgotten.

'What?'

'I had a thought,' Harry said.

'Enlighten me, do.'

'You know how you told me you'd be monitoring the calls that come in, the ones that aren't anonymous, because sometimes offenders call in themselves and leave false tips.'

'Yeah?'

'Well, about ten people have sent flowers to the Ruskin,' Harry said. 'And about double that have sent cards, too. You think that there might be something in that?'

Cameron snorted on the other end.

'What, that the killer sent her a card, a little taunt? To us?'

'Maybe it's worth checking out?' said Harry. 'Maybe you could send someone up here to check them?'

'We're focusing on running down leads here,' Cameron said. 'But it's worth thinking about, I guess. Have a read of the cards and send me a photo of anything that seems unusual. I tell you what, we'll talk about it tomorrow, eh?'

'That's still on, then?' Harry said.

'If you want it to be,' Cameron said. 'I'm sorry if you think I misled you. I may only have a week left in this job, but I've always believed that when you go to work you do your job properly. And I'll make sure that this gets handed over to someone who'll work it how it deserves, alright?'

Harry stood in the hospital corridor, listening to the promise, doubting.

'Ok.'

'I'll see you tomorrow, then.'

Harry had arranged to meet Floyd in a Chinese restaurant in Camberwell, one with high-backed booths far from the window, should any passing staff member think anything conspiratorial about two colleagues having lunch together. Such was the paranoia, Harry thought, thinking again of Susan Bayliss, making copies of documents and keeping them under the floorboards, sending parcels to the Department of Health. Of course, she'd been right – for what she was doing they would have had her job and with it all that had ever given her life purpose or meaning. He empathised with her in that respect. He wondered if the fact that she may have been wrong – whilst it in no way defended what the hospital and Mohamed had done – had ever occurred to her. And if, as it seemed now, someone connected to the hospital had murdered her, she'd only come to regret it as hands held her into the chair and her life poured out from her elbow.

He was still thinking about that when Floyd walked in, hair up, boots on, mustard yellow coat and umbrella. Tuesday hadn't seen the email about it being August when deciding the weather.

She sat down opposite him and shuffled to the other end of the booth.

'How are you doing?'

'Shite,' she said. 'You?'

'What's up?' Harry said.

'This whole mess, the thing with Emmanuel. I'd forgotten all about that. Well, I'd not forgotten, but I'd locked it up somewhere in my head. And now I was sat there in the library this morning working on my thesis and there I am, staring out of the feckin' window for half an hour, and it's all I can think about. I had a dream about Susan, as well, last night.'

'I'm sorry,' was all Harry could muster.

'It's not just you, though,' Floyd said. 'I spent the morning trying to concentrate, to get it out of my head, and then this turns up in my inbox.'

She moved to pass her phone across the table, but then a waiter arrived, pale and bleary eyed, and so she snatched it back to safety. Harry ordered them prawn crackers, two set lunches and two Cokes and he swiped their laminated menus. Floyd passed the phone back over. It displayed an email which Harry read, his breath held.

To: TEAM(CARDIOLOGY); TEAM
(CARDIOTHORACICS); TEAM(PICU/THEATRES)
From: *a.price@belgrave.nhs.uk*

Dear Colleague,

I am writing to offer you our thoughts and sympathies following the announcement yesterday of the sudden and untimely
death of our valued colleague, Susan Bayliss. Those of you
who knew Susan will need no reminding of her commitment
and exceptional patient manner, and indeed she will be sorely
missed.

Regrettably, the circumstances of Susan's death have garnered
interest in the public sphere, including from the media, the
police and the coroner's office. I am sure that many of you
must find such interest distressing at this difficult time, and we
would urge you for the peace of mind of yourself and your
colleagues that you do not enter into any discussions with such
interested parties without the presence of a senior member of
trust management. If any of you are, or have been, approached,
please immediately contact me on extension #3449.

Again please do allow me to extend my most heartfelt sympathies to you following this awful news. Do not hesitate to get in
touch should you have any concerns or if you just want to talk.

Mrs Alison Price
Senior Service Manager, Congenital Heart Disease
Belgrave Hospital for Sick Children
South London University Hospitals NHS Trust

Harry was silent for a while, rereading each of the paragraphs
in turn. He wasn't sure which he found more distasteful: the
suggestion that Price, or indeed any of them, had felt Bayliss to be
a 'valued' member of their team, when they had orchestrated her
suspension and besmirched her reputation, or the thought that
any junior doctor might take solace in speaking to her in their

hour of need. In all likelihood, they'd be offered an espresso and a firm handshake and told to man the fuck up and get back to work. Either that or threatened with an entry along the lines of 'struggling to cope' or 'not a team player' in their appraisal notes.

'How did you get this?' Harry asked. 'You're not still on their books, are you?'

'I'm doing my MD there,' she said. 'And I locum occasionally. So they keep me on the list for cardiology.'

'I met Alison Price yesterday. And Elyas Mohamed, and Theo Padmore.'

'Oh, aye. What did you make of them?'

'Mohamed spent the whole time grandstanding, insisting on giving us a tour of the department and telling us how good his mortality results are. He didn't seem too happy when Alison Price turned up. Padmore was fucking terrified, though, as if a single word in the wrong place would get him sacked on the spot. I see what you meant when you said the technology's much more advanced than the culture.'

Floyd shook her head.

'I only met Theo once or twice. He's a good guy, but ambitious. His job is his life. To be fair, though, you could say that about most heart surgeons.'

It was certainly true of Bayliss, Harry thought.

'What about Price?'

Floyd laughed.

'The smiling face of the NHS in the twenty-first century, eh?' she said, pointing at the now-blank screen of her phone. 'I'd almost stopped thinking about it before that thing turned up.'

She looked up at the ceiling and shook her head.

'How'd she do it, Harry? I bet you certified it, didn't you? Tell me it was peaceful, aye? Couple of milligrams of fentanyl in her arm or something?'

Harry took a deep breath in and the waiter returned with Cokes and prawn crackers.

'Did you bring the A&E notes for Emmanuel Abediji?'

Floyd opened her mouth, a wounded look on her face.

'I'll answer your question, I promise,' he said. 'I just want to know.'

'I took down the relevant parts,' Floyd said. 'Entirely anonymised, of course. You wanted to use this as a case presentation for a project you're doing about human factors in resuscitation.'

'Of course I did,' said Harry. Had the subject matter not been a dead child, he would have smiled.

'Well?'

Harry almost lied to her, and then he didn't. He thought about that email, read it again in his head. There was only one possible motivation behind any cooperation between Mohamed and Price, which was that the cardiothoracic department at the Belgrave was attempting to control the information flow of everyone they could. And, what reason would exist for doing that, if they had nothing to hide? Harry had worked with Floyd numerous times, and she was one of the golden ones, the doctors who'd stay three hours after their shift finished to assist with a challenging patient, who colleagues breathed a sigh of relief for when they saw them on the rota.

'If I tell you something, you keep it between us,' he said. 'I'm not supposed to tell you this. In fact, I'm probably breaking the law. And I could lose my job, even though I don't technically work for them. So this doesn't leave the table. I'm only telling you because it's obviously affected you as much as it has me. So we're in this together.'

'Of course,' said Floyd.

'Not to Dr Jaffry. Not to Manny. Not to anyone.'

'Manny fucked off to Australia two months ago. But good memory,' Floyd said.

Harry shook his head and lowered his voice.

'Bayliss didn't kill herself. She was murdered. It was staged to look like a suicide. If it wasn't for that, then we wouldn't be here, and the Met wouldn't be sniffing around the Belgrave.'

'How?'

'I don't think you need to know that.'

Floyd's mouth screwed up. 'Y'know, this week alone I've told three mothers their child's cancer is incurable. I think I can handle whatever gory detail your pea-headed chauvinistic brain thinks I can't.'

'They pinned her to a chair, opened up her brachial artery, slashed her wrists post-mortem, and poured antidepressants down her throat.'

'They?'

'The killer,' Harry said. 'Just one person, or so we think.'

'We?'

'The police. Figure of speech.'

Although it wasn't, of course. And just like that, he was back into the whirlpool he'd fought Noble for a few days to avoid, but could not escape.

Floyd closed her eyes and tipped her head back slightly, one arm at her side, and Harry briefly thought she was fainting, or having some kind of seizure. Only when he saw the bracelet at her wrist did he realise she was saying a rosary for her dead friend.

'I knew it couldn't have been true, that she killed herself,' she said. 'If you'd known her, you'd've said the same. Trust me. She had this conviction. Once she hung onto an idea, she'd not let it go.'

And that steadfastness had got her fired, Harry thought. Because however surely Mohamed, Gilmartin and Price were attempting to protect the department's reputation, it didn't change the fact that there was no evidence any of the four children who'd died under Mohamed's care had died as a result of his, or anyone else's, negligence. He thought of Noble, sitting down with the experts called in from the Department of Health, showing them Bayliss's copies of the operation notes the Belgrave had conveniently misplaced. To Harry, they had seemed innocuous, but perhaps one of the expert witnesses would find a silver bullet that brought Mohamed crashing down. That, though, would raise more questions than answers – such as how the anaesthetists and the nursing staff had been persuaded to perpetuate the story, or why, even if Mohamed was a negligent showboater, he would go as far as to murder an ex-colleague when she had already been discredited.

'Let's go through it then,' Harry said. 'Emmanuel Abediji. Right from the start.'

She spoke and he read for a while, spooning black bean sauce and egg fried rice into his mouth as he did. It was much the same story as he'd got from Bayliss's notes and the inquiry. He'd collapsed at home, seemingly suddenly unwell, and arrived in A&E with what doctors called 'pump failure' – his heart function so poor that his lungs were filling with fluid from the back-pressure. None of the usual treatments – diuresis, vasoactive drugs, positive airway pressure – had worked. Floyd and her team had spotted the surgical scars, noted the history and done an echocardiogram, which only confirmed that he was almost dead, without giving them much useful information. His heart rate had plummeted, a pre-terminal sign. They tried to insert a temporary pacemaker through a wire fed into his heart, but that hadn't worked, either.

'And that's when we rang him up,' Floyd said.

'Rang who up?'

'Mr Mohamed. Told him his patient was in acute cardiac failure, asked him for a transfer to Belgrave for ECMO or a surgical option.'

Harry whistled. ECMO, which involved connecting the child to a heart-lung machine through tubes the size of hosepipes running into their neck, was a real last resort, a final roll of the dice. It could only be done at the most specialist of hospitals, like the Belgrave, which was perhaps twenty minutes' drive away, maybe ten in an ambulance on blue lights.

'He said he wasn't sure. Gave all kinds of bullshit excuses. Said he needed to come over and see Emmanuel for himself. Said he had a busy list that afternoon, and that their ICU team could manage him. Didn't listen to a word we said. Dr Jaffry spent fifteen minutes on the phone persuading him to accept the referral.'

'He didn't go to Belgrave, did he?' said Harry, knowing full well the answer.

'No. He arrested about two minutes after Dr Jaffry hung up the phone.'

And then that was that. An hour of CPR, every drug in the cupboard thrown at him, every test and imaging modality they could possibly have used, and nothing had been able to restart Emmanuel's heart.

'Have you seen his post-mortem?' Floyd said.

'No. Not yet.'

'Dr Jaffry had them send it to us. It didn't find a specific cause of death. The valve seemed normal. The aortic annulus was narrowed, with scar tissue, but not enough to cause such an acute deterioration. The pathologist suggested an acute arrhythmia.'

It made sense. Harry leafed through the notes, finding the ECGs, the electrical tracings of Emmanuel's heart. Before it had stopped, it had been all over the place, the rate alternating between forty and two hundred beats a minute, both significant extremes.

'Ah,' Floyd said, 'those bloody ECGs.'

The most recent one showed a corkscrew-like pattern he hadn't seen in a long time.

'This is torsades,' he said. The name came from the French word for twisting, based on the pattern on the ECG. It was a rhythm that tended to precede cardiac arrest, but Harry had picked it up because it didn't quite fit. The main causes were chemical imbalances, and drugs.

'Yeah,' said Floyd. 'He had two or three runs of it. Never worked out what caused that, either . . .'

Harry shook his head and ate some more, and thought. Most of the time, when they had tricky patients who they fought hard for yet still lost, one of the best ways of coping was to sit around the table and see what they could learn from it. It didn't stop the second-guessing, but it helped. But for Floyd and the others who'd tried to save Emmanuel Abediji, they didn't know what they'd missed. He'd just died one morning. Across the table, Floyd was reading Price's email again.

'Forward that to me,' Harry said. 'Then delete it. Honestly.'

'They're trying to cover up something, aren't they?'

'Sure looks like it,' said Harry. 'But I don't have a fucking clue what it might be.'

Silence fell, and they watched their food congeal on the table in front of them. Outside it rained.

He didn't really notice the weather as he ambled back to the hospital, where his bike was parked, his heart racing. He'd made excuses towards the end of the meal, after his head had started to drop and his skin had started to itch, and he'd swallowed a pill in the toilets, like a teenager at a nightclub.

It was like the glory of a nicotine hit if you hadn't smoked in months, only amplified and magnified, the tingling in his fingertips, the glow of the world around him. The wholeness he felt. On his last shift in A&E, after the overdose and the trauma call, he'd clerked in a thirty-five-year-old man dying of emphysema, victim of a faulty antitrypsin gene, still smoking because why quit now? If the compulsion was even a fraction of what Harry himself felt, he could not judge others. The man had blamed his parents for starting him smoking and his fiancée for enabling him to continue. In these moments Harry thought about his own life. His inherited addiction, Noble and their mutual dependency, how the people he chose to surround himself with made it too easy for him. But thirty-four years of existence had taught him that the responsibility was his alone. To better himself, to surround himself with better people.

So he called Beth.

'Hey,' she said.

'How are you?'

'Good. Ward's quiet. Two discharges today, just doing the paperwork now. Everyone's talking about you.'

Harry laughed, more an exhalation.

'Who's everyone? The patients?'

'The nurses, the other SHOs,' Beth said. 'I've been banging on about it for the last few weeks, you see.'

'What about me?'

'Just asking me how it went, how many people have called in. That kind of thing. Which, y'know, I wasn't really able to tell them, given the only communication you've had with me since you left yesterday have been single-word texts.'

The air was sucked out of Harry's chest, and all the rest of the guilt rolled into one. Of course, he'd been too busy, either with the Bayliss case, or with Tammas, or on his foraging trip around South London for his pills.

'I'm so sorry, Beth. I really am.'

'I'm just worried about you. You can't relax. It's like you don't even know how.'

'I can relax tonight,' Harry said. 'You're off, aren't you? Let's meet. I'll come to yours. And how about I take you out for dinner? You choose the place.'

'And if there's some break in the case?' Beth said, a venom in her he'd never heard before, which worried him, because he knew her to have a tolerance far beyond any other woman he'd ever met. 'If Frankie Noble calls you up and says she needs your expert opinion?'

'Then I'll just tell her nothing can be that urgent,' said Harry, already working it out.

'What are you doing this afternoon?'

For an instant, Harry considered lying, but he had promised a long time ago that he would never lie to Beth, that she deserved far better than that. Of course, lies of omission, like the fact that he'd been on amphetamines for their entire relationship, didn't count.

'The police are going to see the woman who interrupted us yesterday. Olivia Roberts's mum. She's gathering the rest of the families together and we're going to talk to them.'

Beth was silent.

'I'll be done by seven. Even if we're not done, I'll make my excuses. Half-seven.'

Silence still. A begging man in the rain outside a hospital, ramming his mouth into a wet phone.

'Book a table for half-seven and I'll be there!'

'For God's sake!'

The admonishment hurt him, but it was laced with wit, some kind of humour that escaped him.

'What?'

'Anywhere worth eating out in Brixton doesn't take reservations,' Beth said. 'You should bloody well know that by now.'

At the end of the sentence she began to laugh, and in that moment all Harry wanted to do was wake up in bed with her and work through another box set, with a case and a half of Stella and two delivered pizzas. And fuck three times in one morning, which was one of the side effects of heavy amphetamine usage he was able to put up with.

'I'm sorry,' Harry said, almost laughing himself. 'Honestly, babe. Is that alright with you?'

'If it's an evening, with you and me. Just us. And you turn your phone off.'

'You can take the SIM card out if you want,' Harry said.

'Bullshit.'

'I'm deadly serious. Does half-seven work for you?'

'Short of any more emergency admissions, I'll be away at five,' Beth said. 'And given we haven't had a free bed here in over two weeks, I'd say the chances of that are pretty minimal.'

'You're not working tomorrow, are you?'

'Well guessed,' said Beth.

'Well remembered.'

'So the beers are on you as well, then. Half-seven, in the market. The side by the railway station.'

'I'll be there.'

The rain changed direction and he took a step backwards, into the protection of the alcove.

'You better be,' said Beth. 'Or you're dumped, you do realise that?'

Harry could find no reply to that.

'I'm joking!' Beth said. 'I'll see you later, babes. Love you.'

'Love you too,' he blurted, without thought. Not because he meant it, he realised in the split second after the syllables had left his mouth, but because he didn't want her to be hurt, and he thought perhaps he could reduce that hurt. And it wasn't a lie, not really.

'See you later, Harry,' she said, her voice breaking. And then she hung up.

Noble was waiting when he stepped off the bus opposite Peckham Police Station, her pale face behind the windscreen lit with the purple glow of the new crutch, the e-cigarette.

'Afternoon,' Harry said.

Noble said nothing, just pulled out and turned left onto Queen's Road. Harry thumbed through emails on his phone. A new annual leave form, the forwarded email from Floyd, and spam from take-away restaurants.

'Sorry. Mind's in a hundred places,' said Noble.

'That's ok.'

'Y'know, I can't bloody stand doctors.' She looked over at Harry, 'Present company excepted.'

Harry laughed.

'Fun afternoon, then?'

'They didn't give a single straight answer to anything. Prefaced everything with a, "oh, in case of this, one could see it this way".

Like they were in court. Is that what you have to put up with in hospital? Or is it just the inquiry bods high up the ladder who are full of shit, is that what you're gonna tell me?'

The car stalled and Noble hit the dashboard, fist clenched. The noise and the slight jolt in his seat reminded him of the wee hours, that morning, his Audi running off the road, chewing up turf, hitting the fence. He couldn't remember whether or not he'd damaged the front bumper. He needed to check that when he next got home.

'Sorry,' Noble said. 'I just needed to get that off my chest.'

She restarted the car, the traffic swerving around them. Uniformed schoolchildren stood in packs around the high-street fast-food shops, clutching chicken boxes and greasy kebabs, the cardiac patients of the future. Eventually they pulled off, the frustration still clear in the way she drove, weaving angrily in and out of the bus lane, tutting at all the other drivers.

'They aren't giving you straight answers because there aren't any straight answers,' Harry said once she'd let out a few heavy sighs. 'It's not like forensics, where you can stand up and say it's fourteen million to one against the DNA belonging to someone other than the defendant.'

'Yeah, well, they were still a complete waste of time.'

'What was their conclusion? You showed them the notes we found in Bayliss's flat, right?'

'Yeah,' said Noble. 'They agreed with you. No evidence from those notes that Elyas Mohamed was negligent in his clinical skills. They said the first two, Abdul and Jayden, were standard complications of major heart surgery, and the second two a complete mystery.'

Harry thought about that. Sometimes it happens, in both children and adults, the heart just stops working, a life snuffed out. There were a whole host of rare congenital ion channel pathologies, conduction defects and the like, which could be responsible. But he still couldn't shake the coincidence.

Jayden and Abdul he could believe. A very bad week at the office, but Harry had had bad weeks, too. Two patients, operated on by the same man, dying suddenly in the middle of the day. It seemed too easy just to put it down to statistical clustering, the apparent non-randomness of truly random events.

'Did you ask them about what Bayliss was saying?' he said. 'Whether Mohamed was doing large operations on children too young?'

'Yeah,' Noble went on, 'they said something like, "The place for that debate is conferences and scientific journals, not criminal investigations." Said it a couple of times.'

'What time did you arrange with Michelle Roberts again?' he asked.

'Five. So we're already late.'

Harry shrugged his shoulders. If she was willing to follow him and his girlfriend into a restaurant, he was ready to bet she wouldn't mind slight tardiness. He felt a sudden desire to relax – a burger and a few beers out in Brixton later couldn't come soon enough. He'd stop at the flower stall outside the station on the way, too. And though he knew her accusation about Noble's motivations for spending time with him had been made in anger, he wanted to placate them nonetheless. It would be good, for him as much as for her, to have an evening together, away from all of this. And before things began to get off the ground with Zara and the TV appeal.

'Your lunch date drag anything up?' Noble said.

The traffic was moving so slowly that Noble had no trouble whatsoever reading the email Alison Price had sent around the Belgrave.

'Jesus,' she said. 'When did she get her sugar-coating?'

'From what Amy was saying, I think the rest of the department see it for the bollocks that it is.'

'Her name popped onto my horizon yesterday,' Noble said.

'What, Price?'

'Yeah,' said Noble. 'She rang me up and gave me the hairdryer treatment about interviewing Guzman without informing the hospital, as she's a member of hospital staff. Apparently she's an interpreter.'

'How'd you respond to that?' Harry said, grinning.

'I told her where she could shove it. If that hospital doesn't want bad press, it shouldn't have tried to fucking scapegoat one of their doctors.'

'I know it's shit how someone leaked Bayliss's mental health issues to the press,' said Harry. 'And the way that hospital treated her was awful, of course it was. But right or wrong she was on fairly hefty doses of antidepressants. You can get paranoia in severe depression, you know.'

'Well somebody killed her for a reason, didn't they?' said Noble.

Of course, that was the rub all along, and why Noble's team was still following the line of enquiry – Bayliss was the perfect scapegoat for a hospital cover-up, because she could have been scapegoated with the truth. She was stressed, she was struggling to cope, and once she had that stigma, her entire experience was invalidated, Harry thought, feeling another streak of pity for the woman. It made him glad that pretty much every consultant he'd ever worked for had been thoroughly decent.

'I can't get my head around it,' Harry said. 'If his surgeries did kill those children, it wasn't through negligence. Unless we're all missing something.'

'But someone still killed Susan Bayliss,' Noble said. 'Let's face it, that's about the only thing we're fucking sure of.'

They turned off Blackheath Road and headed downhill, towards the Thames, skirting the western border of Greenwich Park, each side-road a sloping residential crescent. Noble pulled to a stop, put the handbrake on and killed the engine and bent forward over the steering wheel, head in her hands.

'You ok?'

Noble clicked her neck.

'Yeah. Just not really looking forward to this.'

Harry looked up at the house, a tall Victorian terrace with a big, imposing black door and wrought-iron fencing around the front garden, and eight grieving parents inside it. Rain bounced off the windscreen and rolled down the street towards the brown river and the grey sky.

'Neither am I, really,' he said.

Michelle Roberts answered the door, rushing them in from the rain.

'Hardly bloody August, is it, eh?'

Roberts shook Harry's hand. She had gone to considerable

effort, her make-up perfectly placed but understated, her hands soft and moisturised. There was a stiffness in them though, and as she released her grasp he looked down and recognised the tell-tale swellings of arthritis. He stole a glance at her other hand, and Roberts caught him looking.

'Rheumatoid,' she said. 'Doesn't really bother me, though. I've got a great consultant.'

Some people get all the luck, Harry thought.

They came through into the hallway, Roberts grabbing Harry's coat and Noble's parka, placing them onto a mahogany coat stand by the front door. Harry's first impression of the place was how fastidiously clean it was, and of course there was a shoe rack next to the door for guests, already piled with the rest of the attendees' footwear. Noble and Harry duly obliged, their socked feet sinking into deep carpet as Roberts led them through into a sitting room, opening into a sparkling conservatory. On a sunny day it would have positively shone, but with rain bouncing off the glass the atmosphere was much more subdued. And that probably also had something to do with the room full of people staring straight at them.

Harry got the distinct impression that Roberts had been holding court, making small-talk, and that the conversation had died the moment she'd left the room to get the door. Their faces moved slightly as Roberts did the introductions.

'Thank you so, so, much for coming. This is Detective Inspector Noble and Dr Kent. They're investigating what happened to Sue.

'This is Sonja and Will, Jayden's parents. They've come an awful long way.' Will Capp, wearing the most sullen of expressions, had the red eyes and ruddy face of a fairly seasoned drinker, and Harry wouldn't have been surprised if there were antidepressants in the mix too.

'And Gervais, he's Emmanuel's dad,' Roberts continued. 'And Bismah, Abdul's mum, and this is Ali, her other son – English isn't her first language, you see, so Ali helps her out sometimes, don't you?' Ali, a teenager with zigzags shaved into his hairline, shrugged embarrassedly.

'And of course this is my darling Euan –' she kissed her husband on the cheek – 'and Ollie's little brother, Preston.' The child, with a bowl of white-blond hair, had been toddling around, the only source of life in the room. Michelle Roberts grabbed him and ruffled his hair and Harry tried to ignore the way he'd been described. Even the living room existed as a temple to her dead daughter, photos adorning every wall and table, Olivia in the arms of her parents, Olivia on the beach, Olivia with yoghurt on her face. As coping mechanisms went, it wasn't the worst.

There was another figure in the room too, one Michelle hadn't introduced, leant against the back wall. Noah Skelton, dressed in a three-piece suit, tapping on his BlackBerry. Harry gave him a look that said he'd clocked him from yesterday.

'Who's for tea or coffee? Or there's freshly squeezed lemonade,' Michelle Roberts said, gesturing over to a pitcher resting on the conservatory table. 'And help yourself to something to eat.'

In a bizarre attempt at normality, Roberts had put out an array of cakes, biscuits and a plate of fresh fruit, which the other parents had barely touched. The gathering looked like a moving-in party in the strangest of neighbourhoods, and Harry shared a nervous glance with Noble before they both accepted the offer of tea and took slices of carrot cake in paper napkins. Michelle Roberts went to take Preston upstairs to his room, and while she was gone Harry felt the air in the room gather weight. It felt wrong to discuss the matter at hand with a slice of cake in his hand, more so without the woman who had gathered them together. Noble evidently felt the same, as she launched into small-talk. Apologies about lateness, oh, but well, you've come further.

She asked them how their respective workdays had been, whether they'd had difficulty getting time off. Gervais Abediji apologised on behalf of his wife, who had not felt strong enough to come and talk about her dead son.

'In fact, Chioma's not been well,' Gervais said. 'Not well at all.'

Harry said it was fine, and Noble looked distinctly uncomfortable. Will Capp muttered something about having been off on the sick for as long as he could remember, and Sonja rolled her eyes and said her job at Sports Direct had been pretty good since 'it all happened'. Bismah said nothing and Ali had explained that he had Tuesday afternoons off at school, and Euan Roberts said that he was glad they had come tonight as he was flying the Hong Kong route the following morning. He'd checked his smartphone at least ten times since their arrival, and Harry was rapidly concluding that the way Euan had eased his loss was perhaps by detaching, dissolving into his job. He'd noticed a captain's uniform dry-cleaned in the kitchen, and an umbrella with the logo of a Middle-Eastern airline in the hallway, which explained how they could afford to have a garden and a conservatory in Greenwich. As Michelle Roberts re-entered the room, Harry thought about the unlikely mix of people in front of him, like you might find in a Tube carriage late at night. A group unified only by a singular tragedy.

'First, let me say how sorry I am for what you've all been through,' Noble said. 'I can't possibly imagine what it must be like.'

There were nods and thank yous.

'We just want to help in any way we can,' said Abediji. 'If we can help you catch whoever killed Susan.'

Harry turned around and Noble shot him a tired look.

'I don't know what information you're hearing, but we aren't yet sure about the circumstances of Susan's death.'

Harry looked at Noble, but saw that she was staring across the room, straight at Skelton, who was now admiring the thick carpet. Maybe he'd somehow found out that the police were treating Bayliss's death as a murder – defence lawyers tended to be well connected. Michelle Roberts opened her mouth, ready to speak, but Noble kept on, her voice ratcheted up a decibel. Harry was sure that she wanted the room to know who was running this conversation.

'If I could ask you all what contact Susan had with each of you, individually or as a group?'

Roberts said, 'You mean, in the hospital, or . . .'

'I mean recently, after, um . . .' Noble trailed off, her eyes dancing saccades as she tried to find the words.

'After your children died,' said Harry.

The air hung heavy for a while, before Michelle spoke up.

'Well, I may as well start, then,' she said. 'It was a month or so after Ollie went to the angels. I was out on the high street, it was Euan's first day back at work, and I was getting something for dinner, and she just called me. Right there in M&S. And said she'd only just heard what happened and she remembered us and she just wanted to say how awfully sorry she was.'

Harry nodded.

'And then she called again, a few days later. She wanted to know if Ollie had a post-mortem, what it had showed, whether there was any clue to the cause of death. I'd said that they told me they had no idea, that it wasn't a heart attack, or an infection, or a problem with the valve. That they suspected some kind of funny heart rhythm.'

Michelle wiped a tear away, and Sonja Capp passed her a tissue, and she sipped at a cup of green tea. The same story as Emmanuel Abediji, Harry thought.

'Did she say anything else?' Noble said.

'That was just the start. She told me Ollie wasn't the only one, that there were other children Mr Mohamed had operated on who had died too, and she was trying to work out whether something was going wrong at Belgrave. And that we could help, but we'd have to keep it quiet because the hospital was already trying to cover something up.

'Then we stayed in touch. She kept updating me, said that she was compiling records, and she was going to send them to NHS England or whoever. The last I heard of her, they'd suspended her and they were trying to shut her up. And then . . .'

'Did she mention anything about Olivia's operation specifically?' Harry said.

Michelle Roberts nodded.

'When Mr Mohamed sat us down, he told us that surgery was pretty much the only option, that Ollie was going to die if we didn't let him operate. I believed him. He's a consultant, why wouldn't I?' She looked from Harry to Noble, as if searching for agreement to the decision, which, in her mind, had caused her child's death. 'But Bayliss said it wasn't quite like that. She said she'd been to see Ollie with Professor Gilmartin and that she was on the mend, the antibiotics were working, and maybe the operation wasn't really that necessary . . . And then, I asked her what that would mean, and she said that kids who have heart surgery are at a higher risk of sudden death, and that maybe, if she hadn't had the operation . . .'

The dam in her mind burst and she erupted into tears, comforted on both sides by her husband and Sonja Capp, and Harry rushed forward, squatting so he was at her eye level.

'Michelle,' he said. 'I can't begin to imagine what you're going through. But let me tell you this, your daughter's death is not your fault. Whether or not it could have been prevented. You were doing what you thought best for her, and the way things turned out is not your fault. Ok?'

Roberts nodded.

'Thank . . . Thank you. I needed to hear that. Thank you.'

Harry found himself holding Mrs Roberts's hand as she wept a little, the other parents looking at each other or at the floor. Euan Roberts left the room silently and came back with a box of tissues, a tired look in his eyes like he'd done this too many times.

'She said . . . something about . . . He wanted to operate on her because she was high-risk. Because it would impress people. But she didn't think he needed to, and she said maybe if he hadn't, if he'd waited for her to get better, then maybe done it later, it might have been different.'

They took a moment to process that, to pour more tea. Euan Roberts found a chair for his wife to sink into. Harry began to count the days backwards. It had been four months since Olivia had died, and if such pain ever faded in intensity it would not do so for some time. He looked around. The faces in the room were bleak, the jug of lemonade and trays of cakes mocking them from their gingham tablecloth.

Harry noticed Noble take out her pocket-book and check it.

'You spoke to her on Saturday evening, didn't you?' she said.

'Yes. We've been chatting ever since she was suspended. We were talking about options, where we go next. A judicial review of the DoH inquiry, a lawsuit against the hospital, a lawsuit against Mr Mohamed, or even a private prosecution. We'd arranged to meet up and talk about it on Monday evening.'

'Ok,' said Noble, 'thanks.'

Harry retreated from near the families back to Noble's side, quietly impressed by how she had moved the conversation back to the facts, the investigation, and away from the grief. It seemed cold, but it was pragmatic.

Gervais Abediji was next, speaking through bared teeth, his knuckles pale around the back of the chair he leant on. Harry observed him and tried to recall if he recognised him from Emmanuel's brief time at the Ruskin, but he didn't.

'She popped around, out of the blue. Few months after he died, just knocked on the door. I hardly recognised her, all the stress we've been under . . .

'Anyway, sorry. She asked us if we wanted to make a complaint against the hospital, for what happened to Emmanuel. I'd tried to ask the consultant, Mr Mohamed, why the operation had gone wrong, and he'd always fobbed me off. Said "these things happen". But then Susan said there'd been some other option, some minor procedure with a balloon or something, but Mohamed had wanted to do the big operation, the valve transplant. She said she thought he was trying to make some kind of a name for himself, become famous or something. That maybe if they had waited, done the balloon and kept him on the life support for a bit longer, the operation wouldn't have been as difficult. Emmanuel would have lived.'

Harry felt his heart thumping. Noble looked across at him.

'Did you make a complaint?' he said. There had been no record in the inquiry or Bayliss's dossier.

'No,' said Abediji. 'Not because I didn't believe her. Because of my wife. Chioma – well, she had suffered from depression for a while. Since Emmanuel was born, actually. And since the Lord took him it's become much, much worse. I didn't want to put her through that. I couldn't do it to her.'

He shook his head.

'I wish I had now. Now all – this has happened. I wonder if I had, if any of it could have been . . . Oh, Lord forgive me. I'm sorry, I need a fag.'

Abediji turned abruptly and pushed his way through the crowd to the door. Harry took a deep breath. He wasn't sure he was capable of hearing two more such stories, but he had no way to escape.

The Capps went next. 'Susan was at Jayden's funeral,' Sonja said. 'She was the only person from the hospital who came, we both really appreciated it. She'd been great when he was ill. We didn't speak to her at the service, or at least I don't think we did . . . It's all a bit of a haze, really. I think she was there at the crematorium, too . . . My Lord, it was terrible. When we got him back, there was hardly anything there. Just a handful of ashes. Bloody awful.

And Will had said nothing and stared out the window, an antidepressant glaze on his eyes, and Sonja had told of the phone call, how she had immediately remembered Susan – who'd checked in on Jayden twice a day whenever she'd been at work, when the consultant surgeons were nowhere to be seen. Bayliss had asked them how they were coping, and if Sonja was honest, she wasn't really coping at all. She was going to work and going home and taking benzos to get to sleep, and Will was on the sofa when she woke up with two six-packs of Tesco's lager and watching Jeremy Kyle and when she got home there were two cans left and he was watching Judge Judy. And so Susan had driven all the way down to Eastbourne to buy her a coffee and see how she was doing.

And while she was there, she'd told them that Mohamed should have referred Jayden to Professor Gilmartin from the very start, because he was obviously such a difficult case, but by the time Gilmartin was called from the meeting he was in, over to the hospital, up into the operating theatre, changed into scrubs, Jayden had been bleeding for twenty minutes, and the damage had already been done.

Finally, Bismah Mubarak had, through Ali's hard South London vernacular, told them about how Bayliss often stopped by to check on how the family were doing, what with having four children and a father who was working a day job at a convenience shop and a night job as a minicab driver. Ali was telling it third-hand, but to Harry the tale seemed similar to Michelle Roberts's, Bayliss explaining to the grieving Mubarak family that perhaps an open operation wasn't as necessary as Mohamed had made out, just as she had with the Abediji family, too. And with all the guilt and grief which that implied. Indeed, as Ali translated for his mother, Michelle Roberts had quietly broken down yet again, sobbing into napkins still holding crumbs of lemon drizzle cake.

Harry could empathise. He knew how long it took to shake that guilt. It had hung on him after what had happened to Tammas, invading like mould into every corner of his being, even though the fault had lain with the traitorous bastard who'd pulled the trigger, not with him. Or so he'd been told, by his friends and his shrinks, until he began to believe it.

'Do you all believe her? Completely?' Noble said once they were all done.

It was Gervais Abediji who spoke first. Harry hadn't noticed him return to the conservatory.

'I remember her, because she gave a shit. Whenever Mr Mohamed spoke to us, it was like what was going to happen was a foregone conclusion. That he had made the decision, and was telling us, not asking us.'

Harry nodded, and looked down at Abediji's hands, where the knuckles were turning white again.

'I don't know what happened. I believe her,' he looked straight at Noble, 'but part of me wishes she never called. Losing my son is hard, but I do not think I am any better off thinking that we could have somehow prevented it. Or that Mr Mohamed might somehow be responsible . . .'

'Gervais, we can't think like that,' said Michelle Roberts. But Abediji wasn't calmed, and shook his head, looking Harry dead in the eyes as he spoke.

'Because as God is my judge, if I find out that he was, I'll kill him with my bare hands.'

'Fucking hell,' said Harry, getting back into Noble's car, drenched from the rain.

'I've had better afternoons.'

Noble leant back, produced a cigarette from thin air and smoked it down to the nub.

'Take it you don't want one?'

'I'm bloody tempted.'

He could use a drink. Something to take the edge off the conversation. He looked back up at the house – the parents were yet to disperse, and Harry wondered what the conversation was amounting to. The most depressing afternoon tea in the country, perhaps.

They were about to head off when someone tapped on the passenger window, and they both looked up, Harry recognising instantly the dark blue suit of Skelton, the solicitor. He lowered the window.

'What do you want?'

The rain was soaking his hair and his suit. He gestured towards the back seats, and Harry looked across at Noble.

'Get in,' she called.

Skelton did so, brushing water off his shoulders.

'Well?'

Harry turned around in his seat.

'Look,' Skelton said. 'I don't want any trouble. I've represented Susan for a while. When the families said they wanted someone, she recommended me. Our firm handles malpractice as well as criminal work, so I guess—'

'I don't care about your CV,' Noble said. 'What do you want?'

'I just wanted to let you guys know about something. In case it's relevant.'

The staccato of rain on the car roof.

'Susan called me on the morning she died,' Skelton said. 'She wanted to know if there were any forensics laboratories I'd worked with who could arrange some testing.'

Harry looked across at Noble. From her expression, he was pretty sure it was the first she'd heard of that, too.

'Did she want anything specifically?' he said.

'Yeah. She wanted to know if I had any contacts who could do a toxicology screen on a blood sample.'

'Did she say why? Or who?' said Noble.

Skelton looked at the floor.

'Well, it was about two in the morning. Susan did that recently, stay up late. Usually, err, drinking. I told her I'd think about it and get back to her.'

'This was Saturday morning, yeah? Friday night?' Noble said. The weight of that implication on Skelton's conscience was obvious in his face. Twenty-four hours later, Bayliss was dead.

'Yeah.'

Harry's mind went back to the Chinese restaurant and Amy Floyd, the mysterious ECGs and the crowd of doctors around Emmanuel Abediji in the Ruskin's A&E department.

'Did she mention who she wanted to run the test on?' he said. 'Anything about a funny heart rhythm or anything like that?'

'What's that? She didn't say anything about what she wanted to do the test on, just if I knew of a lab that could do the test.' Skelton brushed water from his hair and opened the door. 'Look, I just thought you guys should know about that conversation. If I'm honest, I think I'm out of my depth here. I liked Susan. She was a friend of a friend, so when she asked if I'd represent these families, I couldn't say no, but now, with what's happened . . .'

He tailed off, and before either of them could say anything he was out of the car door, slamming it behind him, and running back up into the house.

Noble drove around the corner and parked on a side street where they could talk. Harry expected her to lean over and open the glove compartment where she kept one of her hipflasks, and scratch her own itch. He took a bottle of water from his door bin and gulped down a pill, the veil of fatigue briefly lifting.

'What do you think, then?' Noble said.

'About what?'

'About the fucking Israel-Palestine crisis, Harry.'

He rolled his eyes and willed himself a minute closer to his date with Beth.

'I think that fucking hospital is covering for Mohamed,' he said. 'I think he was way off the reservation with those operations. And that when Bayliss called him out on it he tried his best to get rid of her.'

'And he succeeded.'

Harry shook his head.

'I can't see it, though. Bayliss was fucking brave to blow the whistle, to go to the parents. Encouraging someone to make a complaint against her own boss. I can't see her doing it based only on her gut instinct, on conjecture . . .'

'What if it's not based on conjecture?' said Noble.

'Everything we've seen so far gives us absolutely nothing incriminating Mohamed for those kids' deaths.'

'What if Bayliss had something more? Cause I'm beginning to think she must have done.'

'If she did, why wouldn't we know? Surely she'd have given it to the DoH? Why wasn't it in her dossier?' asked Harry. 'It doesn't make any sense. Unless she was privy to something else, but she couldn't prove it.'

'The toxicology?'

'Maybe,' said Harry. 'I told you I met up with the doc who treated Emmanuel in A&E. Before his heart stopped, he had a funny heart rhythm. Called torsades de points. It's caused by a few things – chemical imbalances, heart failure – but it can be caused by drugs, either ODs or poisons. I wondered if that had been tested for, actually. Maybe Bayliss was wondering that, too. If it could have been a drug error, a dodgy prescription or something.'

'But even then, why would the hospital cover it up? Surely it'd put Mohamed in the clear?'

'Maybe someone prescribed the wrong drug, I dunno. Or the wrong dose. As an outpatient or something. Doesn't really make sense either way. Do you know if they had forensic post-mortems?'

'Haven't seen the PMs yet,' said Noble. 'I'll get on it as soon as I can tonight.'

'Send them to me,' said Harry.

'Will do.'

'Still doesn't give them anything to cover up, though. Nothing bad enough to kill a woman over, certainly.'

They both looked ahead and said nothing for a while. It started to rain again, bouncing down on the roof of the car and running down the windscreen. Noble lit a fourth cigarette and wound the window down slightly. He thought about what she'd said and realised that she was right. The hospital had already painted Bayliss as crazy, both within the medical profession and in the press. No-one was going to believe her alive, but dead, an investigation was almost guaranteed.

'Do you think whoever did it thought they'd get away with it? That we'd buy the suicide?'

'I dunno,' said Noble. 'It's a complex scene. The staging seems preplanned, but actually everything the killer used was to hand. The kitchen knife, the pills. The killer puts her in the chair and cuts her elbow, and then does the rest – the wrists, the tweet, the pills – post-mortem. Cleans it up using make-up wipes from her bathroom. They were improvising.'

Harry nodded. He was back at Bayliss's house now, remembering the metallic smell of her congealing blood, the books on the shelf, and the August wind wafting in through the open window. Noble was quite right – it was a scene of contradictions.

'D'you think it could have been a doctor?'

'Probably a degree of medical knowledge to go for the brachial artery, know where it is,' Harry said. 'But not enough to know that she wouldn't bother with sertraline.'

Noble nodded.

'So like a hospital manager's level of knowledge, then?'

She smiled and Harry couldn't help smiling too. They had both appreciated that about one another in the good old days, the ability to salvage a grain of humour from the darkest conversations.

'Ha,' he said. 'That'd be too easy. And it goes back to what we were saying. If the hospital were trying to discredit her, they'd already done it. Killing her achieves nothing. And I don't see a doctor doing this, but I've been wrong before. I'm not saying they're not capable, I'm just saying it doesn't feel like that. Not that my opinion has any weight, I'm sure. In my brief experience.'

'Your opinion always has weight with me, Harry,' Noble said, and they both went red and said nothing more. She started the engine and asked him where he wanted dropping, and he didn't reply because his head was somewhere else. First remembering their relationship, the takeaway curries they'd gorge on whilst she picked his brain on whatever had crossed her desk that week. Domestic violence, gang revenge murders, a nursing home worker who'd bumped off an elderly resident and tried to claim the insurance. He missed that. And then thinking about Elyas Mohamed in his office, looking out at Kennington Park, what he was spending the evening doing.

'Maybe we've been looking at this the wrong way,' he said.

'What do you mean?'

'What if it was never about silencing her? I mean, the horse had already bolted, the moment she went to the DoH. What if it was revenge?'

Harry watched that idea spin in her eyes as they pulled up to a red light.

'It'd put Elyas Mohamed at the top of the list, wouldn't it?' Noble said.

Harry shrugged.

'You said yourself, it looks like he had it in for her,' Noble repeated. 'And Padmore said she'd damaged his reputation pretty badly.'

'Enough for murder?'

'If someone's got the wrong wiring, anything can be enough,' she said. 'You should know that by now.'

She looked across at him, a defeated grin on her face. Perhaps this was only the second time he'd assisted to such an extent with a police investigation of an actual murder – other than Zara, of course, which was halfway there, and until very recently had comprised mostly of the police assisting him, or rather trying to find reasons not to. Again his guilt at actually enjoying it nagged at his psyche, and as Noble slowed down, trawling the streets just west of Greenwich Park, he thought, well, it'll end soon. It was far too late to back down now.

'There's a briefing tomorrow,' she said. 'Half-twelve. I'd like you to be there, if you're not working.'

'I was gonna meet Dave,' Harry said.

'I'm sure he can come over to Peckham. Claim it on expenses.'

Harry smiled. Thought again of Zara and the flowers and cards outside her hospital bed. If she was conscious of it, she almost certainly didn't have the cortical function to process it into what it was, a show of love, with all the positive emotions that connotates, but it warmed him nonetheless.

They drove another five minutes in silence again.

Then at a red light, Noble said, 'I've stopped drinking, Harry.'

'What?'

'Six months on Friday.'

Thunder sounded somewhere in the distance and all Harry could manage was a staggered, 'Well done.'

Brixton Village. Men in denim and drainpipes with loop earrings and chest-deep beards, girls in dungarees with oversized headphones, fad food from all over the world, and Beth striding over to him, that infectious grin on her face, and Harry trying to expunge all the other thoughts from his head as he held her and kissed her hard on the mouth.

'Hey, TV star.'

'If you say that one more time, I'm going home,' Harry said.

'How was seeing the families?' said Beth.

'I don't want to talk about that,' said Harry. 'And neither do you. How was your day?'

'Alright. Yvonne's started saving her shit in her pockets so she can throw it at the nurses, so she has to be searched when she comes out of the toilets. The beauties of mental health.'

He laughed.

'Where are we eating? I'm starving.'

'Bukowski.'

'Good call,' Harry said in a mock Australian accent.

They strode over to the other side of the market, crossing Atlantic Road and the railway arches with their thirty-year-old grocery shops and fishmongers, local institutions who Network Rail were trying their best to evict for more profitable clientele. They talked a little bit more about their day, Harry about the *Crimewatch* stuff and the lead they had and the gifts Zara had received, and she about Bethlem and the other inhabitants of the triage ward she was responsible for. They ordered craft beers, and as Harry tasted it he thought of Noble's declaration, and wondered why she'd told him like that, as if maybe she expected him to leap straight into her arms and tell her all was forgiven. Not when he had this, he thought, as Beth read out the ingredients of every burger on the menu in a mock Nigella Lawson voice, sending him into stitches. This was no comparison to cleaning vomit out of a thirty-five-year-old woman's hair at four in the afternoon.

'Fat Gringo,' she said now. 'I know I had it last time, but it's so good.'

Harry smiled and chose something slathered in chilli.

'You've got tomorrow off as well, don't you?' Beth said.

'Yeah.'

'Let's go somewhere,' she said. 'How about Brighton? Or we could take your car, see if we can find a last-minute spa day or something. Get you pampered.'

It sounded like hell, even if a vision of himself with cucumber slices over his eyes was somewhat amusing.

'I'm meeting Dave to talk about the appeal,' he said, leaning over and rubbing her arm, 'But how about a lie in, and I'll cook you breakfast.'

Beth tried and failed to hide her disappointment.

'Sure, why not. You'd better cook the eggs right.'

He smiled.

'How about lunch?' she said.

Harry went red and mumbled.

'There's a briefing on the Bayliss case,' he said. 'I told DI Noble I'd be there.'

'For God's sake! You bailed on me yesterday, you're bailing on me tomorrow, too.'

'I'm not bailing,' Harry said. 'We never agreed any plans, and I was always going to see Dave.'

'How often do we get days off together, babes?' Beth said, slurping. 'With your crappy rota, and your police work on top of it. And when we do have them, you're finding other things to do.'

'This Bayliss case is bad timing,' said Harry. 'I'm sorry. I'd love to see you more. Hey, I'm working Thursday and Friday night, then I'm off at the weekend. We'll do something.'

'You'll spend all Saturday sleeping.'

'Yeah, we can have curry and red wine at nine in the morning. Then I'll have a wee nap, and I'll be good to go.'

She didn't laugh.

'I'm worried about you.'

'I'm fine. You know what I'm like, I can't say no.'

'Only to your ex,' said Beth. 'You say no to me enough times.'

Harry had to stop himself telling her to fuck off, instead sipping his beer and waiting. His stomach twisted. He checked his phone and saw a text from Michelle Roberts. *Thanks for coming tonight. Sorry if it was a bit tense. Hope it was useful. M. x*

'I'm sorry,' Beth said. 'I didn't mean that.'

'It'd be the same if it was any other detective,' said Harry, not quite sure it was true. 'It's a complicated case. The parents, the hospital, the whole thing.'

'Whatever,' said Beth. 'I just want to feel like you want to spend time with me, if that's not too much to ask?'

'It's not too much to ask,' he said, kissing her, and deciding to change the subject. 'You're going off psych, then?'

'I like it, I like the social aspects, but it's just so under-funded,' she said. 'Most of the time I'm on my own, and I don't have enough time to get to the bottom of people's issues. But hey, you know how much I like a fight I can't win.'

Makes sense why you like me, then, Harry thought.

'How about you. You won't be stuck in A&E your whole life, will you?'

'I kinda like it. The camaraderie's good, and if you get a difficult patient or a difficult relative they're only your problem for four hours . . . And the consultants are good, they're supportive, the nurses are good. And y'know, I'm only doing two doctors' jobs every other shift . . . I guess one of the upsides of a recruitment crisis is that you end up meeting a lot of new people.'

Beth shook her head.

'We have a name for what you're experiencing,' she said. 'Stockholm syndrome.'

Harry laughed.

'Seriously though, you can't be an A&E reg forever,' said Beth. 'And the sooner you get back on the training ladder, the easier it'll be.'

'I know that!' said Harry. 'But ICU's hardly better, is it?'

'Let's go somewhere they don't treat us like shite, then!' said Beth, 'Australia's still recruiting GPs. New Zealand, too. You can cycle round the southern Alps, I could keep animals.'

'I couldn't leave . . .'

'Why not? What's keeping you here?'

Harry thought about that one. Beth looked at him, evidently expecting an answer, but he had none to give that wasn't embarrassing. If he said the police work, she would equate that with Noble, and hit the roof or get passive-aggressive. He couldn't say Zara, because that made him sound like a creep, even though it was true. No-one else was advocating for her, bringing people like DS Cameron to task for letting their guard drop. He couldn't say his family, because he had none.

'Peter,' he said. She had no response to that, just sipped her beer and looked at the table. Harry felt furious with himself. Why couldn't he have just humoured her, fantasised about emigrations he knew he would never make, just to keep her happy? Why did he have to kill the mood?

'New Zealand would be far too quiet,' he said. 'You know me. I need a city.'

'You've never tried anywhere else but London.'

'Portsmouth? Frimley Park?'

'That's not the bloody countryside!'

Harry came close to pointing out his only experience of rural living was a forward operating base in Afghanistan, but stopped himself.

'Well, not New Zealand then,' continued Beth, 'Australia. I could be a GP in the Australian outback somewhere, serving the Aboriginal communities. You can work in the local hospital. Think about it, barbecues every other night, a fridge full of beer, week-ends on the beach. We could have a farm . . .'

'Fuck it,' said Harry, 'Let's book a flight.'

Beth laughed.

'I wish.'

'Be careful what you wish for. One condition, though.'

'What?'

'No fucking farm. Ever.'

It had been dark for about two hours, not that there were any windows in Noble's office. Her desk was an absolute tip, covered by report after report from her team members. Confirming Guzman's alibi, data which put her, or at least someone using her phone, on a night bus leaving Dalston at 03:42, and the interview with the accountancy student she'd spent the night with whilst her girlfriend was being murdered. That played into Noble's thought process, too. The killer would probably not have been sure that they wouldn't be interrupted, which made her more and more certain it hadn't been particularly premeditated. Or if it had, the killer had been forced to do it that evening. It was the work of an intelligent person, surely, but not necessarily one who'd planned to do it.

Or persons, she thought. Some of the detectives were convinced that it had to be more than one, one to hold her down whilst the other cut her elbow. Bayliss was slight, couldn't have weighed more than eight stone, so Noble reckoned it could have been done alone, particularly if Bayliss hadn't expected the initial attack. By a killer who was reasonably medically aware, but not forensically aware, given that the post-mortem wrist wounds and pills had been rapidly uncovered. Multiple killers was a possibility, of course, but a distant one.

She thought about the fear that Bayliss must have gone through, thrashing in the chair, and how the person who'd inflicted that fear deserved to be scared themselves, preferably in a category A prison corridor with a couple of screws looking the other way. Then she stared down at the pile of reports. The answer was somewhere in there, waiting for the right pair of eyes.

The knock at the door.

'Come in.'

It was Grenaghan.

'Evening, Frankie. Not surprised you're still about.'

I'm stunned you're here after five o'clock, Noble thought but didn't say.

'How's it going?'

'Not too bad, sir. Had a tough one this evening.'

'The parents?'

'Yeah.'

Grenaghan sat on the edge of her desk and shut the door behind him. Noble wondered what she was in for, either the you-did-your-best-but-we're-passing-the-case-on-to-Special-Projects lecture, which would be a fucking blessing, or one of his odious pep talks. She'd never been victim to one herself, but the Homicide & Serious pub gossip was rife with bitching about Grenaghan's sermons, featuring in equal measure biblical imagery and anecdotes from his time in Armagh, how if they thought they were up against it now, at least they weren't checking under their cars for tilt bombs.

'I had an interesting phone call from the assistant commissioner,' he began. 'Who'd himself been called by the Belgrave's chief executive. She accused you, by name, of conducting a systemic program of harassment towards trust staff. Including an accusation that you interviewed staff members on the hospital wards, with patients and relatives present, that you intimidated junior members of staff, and that you threatened one of her managers when she phoned you to discuss this issue.'

'Sir, I—'

Grenaghan raised a hand.

'I just want to hear your side of the story.'

Noble inhaled and explained how Mohamed had offered, actually more insisted, to take them on a tour of the cardiac unit, and how the interview itself had taken place in his office. And with Padmore, Price had been the one doing the intimidation, not her.

'This woman Price is running some kind of damage control operation, I think. She was doing her best to answer Padmore's questions for him, and she tried to have a go at me for interviewing Guzman without her present. I don't think they have a clue that it's a murder inquiry, sir.'

'Why did she care about Guzman?'

'She's a hospital interpreter. That makes her a staff member.'

'Hmm,' Grenaghan said. 'Are you viewing her as a suspect?'

'Of course. Not yet strongly.'

Noble felt her face start to burn. She couldn't be arsed with a bollocking, and she really couldn't face being asked to apologise to Alison Price. Not with the shambles of the investigation as it was already. Christ, today had already been a six at least, and it was rapidly approaching an eight. She'd call Everscott the moment she got into the car to drive home.

But then Grenaghan broke into a devilish grin.

'Keep up the good work, Frankie,' he said. 'If the Price woman gives you any more trouble, let me know. You know where I am.'

'Thank you, sir,' said Noble, the burn replaced with a small smile, perhaps the first today. She followed him from her office, heading for the coffee machine.

Harry and Beth moved on to a craft beer place around the corner and drank until closing time, swapping anecdotes, debating the relative merits of the various burger pop-ups in Brixton, and planning a hundred holidays in addition to their inevitable emigration.

The hotel made of ice in northern Finland, scuba-diving across Balinese coral reefs, a road-trip across the Deep South, stopping in honky-tonk bars and bourbon distilleries. When they staggered into Beth's place, she berated him for making such a noise that he'd wake up her housemates, both of whom had shifts starting at eight tomorrow, and he giggled and forced her down onto the sofa, one hand up her shirt, another tugging his belt free, and she laughed and told him there was no chance they were doing it in the living room, so he picked her up like a fireman and carried her upstairs and dumped her on the bed and they shagged for forty-five minutes, alternating positions, and he thought of nothing but her body and the taste of beer and chilli in her mouth and how she was right, he needed to loosen up more.

After that, Harry slept for maybe twenty minutes. After that, the same time staring at the ceiling in the blue half-light of half past one. He shifted in the bed, rolled over and looked at his phone.

Noble had emailed him a file containing post-mortem reports on the four children. He rolled over again, and beside him, Beth stirred.

'Stop moving, you're waking me up.'

He wouldn't sleep for a while now – an effect of using the pills full-time rather than just when he was tired was that they maintained a constant concentration in his blood, so when they wore off he got the pains and the shortness of breath, the withdrawal symptoms, but he didn't fall asleep.

So he grumbled, 'Sorry', took her laptop and went downstairs, thudding down the steps in the dark, into the living room, bringing a chair up to the table, booting up the computer and typing in her password. A journey into the kitchen yielded a glass and a bottle of Jameson's Beth kept for when he stayed over sometimes.

Perhaps the last cogent thought he remembered that night was to wonder if Bayliss had spent her last morning alive doing the same, reading the litany of dead children, and thinking of how it might have come to pass.

At the desk, in the dark, the screen glowed into his pallid face.
He read.

SIX

Wednesday, 27 August
Morning

She found him slumped over the desk, her laptop out of charge, starchy drool hanging from a corner of his mouth.

'Fucking hell, Harry.'

Beth was in her pyjamas with a glass of water in one hand, standing next to one of her housemates, Reshma, in cycling gear, who was retrieving her bike from the living room. In his dream, Harry had been chatting to his dead friend James, but with Susan Bayliss slaughtered in the chair next to them. So it took him a moment to reacquaint himself with the room. In the months after James had been killed, Harry had seen him often, his brain usually awash in a maelstrom of alcohol and amphetamine. Since then he only appeared on particularly dark nights.

'Sorry,' he rumbled.

Reshma laughed, pointing at the Jameson's.

'You had a heavy one, then?'

Beth nodded, last night's make-up still on her face.

'Have a good day,' Beth sang. Harry's meninges pulsed with pain. He'd been up reading until about four – well, reading until two, and then staring at the screen.

'You too,' Reshma said, wheeling her bike out of the door. 'Oh, some pills fell out of your coat, Harry. I put them on the radiator.'

Shit, he thought.

Beth swiped them as the front door slammed closed, and as Harry woke fully he turned to see her holding the translucent orange bottle, inspecting the label.

'Never seen aspirin in a bottle before,' she said. 'D'you get these prescribed?'

'Yeah,' Harry said, thinking of a lie. He was far too young to be on them for heart problems, and the line he'd used on Noble about cluster headaches was unlikely to work on Beth. But he didn't get the time.

'Well, great! My head feels like it's got a chainsaw inside it.'

She set the glass of water down and popped open the child-safety lid. Harry scrambled out of the chair.

'Umm, don't do that,' he said.

'I'm only gonna have two,' she said, dropping the pills into her waiting palm.

He briefly thought about just letting her take them, but couldn't do it.

'Just give them back!'

The room was crisp now, and Beth's face hardened as she looked from him down to the pills, and the corners around the label, which she peeled off.

'Oh, babe,' she said.

'It's not what you think!'

She put the pills back on the table, and Harry waited for the explosion. He was the definition of a fool, someone who didn't deserve a woman who cared for him like she did, but who none-theless did his best to fuck it up beyond recognition. But she didn't berate him. Instead she put on the face she no doubt used when she was trying to persuade paranoid schizophrenics to consent to a depot injection of some mind-numbing tranquilliser. In that moment she had gone from girlfriend to carer, roles she no doubt saw as equivocal.

'Babe, if you're on antidepressants, you don't need to hide it from me. You don't need to hide it from anyone.'

He closed his eyes and was painfully aware of his insignificance and his fallenness, like an astronaut looking at the world from space. In the moment he heard Noble again, telling him she was sober. Six months on Friday. If she could find the courage to admit she needed help, so could he.

'They're not antidepressants,' he said, opening his eyes. He at least owed her that, looking her in the eyes when he told her.

'They're amphetamines.'

Her mouth dropped open.

'You're prescribed them?'

He shook his head.

'You prescribe them yourself! Oh, Jesus!'

He shook his head again.

'Well, I did these ones. But only because I ran out. Normally I get them online.'

Now she exploded.

'Online! So you don't have a fucking clue what you're taking then, do you?'

The devil in him wanted to say, whatever they are, they do the bloody job, but he stopped himself.

'So what is it?' she went on, 'You take them to keep yourself going, and then it's whisky at night to get to sleep. Jesus, you know how this ends, right? Or have you never seen them in A&E? Cause if you haven't, pop over to the Maudsley and ask to take a look. They'll drive you completely fucking crazy. That's if you don't have an MI or a stroke first! Do you have any idea what your blood pressure is? Have you measured it?'

'No.'

'How long's this been going on for?'

'Months,' Harry lied. It was closer to two years, but she didn't need to know that. 'I'm an idiot.'

'You're more than a fucking idiot, you're a danger.'

'I'm not a danger to the patients. I always keep myself alert when I'm working.'

'By taking fucking speed!'

Harry felt tears begin to well but stopped, reaching for her glass of water and sinking half of it. She ran to him but he pulled away.

'Who knows?'

'Only you,' said Harry.

'You're shitting me. What about Peter?'

Hearing someone else use his first name felt wrong, but he ignored it.

'He knows. He understands. You know what he is to me.'

'I've got a right mind to leave you swinging in the fucking wind, Harry. I can't believe this!'

'I'm sorry.'

'For what?'

'For lying to you.'

'You're a fucking idiot!' she repeated, then took a moment, pacing left then right, putting her hands on her hips and blowing air out.

'I'm going to cut down, I swear.'

'I can't believe I'm hearing this! *Cut down?* You're taking speed,

Harry, not fucking having a few too many glasses of wine on a weekday. Have you heard yourself?'

'I know, I know . . . I was going to, it's just with all this stuff with Zara, and then this thing with the Belgrave came up, and—'

'Zara is nobody's problem but yours! And if you needed time off, to slow down, why didn't you say no to Frankie? Would that have been so hard?'

'It'll be done in a week,' Harry said. 'You're right, the Zara stuff can wait. I'll cut down, I swear.'

She folded her arms. Became a shrink again.

'How many are you taking a day?'

'Four. Maybe five.'

If you averaged over the last two years, maybe, including the first nine months when it had been one a week. Which meant it wasn't technically a lie, just a pertinent bit of spin.

'When was the last day you didn't take one?'

'Sometime last week. Maybe the week before.'

'You're lying.'

'No.'

After the first one, it became much easier. Omission or commission, it was all the same.

'You're addicted.'

'No I'm not.'

'You're in denial. You've no insight. None whatsoever. This is scary, Harry. Really fucking scary.'

Insight was the big word. If you didn't have that, they could section you and lock you up. The further down the path to insanity you were, the more likely you were to think you were fine.

He sat down on the edge of the sofa.

'I've got enough insight, Beth. Grant me that. I know I've got a problem. I've just been putting off dealing with it, that's all.'

'Cutting down won't work. Not with amphetamines. You need to stop. You'll probably have to withdraw.'

'Ok,' said Harry. 'How long does that take?'

Her face was still flushed, but the muscles in her folded arms were relaxing, perhaps involuntarily.

'You've got days off next week, haven't you?'

'Tuesday to Thursday.'

'I'll take leave. Shilen owes me a swap. You cut down as best you can until then, and then we'll go up to my parents' place. You go cold turkey, I'll take care of you.'

They'd been before, a cottage in Norfolk, stone's throw from the beach. There were worse places to hallucinate for a few days. It sounded like a different reality, like he'd need to fake his death in order to do it. But he said yes anyway.

'Thank you.'

Beth stepped closer.

'And I'll set you up with one of the addiction consultants, in absolute confidence. He won't tell a soul.'

'Whoa, whoa, no way.'

'You're in no position to negotiate!' Beth yelled, pointing at the orange bottle, which sat on the table, judging him.

'Is this what you want? To live like this? Is this what you want your life to be? Cause if you look me in the eye and tell me that, then I am out of here, ok?'

He looked at the ceiling and said a prayer that it might fall in on him.

'If you tell me you want to stop, and you mean it, then you get one chance. I'll be with you every step of the way, but if you fucking lie to me again, then we're over. Understood?'

'I want to stop,' Harry said. Stop everything. The pills, the work, the guilt.

She put a hand on his.

'Do you? Promise me.'

'I do. I promise.'

'You've got one chance, alright? Sort yourself out. Put all this bullshit with the police into place, and then next week, we'll get you clean. Ok?'

'Ok.'

'I love you, Harry Kent.'

Harry's heart was thumping. He needed another dose, soon.

'I love you too.'

Noble was drinking coffee alone in her office, working on the spreadsheet for that day's task, when McGovern knocked on the door.

'Come in.'

'You probably wanna see this, guv.'

A group of detectives were sat around a computer, the screen showing a browser with ITV's breakfast show streaming live, the correspondent narrating over an image of Bayliss that looked a few years old.

'Police are yet to confirm whether Susan Bayliss's death is being treated as suspicious, calling it "unexplained at this time", but sources have indicated that it appears to be a suicide. This, of course, throws new light on the inquiry into the deaths of a number of children following heart operations at the Belgrave, the hospital Bayliss had recently been suspended from.'

The segment ended and the camera focused on a studio anchor, who addressed the camera.

'And the mother of one of those children joins me now by telephone.'

A girl's photo, which Noble recognised from the Roberts's house as Olivia on the beach, now came up on one half of the screen, the ticker across the bottom identifying the caller as Michelle Roberts.

'Jesus Christ,' one of the detectives whispered.

'Good morning, Mrs Roberts. Thanks for joining us. This must be an incredibly difficult time for you.'

'Thank you,' Roberts said. 'It is.'

'Did you know Susan Bayliss, then?'

'Yes, very well,' Roberts said. 'When my daughter was in hospital, she looked after her, following her operation. She was by far the most considerate person there, always very kind, always happy to take you for a cup of tea or something. As soon as she found out Ollie died she was brilliant, very supportive. She was the only person from that hospital to get in touch, find out if we were ok.'

'So were you quite surprised when she was suspended?'

'No, not really. That's what I want people to know,' said Roberts.

Oh God, Noble thought. The very last thing they needed was an accusation of murder on breakfast TV, or any other accusation for that matter. Bizarrely, she hoped that the solicitor was somewhere in the background to make sure nothing of that kind was said.

'By then, a few of us had got together to demand an explanation from the hospital as to why our children died. Bayliss got in touch with us because she thought the hospital were covering up the mistakes that led to our children's deaths. And she'd decided to take it to the Department of Health, and she knew it was going to cost her her job. But she did it anyway. She was one of the bravest people I've ever met, and now . . .'

'Wow, it certainly sounds like a really difficult time,' the anchor repeated. 'You're still carrying on with your campaign, I can see. You've been getting quite a lot of attention on social media.'

Roberts sounded as if she was fighting back tears.

'If there's one good thing that's come out of this tragedy, it's that more people are taking us seriously. And we call on the Department of Health to start a fresh inquiry into what happened at that hospital.'

'Thank you for speaking to us, Mrs Roberts. Again, I'm very sorry.'

She moved on to speak to some think-tank suit about protection for whistleblowers.

'Dr Siddiqui, this isn't the first time an NHS whistleblower has died in tragic circumstances, is it?'

'Could've been worse,' McGovern said.

'Could've been,' said Noble.

The briefing wasn't until half-twelve, and Beth had left already, so he was in limbo. He didn't fancy heading to the police station and just waiting around. Nor did he feel he could head home and pretend to sleep. Not with the two pills he'd taken almost immediately after she'd left him buzzing around his system. He felt rotten, and it reminded him of one of the worst days in his life. About two years ago, the affair he'd had with his best friend's wife had been revealed, and after James had confronted him he had felt like a husk; it had taken all of his might not to just drink himself into oblivion, or worse. Instead he'd punished himself with a ten-mile run and then a one-mile swim. And that night, he'd still felt consumed by guilt and shame. This didn't feel too much different. Distraction was about the only solution that came to mind, and all the better if it was something of worth.

So he reread the post-mortem reports of the four dead children and came to the very same conclusions he had the first time around. They went into specific detail as to the normality of the hearts on examination, but compared to previous post-mortem reports he had read they seemed a little slapdash. Harry had attended an entire weekend of child protection training as part of his accreditation process for becoming an FME, and that had included a seminar on the procedures to be followed after the death of a child. One fact he remembered was that all sudden deaths of children were to be treated forensically until proven otherwise.

The same pathologist was listed on three of the PMs, and a quick search identified him as Dr Clemens Utting, a specialist cardiac pathologist at University College Hospital in Bloomsbury. The more Harry read over the reports, the more he became convinced that the job had been less than comprehensive. He wasn't sure though, so he rang someone who would be. And in the first bit of luck he'd had in a while, Megan Wynn-Jones picked up straightaway.

'Hello?'

'Dr Wynn-Jones, it's Harry Kent. We worked on the investigation into Keisha Best's suicide last—'

'Of course I remember you, Harry. What can I do for you?'

Wynn-Jones had performed an autopsy on a seventeen-year-old girl cut to pieces by a train, the girlfriend of a gang member whose life Harry had saved after he'd been shot by the police. She had long held suspicions that the suicide had had more to it, but not until Harry had become interested had anyone taken them seriously. Since then, they had stayed in touch, and Harry had been aware that he could call in a favour if the need arose.

'It's a little sensitive,' he said. 'Can I rely on your confidence?'

'Do you need to ask?'

'Thanks. I'm looking at two PMs at the moment. Two children who died, both sudden cardiac arrests in the community following heart surgery a few months prior. The guy's given the cause of death as arrhythmia in both cases. But he's not run any toxicology tests, or electrolyte analysis, or even talked much about the systemic examination. He's just listed the histology of the heart.'

Static through the phone.

'Are you sure?' said Wynn-Jones. 'That can't be right . . .'

Harry felt a small buzz at the validation of his suspicions.

'What do you mean?' said Harry.

'That's almost mandatory in a sudden cardiac arrest. Even in an adult, if they were coming for a PM I'd run a tox screen. In a child, absolutely. And electrolytes, too.'

'So it's standard practice to do them?'

'It's almost malpractice not to,' said Wynn-Jones.

'Thanks, Megan,' said Harry.

He hung up, looked at his phone and then his laptop. On Emmanuel Abediji, the post-mortem barely stretched to two pages, far short of the usual five to eight. Olivia Roberts's wasn't much longer. He went to the browser tab on which he'd searched for Clemens Utting's name, and scrolled down the search results, finding a short biography on the website of the *Journal of Cardiovascular Pathology*, where he was an editor. He read.

Dr Utting graduated from the University of Freiburg, Germany, in 1983, before undertaking postgraduate training in Kiel and Berlin. He moved to the UK in 1992 to undertake research at the University of Cambridge, before being appointed Consultant Pathologist at the Belgrave Hospital, London in 1999, being made Clinical Lead for Pathology in 2004. He moved to University College Hospital in 2011 and took up a role as a Reader in the Department of Pathology at University College London.

Twelve years at the Belgrave, he thought. Medicine was a small world, and specialties even smaller. It was likely that Utting was one of fewer than five cardiac pathologists in London, and the majority of those would have spent some time at the Belgrave, the largest congenital heart centre in the country. But coincidences tended not to sit well with police officers, and that had rubbed off on Harry during the last two years of surrounding himself with them.

He called Noble.

'Hey.'

'I read the PMs,' he said.

'And?'

'Nothing interesting, nothing that changes the game,' said Harry. 'But they're bullshit.'

'What do you mean, they're bullshit?'

'I told you yesterday. Every sudden death in a child should have a full forensic PM. Things like toxicology should have been routine, but weren't done. Seems almost like the pathologist decided it was natural causes and didn't bother.'

'Any evidence it wasn't?'

'No,' Harry admitted, 'but the PMs are far from thorough – substandard even. And I spoke to my friendly neighbourhood pathologist, who agreed.'

'They didn't do toxicology?'

'No.'

'Do you think Bayliss knew that?'

'Maybe,' said Harry.

'Who did the PMs?'

'That's the interesting part. It's a guy called Clemens Utting. He works at UCH now, but between 1999 and 2011 he was the head of pathology at the Belgrave.'

'Shit.'

'Shit indeed.'

'What should we do? If Bayliss was interested in toxicology, we really ought to follow up on that. We need a successful prosecution when we break this, so we've got to dot the i's and cross the t's, especially if we're looking at Mohamed for this. Any chance they kept samples? Or that we could get a second PM?'

'They should have kept samples,' said Harry. 'But as regards a second PM, I can't imagine persuading Michelle Roberts to exhume her daughter will be that pleasant. And Emmanuel was cremated, wasn't he?'

What was it Gervais had said? *There wasn't much left. Just a handful . . .*

'Ah, shit,' said Noble.

'Well let's hope they kept samples,' said Harry. 'I was thinking of maybe trying to find that out. Speaking to this Dr Utting.'

'I can't spare a detective,' said Noble. 'Like I said, we're focusing on the staff at the Belgrave. That's taking all my resources.'

'Well, I'll go myself, then,' said Harry.

Noble sighed into the phone.

'You're getting a kick out of this, aren't you?'

Not a kick, thought Harry, but something. A release, perhaps. If he was thinking about dead children and post-mortem reports, he wasn't thinking about Beth, her anger and his lies.

'Well, report back to me,' she said. 'And be back here for the lunchtime briefing.'

'I will be.'

He took the Northern line up to Warren Street and crossed over to the red-brick buildings of the university. The office he sought was on the second floor, with a view of the main quadrangle. He'd called ahead, so he knew he was expected, but he hadn't been especially candid in his introduction. He was a forensic physician working with the Metropolitan Police who had a few urgent queries about a current case. The man he was visiting was intelligent enough to realise that the query probably wasn't through the official channels, but interested enough not to care.

The office was on the third floor of one of the building's arms, facing out onto Gower Street, off a corridor behind a reinforced steel door. He gave the security guard details of his appointment and toyed between his NHS ID card and his Met one, eventually choosing the latter. After all the effort of his bullshit so far, it felt a shame to be turned around now. It worked, and Harry knocked twice at the office door, feeling only a little nervous, or maybe that was the pills' doing, giving him the occasional run of palpitations.

The door opened, and Harry was struck by the utter chaos of the office. Every desk or shelf was covered in stacks of papers, books and journals, the floor cluttered with overflowing wastepaper baskets. Even the filing cabinets were piled high with more paperwork and general rubbish – the only order to be found was at a solitary workbench by the window, on which sat a double-headed microscope, an iMac, and a pristine collection of histology slides, each of which, Harry surmised, contained a sliver of muscle tissue from a child's heart. Spinning around in his chair to face his visitor was Dr Clemens Utting, Consultant Cardiac Histopathologist. Utting was the wrong side of fifty but looked positively ancient and as decrepit as his office in a chequered shirt with one collar in, one collar out of a beige jumper, a coffee-stained white coat, and a beard that suggested he'd been kept hostage somewhere for years.

'Morning,' he said.

'Morning. I'm Dr Kent.'

'Ah yes, the mysterious forensic physician,' Utting said, his accent clipped and musical. 'If that is such a thing. The web article I found described you as some kind of surgeon.'

Harry slid his ID card into Utting's spindly fingers, and explained. 'That's the old name for the role. I'm a Force Medical Examiner. And, what internet article, if you don't mind my asking?'

Utting didn't strike him as the kind of man who watched *Crimewatch*.

'There was something from last year – some court case you were giving evidence in.'

'Right.'

'It was only because I found that, and it was from the *Independent*, which is a publication I find reputable, that I agreed to meet you.'

'Well,' Harry stuttered a little, 'thank you.'

'Coffee?'

'No thanks.'

'Suit yourself. So what are you doing here?'

'I'm providing the police with some medical advice into a murder investigation that's currently ongoing.'

'Haven't you anything better to do with your time?'

Harry chose not to answer that one. Utting sipped his coffee and then spoke anyway.

'So, go on then. What does a Force Medical Examiner –' he said the words with European sarcasm – 'want with me and my collection of pickles?'

He pointed at the fixed half-hearts in pathology pots on his workbench.

Harry reached into his bag and brought out the four post-mortems he'd spent the best part of the night reading. Utting, evidently interested, reset his wire glasses on his nose.

'You wrote the pathology reports for two sudden cardiac deaths in March and April, Emmanuel Abediji and Olivia Roberts.'

'I'm not so good with names.'

Harry passed the reports over and Utting looked over the frontsheet of each. How he was remembering them Harry had no clue. Perhaps the dates or the sizes of the hearts.

'Ah, yes,' Utting said. 'Why are you having an interest in these? There is no way these are criminal cases, surely?'

'Well, that's what I wanted to ask you. You listed the cause of death in both these cases as presumed cardiac arrhythmia.'

Utting nodded and took Harry through the process for both. He had performed both post-mortems, and Emmanuel's examination had been completely normal. Olivia's lungs had contained a reasonable amount of fluid, suggesting she had experienced acute heart failure before she'd died. But no brain haemorrhages, no pulmonary emboli, nothing that could kill a child in an instant. Utting had examined the hearts at the autopsy, having been well informed about the surgery both of them had undergone. The valves in both cases had been well healed with no signs of wall breakdown, infection or blood clots. Likewise, there were no areas of scar tissue which could have caused an arrhythmia in either of them.

'You were aware they had both recently undergone cardiac surgery?'

Utting looked down at his notes again.

'They both had prosthetic valves, I recall. But I don't remember it being particularly recent.'

'It was three months in Olivia's case. Three and a half in Emmanuel's.'

'Ah.'

Harry looked across the office, trying to get the measure of this man. He wondered whether the aloofness was his personality, or because he was in some way mocking Harry, playing the fool.

'So why did their hearts stop working?' Harry said.

'Good question,' said Utting. 'I'd tell you if I could. And I guess perhaps you've come here in the hope that I could share with you some hidden truth that was not in my reports.'

The room was suddenly stifling. Utting leant against the lab bench with his arms folded.

'The reports don't have much.'

'I beg your pardon?'

'They're not that detailed,' said Harry.

'Well, they were both young children who were otherwise fit and well, apart from their heart problems.'

'You're aware of the guidelines that all sudden deaths in children should be given a forensic post-mortem?'

Utting's hand came up to rest in his beard.

'Yes, I am. And you're aware that I'm a consultant pathologist of almost forty years' experience. So I feel that I am experienced enough to know when the guidelines are appropriate and when they are not.'

'Would you elaborate?'

'With pleasure,' said Utting, flamboyantly pointing at a report on his desk and the corresponding heart slivers on the microscope. 'Take this young man, for instance. Undiagnosed hypertrophic cardiomyopathy, died warming up for a football match at age fifteen. I decided that there was sufficient ambiguity to run the full panel, and we revealed he had taken cocaine the night before. These two cases, I did not feel that the cause of death was in any doubt. Indeed, as you say both of them had had previous cardiac surgery. You may not be aware, Dr Kent, but this predisposes them to a sudden cardiac arrest.'

Harry said nothing for a while. Then he decided that he hadn't come here to make friends.

'You worked at the Belgrave for twelve years,' he said.

'You have access to the internet,' Utting said. 'Well done you.'

'Did you know Elyas Mohamed?'

'Of course.'

'Who operated on Emmanuel Abediji and Olivia Roberts. Who was investigated by the Department of Health for alleged negligence, and who your post-mortems happened to put in the clear.'

Utting stared at him hard, shaking his head. Outside, an ambulance or a police car screamed past, car horns blared, brakes screeched.

'That's what you think? That I did a rush job, that I was not thorough because I was covering for some old boy pal?'

Harry said nothing.

'You couldn't be more wrong . . .' Utting said, turning his back. He turned on his heel, walking with a limp towards his computer, then about-turning once again and slamming shut the filing cabinet.

'*Scheiße*!'

Harry's phone buzzed. Utting seemed furious, but more at himself than at Harry, which made him excited. If he was getting to him, there had to be something worth getting to.

'Let me tell you why I left the Belgrave,' said Utting. 'Having worked there for twelve very happy years, I was no longer willing to remain at that institution.'

Harry switched on his internal dictaphone.

'That place has turned into something tantamount to human experimentation. Every patient that comes in they see as a potential news headline, a case study in a top journal, a research grant, a ticket to some conference in Honolulu. In a few, shall we say, controversial cases I gave my considered opinion, and was told, as I was not a surgeon, to report the biopsy and play no further part in the discussion. That is not the kind of medicine I wish to be a part of. So believe me, I would be the first in line to see that place get a good shakedown from the DoH.'

Utting was close up to his face now, and Harry could smell the must coming off him.

'So why didn't you do a proper examination on Emmanuel and Olivia?' said Harry.

Utting kicked a filing cabinet.

'The same bloody reason anybody doesn't do anything these days!' he seethed. 'Cost-cutting! Efficiencies! A toxicology screen is two or three thousand pounds, and you can double that for a genetic assay. I have three PhD students, and if I want to keep them on I have to keep this department's outgoings at a minimum. I don't know when I gave up fighting the *verdammt* administrators, but the first time I got away with it and no-one noticed and it kept them happy . . . There's hardly any paediatric pathologists about these days, not since the shaken baby stuff. They're all too scared of getting struck off. So they corral me into doing it, when all I really care about is heart structure, and my bosses would have a fit if I tried to run a test like that. They reckon a university hospital's prime objective is to save more money than they did last year.'

As the pathologist spoke, the pain in Harry's thumping chest grew larger and shot down his left arm. He tried to channel his anger into something constructive, thought back to the conversations with Noble. If someone at the hospital had prescribed Emmanuel or Olivia the wrong drug, and then covered it up . . . There were gaps in the logic, but as Noble had said, they had to be thorough. Particularly as less than twenty-four hours after she'd suggested running a toxicology test, Susan Bayliss was dead.

'Do you still have samples?' he asked Utting.

'Heparinised blood in the deep freeze. We keep it in case we identify a genetic mutation in a relative and we want to re-test.'

'Can you run toxicology? And electrolytes? And everything else you left out? I can ring the SIO if you need that authorised.'

Utting sank into his chair and looked up at him, licking at the grey hairs of his beard.

'Yes.'

Harry went to speak, but Utting was still in thought.

'I'll do it. I should have done it.'

Harry had to stop himself agreeing. He wasn't sure what made him angrier: the thought that this man had been sloppy purely out of toeing some policy line, or as part of some multi-hospital cover-up. When Utting spoke again he was quiet.

'I was like you once.'

'I beg your pardon?'

'Young and idealistic. I thought that there was never an excuse for doing anything other than the absolute gold standard. I saw people who made decisions to the contrary and looked down on them. I thought they were some kind of lesser breed of doctor, that in some way they cared less than me.'

Harry said nothing.

'When you get older, you'll learn that you are probably right, but if you fight them every time you will lose your friends very quickly. And then you'll be outside the system, where you cannot effect a single change. So you have to tolerate one small thing, and then the next, in the knowledge that when it really matters, you will be there to make a difference. So there you are.'

'How long do you think it'll take to get the results?' said Harry.

'A day or two, depending on the samples. Certainly I can have something qualitative in that time.'

Harry took one of his business cards from his wallet and passed it over.

'Call me when you know,' he said.

'I will.'

'Thank you.'

Utting nodded solemnly, crumpled further into his chair, and looked at the rows of pickled hearts.

Noble had managed to get out of the building shortly after fielding about ten phone calls from Grenaghan and the eight detectives at the Belgrave, who were systematically interviewing the fifty staff of the cardiac unit. They were bringing in a good deal of information, but it was low quality and of little use. No-one really liked Elyas Mohamed, but no-one really liked Susan Bayliss, either. Not that they especially disliked her, either. She was just there. Maybe it was people's natural reluctance to speak ill of the dead, or fear of being put in the frame if they criticised her, or not wanting to grass up their mates. But as Noble rehearsed the afternoon's presentation in her head, chewing on the end of her e-cig, she realised it was going to be much the same as the previous day's.

She'd barely been outside five minutes when DC Acquah found her.

'Guv?'

Acquah knew her smoking spot, which was never good news. Worse still, she had a mobile phone in her hand.

'Who is it?'

'Greenwich.'

'What the bloody hell do they want?' Noble said.

'Michelle Roberts made a 101 call earlier this morning,' Acquah explained. 'Said that she thought she'd been followed on the way home from shopping, and that someone was in the garden, looking around the house.'

'Jesus,' said Noble. Serves her bloody right, she thought. Ringing up, or perhaps even visiting Roberts again was high on her list of actions. Mostly to try and foster an understanding that the police were on the family's side, that they all wanted the same thing – to find out who'd killed Susan Bayliss. But as tempting as it would be to say that Roberts had brought any unwanted attention on herself, Noble's immediate thought was safeguarding. If the killer had felt threatened by Bayliss, and had thought – either rationally or irrationally – that the best course of action was to eliminate her, then who was to say they wouldn't treat Michelle Roberts the same?

She took the phone and was soon talking to the Greenwich duty inspector.

'We sent a response unit to do a quick go-over of the immediate vicinity and search the house and garden,' the inspector said. 'They found no present threats. We've reassured her about security – keeping the doors and windows locked – advised her to perhaps go and spend some time with a friend or a relative, if she's particularly concerned. The usual spiel.'

'Thanks for letting me know.'

'Well, she mentioned you'd been around to visit yesterday. So my officers flagged it up with me.'

'Well, good on them,' said Noble. 'Have you got any units who can do a few drive-bys throughout the day, maybe check up on her in the evening?'

'I'll do my best, but you know how it is. Haven't got enough cars to do anything.'

Noble actually believed this one, even though the old under-resourced line was all too often a stock excuse for lazy coppers. She thanked the inspector again, gave the phone back to Acquah, told her to piss off, lit a new cigarette and rang Wilson.

'Guv?'

'What you up to, Mo?'

'Small personal errand.'

Noble grinned. Wilson had joined CID from Trident, the Met's gang intelligence unit, and still maintained a network of snitches across South-East London, who he occasionally had to squeeze from time to time. Whilst it was unlikely to be useful on a case like this, she knew that other investigations who needed that kind of intelligence would often contact Mo, and so she wasn't surprised if he was AWOL for a few hours.

Briefly, she explained the events of the morning.

'You in the car, or on the bike?'

'Car.'

'And your plans for the afternoon are?'

'Paperwork. There's an attempt murder charge being filed against one of my customers from the weekend, CPS want a few bits and bobs.'

'How about you drive over to Greenwich and do your paperwork in the car there?' Noble said. 'Check in on a cup of tea with Mrs Roberts every now and then?'

'I guess I could do that,' Wilson said. 'This Mrs Roberts, she's married, I take it?'

Noble laughed properly for maybe the first time in days.

'Yeah, she is. Her husband's just flown to Hong Kong though, if I remember correctly.'

'Interesting.'

'Yeah, and she's a grieving mother with pictures of her dead kid all over the living room. Don't forget to include that in your porno fantasy, you sick bastard.'

Wilson laughed and hung up.

Harry bumped into Noble as she was heading back into the station. Cameron had arrived, and had texted to say he was waiting in the canteen.

'Good job,' he said.

Noble scowled.

'Yeah, maybe. You need to fill me in on your trip up to UCL,' she said. 'How about a quick lunch before the briefing?'

'That'd be alright. I'm seeing Cameron now. Should be done in half an hour, I guess.'

'I'll come and find you,' Noble said.

As he headed down the corridor he checked his phone and saw a voicemail from Beth, and played it.

'Harry, it's me. I'm still getting over earlier. I'm still angry, but you have my support and my love. But you really need to get help. I've emailed you a link to the Practitioner Health Programme. It's a confidential service run out of the RCGP. Doctors for doctors, entirely discrete. They have a special clinic for addictions, and you can self-refer. It's what you need, Harry. Call them tonight, and we can talk about sorting you out once I've cleared my head a bit, ok?'

He paused outside the canteen as two coppers walked past, taking the piss out of something. His finger hovered over a half-written reply, but he didn't know what to say so he went into the canteen. Cameron was sitting with a half-eaten steak pie in a poly-styrene tray before him, the case file on Zara stuck on the table. Far too thin for a crime three years old.

'There's good news and bad news,' Cameron opened with. 'Which do you want first?'

'The bad,' said Harry.

'We still don't have a name,' said Cameron. 'We've got a few good leads, but no-one's ID'd her. I'm sorry.'

'What about the good news, then?'

'We've got significantly more information than we had this time last week,' Cameron said. 'We had sixteen calls in total, reporting that she frequented Waterloo Station.'

'Waterloo,' he repeated.

'Sixteen calls is pretty significant, Doc,' said Cameron. 'Especially when we're talking about something that happened three years ago.'

Harry had repeatedly asked DS Cameron not to call him that, but Cameron had never relented. He suspected it might be slightly spiteful – Harry had spent a lot of time, over email, telephone and in person, trying to persuade the Specialist Case Investigation Team to take on the case, and he got the impression that Cameron would rather be working one which had a higher than miniscule chance of being solved.

'What did they say?' Harry asked.

'Five or six came from station workers, said they recognised her from the entrance on Waterloo Road. Said she used to beg there. Lots of the sandwich shops hand out their unsold food to the homeless when the station closes, and some of the staff remem-bered her. We had two or three say that same story. Funny how much people can remember, eh?'

Harry looked up and stared straight at Cameron, who was gulping from a bottle of Diet Coke. All his attention was fixed on the precocious detective now. Maybe he was tired, maybe he'd been dejected by Cameron's initial statement that they hadn't managed to identify Zara yet, but now his excitement was real. He had been fascinated by this girl for three years and right now, between slurps of Diet Coke, this man was telling him the first new piece of information they had had about her life in all that time. Harry felt like he'd just popped five of his pills. He could feel his heart in his chest, and he was sweating a great deal even for the sweltering heat of the stuffy canteen.

'Nobody remembered her name? Nobody recalled speaking to her?'

'We had one call, from this woman,' Cameron said. 'Gave her name as Mary, sounded like an Irish traveller according to the call-taker. She said she'd shared a hostel room with her for a few weeks at Archbishop's Hall. It's a crisis centre, over towards the Elephant.'

'She must have known her name!' Harry said, too loud. 'If they shared a room for weeks, she must have!'

Cameron looked down at the table between them.

'Mary said she was short of money,' he said. 'She said she'd only give the name if we were willing to pay for that information.'

Harry slapped the table.

'Fuck's sake,' he said.

'*Crimewatch* has a policy of not offering money,' said Cameron. 'There's plenty of cranks who call up, even if they know bugger all.'

'I'll pay,' Harry said. 'She left her details, surely?'

'No she didn't,' said Cameron. 'She refused to, once she was informed that she wouldn't be getting any money.'

The detective drained the rest of his Diet Coke, sucking the last drops of moisture from the bottle, and Harry regretted not taking up his offer of a cold drink. The frustration made him want to get into the gym and hit the bike or the rowing machine, work out the anger. Somebody in London knew what had happened to the girl with the pink hair, namely whoever had strangled her, fractured her skull, and left her to die in an alleyway. But he'd always believed that there had to be someone else who knew who this girl had been before that had happened. Harry didn't know whether to feel vindicated that such a person existed, or exasperated that they would throw their knowledge away for the want of material gain.

'What about the other calls?' he asked.

'A handful of single identifications from all over the country,' said Cameron, looking down at his notes. 'Lincoln, Cornwall, Scunthorpe, Falkirk. Two callers who work at the same hotel in Brighton wondering if it might be a girl who used to keep the bar there, but we traced that woman, and she's in Australia. We'll follow the others up, of course, just in case. An old man from Liverpool called in, said it was definitely his granddaughter, gave us all a hard-on for a while. Turns out his granddaughter was there with him, and the poor bloke's got Alzheimer's.'

Cameron sat staring at Harry, as if baiting him to react.

'No-one called from Clapham? Or Battersea?'

'Nope.'

The girl they called Zara had been found not far from Lavender Hill, and yet nobody had called in from that area. But she'd been seen in Waterloo and had perhaps stayed in a homeless shelter nearby. It was more information than they had ever had before, but it wasn't enough. Still, it could direct their investigations. If she'd stayed in one homeless shelter near the South Bank, the chances were she'd stayed in others. The main commuter train line from Waterloo ran through Clapham Junction. Harry had visited plenty of shelters around there, but he hadn't gone as far north as Waterloo. If nobody recognised her, they could start taking names of residents and then checking them all.

In all the excitement, Harry realised he'd stopped listening.

'Christ, you really are on a different planet, aren't you, Doc?'

'Sorry. I've got tangled up in something.'

Cameron laughed.

'I was hoping you'd be more pissed off,' he said.

'Why?'

'So I could make your day with this,' Cameron said, passing Harry two sheets of paper, clipped together. The top one was a printout from the website of a church, St John the Evangelist, the address listed on Lambeth Road, on the southern side of Waterloo Station. The page featured the biographies of the pastoral team, and Harry read the names, scanning the photos. The second page was a call log from the police call centre, dated Monday, 25 August, the night of the television appeal. It listed the caller's name as Frank Barnabas. Harry immediately flipped back to the website printout, finding the photo of a young black man in a clerical collar. He returned to the call log, reading the call-taker's summary, the bullet points flying off the page.

Caller was working as a street pastor on homeless outreach project, Easter weekend 2011. Unable to remember exact date or subject's name. Accent/name Eastern European, unknown language/nationality. English good.

Caller remembers encountering subject in railway arch btw. Westminster Brdg. Rd., STH. Remembers subject was cold and exposed.

Caller escorted subject to St John evangelist church. Had meal with subject. Conversation lasted ~2hrs. Provided subject with warm clothes and shelter.

Caller willing to be interviewed. Gave work address as St John's church Lambeth Rd. SE1 See other contact details below.

Harry looked up at Cameron who was grinning.

'He said he's got no idea what her name is,' Cameron said. 'But he remembers speaking to her at some length. Said that he'd be more than happy to have a chat with us, see if there's anything else he remembers about her.'

'They spent an evening together?' Harry said, rereading the call log.

'She slept in the church that evening,' said Cameron. 'Apparently the churches round Waterloo have a rota system. One of them's open each night for anyone they find on the streets.'

'But he can't remember the name?' said Harry.

'No,' said Cameron. 'He said he'll try and remember who else was working that night, see if any of his colleagues remember. But it's doubtful. And they didn't keep records. He did say she was East European, though.'

They communicated with Zara by asking her to move her eyes left or right in response to questions, one of the few voluntary movements she had left intact, and she understood enough English to do this, but she tired too easily to spell out a name. He was fairly sure that she was foreign, and that English wasn't her first language. For a start, all UK missing persons matching her age and description had been checked, and she wasn't one of them. Finding out her first language might help Niebaum and his team a great deal.

Harry was undeterred.

'This is fantastic!' he said. 'When are you gonna interview him? Tomorrow?'

Cameron shuffled on his seat, licking his lips. Harry knew relatively little about the detective – he had come to meet him through Noble, whom he had repeatedly badgered during their relationship to get someone in the Met to take up the case. The Specialist Case Investigation Team consisted of about twelve senior detectives to cover the last thirty years of crime in Greater London, so they had a long waiting list of casework, and Noble had managed to put the girl with the pink hair on the list back in October. Harry had got the call from Cameron in July, letting him now that SCRU was looking into the matter, with the idea for the TV appeal, and things had gone from there. But in all the time they'd met, Cameron had seemed distracted, like he didn't really care. Harry had met other police officers and doctors like that, where the job to them was like any other. They might as well be working in a cardboard factory, as long as the money came in at the end of the month.

'We've got other active cases,' Cameron said. 'I told you on the phone, the last half of this week's gonna be hell. Friday's a possibility. If I don't get to do it myself, it will be the first thing on the desk of my replacement, I promise you that.'

'This is the first new piece of information about what happened to Zara in three years!' Harry protested. 'I can't believe it's not a priority.'

Cameron got to his feet, picking his bag up off the floor. All the pleasantness was gone from his face.

'This is a priority,' he said, 'but as I'm sure you can appreciate, there are other matters which I've got to wrap up, and—'

The door to the canteen flung open and Noble was standing there. She was fitting a Kevlar vest over her blouse. Behind her, detectives rushed out of the station, towards the car park. She made eye contact with Harry and immediately he was up, running towards them.

'What is it?' he called as he followed behind, out into the bright light of the car park. The reply came over her shoulder.

'Someone's attacked Michelle Roberts.'

Outside, McGovern and another detective were piling into the back of a patrol car, shouting at the uniform to fire it up and drive them over.

'Is she injured?' Harry asked, running towards his own car, which was parked around the other side. He fumbled in his trouser pocket to grab the key, unlocking the boot.

'Don't know! Are you coming, or what?'

'I'll grab my kit!'

The boot flew open, and he reached inside, grabbing the emergency medical bag that lived there, looping its strap around his hand. He slammed it shut and ran towards Noble's Volvo, which she was already backing out of its parking space. Pressed the button on his keyfob through his coat pocket and didn't bother checking if his car had locked. Slid into the passenger seat of Noble's car, threw his pack onto the back seat, and strapped himself in.

Noble hit the blue lights in the grille and backlights as they pulled out onto Queen's Road, tracing the same route they'd taken last afternoon, for tea and cake with the grieving parents.

'Shit,' she said.

'What is it?' Harry said. The SatNav in her car put the time to the address as ten minutes. On blue lights they'd halve that, especially with light afternoon traffic.

'Roberts called us about two hours ago,' she shouted above the sirens. 'Said she thought someone had followed her home this morning. Uniform responded, said the area was clear.'

'Jesus.'

'She's just called 999, said someone's trying to break the door down. She's taken her son and locked them both in the bathroom.'

Harry's mind shot back to Preston, the excited toddler running around with the bowl haircut.

'Fucking hell.'

'I sent Mo down to hang around, check things out,' Noble went on, her mind active, speaking all her thoughts out loud. 'He's just around the corner, thirty seconds, max. He'll be there by now!'

They ran a red light, the patrol car with McGovern and the other detectives ahead of them, clearing the traffic, lights blazing.

'You got Mo's number?' she repeated.

'Yeah.'

'Call him!'

Harry did so, trying to slow his heart rate down as he found Wilson in his contacts. He didn't know why Noble had grabbed him from the canteen on her way out of the station. Perhaps later she would say it was in case there were injuries, but her confusion at him getting his kit from his car weighed against that. Maybe it was just that it all seemed to be going to shit, and she wanted a familiar face, someone she thought she could count on. No, Harry scolded himself. She *could* count on him. Whatever had gone past, now, sirens wailing, charging into the unknown, he was behind her.

Wilson's phone rang, and rang, and rang, and nothing else.

'No answer,' he said.

'Come on!'

Noble grabbed the radio console, steering with one hand, then dropped it to change gear.

'Shit, Harry, hold that up at my mouth, yeah?' Into the handset: 'Control, this is Acting DCI Noble. Can I have an update on the 999 call from Wellington Terrace, please?'

'Roger that, one second please.'

Radio static, more blue lights, past New Cross, heading uphill.

'This is Control. Caller reports an individual attempting to break down the front door, erm, caller advised to retreat to safest location. Child present at—'

The radio communication was cut out immediately by the high-pitched, repetitive tone of the panic alarm, the worst sound any police officer can hear. Harry just happened to be watching Noble's pale, determined face at the moment she heard it, and he watched the jaw slacken, the lip curl in worry. When an officer presses their panic button, the radio channels cut out for ten seconds, broadcasting the caller's distress call to all units in the area. Noble and Harry followed protocol and remained silent. Noble even killed the siren, as did the car ahead.

Static.

'—need assistance.'

Static.

'Help.'

Static.

'Now.'

Harry had never heard Moses Wilson sound so weak.

'Mike Delta One Four Nine, are you injured? What's going on?'

Every officer in the borough could hear Wilson breathing heavily and saying nothing.

Noble hit the siren and the tyres screeched as they accelerated through another red light, onto the Deptford Bridge roundabout. She was whispering something under her breath.

'Come on, Mo, be ok. Tell me you've just dropped your fucking radio.'

Radio silence and screaming sirens. Harry thought of the narrow house in Wellington Terrace, the heavy wooden door, picturing Michelle and Preston Roberts cowering in the bathroom. There would be other police units closer than they were, response cars from Greenwich and Lewisham, who should already be on scene. Another priority call cut across the radio traffic, filling the car with the speaker's urgency.

'All available units, please respond immediately to 3 Wellington Terrace, SE One-Zero.'

'Give me the radio again!' Noble demanded. Harry held it at her mouth.

'Control, get an ambulance to him!'

'LAS already dispatched, confirmed.'

'What's the status of the 999 call?'

'Caller not responding, ma'am.'

Noble flung the radio into the footwell and it bounced around on its flex.

'Fuck!'

Having the patrol car clear the path for them was helping with time, and Greenwich Police Station flew past them on the right, the railway station on their left. Another patrol car was joining the convoy, adding to the light and noise. Harry tried his best to think. In Afghanistan, rushing to the scene, he would have briefed the team of two paramedics, one nurse, and four RAF infantry, about the plan. Here he just had his personal kit, and no information at all on the number or severity of casualties. Wilson sounded seriously injured. Worst case scenario, Michelle and Preston were too, which made three critically injured patients. Just as Noble was, he began to think himself into the moment, plan for the inevitably chaotic scene he was about to enter.

'This is Romeo Golf Twenty,' a terrified female voice said. 'We are on-scene. We have an officer down on the ground floor, require urgent assistance and paramedics. Officer is unresponsive. We can hear cries for help upstairs and are making our way there.'

The running commentary carried on as they shot up the residential street on the eastern border of Greenwich Park, heading steeply uphill.

'I'm gonna find this bastard!' Noble shouted as the car in front of them turned. 'I'm gonna find him, and I'm gonna fucking kill him!'

'Priority call, we have one injured female in the upstairs bathroom, appears to be multiple stab wounds. There's a young child, appears uninjured. Repeat, we have an officer down in the front hallway and a female with stab wounds in the upstairs bathroom. We need urgent backup and medics.'

Noble turned into the Roberts's street and Harry saw the array of police cars ahead, two response vehicles already arrived, and McGovern and Bhalla and the two Southwark PCs charging out of the car, batons drawn. A paramedic car was arriving from the other side, too. Noble had the door open before she'd even stopped, pulling her personal radio up from her belt. Harry spun out of the other side, opening the back door and grabbing his kit off the seat.

'Talk to me, Mo!' someone cried out.

Harry looked up at the house, his pulse throbbing in his temples. The front door had been kicked, or rammed, off its hinges, splinters from the broken lock glinting in the light. Moses Wilson lay on his back, head and shoulders in the hallway, bottom half in the living room, frothy pink foam dripping from his mouth, blood matted in his hair, an extended ASP baton dropped by his right hand, DC Bhalla cradling his head, one of the Southwark PCs opening up a first aid kit.

'Medic coming through!' Noble called, clearing the way for Harry.

He set his bag down to one side, pulling a pair of gloves from a side pocket and slipping them on as he surveyed Wilson's condition. He was breathing quickly, the pink foam bubbling as he did. That was bad news. It meant a wound to the heart, lungs or both.

'Mo! Can you hear me?'

About him blood seeped into half-inch-thick cream carpet, underneath his back a growing pool.

'Give him some space!'

More officers charged past them into the house, screaming, 'Police!'

'Get his vest off!'

The PCs didn't need telling twice, unclipping Wilson's stab vest and throwing it onto a leather sofa. Once they were done, they took a limb each and dragged his limp body into the middle of the room so they could work on him from all sides. Harry set about removing Wilson's bloodstained T-shirt with trauma shears, pulling off the fabric to expose the chest. Trauma patients like this were easy. Find the wounds, stop the bleeding. Harry had treated his friends before, on the battlefield. He could do it again.

The injury was a few inches under his left armpit, between the ribs, and just wide of where the vest would have saved him. Maybe his arm had been swinging up to defend himself, and the knife had caught him under there. The hole was diamond-shaped, and bubbling blood, and when Harry saw it he felt sick. The area was only a few centimetres above his heart, and if the knife had penetrated at all, it could have gone straight through. Harry grabbed a PC's hands and folded them over the wound.

'Press as hard as you can!'

He went to the pack and got out a dressing to control the external haemorrhage, but in reality it was the internal bleeding he was worried about, especially if the heart was punctured. He flicked Wilson's face, listened to his lips, checked he was still alive. Moved the copper's fingers out of the way, and placed a gauze pad over the wound, sealing it on three sides. Then he stepped back to assess things. Checked the rest of the chest, the neck, and the other armpit for other injuries, listened with his stethoscope to ensure the lungs hadn't collapsed.

Wilson was critically unwell, but there was Michelle Roberts, too, wounded and upstairs. Multiple stab wounds, the officers had said over the radio.

A paramedic arrived, laden with kit, face shocked.

'Stab wound, left thorax,' Harry said. 'I'm a doctor. Get him on oxygen and get a line in, a big one, and don't fuck it up. Keep listening to his chest. If the air entry reduces, do a decompression.'

The paramedic nodded to all of that.

'Where are you going?' she said.

'There's another one upstairs.'

'Ok. HEMS are en route.'

Thank fuck for that, Harry thought. The air ambulance team would have at least one doctor and a paramedic, all with extensive trauma experience. They were exactly what was needed, except they were taking off from a helipad in Whitechapel, and Moses Wilson and Michelle Roberts were in Greenwich, bleeding out.

Harry picked up his bag, left Wilson with the paramedic and headed further into the house. He found Noble in the front hallway, giving orders.

'Victim reports suspect dressed in black hoodie, grey trackies, white trainers, making off on foot via back gardens, headed in direction of Greenwich Park. Broadcast immediately.'

Harry pushed past her and headed up the stairs. If Roberts had given that description, at least she was still talking, which was good. Downstairs, Noble carried on, barking into the radio.

'I want all exits of Greenwich Park secured with officers there. I want Air Support, and mobilise four response units to the local area.'

At the top of the stairs, Harry was greeted by the sight of a bathroom door swinging open, the middle of it destroyed completely, two police officers with a rudimentary first aid kit, spots of blood on the floor. He swung around and took it in. Curled up like a child, Michelle Roberts sat by the radiator behind the bathroom door, wailing inconsolably. There was wood and blood all over the varnished mahogany. Preston in the empty bathtub, not a spot of blood on him. She had barricaded herself against the bathroom door to stop the attacker getting in, and he had stabbed her through the door, which was a good inch thick, which told them something about the weapon used. As he tried to assess the casualty in front of him, that fact didn't bode well for Moses Wilson's heart.

One of the police officers was trying to tug Roberts's arm away. Blood was smeared all over her flower-patterned summer dress, and on the bathroom tiles.

'Michelle, it's me, it's Harry. Where are you hurt?'

She looked up at him with terrified eyes, as if everyone in this room might try to hurt her child. How many knife blows had she taken, refusing steadfastly to move from that door?

She whimpered and said nothing.

'Let me look at you.'

'He tried to kill me,' Michelle said.

That was awful, but it reassured Harry. If she could speak in a full sentence, then she wasn't dying just yet. And whilst there was blood on her dress, it wasn't pouring out of anywhere obvious.

'Where did he hit you, Michelle?' Harry tried, a touch more direct.

'I don't know!'

Harry looked up at the slices hacked out of the door, some of them tinged with red.

'Was your back to the door, or your side?'

'My back,' she said, and pointed, and Harry said, 'I'm going to need to take this off so I can take a look.'

The biggest of the stab wounds had gone into the meat of her deltoid, but it was oozing, and the others, along her face, her back, her buttocks, were glancing blows, cuts, grazes. Quickly, but thoroughly, he checked the areas where a missed injury would kill – neck, thorax, abdomen, pelvis – just like he had done countless times in the back of a Chinook. There was smeared blood, but no critical injuries. In his head he thought of the grey colour of Wilson's lips and his laboured breathing, and how he really needed to be downstairs, with him.

As if on cue, two paramedics arrived, stomping up the stairs behind him.

'You good here?' he called to them.

'Harry!'

It was Noble's voice, from below. He ran. Down the stairs and into the room where Moses Wilson lay, all his colour gone, the dressing he'd applied soaked in red, the paramedic beside him, hands interlinked, performing CPR on his bare, exposed chest.

'He just stopped breathing!' she said. 'Just now!'

Harry's own heart sunk. He knelt by Wilson's head, placed two fingers on where his carotid pulse should be, and looked to see the interventions the paramedic had carried out in the minutes he'd been gone. High-flow oxygen and a plastic oral airway in his mouth, a needle in the ribcage to decompress any trapped air. Shit, Harry thought, shit shit shit. Wilson had died in front of them. He had a penetrating injury to his chest. There was only one course of action that could save him now, and those thoughts slotted into place, logically, like a key into a lock. There was no pulse at his neck. It had to be done.

'Stop doing compressions,' he said. 'Come here.'

The CPR wouldn't work for Wilson, whose heart hadn't stopped because of a heart attack, but for one of two reasons. Either he'd bled to death, which neither Harry nor anyone else could do anything about, or his punctured heart had formed a blood clot so tight it could no longer pump blood out, which he could fix. Harry looked down at his patient. The jugular veins in Wilson's neck were engorged with blood, which made the latter diagnosis more likely. He dumped his bag again, pulling out a yellow packet he had never before opened in anger. He had last checked its contents maybe a month ago, an afterthought.

'You ever seen a thoracotomy before?' he said.

'No,' said the paramedic, unwrapping a chest seal and fixing it over the wound.

'Well you're about to,' he said. 'There's the kit, here. You ready?'

She nodded.

'Let's go, then.'

Harry started with a scalpel, making one hole between the fourth and fifth ribs on Wilson's left side, widening it with his finger, feeling the pop as he went through the pleural lining. Swiftly, he stepped over Wilson and did the same on the other side. It was a rush job, but it had to be. Every second he delayed was a second Wilson's brain was starved of oxygen.

'I need a pair of hands!' he called out. 'Get fresh gloves on!'

The two police officers didn't need telling twice.

Harry cut into the first hole with his scalpel and cut through flesh and muscle, linking it in one straight line with the other. Then he went in with sterile scissors, cutting the muscles in the space between the ribs, east to west, using all his strength to go through Wilson's breastbone.

'Get your hands in there!' he ordered, folding the officers' hands over opposite halves of Wilson's ribcage. 'Now pull them away, like this. Give me space!'

Inside Wilson's chest Harry saw the heart, quivering, tense. He placed his hands around it, pulling it slowly to the centre of the chest, where he could see it better, and lifted up the pericardium, the fibrous bag in which it sat, with his left hand, whilst wielding the scalpel with his right. He'd done this procedure twice before, both times in the A&E Resus at the Ruskin, both times on young men who'd been stabbed in the chest, both times unsuccessfully.

He made the cut into the fibrous tissue, down, and then across, an upside-down T-shape. Then he reached in and felt for the clots, pulling them out, dropping them onto Wilson's belly. The puncture wound was small, but obvious, in the side of the right ventricle. There was fresh blood in the chest cavity, too, now starting to clot as it began to contact the air. More paramedics had arrived, and now Harry was done with the hardest part of the procedure he barked orders.

'Get an IO line in, and an IV!' he shouted. 'Give him 250 of saline!'

Blood was beginning to flow, now the clots were gone, and Harry rested Wilson's heart on his left hand, squeezing it gently with his other, pumping the blood out for him. Around him, the coppers did their best to keep his ribcage open without looking inside. In hospital, they had rib spreaders to do the job, but they were too big and heavy to fit into his pack. Somewhere above them, the noise of an approaching helicopter heralded the arrival of the HEMS team. At least the garden was big enough that they wouldn't have to worry about finding somewhere to land.

On the sixth or the seventh squeeze, Harry felt blood rush against his hand from the puncture wound, and let go. The heart was pumping fast, and struggling, but it was there. But as it restarted, so did the bleeding from the stab wound.

'Suture, now, please!'

The paramedic passed him the needle, and Harry stabilised the heart with one hand, and held his breath as he went in for maybe the most important stitch he'd ever placed. The helicopter was loud now, coming in to land. Maybe he should have waited for them. But maybe if he had, Wilson would be beyond rescue.

He put the stitch in, tied it off and watched. The heart began to beat, again fast, again weak, but there. He grabbed the paramedic's hand and slid it inside Wilson's chest, curling it around the aorta.

'Compress that,' he said. It would keep what blood Wilson had left between his heart and his brain, where it was needed. Harry relaxed and kept pumping and breathed for perhaps the first time in a minute, looking up, taking the bigger picture in. The paramedics had placed a monitor on, which showed an ECG trace, and they'd managed to drill a line into the humerus, too. Harry tried to think of the next steps. The HEMS team would need to get him intubated, and start a blood transfusion too. They'd need an IV line for that, so he got another paramedic to take over the cardiac massage, took a cannula from one of the paramedics and sited it in the jugular vein, still engorged, securing it in with tape. As he finished up, the deafening sound of rotors filled the air, and he looked up to see the red HEMS helicopter touching down in the garden, the downdraft making mincemeat of Michelle Roberts's carefully crafted flowerbeds.

A copper came into the room, one who'd been helping Michelle.

'Jesus Christ,' he said, and vomited behind one of the sofas. Given that Harry had already contaminated the scene by performing open heart surgery, forensics probably didn't matter any more.

'Over here,' another copper said, bringing with her the HEMS team in their orange jumpsuits, through the conservatory door. Harry recognised the doctor, Louise Verger, a consultant anaesthetist at the Ruskin, but he had no time for niceties. He started speaking as he switched with the paramedic, pumping Wilson's heart between his hands.

'He's been stabbed in the left axilla. Cardiac arrest witnessed by LAS, I was here about a minute after. Down-time's less than five. He's got a single wound in the lateral wall of the right ventricle which I've sutured.'

'Bloody hell, Harry. Good work.'

Keep pumping, Harry told himself.

'There was a massive haemothorax, about two litres came out when I opened his chest. We need to fill him.'

The flight paramedic was already there, replacing the fluid bag with a unit of O-negative from the fridge-pack the helicopter carried. Through the IV line in his neck it would get into his heart almost immediately.

'He's got a carotid pulse,' the HEMS paramedic said. Harry pulled his hands out of the chest, watching the dark blood shoot down the tubing and into Wilson's neck. Around him, police officers were covering his legs in blankets to keep him warm. He looked down at the monitor, seeing the furious, fast beating of a heart trying its best to survive.

'Give another unit of O-neg and I'll intubate him,' said Verger, moving around to Wilson's head.

'He's a detective,' said Harry. 'He's a friend.' He didn't know why he said that. Most of the people whose chests the air ambulance staff opened were drug dealers or gang members, and they fought just as hard to save them.

'Ok,' said Verger as the paramedic laid out kit for her. Harry kept looking around for what more he could do. Behind them, a second HEMS doctor had emerged from somewhere.

'We've got a female, late thirties, multiple lacerations. She's got a nasty shoulder lac which I've dressed, but she's haemodynamically stable. LAS can convey.'

'Ok,' said Verger. 'Why don't you go with her, just in case.'

In all the chaos of Wilson dying on him, Harry had completely forgotten about Michelle Roberts. Now a couple of officers were heading out of the house, one holding Preston in her arms, shielding his eyes from the macabre sight before them. Noble was following, and Harry traced her eyes down to Wilson and his open chest, and she had to turn and retch.

'We've got a blood pressure,' said the HEMS paramedic. Harry looked, and saw the monitor. Wilson's heart was pumping by itself, but even that wasn't a guarantee. He helped draw up drugs, clot-protectors, antibiotics, whilst Verger anaesthetised Wilson and put a tube down his throat so they could breathe for him, all the while giving another blood transfusion. The HEMS team were going to drive him to the Ruskin in a ground ambulance – it was too risky to fly someone in such a critical condition.

'You're coming?' said Verger.

Harry looked at Noble, who was giving orders but always staying within sight of her sergeant. Harry had no idea how much time had passed since they'd arrived at the house, nor what had happened in that time. If the attacker had been found, or identified, or got away.

'Go,' Noble told him. 'And call me!'

Harry nodded and headed to the back of the ambulance, pulling off his bloodied gloves and dumping them into a clinical waste bag. As the paramedics got the ambulance trolley out, loaded Wilson on, and closed the doors, Verger went to grab Harry and let him in the side.

'What the hell are you doing here, anyway?' she said.

'Don't ask.'

It was a long time since Harry had seen so many police officers in the Ruskin's A&E department.

Wilson had been taken through already. He'd been ok in the ambulance, though they'd gone through three units of blood trying to maintain his blood pressure. Halfway through, he'd started bleeding from one of his mammary arteries, and they'd had to briefly pull over so that Verger could clip the artery closed. On arrival, they'd been met by a trauma team – anaesthetists, surgeons, specialist nurses who'd given Wilson the once-over before transferring him straight to theatre, where the cardiothoracic team would finish the job Harry had so messily started. Now Verger and Harry stood in the middle of Resus, not doing much. The other HEMS doctor and the paramedic had arrived with

Michelle Roberts, and a second trauma team were dealing with her now. He'd heard that she was stable, and that the worst-case scenario was losing an eye. Both Wilson and Roberts had police escorts, armed with Tasers, in case their attacker decided on a suicide mission to return to the hospital and finish the job.

'He's just arrived in theatre,' a junior anaesthetist said as she ran back to the Resus cubicle to grab Wilson's notes. 'Still with us. For now.'

'Good job out there,' Verger said. 'Not a lot of people would have the balls to do that by themselves.'

Harry said nothing. His senses were still heightened, trying to filter out all the sights and sounds of the A&E department, the other, less unwell patients who'd been unceremoniously abandoned as the doctors had flocked to aid Wilson and Roberts. The curtains were drawn around Roberts's cubicle now, but some of the trauma team were starting to leave, their services unneeded. That was a good sign.

More and more police began to arrive, most asking for Wilson and being told that he was in theatre and they'd send word the moment they knew anything. They asked the obvious question. People wanted numbers, statistics, and whilst Harry knew them, he also knew the docs and nurses wouldn't reveal them. The journals said fifteen per cent of people with Wilson's injury would survive, but that was a useless statistic, because there was only one that mattered to him and his colleagues. A hundred per cent, or zero.

'If I'd known you guys would be so quick, I'd have waited,' Harry said, not sure if it was true. He was seeking validation from a senior, which given the circumstances, he could forgive himself for.

'And if you had, we might not have got him back,' Verger said. 'It was the right call.'

Verger disappeared and Harry felt a wave of exhaustion come over him. With all of the madness of the last – how long was it even? An hour? Two hours? – he hadn't wasted a moment's thought on what this meant for the investigation. He remembered sitting in the corridor at UCL, watching Michelle Roberts on breakfast TV. Someone had seen that, and it had brought them to rage. Enough rage to break down a door, to attempt to murder a police officer, and to try and stab a mother to death in front of her child. The violence he had seen at the Roberts house, apoplexy personified, was undoubtedly the same rage that had been inflicted on Susan Bayliss, and then tempered by the staging as a suicide. But this madness couldn't be so simply that of professionalism, or of cover-up. This was a proper psycho at work.

Two more detectives arrived, this time asking for Harry by name. They were from Homicide & Serious, the MIT that covered Lewisham and Greenwich. They needed a statement, so they sat Harry down in a quiet room – a cup of tea was produced from somewhere – and asked him questions. Harry couldn't answer many. His memory of the whole situation was blurred entirely, jumbled up in time and space. He knew he'd gone up to see Michelle Roberts, maybe once, maybe twice, and that he'd been called down when Wilson had stopped breathing, and from then on he knew nothing. He remembered thinking that the knife had to be fairly long to have penetrated through the door. He couldn't tell them anything about the injuries that they didn't already know.

After the police interview, Harry wandered back into A&E. Verger had gone, been picked up by the HEMS aircraft so they could fly off to their next mission, but she'd left a note for him, saying that she would get in touch with his superiors to commend him and that she'd let him know when the case would be discussed back at the helipad. Harry didn't care about debriefing at the moment. He wanted to find Noble, find out what was being done to catch the person who'd done this. The man – it had to be a man – who'd fled through the garden.

None of the officers in A&E had seen her, so he wandered out to the hospital forecourt, where a number of unmarked cars were pulling up. There was a waiting party of police, beside Grenaghan, the superintendent, and Noble was amongst them. Harry tried to catch her eye, but she was focused on the cars: black BMW saloons. Harry wondered who it was, but found out soon enough. The Assistant Commissioner emerged from one in full uniform, complete with shoulder braiding, surrounded by aides and suits. She too, of course, would be told that Wilson was in theatre, and she couldn't pay a visit, but maybe it was just to show face, show support. In the rear of the echelon, Harry saw a face he'd hoped never to see again, that of DCI Marcus Fairweather, lead for the Professional Standards Directorate.

It made sense. Michelle Roberts had contacted the police with concerns, officers had been dispatched, she'd been reassured, and two hours later someone had tried to murder her in her own house. Of course there would need to be an inquiry, but Harry couldn't help wondering if it could wait until DS Wilson was out of surgery before it started.

Harry leant against the wall of the hospital, his heart still racing, his temples still pounding, his stomach still sick, and it was a while before he realised what he was undergoing. It was no longer the shock of the incident, or the adrenaline rush of the incident, but the familiar feeling of early withdrawal. He listened again to Beth's voicemail, and became all the more determined to stop, and felt all the more ashamed as he snuck back towards his locker to retrieve some pills.

Noble called him as he was coming out of the changing room, and they rendezvoused on the ambulance ramp outside A&E.

'Any word?' she said.

Harry shook his head.

'Don't bullshit me. Will he make it?'

'I don't know. We got to him quickly, didn't we?'

'I guess.'

'How are you?' Harry asked. A human, genuine question. She was almost shaking too, and static crackled on the radio.

'Been better,' she said. 'We think he was already inside when Mo turned up. He wasn't expecting to be interrupted so quickly. Mo surprised him, took the door down, he took Mo out and fled out into the garden and cut into the park. Mo probably saved their lives.'

'I'm sure he did,' said Harry. 'Did you get him?'

Noble threw her cigarette butt on the ground and stamped on it.

'No,' she said. 'We did a ground and air search of the park, but found nothing matching the description. All Michelle could give us was clothes. No ethnicity, no height or build. She saw him running from the bathroom window. There's no fucking CCTV in the vicinity, no vehicles making away at speed, fucking nothing.'

'Are you still looking?'

'It's not me,' Noble said. 'We just had that chat now, with Grenaghan. Greenwich are leading the manhunt, they're gonna have the Incident Room open for twenty-four hours. He's taking over the Bayliss investigation, with me as deputy SIO.'

Harry didn't know whether she was pissed off, relieved, or both, so he said nothing.

'What now?'

'Christ knows,' said Noble. 'There's a meeting at six, at Peckham. You've got blood on your shirt, Harry.'

It was starting to rain again, spits of water.

'Shit, I'll go change.'

'This has fucked it all up,' Noble said., 'I thought we were getting somewhere. Shit. It's gotta be connected to Roberts going on TV this morning. Someone saw that and fucking snapped.'

'What was Roberts saying?'

He remembered watching it on the way to meet Utting, but had forgotten the detail. Which seemed reasonable given the circumstances.

'That the hospital were refusing to investigate her child's death, and they were covering up three more who'd been operated on by the same surgeon. That they'd threatened the police and were refusing to cooperate with the investigation into Bayliss's death, and that they'd hounded Bayliss out for giving information to them about their own children.'

'None of that's untrue,' said Harry. 'Did she mention Belgrave? Mohamed?'

'Not Mr Mohamed,' said Noble. 'But one or two of the news articles ID'd him as the surgeon.'

They paused for a while.

'Do you think he's got that faulty wiring? To react like that to someone slandering his name?' Harry said. He didn't himself, but at the moment the pool of suspects seemed vanishingly thin.

'I don't know. But he's in our sights at the moment. Whoever it is, we're gonna find them and put them away.'

'What can I do to help?' Harry asked.

Noble finished her cigarette and scrolled through her phone. She'd received at least ten texts during their conversation, and right at that moment Harry did not envy her one bit. Right now, the only thing stopping him from going home and sleeping was himself.

'Once Michelle Roberts's statement has been taken, we could do with a documentation of her injuries, for Forensics. I was going to call the duty FME, but if you're here . . .?'

'I'll get it done,' Harry said. 'You'll need someone to bring my car over.'

They started to head back into the main hospital, but, still sheltered from the crowds, Harry fought off the urge to hold her, to tell her everything was going to be ok, that she'd do fine. Instead he just said, 'I'll tell you when I know anything.'

'You better had.'

'Good luck, Frankie.'

Her phone rang, she picked it up, and headed off.

Michelle Roberts was upstairs at the Ruskin, on the oral and maxillofacial surgery ward. When Harry arrived, she was still being seen by the detectives from Greenwich, so he sat at a computer and brought up her notes. The more major injuries, to her shoulder and lower back, were purely muscular, as he'd suspected, and the trauma surgeons thought these would heal without needing an operation. One of the facial injuries was more serious though, and Harry got a good idea of it as he read the report of her CT scan. The knife had gone into her right eye socket, causing a blood clot that had had to be drained with a needle under local anaesthetic. The eye surgeons were reviewing her too, and it had been decided to keep her in overnight for observation.

When Harry had finished reading, he picked up the phone and called down to the surgical ICU.

'Hi, can I speak to one of the doctors, please?'

'Who is this?'

'Harry Kent. A&E reg.'

He used to work on the ICU, so he knew most of the doctors. The one who picked up was Ali Hussein, a former colleague.

'Afternoon, Dr Kent. Are you sure your first name's not Clark?'

'I'm sorry?'

'As in Clark Kent? Superman?'

'I'm not following.'

'How about this then, Harry? Did you have your red under-pants and your cape on when you cracked that copper's chest open this afternoon? What was it, Harry, FCEM revision too boring for you, eh?'

'Very funny,' Harry said. 'How is he?'

'He's stable,' Hussein said. 'We got him about half an hour ago. They had to shock him once or twice in theatre, when they were repairing the wound, but other than that he's been good. Lactate's reasonable, pH is ok, too. Cautiously optimistic.'

ICU doctors always were optimistic, despite the fact a quarter of their patients didn't survive the admission.

'You've got my number, don't you?' Harry said. 'Let me know if anything changes.'

'Of course. And bloody good job, mate.'

'Thanks.'

The two detectives left Roberts's room, nodding to the two uniformed officers who'd been assigned to protection duty, both with Tasers ostentatiously displayed on their belts.

One of the detectives approached Harry. 'You the doc who worked on Mo at the scene?'

He nodded. They patted him on the shoulders.

'Owe you one, pal. You ever need someone nicking round Greenwich, let us know.'

Harry approached Roberts's side-room, flashing his ID card to the police guards. He'd changed into spare clothes and taken his forensic kit from his car. The officers signed him in, and Harry entered the room.

'Hi, Michelle.'

Roberts had her knees up to her chest in the hospital gown, wound dressings visible across her right shoulder and the right side of her face, the cheek, the scalp. A big gauze pad lay over the under-side of her right eye, which was swollen and purple, like a boxer's. A centimetre higher and she might well have lost the eye. At the house, Harry hadn't appreciated the facial injuries. They had no chance of killing her, so she hadn't been a priority. But now he could see the extent of the trauma, and pictured her, holding the door shut with her shoulder, all of her weight in it, and he felt cold.

There was a plain-clothes copper with her, one of the family liaison officers, who sat cross-legged on a chair at the head of the bed. Michelle looked up slowly at the new arrival, bloodstained tears seeping from her injured eye. He couldn't stop himself from reviewing the charts at the end of the bed. Observations stable. Drugs, a few: co-codamol, co-amoxiclav, methotrexate, gabapentin, amitryptiline. The last few made him think, until he remembered she had rheumatoid.

'Hi,' Harry repeated.

She looked up.

'Harry!' Michelle said. 'You were at the house, weren't you?'

He wasn't surprised that she was unsure, given what she'd been through.

'Yes, I was.' He gestured to the end of the bed. 'Can I sit down?'

Michelle nodded and sobbed a little and reached over, and her eyes pleaded.

'I told you they were out to get us. You believed me. Why didn't they?'

The FLO stood up and came over, speaking in a low voice.

'She was all over the place with the Homicide & Serious lot,' she said. 'Wailing and screaming, the poor thing. I think the doctors gave her something to calm her down.'

Harry took Michelle by the hand. 'They did,' he said. 'That's why Mo – sorry, DS Wilson – was there so quickly. DI Noble had him on stand-by around the corner.'

'Did he save my life?'

'Probably. We think he confronted the attacker and prompted him to flee.'

Roberts cried again, and Harry rubbed her back. He had met this woman only a few days ago and now felt a sense of responsibility for her. He wondered if he could have done anything to prevent the brutal attack which had almost killed her, if he could somehow have persuaded Noble to take her theory more seriously.

'When can I see Preston?'

'As soon as we can,' the FLO said. 'He's on his way over from the hospital now.'

'Make sure it's not the Belgrave!' Michelle whimpered.

'Don't worry, love, he's at Lewisham General. There was a bit of a mix-up.'

The FLO, whose name was Connie, took Harry aside and explained. In all of the confusion, the Greenwich detectives had taken Preston to the local hospital for a check-up, without realising the paramedics were bringing his mother to the Ruskin. Euan, her husband, had been contacted in Dubai, where his flight had stopped over, and was now on a plane back towards London. Normally, they would try and arrange for Roberts to be with her family, but they all lived in Scotland and were not much in contact anyway.

'We're bringing Preston over as soon as we can. Should be here in half an hour.'

'I want him.'

'He's coming,' Connie said. 'The doctor needs to write down all of your injuries. You know him, don't you?'

'Yes.' She looked at Harry then at Connie. 'He helped me. He believed me. He was the first one who believed me that someone wanted me and Susan shut up, and look what's happened now.'

'I'm sorry I couldn't help you more,' Harry said.

'Don't worry,' said Roberts. 'The other parents, are they in danger? Will they—'

'They're under police protection too,' Connie said.

'Ok,' said Harry. 'I just need to record all your injuries. It won't take long, I promise. If you've any questions, just ask me to stop.'

'Ok.'

Sometimes, if the patients consented, Harry did this with a dictaphone, recording his description of the injuries as he photographed them, but with Roberts in the state she was in he thought it best to use the old-fashioned way of writing it down. He moved thoroughly, head to toe, removing the dressings where appropriate and describing each in cold, scientific prose. *Laceration in right zygomatic region, direction supero-medially (2 o'clock as viewed from AP), 67mm x 4mm. Correlated with CT scan report of orbital injury and associated haematoma.* Then, he held a ruler up in front of the injury and photographed it with a compact camera. This he repeated for each stab wound, the one to her cheek, five or six to her shoulder, other glancing blows to her back, two on the upper part of her right buttock. In all, Harry documented fourteen separate injuries, without counting the abrasions and splinter cuts all over her right-hand side.

'That's it,' said Harry. 'All done.'

He wasn't processing it, of course. There wasn't space in his brain. It was just action, input and output.

'How's the police officer?' Roberts asked.

'He's in intensive care,' said Connie.

'Does he remember who it was? Can he describe him?'

Connie mumbled something and Harry said, 'Umm, he's not able to talk just yet.'

'God, I wish I'd seen his face,' Roberts said. 'I wish I'd seen him. D'you think it was him? Mr Mohamed? It could have been, y'know, the more I think about it . . .'

Connie leant onto the bed and took Roberts by the hand, and Harry awkwardly backed away, replacing his equipment in the bag.

'Don't think about it. That's our job, ok, Michelle. You concentrate on getting better.'

There was a knock on the door, and as Connie moved to open it, Harry felt the veil of sleep descending, the familiar exhaustion. His eyes closed, and he worried for a second he might collapse. Two detectives came in, smiles on their faces, one holding Preston's hand. He too was grinning from ear to ear, a Fruit Shoot in one hand, blissfully unaware that he had spent ten minutes that afternoon hiding in a bathtub while his mother shielded him with her own body against some murderous psychopath.

He ran onto the bed, into his mother's arms, and the sound of crying as Harry exited the room was a joyous one.

Harry felt cold as he stepped into the lift, bustling with patients, relatives and staff, heading down towards the main hospital corridor. He hadn't eaten all day, and he was starving. So much had happened it was difficult to process. There was Beth, there was Cameron and his news about the man who'd known Zara, and then there was the madness of the afternoon.

He wandered aimlessly through the hospital canteen, unable to bring himself to search the grey hot food vats or the flat-packed sandwiches for something to eat. After some time had passed he found himself outside the doctors' mess, staring aimlessly at his phone, not knowing who to call or what to say. And then he finally broke and put his head against the wall and cried for a while. Just sobs and shakes, the defeated quivers of a man who had reached his breaking point. It was five o'clock on a Wednesday. Someone would find him soon.

'Harry, is that you? Are you alright?'

He looked up, and though most of what he could see was flashing light, he made out Amy Floyd's face.

'What's happened, Harry? Whatever's the matter?'

'I can't sleep,' Harry said.

'You look awful.'

'I need to sleep.'

'Ok,' Floyd said. She took him by the arm, and led him out to the corridor that led to the on-call rooms. He was vaguely aware of her fighting with the administrator, getting the keys. Images were passing in front of his eyes: Wilson with his chest open, Bayliss in a pool of blood, the pathologist in his white coat, Beth's face, twisted in anger. Floyd back now.

'I've got you a room, pet, c'mon.'

She opened the on-call room, the prison cell, and sunk Harry into the bed, resting his forensic bag on the floor. And then she shut and locked the door, and he was on his back on the bed, his arms above his head, and Floyd was taking off his shirt, and then she was kissing him, and then they were naked on the bed entwined, and she was forcing him inside her, her scrubs drenched in sweat, her tongue inside his mouth, and then he opened his eyes and she was there but with the face of Susan Bayliss, and he looked down and saw her elbows and wrists and there were the wounds, black congealed blood draining out onto the bed and the floor.

He opened his eyes again, and she was gone, and Floyd was back, or was it another face? Was it Frankie, with those pleading, scared eyes that only he could really see?

Some time later it all faded away.

SEVEN

Wednesday, 27 August
Night

Harry woke up to the drilling sound of his vibrating phone on the table by the bed.

'Hello?'

It was Noble.

'You alright, Harry? You haven't answered my texts.'

The windowless room was completely dark, just a line of light coming in through the door. Harry stretched and clicked his neck and looked at his phone. It was coming up to half-nine.

'Shit. Sorry. I fell asleep.'

'Right,' said Noble. 'I was just waiting on that report about Michelle Roberts's injuries.'

'Yeah,' said Harry. 'When do you need it?'

'Not soon, you can do it tomorrow. But gimme a headline or something.'

'Sure,' said Harry. He scrabbled around for a light switch, trying to clear the fog in his memory. Hearing Noble's voice brought up an unpleasant feeling, and it took him a while to remember the nightmare from last night. His scrub bottoms were sticky and warm. The dreams were getting worse. This had to stop.

'She had fourteen separate injuries, mostly right-sided. The wound morphology suggests a long, thin instrument – jagged edges, probably not a kitchen knife. Stiletto knife, perhaps, or a screwdriver, an awl, something like that. That'd fit.'

'Forensics said something similar based on the marks in the door,' Noble said. 'A screwdriver. They think that's how he got in, and it was Mo who kicked the door down. Interesting he used it as a weapon, too. Just wanted to check that. Cheers.'

'How's it all going?' Harry said. He eventually found the light and switched it on. It blinded him.

'Back to the start, really. We're no longer convinced this is a cover-up, but someone who's been angered by what Bayliss and Roberts were saying. The level of violence, it has to be someone who's unhinged, maybe even psychotic. There was some restraint in the Bayliss killing, but this is mental, so whoever it is, he's getting worse. So we're going through all the cardiothoracic staff at

263

Belgrave, looking for any of them with criminal records, or histories of mental instability. We're looking at former patients, parents of patients, anyone who might have an over-valued sense of loyalty to Mohamed or the hospital and be willing to defend its reputation with violence. This offender's got to have a history, either criminal conviction or psychiatric treatment.'

It made sense. The killer's actions were becoming less and less rational, which pointed towards somebody mentally unstable. Which limited an investigation that was light on forensic evidence and heavy on motive, as the motive might only make sense to the offender.

'How you feeling about the case going to Grenaghan?'

'It's attempted murder of a police officer,' Noble said. 'It's going to go upstairs, and I'm glad for it. Grenaghan can ring up the AC and get whatever resources he wants. I can't.'

'Ok,' said Harry. 'What are your plans for tomorrow?'

'Why, what are yours?'

'Helping out in any way I can,' said Harry.

'I'll let you know. Between you and me, it's looking like we're bringing in Mohamed for questioning. It might be good to have you there.'

'Ok. I'm working the night shift tomorrow, so you've got me until six.'

'Great,' said Noble. 'Don't you need to sleep?'

'I'll think of something,' said Harry.

'Any news on Mo?'

'Not yet. You'll be the first to know.'

'Good. 'Night, Harry.'

Harry managed to find clean scrubs – putting the ones he'd messed in the bin, not the laundry basket – and went to his locker to get changed, then up to the ICU, where there had been no change in Wilson's condition. His chest had been closed with a long series of staples, and it would be an ugly scar. If he survived, he could say goodbye to any sideline as a topless model, that was for sure. A bag of platelets was running in, to help his clotting, and a drain took blood and fluid out of his chest. Harry got out of the ward before Dr Hossein could make any more bad jokes, went out and hailed a taxi to Peckham Police Station. He looked up and saw the lights on the first floor, the Incident Room working overtime, the car park full. He would have to find out where his medical kit had ended up. With luck, someone would have picked it up.

He took one pill on the drive down to Kingston, just to avoid a repeat of the other night's mishap, and to keep him awake whilst he waited in the drive-thru McDonald's in Streatham for his first meal of the day. He ate two large Big Mac meals, one after the other, trying to work out all of the calories that he must have lost during his attempts at resuscitating Wilson, and the rest of the chaos. And he thought about what Noble had said, about the state of mind of the person they were looking for. He spent maybe fifteen minutes digesting the carbo-hydrates and thinking about that, picturing all the people they'd met so far, screwdriver in hand, hacking through the bathroom door in Michelle Roberts's house. Elyas Mohamed. Theo Padmore. Noah Skelton, perhaps. Even Alison Price, the overweight manager. That one he couldn't imagine, but stranger things had happened.

He got to Marigold House a little after ten-thirty. It was a fairer evening than the last time he'd been down, though black clouds still formed a layer across the night sky. Sweat clung to Harry's clothes as he got out of the car, and he was aware of his own smell – the clothes weren't clean, but they were all he had in his hospital locker. There was a shower at Marigold House he could use if need be.

When he got to Tammas's room, he moved to open the handle without knocking, as was his habit, but through the small window in the door he could see another figure, a squat Asian woman in a woollen jumper. He had never seen the woman before. There were few staff at Marigold House, and he knew all of them by face and name, or at least he thought he did. He knocked, and one of the duty nurses he knew well, Sandra, opened the door.

'Oh, evenin', Harry. We wasn't expecting you.'

'I can come back if it's not convenient.'

'No, it's no problem,' Sandra said. 'This is Dr Agrawal, one of our doctors.'

'Hello,' Agrawal said. This made Harry concerned. Marigold House was nurse-run and nurse-led, with most of the actual day-to-day done by care assistants. Doctors were only called in out-of-hours if residents were really unwell.

'Is that. You. Harry?' Tammas said. His voice was strained but strong.

'Yeah, it's me, boss. You're throwing quite the party, eh?'

'There's blood. In my piss. Apparently. They're just. Making. A fuss.'

'Are you Peter's son?' Agrawal asked.

Harry had got that question before. Though Tammas was only fifteen years or so older than him, the injury had aged him somewhat. Atrophy the mimic of time.

'No, I'm an old friend.'

'Ok,' said Agrawal. 'We're going to send urine and blood samples to the hospital to see if we can find out what's causing this infection. I've given him some stronger antibiotics by injection as well.'

'Took her. Bloody ages. To get a line. In. And it's only. A wee. Blue one. Bloody GPs.' He gave a rattling laugh. 'You know. What they say. Bottom half. Of medical school. Has to get a job. Somewhere.'

'Don't listen to him,' Harry whispered. 'He's like this with everyone.'

'So I've heard . . . Anyway, we'll have to watch him fairly carefully. I'm going to swing by tomorrow morning, and I've got the nurses to put him on two-hourly observations.'

Sandra smiled, although Harry knew that she'd secretly be cursing the task. It meant getting up every other hour throughout the night to take Tammas's pulse, blood pressure, temperature. It was a necessary effort though – being bedridden and dependent on a ventilator, it would only take a small insult to send him over the edge.

'If it doesn't get better, we'll have to get you over to hospital.'

'I'm not. Going. To bloody hospital.'

Agrawal said nothing, and Harry thought it wise not to intervene. They would cross that bridge when they came to it. The nurse took another round of observations, and Harry tapped his feet, waiting for the rigmarole to be over. He chanced a look at Tammas's notes, but was spotted, which gave rise to another spluttering rant, interrupted by his ventilator.

'Don't you. Bloody. Dare. Look at that. Harry. Who. The bloody. Hell do you. Think. You Are.'

'I'm just looking out for you, boss.'

'If I want. You. To look out for. Me. I'll bloody. Ask you.'

'Ok. Sorry.'

After that, they hurried out and left Harry to it.

266

'Sorry. Harry,' Tammas said. 'Catheter. Infection. Makes me feel. Like a. Ninety-seven. Year-old. Woman.'

'It's alright.'

'How're things?'

'I think I might have fucked up.'

'This'll. Be. A long one, then?'

'I'll do my best . . .'

'In that case. Get me some. Of that Talisker.'

Harry glanced across at the door and then at the cabinet.

'Oh. For fuck's sake. If you can. Think of. A single. Physiological. Reason why I. Can't have—'

'Alright, alright . . .' Harry said, pouring a measure out. Fuck it, one for him as well.

They sat in silence for a while. Harry looked at his old friend, trying to gauge his condition. This was one of a doctor's most vital skills, to look at a patient and, from a variety of subtle cues – their colour, the sweatiness of their palms, the way they breathed, the size of their pupils – make an immediate, subconscious decision as to how sick they were. Harry was fairly adept at it with strangers, but to look at Tammas, a man he'd known for fifteen years, and do the same proved impossible.

'You. Didn't drive all. This way for. Whisky,' Tammas said.

So Harry talked. He told him about the attack on Michelle Roberts, how he'd been to see her the evening before, and was now thoroughly embedded in a major police investigation. About the emergency thoracotomy, which Tammas had taught him to do, and how that might well have saved Wilson's life.

'Sounds like a good. Day's work,' Tammas said.

Harry detected no hint of pride and had expected none. He had instilled in Harry that nothing about medicine should be heroic – just the recognition of pathology and the provision of the appropriate treatment. He would have approved in this case for that reason alone.

'What are. You really here. To talk about?'

'The pills. It's got a bit out of hand.'

'Has. It really?'

Harry nodded silently. He took the last of his whisky and went to wash the tumbler out, lest he be tempted by another.

'Ever heard. Of. Eric Moody?'

Harry shook his head.

'British Airways. Pilot,' Tammas said. 'He took. A 747 through an. Ash cloud in. Indonesia. Lost power. To all the. Engines. Addressed the. Passengers and said. We have a small problem. All. Four engines have. Stopped. We're doing. Our best to. Start them. I trust. You are not. In too much distress.'

'Jesus,' said Harry.

'It won. An award. For the understatement. Of the century.'

'Right . . .'

'But I think you. Might be. In contention for the crown. If you think. Your pills. Are a little. Out of hand.'

Harry didn't feel like laughing, although a wide grin had spread across Tammas's pallid face.

'How many. Are you taking?'

'Ten a day, at least,' Harry said. Head in hands. Tammas was the only person he could admit this to, and even then he couldn't look him in the eye. It was as if saying it out loud made it real.

'Five milligrams?'

'Ten.'

'Jesus. Christ. Are you still. Getting them. Off the internet?'

'Mostly. I had to, umm, get some from the pharmacy the other day. I ran out, I fell asleep at the wheel . . . It was an emergency.'

'You. Self-prescribed?'

'No, well, I. I prescribed them in your name.'

'How. Fucking. Dare you.'

'I'm sorry.'

'You stupid. Bastard. Harry. I'm not. Giving you. A bloody character. Reference. When you're at. The GMC. I'll sell you. Up the fucking. River.'

Tongue-in-cheek as it was, that hurt him. Two Januarys ago, when his friend James had been murdered, the police had briefly suspected Harry of being responsible. They had visited Tammas, who had told him that Harry had always been a little jealous of James, and was short-tempered, and had had an affair with James's wife, which had caused them to narrow their focus quite considerably. Harry would ordinarily have struggled to forgive his boss for that, had everything he'd said not been true.

'Have you had. Any chest pains?'

'Occasionally.'

'Paranoia?'

'Shut up, boss. I know the risks. I know what to look out for.'

'Physically. Maybe. But how will you know. If you're. Going mad?'

'I'm gonna get this sorted.'

'How?'

'Beth's parents have a cottage in Norfolk. She's been trying to get us to go there for a weekend for ages. I'm going to cut down the rest of this week, then we'll go there and I'll withdraw. She'll look after me.'

'And. Then what?'

Three words which were so beyond Harry's comprehension that he just stared at the window for a while, then at the paintings of glens and mountains that adorned Tammas's room.

'I don't know.'

'Why. Not go tomorrow?'

'I'm working tomorrow night. Night shift, Resus.'

He didn't mention the stuff about the investigation. If Noble called and said she needed his help, to re-interview Mohamed or anything to do with the hospital, he would be there like a shot. It was not up for debate, so Harry saw no point in bringing it up and letting Tammas try and dissuade him from it. He didn't entirely understand himself why he had to act, why he couldn't just leave the whole thing alone, so there was little hope of Tammas doing so.

'Right. Just remember. This is not in. Isolation. You might give these. Pills up. But then. You have to look. At your life. Because work. Will still be there. Zara. She'll still be there. Too. Unless she's woken up. And told you. Her post code. And her favourite movie. And that it. Was Professor Plum. In the library. With the. Candlestick.'

'That's not funny.'

'Maybe not. But it's true. This is. A response to. A force. Acting on you. It's not. Just random. You won't. Be sorted. Unless you find. Out what that is.'

He prepared the defences, but before any of them reached his lips another part of his brain interjected with the rebuttals. He could say that the pills were only because he was working two jobs with conflicting hours, with the police and with A&E, but of course the only reason he did so much with the police was in the hope of recruiting more interested parties to deal with his private obsession about the nameless young girl. Or he could argue that everyone had their breaking point, that certain things could break any man, fall into the asinine trap of blaming his upbringing, his absent father, or his alcoholic mother. That would be an utter betrayal. The only reason Harry was where was he was today was because he had decided for himself that where he came from would be a part of him, but would never define him. The man who had made him realise that was lying in front of him now, ventilated and still. And perhaps he was teaching him the same thing. The forces acting upon him could not be changed, but his reaction to them could.

'I'm hot,' Tammas said.

Harry leant over and felt his brow. It was feverish.

'Do you want me to get the nurse?'

'No. There are. Some ice cubes. In the freezer. Get a couple. Would you.'

Harry went over to the freezer and opened it and put the ice cubes in a plastic cup.

'Do you want me to pop them in your mouth?'

'No. Leave them. In the cup.'

'But how are you going to—'

'Now pour in. The whisky. About a quarter. Full. There's. A good boy.'

Harry laughed and poured it in, but he only barely covered the cubes. He was worried about this infection. As the GP had said, it was a fine line from how sick he was to needing hospital admission, and with Tammas's spinal injury, diagnosis was much trickier. His kidney infection might cause raging pain in the average person, but he would have no idea.

Tammas dimmed the lights by voice command and Harry moved to the armchair by the window.

'You're. Staying, then?'

Harry nodded.

'Feel free to come over here and kick me out if that's not cool.'

'Piss off. Goodnight.'

Silence and pumping air for a few minutes, then Harry asked, 'Did that pilot land the plane?'

'Of course he. Did. No-one would think. Him a hero. If he hadn't.'

EIGHT

Thursday, 28 August
Early Morning

Noble thought that raids like this were always better if they were done at dawn. It meant getting everyone down to Sevenoaks for five in the morning, but it wasn't just for the atmosphere. Circumstances had forced their hand. The decision had been made at about midnight, and a quick phone call to Belgrave had informed them that Mr Mohamed was scheduled to begin his clinic at eight o'clock that morning. So the plan had been drawn up. Grenaghan had called a magistrate he played golf with for a midnight warrant, and a team of detectives had volunteered for night duty and worked through to the wee hours to get the paper-work in order. Noble had been delegated to lead the search, so she had been given permission to sleep. She had done so for about four hours on the floor of her office, and now sat bleary-eyed in the passenger seat of her car, sipping coffee from a takeaway mug. As they were out of jurisdiction, they had a uniform sergeant and her mate from Kent Police just to keep an eye out. Fortunately, they had made themselves useful by doing a coffee run.

'I still think we should've hard-stopped him on the A2,' McGovern said, 'That'd scare the living shite out of him.'

Noble grinned.

'Yeah, tempting, isn't it?'

Noble knew full well that her colleague understood why they had to be sitting here at six in the morning in the commuter belt. The attempted murder of a police officer and the attack on Michelle Roberts had been the third story on the ten o'clock news yesterday, after drowning refugees and war in Ukraine. Even the BBC reported that police 'had not yet confirmed a link with the ongoing investigation into the death last weekend of Susan Bayliss, formerly a doctor at Belgrave Hospital in London, where the alleged target of the attack's daughter had been treated.' Apparently, the tabloids were showing no such restraint, with headlines like *Grieving mother attacked by knifeman – HOURS after accusing hospital doctors on TV.*

With that kind of media attention, searching and questioning Mohamed during working hours at the hospital or in any kind of public place was a bad idea. As antisocial as it was, doing the search and picking up Mohamed whilst he was still at home was the best way to reduce the risk of pouring more petrol on the flames. Indeed, apart from the locals, they were all in unmarked cars. The search team were in a van parked in a retail park back in Sevenoaks, waiting for the call to arrive, as all the laybys along the country road off which Mohamed's house lay were now taken.

'D'you think he did it?'

'I don't know,' Noble said. 'I always thought his arrogance was just overcompensating. Like we said at the briefing, whoever did this is properly enraged by what Roberts and Bayliss were saying. He restrained himself with the first one, but now he's gone proper psycho. If he did lose it yesterday, then when we push him he'll probably blow a gasket again. And then he's ours.'

'I like the sound of that, guv,' McGovern said.

But both of them knew this was wishful thinking. The silver bullet that had made their decision and got them the warrant had come from some good old-fashioned police work late last night. Grenaghan had ordered that all known persons of interest in the investigation had their vehicle registrations checked and cross-referenced with the network of Automatic Number Plate Recognition cameras situated around London. Mohamed's had been one of the first to be checked. His X5 had been spotted several times, apparently driving from Sevenoaks towards Greenwich at lunchtime. It had been pinged eastbound on Nelson Road, the northern border of Greenwich Park, at 14:42, half an hour before the attack on Roberts. No more pings until 15:56, when the car was spotted going southbound on Tunnel Approach, then back along the A2, and presumably all the way back to the sleepy hamlet of Ide Hill. Gableview, the house was called.

They had a man with a motive who was in the area of the attempted murder during the time of the attack. According to Grenaghan, the magistrate had needed no persuading whatsoever.

'Lights are on upstairs,' DC Bhalla said over the radio. He and DC Wilders were positioned at the end of Mohamed's driveway with their headlights off, a pair of binoculars each.

'Let me know when they're on downstairs,' Noble said.

Five minutes later, they were. The sun was just appearing, low and orange above the oaks and conifers to one side of the driveway. As they approached, she got an idea of the size of the house. It had to be worth more than a million, but she guessed heart surgeons had little trouble getting mortgages.

They stopped at a black electric gate set into thick hedgerows, in convoy. She and McGovern first, Bhalla and Wilders behind, and then the local uniforms. The search team were on their way. She got out of the car, looking through the bars of the gate, seeing the lights on in what looked to be the kitchen. Mohamed had a separate garage near the gate, and there was a swimming pool in the background. Noble reminded herself to search the cars quickly once they'd gone in. She kept her finger down on the bell for a long time, seeing her own face in the screen of the intercom. It took maybe a minute for a tired, gruff voice to respond.

'Hello?'

'Elyas Mohamed?'

'Oh, God.'

Noble assumed he had recognised her.

'It's Acting Detective Chief Inspector Noble, Metropolitan Police. We have a warrant to search this address. We'd also like you to accompany us to London for questioning.'

'You do know I have a clinic this morning?' Mohamed said. 'Eighteen children with families travelling from all over the South of England. You do know how much disruption it'll cause, to cancel that at such short notice?'

'We've informed the hospital.' Noble lied. Someone had been tasked with letting the odious Mrs Price know they were picking Mohamed up, but she didn't really care if it happened or not.

'Am I under arrest?' said Mohamed.

'Shall we discuss this inside, Mr Mohamed?'

There was a buzz and the gates began to open. Noble got back inside the car and McGovern drove them through, serenaded by birdsong and the sounds of their convoy crunching on gravel.

When she knocked, Mohamed opened it on a chain. He was half-shaven, wet haired, and in a hastily buttoned Lacoste shirt.

'I've just called my lawyer,' he said. 'I want to see this warrant.'

Noble rolled her eyes. The rest of them had lined up behind her, holding boxes of gloves and evidence bags.

'It's in the car. Do you think we'd have come all the way down here without one?'

Mohamed said nothing. McGovern passed the warrant to her, and simply showing him the name and address on the front page was enough. He shook his head as he opened the door.

'Please be quiet, my family are asleep upstairs.'

'We'll do our best,' Noble said. 'I'd advise you to take a seat whilst we conduct the search. We'll do upstairs last of all.'

'The whole house?' Mohamed said.

'Yes, the whole house. And the other buildings, and your vehicles. And the contents of any computers or other devices present at this address.'

'This is ridiculous. This is harassment!' Mohamed said to no-one in particular as he retreated into the kitchen and sat down at the table, head in his hands. Quickly, the team set about divvying up the search – they would do his office and the cars first, as they were on the ground floor and unlikely to wake Mohamed's children, and most likely to yield useful information. Noble gave the two DCs assigned to that task specific instructions to check SatNav devices or smartphones closely for recent journeys made. She wasn't expecting Roberts's address to be saved, but if he'd kept his location services switched on on his smartphone, then Technical could very easily trace that and put him at the crime scene. McGovern would stay and supervise the search once the team arrived, with Noble and Bhalla driving Mohamed back to Peckham.

As they were spreading out, Mohamed's wife arrived, wrapped in a dressing gown.

'What's going on?' she said. 'Who are these people?'

'The police,' said Mohamed. 'They want to take me in for questioning.'

'Have you called Shad?'

'Of course. He's on his way.'

Noble presumed that was the solicitor. Mrs Mohamed turned to her with pleading eyes.

'He's done nothing wrong. That viper tried to destroy his career. She was troubled, you should—'

'Shut up, Penny.'

She did so, and went over to her husband, but then turned back to Noble.

'It's six-thirty in the morning!'

'I'm sorry for the inconvenience.' said Noble.

'Take the kids to school early, drop them at the breakfast club,' Mohamed said. 'Then go to your sister's or something. Or Tanya's. I'll be back as soon as I can.'

'You're going with them, then?' said Penny. 'Do you have to?'

'Good question,' said Mohamed, turning on Noble. They looked like a Rembrandt portrait, he in the high-backed wooden chair and she at his shoulder.

'We intend to interview you under caution. This means you would be attending voluntarily, but with the same rights as someone who was under arrest. However you would be free to leave at any time.'

'And if I choose not to come?' said Mohamed.

'Then I'll arrest you,' said Noble.

'You can't do that!' Penny cried. 'You don't have any evidence!'

'They have a warrant,' Mohamed said, before turning to Noble. 'Not really voluntary, is it?'

That was strange, and got her excited. She'd expected him to put up more of a fight, but he didn't. Maybe because he knew she had something, because he was guilty. And he didn't want to find out what they had on him in front of his wife. There was anger behind his soapstone eyes, and she could see that it was driven by the humiliation of the search. Not for the first time, she wondered if that anger could be magnified to the rage which had nearly killed Moses Wilson and Michelle Roberts.

'May I go upstairs to get dressed and finish shaving?' Mohamed said.

'I'm afraid I must ask that someone escorts you. I hope you understand.'

Noble nodded to DC Bhalla. Mohamed shook his head repeatedly as he stood.

'You've got it all wrong,' he muttered as he headed out, Penny in tow.

'What do you think he meant by that?' McGovern whispered once he was gone.

'I'm sure we'll find out,' said Noble.

Harry woke up next to a still-sleeping Tammas, drove home and slept for another few hours. Then he showered, shaved, put on a fresh, ironed shirt, and took a pill. Just one. He would try and just take seven today, eight maximum.

He had a missed call from Noble, so he returned it.

'How's it going?'

'Ok. I've just spent an hour watching my two best room-guys give Elyas Mohamed a bashing.'

'You picked him up?' Harry said.

'Yeah,' said Noble. Quickly, she explained to him Mohamed's car's movements on CCTV, and the search of his house. It sounded fairly convincing, but it was going to require some pretty heavy evidence to begin convincing Harry that Mohamed, cocksure as he was, was capable of the brutal crimes they were investigating.

'Anything on him yet?' said Harry.

'No. We've swabbed him for DNA. He says he's never been to the Bayliss flat, so if we find him there, we've got him, but that'll take days to come back. He's answered no-comment to every other question, the slimy bastard. Roberts is in no state to give an ID – she can't remember seeing a thing, Wilson's still in a coma. I need some bloody leverage.'

'Hmm,' said Harry. In the shower, his mind had been going over the case meeting, the one where they'd discussed the plan to go over everyone from the cardiac department at the Belgrave, and then he'd thought about their very first trip to the hospital. There was a thread left unsewn.

'What?'

'Your interviews. Have you spoken to Theo Padmore again yet?'

'No. Do you think we should?'

'I still think he was holding something back when we spoke to him on Monday,' Harry said. 'In fact, I was thinking of going over there myself, see if I could get through to him. Doctor to doctor, you know.'

There was quiet on the end of the phone for a while.

'Frankie?'

'What the hell are you waiting for? I'm not the SIO anymore, I can't authorise you. I'm not saying don't do it, but you're on your own.'

He wasn't sure. Going by himself was completely against protocol, but he was too far in to back out now, and he had a good friend in hospital and the chance to help find the man who put him there.

He hung up then called the ICU at the Ruskin again. No change in Wilson's condition, no signs yet of awakening. It took him the amount of time he spent drinking a coffee alone in his flat, staring out at the day, which was a good one, to decide on a course of action. He texted Beth, apologising again, and asking if it would be possible to head to Norfolk at the first opportunity. She was working today, and so he didn't expect a reply until lunchtime.

He set off walking. It felt good to be in fresh clothes – for what felt like the first time in weeks but was only the first time in days – on a summer morning. It was just a shame he couldn't expunge the image of Michelle Roberts's bathroom door with the holes in it, or the way she had curled up on her hospital bed, or indeed Bayliss, dead and murdered by that same hand in her own flat. Both cases had a unique component he had never encountered before, in that he was acutely aware of the abject fear both Roberts and Bayliss would have gone through. That was what he thought of when he thought of them, the terror their attacker would have inflicted. For Susan Bayliss, it would almost certainly have been the last emotion she felt.

He was at the Belgrave before too long. There was no sign of a police presence, though Harry spotted what looked like a camera crew outside the main entrance of the hospital. The receptionist told him that Mr Padmore was covering Mr Mohamed's clinic, as he'd called in sick that morning. Harry had arrived at a good time – Padmore was in with his last patient, so Harry took a seat in the outpatient suite and waited, watching kids play on slides, or interactive video games, or being entertained by work-experience kids with red T-shirts. He was feeling tired, and his heart was racing, and his head throbbed, but he resisted the temptation to give in. He thought about Tammas. *You cannot change the forces.*

Soon after that, a young girl bounded out of the room, smiling, her mother chasing after her. Harry took his chance and knocked slowly.

'Yes?'

He walked in.

'Oh,' said Padmore. 'Hello again.'

'Busy morning?'

Padmore nodded, gesturing at the stacks of patient notes on his tray.

'Mr Mohamed called in sick. I was meant to just be on research today, but . . . Thank God there were only two new patients, the rest were just follow-ups. What do you want, anyway? You're not interviewing me again, are you? Because of what happened yesterday?'

'Not in as many words,' Harry said. 'May I shut the door?'

Padmore fixated on the sliver of light from the half-open door as if it were his only escape from a burning room. He said nothing. Harry shut it anyway.

'I should really call Alison . . .'

'Shut up, Theo.'

'I'm sorry.'

'This is not a police interview. I'm not a police officer. But yesterday someone almost killed one of my good friends as well as the mother of one of your patients.'

'That's not necessarily connected to what Susan did, though—'

'Susan didn't *do* anything,' said Harry, lowering his voice. 'She was murdered.'

'What? I thought she committed suicide! Slit her wrists!'

He was sinking into the chair now, face white.

'It was staged. By the same person who tried to kill Michelle Roberts yesterday.'

'This can't be happening,' said Padmore.

'It is happening. And I can tell you now that your boss is currently being questioned on suspicion of that murder, and the attack yesterday.'

Harry watched him process it, twisting the chair one way then the other, and felt slightly guilty about how harsh he was being. Padmore reached towards the phone on the desk.

'I really should inform—'

'Put it down!' Harry yelled, taking another step forward. Padmore went to punch in the extension, and Harry took three steps towards the wall and yanked the phone out of the wall socket, before moving back to block Padmore's route to the door.

'Now, sit down and listen. I know you know something about this that you're not telling us. I don't think you're just trying to save your own skin, I think you started off with some kind of noble intention. You thought all this was just a case of miscommunication and some pissed-off parents, and now it's got a lot bigger and you're freaking out. But things have changed, and you really need to talk. I can protect you, within reason. But if you don't start talking then it'll be the police who are here next, and I can promise you they will not be so understanding.'

Padmore was silent for a while, looking between Harry, the floor, the walls, and the closed door.

'You can protect me?' he said. 'How?'

'Not if you've broken the law, I can't,' said Harry. 'But I don't think you have. I think you're covering for someone, whether you know it or not.' He leant forward, right in Padmore's face. 'Ok? Whatever ship you're on, it's sinking. And if you don't want it to drag you down with it, then you'd better start talking. If you do, and you cooperate with the investigation at an early stage, it might be looked on favourably. They can usually work something out.'

Padmore seemed close to tears now.

'How did it get to this?' he whined.

'You tell me.'

In truth, Harry had no idea if he'd be able to help Padmore when it all came out. All he cared about was that it appeared his suspicions were correct, and he needed to get that information out.

When Padmore spoke, it was low, and he barely took his head out of his hands.

'Susan came to me about most of it, and I didn't believe her. She thought Mr Mohamed was incompetent, gung-ho. Yes, perhaps his ego could do with a bit of a trim, but her concerns were unfounded. I questioned her motivations. She hated him for the way he treated her, she didn't think he was giving her enough theatre time, and I think she wanted to get her own back.'

Harry said nothing. It was just like taking a history in A&E. If you let the patient talk, they'd answer all of your questions before you even asked them.

'Everyone knew it was her who'd blown the whistle, after the way she'd acted in the M&M meeting. You could sense it in the way people acted around her . . . Even the theatre staff gave her the cold shoulder. I pitied her for a while. I think she thought that everyone else thought Mohamed was some tyrant and they'd all rally around her when she stood up to him, but they didn't. We didn't, I should say.

'When it was obvious they were going to suspend her, Mohamed stopped speaking to her – wouldn't let her into theatres, or onto the wards. But then she rang me up, just before she got suspended, said she'd been getting close to some of the families of the dead children, who were campaigning for a new inquiry. Then she made a wild accusation.'

'What?' said Harry. He tried not to betray his excitement. He knew that whatever was to come was what had been weighing Padmore's conscience down for all this time.

'She said that Mr Mohamed had slept with Michelle Roberts.'

Harry wasn't sure he'd heard that right.

'What? When?'

'On the night Olivia had her operation, so she said. He'd gone to see her in the PICU, and then offered to escort her back to her hospital accommodation. And then it had happened, apparently.'

'Did you believe her?'

'I told her she was mad. She said she'd just left Roberts's house and I could speak to her myself if I wanted.'

'How could you say nothing! And after what happened yesterday, how could you just not speak out? Christ, do you have any idea how much this changes things?'

'You don't realise how desperate Susan was at that time. She would have said anything to bring Mohamed down.'

'That doesn't matter!' said Harry. 'How could you? Did you challenge Mohamed about this?'

'Of course not!' said Padmore. 'Do you really think I'd go into my boss's office and just say, oh, by the way, did you happen to

sleep with one of our patients' mothers while she was still in intensive care?'

Seeing the mild-mannered man red-faced and upset took Harry
aback, but he knew he'd touched a nerve.

'I can't believe this,' said Harry.

'It's probably not true,' said Padmore.

'Really? You really think that?'

'I did,' said Padmore. 'But after yesterday . . . After all this. I
don't know what to think anymore.'

Harry stood up.

'I've got to go now. You did the right thing, telling me.' If too
late, Harry thought but didn't say. Assuming it was true, had they
known they could have focused on Mohamed, watched him much
more closely. Perhaps closely enough to prevent the attack on
Roberts and Wilson. One final thought occurred to him as he was
leaving the room.

'What about the notes?'

'Price got rid of them,' said Padmore. 'Everyone knows that.
But good luck proving that one.'

Harry got out of the hospital and hailed a taxi on Clapham Road,
telling the driver to head for Peckham Police Station. He switched
the intercom off and called Noble. It went to voicemail. He scrolled
through his contacts and was about to ring Wilson, before remembering where he was. Eventually he managed to get through to the
Met Police switchboard and get connected to the Incident Room.

'Hello?'

'It's Harry Kent. Is DI Noble around?'

'Afraid she's with the super at the moment. I can get you DS
McGovern?'

'Please.'

McGovern came on the phone, sounding busy.

'Yeah?'

'I've just been speaking to Theo Padmore,' said Harry. 'He said
that according to Bayliss, on the night Olivia Roberts had her
operation, Mohamed visited Michelle in her hospital accommodation, and they had sex.'

'What?!'

'Tell me about it.'

'You've got to be kidding me,' said McGovern.

'Bayliss told him that, a few days after she got suspended,' said Harry. 'I don't know if it's true, but it seems Bayliss thought so.'

'Jesus. I'll get her. Hang on a sec.'

Harry stayed on the line and thought. He had been quick to challenge Noble on the motive for the attacks being to keep Bayliss and Roberts quiet, because the cat was already out of the bag. But this changed everything. The allegations about the hospital would, at worst, just lead to another inquiry, which Mohamed would have undoubtedly survived. But this was an iceberg that would sink even the most well-connected of ships. Sex with a patient's mother, on hospital premises, was a one-way ticket to the GMC.

It also made Harry's blood boil. To take advantage of a vulnerable woman on the very night her daughter had undergone an operation she might not survive betrayed every ethical principle in existence. Lord knows, Harry had made his own mistakes, but that was something else. He could believe it, too.

'Hello?'

It was Noble.

'Hey. How's it going?'

'This is exactly what we fucking need, Harry. I could kiss you.' He ignored that one. 'The smug bastard's been no-commenting all bloody morning.'

'It's hearsay,' Harry said. 'Bayliss told Padmore told me.'

'Come on, Harry, you're not a bloody defence lawyer all of a sudden are you? This gives the guy in front of me, who has no alibi for the time of either attack, who we can put within a fifteen-minute walk of the Roberts house yesterday, one hell of a motive.'

'But Bayliss could have made it up,' said Harry.

'You think?'

'I don't know!' said Harry. 'But if I can say that, a defence lawyer certainly will.'

Silence, as Noble thought for a while. He hoped she got the direction he was pushing in, as unpleasant as it was.

'I guess we should get it confirmed then,' she said.

'I'll come with you. Are you going now?'

'Might as well. I'll see you there.'

Harry hung up and told the driver to head for the Ruskin instead. Without thinking, he reached into the pill-bottle in his jacket pocket, and took one. It was impossible for him to tell how much of the buzz he was getting was from that, or the possibility that he had uncovered the fact that would put the man who had killed one person and tried to kill two others behind bars.

Michelle Roberts remained under observation at the hospital, but when Harry arrived and peeked through the window of her room she appeared to be getting ready to leave, dressed in normal clothes, sitting on the end of her bed. Preston was cross-legged on the floor, playing on an iPad, and Euan was asleep in the chair. Connie, the FLO from yesterday, sat outside looking thoroughly bored along with two uniformed police officers.

'Doctors say she can go home,' Connie said.

'She's not, though, right?' said Harry.

'Course not. We've found a hotel room for them, undisclosed location, where we can keep them under twenty-four-hour protection.'

'Has DI Noble spoken to you yet?'

'Yeah,' said Connie. 'We're not to leave until she's been. Nothing to do with you, is it?'

'Just a little,' said Harry.

He heard the elevator arrive and, as if on cue, Noble strolled in, DC Bhalla in tow. She looked like shit, but she had the same fire in her eyes as Harry felt.

'Afternoon, ma'am,' Connie said.

Noble peered inside and saw the same tableau as Harry had.

'We need to do this with her on her own. No husband.'

'She won't like that, ma'am.'

Harry leant in to Noble and said, 'I can handle that.'

He raised his fist to knock at the door and looked to Noble for permission. She nodded.

It was a startled Michelle Roberts who opened the door, looking around her, first at Connie, then at Noble, then at Harry.

'I'm sorry to disturb you, Michelle,' Harry said. 'I'm afraid I need to examine you again.'

'I thought you did it all yesterday?' Michelle said. 'I'm about to leave.'

'I know. Again I'm sorry. I thought it best that we do it while you're still here rather than disturb you this evening.'

'Why do you need to do it again?'

Harry was aware that Noble was looking at him, seemingly angry.

'We just need to take some more measurements of your injuries,' he lied. 'To get a better idea of what weapon might have been used. It really won't take long.'

She looked teary, perhaps still a little sedated, but shrugged and turned around. There were still dressings around her shoulder and back, but her eye appeared less swollen. The fracture had only been minor, and most likely she would recover fully with no issues to her vision. As they went inside, Euan Roberts, still wearing a shirt with captain's epaulettes, stirred and got up from his chair.

'What's going on?' he said.

'They need to take a look at me again, before I go. Take Preston outside for an ice cream or something and we can meet you there.'

Once they were alone, Harry glanced at Noble, trying to work out if he should hold back. She would make it very clear if he needed to, so he carried on.

'What do you need to look at?'

'I don't need to look at you. We were telling you something of a white lie, Michelle. The thing is, there are a few questions we need to ask you that might be better off heard alone.'

He tried not to sound sombre, but failed. Roberts heard the warning shot loud and clear though, and retreated up to the head of the bed, tucking her knees into her chest.

'Do we have to?'

'We're on your side,' Harry said. 'Don't forget that. But I think you know what we're talking about, don't you?'

Roberts nodded.

Though her anguish was obvious, Harry couldn't help but feel excited that the story was true.

'I'm going to have to ask you to confirm it,' said Noble. 'I'm sorry. But we hope to use this information.'

'Mr Mohamed had sex with me. On the night Ollie had her operation.'

The fact she'd used his medical title made Harry all the more angry.

286

'He walked me to the hospital accommodation. It was late – two a.m., I think. Euan was stuck in bloody Kuala Lumpur. His daughter's having heart surgery and he can't take any time off, no. Sure, he was probably with some slapper of an air hostess. Y'know that's what he's like, he thinks I've got no idea, that I don't notice that he keeps condoms in his fucking washbag.'

'No-one's judging you,' Harry said. 'We just need to know what happened.'

'What happened is I was lonely, my head was on another planet. He saw how upset I was, asked if I'd like him to sit with me, make me a cup of tea. And then, I don't know, he was just this hero who'd flown in and saved my daughter's life, or so I thought . . .'

Roberts burst into tears, and Noble fumbled around the room, looking for a tissue. Harry stepped forward and took her hand.

'It's ok.'

'I mean, I knew it wasn't allowed. I knew it was wrong. I wasn't expecting him to make me breakfast in the morning, or stay in touch. But I thought after Ollie died, he might call to see if I was ok. Or that he'd speak to me when we asked if they had any information as to how she'd died. But he never replied to my emails, never picked up my calls. Bastard.'

'Who else knew?' said Noble.

'Only Susan. She's the only person I told.'

'Euan doesn't know?' said Harry.

'No.'

'You know, if this got out, Mohamed would be finished,' Harry said. Noble flashed him a look but he didn't care – he was adamant that if the outcome of the investigation didn't entail Mohamed being arrested and charged with murder, both completed and attempted, Harry would bring about his fall from grace personally. It would take a single email to the GMC.

'Of course,' said Roberts. 'Susan said as much. She was going to report him for it, get him struck off. I talked her out of it. I don't want my marriage to fall apart . . . Euan and I have our problems, but we're good. We love each other. And it'd be awful for the – for Preston. And not like that, with my . . . my . . . mistake, there in the public eye. You know what the papers are like. They've been bad enough with this whole business, the way they reported on Susan. Made her sound unhinged.'

'Did you threaten him at any time?' said Noble.

'What, with going public about what happened?' said Roberts. 'No.'

'Did Susan?'

'Not that I know of. She wanted to, though. Said it might help him cooperate. But I told her not to. What, you think he did this? To keep us quiet?'

Roberts looked at each of them in turn, but Harry made a point of looking at Noble.

'It's one line of enquiry,' she said.

Michelle Roberts sat up straight in her bed, speaking through cracked, dry lips, a look of determination in her one uncovered eye.

'Then do whatever you have to,' she said, 'if it means getting him. I'll testify against him in court. Even if it means sacrificing my marriage. If it puts that son of a bitch behind bars.'

'Thank you,' said Harry.

Slowly, Roberts began to cry.

Noble called Grenaghan to let him know that Roberts had confirmed the story, and he instructed her to make her way back to the station and get his reaction. She could have anyone she wanted by her side, he said.

'Does that include me?' said Harry.

'If it was my investigation, it'd be an instant yes,' she said. 'But it's not anymore. It'd look a bit strange. And I don't want to give his brief anything irregular they can hit us with in court.'

'I'm coming to the station. I'll watch on the camera feed.'

'With pleasure,' said Noble.

They stepped into the ICU before leaving. When they arrived, the doors were being held open whilst two porters wheeled one of the blue-draped trolleys used to transport the recently deceased to the hospital mortuary.

'Oh, God,' Noble said.

Harry saw her face drain of colour and stepped a little closer to her. This place was hallowed ground for Frankie Noble, being where she had said a final goodbye to her husband.

'It's probably not him,' said Harry.

And it wasn't. Wilson was still in his bed, still heavily sedated, but no longer on a ventilator.

'He pulled his tube out this morning,' said the nurse. 'Gave us all a bit of a fright, but no harm done. The surgeons said the latest echo looked good.'

They watched him for a while, aware that time was against them, as Mohamed waited in an interview room. Mo had a thick line of staples across the chest incision Harry had made, the skin around them raw, pink and yellow and not yet healed. The sight of it took Harry back to the blur of adrenaline that had been yesterday afternoon, the heart-sinking moment when he'd arrived to see the paramedic doing CPR, and the strange stillness that had come over him once he'd worked out what needed to be done, the relief of hearing the helicopter touch down.

Noble, probably thinking something similar, put her hand on Harry's shoulder. He flinched away, unnecessarily harshly, and when he turned she looked wounded.

'Sorry,' she said.

'Me too,' said Harry. 'Let's go, shall we?'

As they moved to leave, he paused to look up at the board of patients' names and matched that with the number of the now-empty cubicle they had passed on the way in. The name of the dead patient was Vincent Proud, the man who had been brought in on Sunday night after overdosing, on whom the A&E team's efforts had been ultimately in vain. Perhaps, if he had family, they had had the chance to say goodbye. He looked back at Wilson, his frame engulfing the bed, by far the healthiest-looking patient on the unit.

The house always wins, he thought. Then he took another pill, and joined Noble at the door.

Harry joined the crowd of detectives hunched around the video monitor who had nothing much better to do than watch Noble and McGovern take a swing at Elyas Mohamed. Word had spread fast about their discovery, and that Harry had been the one who had made it come about. He had expected an awkward atmosphere inside the police station, like walking into an unfamiliar pub and being eyed up by the locals, but in fact he got quite a few backslaps and handshakes, which made him feel even more out of place.

'Mr Mohamed, you are aware that you remain under caution,' Noble began. 'I must inform you that we have received some information which implies you are responsible for the crimes we are investigating, and I am now going to ask you to account for this information. I should inform you that we are very close to arresting you on suspicion of murder and attempted murder. And therefore I very strongly suggest to you that you answer this question truthfully and completely. Is that clear?'

Mohamed looked across at his lawyer, and then said, 'No comment.'

Harry sensed the breaths held around him as Noble waited. The main reason Harry had previously questioned Mohamed's place as prime suspect was because of the lack of motive, or rather a strong enough motive for the risk he was taking. Petty revenge, or to cover up a conspiracy that either didn't exist or was already uncovered. But this, which would definitely have killed his career, ruined his entire life, was something worth killing two women over.

'Did you have sexual intercourse with Michelle Roberts on the evening of the 20th January?'

'What? No!'

He said it so loud it was peppered with static over the speakers.

'I mean no comment!'

But his bluster was fading, and even on the computer screen Harry could see in his face the expression of a chess player who, though ten moves from checkmate, could see defeat was inevitable.

In the room, Noble pushed on.

'In that case . . .' She stood up. 'Elyas Mohamed, I am arresting you on suspicion of the murder of Susan Bayliss on 24th August and the attempted murder of Michelle Roberts and Detective Sergeant Moses Wilson on 27th August. You do not have to—'

'No!' said Mohamed, now breaking down. 'I didn't do this! You've got it all wrong! You've got everything wrong!'

'How? How have we got it wrong?'

The lawyer interrupted. 'I'd like a word with my client.'

'I'd like a word with your client, too!' said Noble. 'I'd like to know why he was in Greenwich at the precise time of the attacks yesterday. And why he's just lied to us about having sex with the mother of one of his patients. You better start talking, Mr Mohamed.'

'I will,' said Mohamed.

'Oh yeah,' said someone behind Harry. 'Start digging that hole.'

Harry leant in closer.

'I need to speak to my client, in private. Right now,' the lawyer said, leaning over to grab Mohamed's outstretched arm.

Noble came out of the interview room and headed straight outside for a cigarette. It was going fucking well, and if her read of the situation was correct then Mohamed was on the verge of confessing either his guilt or the role he played, whatever he knew. He was calculating his options, the strategy where he lost the least. Grenaghan, who was tied up in Greenwich, closing up the manhunt investigation, would be pleased.

She saw Harry bound around the corner before too long.

'What do you think?' she said.

'I think you've got him on the ropes.'

'Just hope he doesn't zip up now his brief's onto him,' said Noble.

She was working on a tactic for that now in her head. She'd make sure he knew and understood he was formally under arrest, and go over in detail the part about 'it may harm your defence if you do not mention when questioned something you later rely on in court.' He'd have to explain to a jury what he was doing in Greenwich at the time of the Roberts attack, and if he didn't tell them now, the judge was within their rights to call it out as bullshit. That might well work.

Noble finished the cigarette and looked over at Harry, who was staring up at the sky, vacant. She briefly wondered what was going on in his mind, both glad to have this man by her side and infuriated that he had given them this break, using nothing more than instinct, memory of the finer details of a conversation everyone had long since forgotten.

Harry reached into his pocket and retrieved a white pill from a familiar orange bottle.

'You've been doing too much thinking?' she said.

'What?'

'Your headaches?'

'Oh,' said Harry. 'Yeah . . .'

Footsteps interrupted them.

'He's talking, guv.'

The crowd around the monitor had grown, and Harry found himself on the periphery, but luckily behind a diminutive pair of detectives. DSU Grenaghan had arrived too, along with the Assistant Commissioner and another bunch of suits Harry assumed were interested, now that the case involved the attempted murder of a police officer.

'My client has a few things he wishes to say.'

Mohamed was sweaty, his tie removed, top two shirt buttons gone, sleeves rolled up, hunched over the table. Perhaps imagining his future, or the lack of it. Maybe the GMC would take pity, given that it was a one-off, not a sustained relationship, and only suspend his registration. Then again, it was a high-profile case with media attention, and that never boded well for doctors under investigation. Justice had to be seen to be done.

'I can confirm I had . . . umm . . .' he coughed, 'sexual inter-course with Mrs Roberts on the night you asked me about. It was a terrible mistake and I regret it greatly.'

Harry thought that last part was genuine.

'Bastard,' somebody whispered.

'What happened?' said Noble.

'She came to the ICU late at night. She was obviously, umm, emotional. The nurses were calling security to escort her back to the hospital accommodation, but I said I was going that way, my on-call room was in the same block. She asked me to stay. My wife and I were, umm, separated at the time. I'm a fool. I really am . . .'

'Who knew about this?'

'No-one,' said Mohamed. 'Or so I thought. I told no-one. In fact, with all this . . . going on, I'd convinced myself that it never happened.'

That was easy to do, Harry thought. As defence mechanisms went, it wasn't the worst idea.

'Mrs Roberts never talked to you about it?'

'No.'

'Or alluded to it? Perhaps when you were discussing her daughter's death.'

'No. We never discussed her daughter's death.'

'Because you were afraid she'd bring it up?'

'No, because I didn't think it would be any help to them,' said Mohamed. 'Well. Maybe. Who knows?'

He collapsed onto the table.

'What about Miss Bayliss?'

'What about her?'

'Did she ever threaten you with that information? Or bring it up?'

'No! I don't think she had any idea,' said Mohamed. 'My God, is that what you think? You think I did this . . . to stop, to stop people finding out . . . God, no, this is what I mean, you've got it all wrong.'

'You're going to need to do a lot of work to convince us of that.'

'The burden of proof is on you, Chief Inspector,' the lawyer said. Noble, McGovern and even Mohamed shot him a look to say, 'shut up'. Someone behind Harry said, 'Prick'. Mohamed appeared to sob for a while, but then sat up straight, rubbed his eyes and looked over at his brief.

'My client is able to account for his movements yesterday,' the lawyer said.

'Please do,' said Noble.

Mohamed did a bit more heavy breathing before starting to talk.

'I received a text message at eight twenty-five in the morning,' he said. 'From an unknown number. It said that they had information that would end my career, and if I wanted to keep it then I should meet them that afternoon.'

'Seriously?'

'My client is happy for his phone records to be investigated,' the brief cut in.

'Where was the meeting?' said Noble.

'Car Park C at the O2 Arena,' said Mohamed. 'At two p.m. The person asked what car I'd be driving. I told them. That's the last I heard. I tried calling, I asked who it was, no-one answered.'

'And let me guess, no-one showed up?'

'No. I drove away after about an hour.'

'You expect us to believe that?'

'Check my phone. It's all there.'

Mohamed got his phone from his pocket and thumped it down on the table.

'I'm sure it is,' said Noble. 'And it just so happens that you're alone, fifteen minutes' walk from Michelle Roberts's house, at the time she's attacked? With no-one to vouch for you?'

'I didn't attack her, I'm telling you—'

'When you knew she was in possession of information that could end your career. As was Susan Bayliss. Two people who can bring you down. One's dead, one's in hospital. My sergeant is in intensive care. What would you do in my position, Mr Mohamed?'

'Someone's setting me up!'

'Can you give us any evidence of that?'

The air around Harry had turned hostile. The respectful silence had given way to murmurs, whispers, opinions. Someone muttered, 'She's getting nowhere.'

Mohamed stood up.

'I don't need any!' he said. 'You need some that I'm connected to any of this, and you won't get it, I'm telling you now!'

The interview ended pretty soon after that, once it became obvious that Mohamed wasn't going to give them anything. Noble stood just behind Grenaghan, and after five minutes or so of whispered conversation the superintendent stood up, gave out a few actions to detectives – obvious things, like checking the CCTV at the O2 Arena, and going through Mohamed's phone to trace the number, and if possible, its owner. After that pretty much everyone else dispersed to their duties. At that, Harry felt an overwhelming sense of relief. A suspect was under arrest and in custody. There were forty-eight detectives across three boroughs working on getting enough evidence for a charge. Harry had done his bit, and now it was time to put his own existence in order.

He waited until the crowd had gone down to approach Noble. She saw him over the shoulder of another detective, and came over once she was finished.

'Thanks for sticking around,' she said. 'And bloody good work on getting that thing on Roberts. He wouldn't have said a word without us hitting him with that.'

'I'm sure that's not true,' Harry said.

'Don't be modest, it doesn't suit you.'

Harry looked at her and smiled, then tried to stop himself.

'I'm busy over the weekend, so I'm going to take a step back from this. I've probably got too far involved already. And . . . well, yeah. It's probably best for everyone if I leave this all to the professionals.'

'I understand . . .' Noble said. She seemed disappointed, and Harry didn't think it was because she'd miss his professional involvement. He thought again of her revelation to him, and briefly considered saying something about that, but couldn't word it in a way that didn't sound patronising or self-righteous. *Look at what little Frankie can achieve now she's sober.*

So he just said, 'Good luck.'

'Take care. Thanks.'

Harry went home and showered. When he came out he had a missed call from Beth.

'Still on for this weekend?' she said.

'Yep. Saturday morning still work?' said Harry.

'Yes. Have you spoken to those doctors yet?'

'No. I'm gonna get off the pills, then I'll make the call.'

'You promise me?' said Beth. 'You will?'

'I promise. I'm clearing my life out. I just told Noble not to contact me anymore. Anyway, they've made an arrest. Looks like things are coming to a close.'

'What about Dave?'

'I'll speak to him on Monday,' said Harry. 'They have a lead which they're following up. I'll take them to task if they don't, but it can wait.'

He wondered if he believed it, but Beth seemed to. The prospect of withdrawal scared him – he had never witnessed one from amphetamines, but he had seen enough cold turkey from heroin, cocaine, alcohol, and the typical array of party drugs, to know how unpleasant it could be. That's why it was important to have Beth on-hand, with a heavy dose of reassurance, and maybe sedatives if need be. It probably didn't sound like such a good idea, isolated in a cottage somewhere, but that was her in a nutshell. There was little she couldn't handle.

As he cycled over to the hospital, Harry's thoughts returned to Elyas Mohamed, and his story about the set-up, the mysterious text summoning him to a car park. It was either a well-planned cover, an alibi without being an alibi, or it was just bullshit. Harry wondered if it really mattered. Nine months going out with a homicide detective had taught him that whilst the majority of cases were open-and-shut, like Pauline Wright bashing her husband over the head with a sambuca bottle, some were more nebulous. They might find a sliver of DNA or some other forensic detail that nailed Elyas Mohamed, they might have to take what they had to a jury and keep their fingers crossed. Either way they might never know whether he really had killed his own registrar or not. Just as they might never know why Olivia Roberts and Emmanuel Abediji had died so suddenly.

Harry didn't believe it yet, not one hundred per cent, but did that matter? Maybe, maybe not. Like he'd said to Noble, he'd done his part. He'd responded to whatever need the killing of a distant colleague had stirred in him, and now it was time to move on.

He never had been much good at that, he thought, as he wheeled his bike into the hospital.

Midnight, and the department was almost full.

'Harry, sorry to bother you.'

It was Narwaz Ali, one of the SHOs on that night. If Harry remembered correctly, she was working in Majors, the area of A&E which held patients who weren't critically unwell but might still require hospital admission. Harry was meant to be covering Resus, not Majors, but such was the nature of the department that all the wards tended to blur into one.

'Don't apologise,' said Harry, 'What can I do for you?'

'There's this patient,' Ali said. 'Eighteen-year-old student, came in with lower abdominal pain about two hours ago. She's quite tender over her suprapubic region, and she's been running a bit tachycardic. FBC looks normal, CRP's a little raised. I wanted to call gynae down, but the reg says it's appendicitis and to admit to SAU . . .'

Harry rolled his eyes. It wouldn't be the first time the gynaecologists and the surgeons had bickered over accepting a young woman with abdominal pain. But he understood now the reluctant tone Ali had used. In terms of hierarchy, Harry didn't outrank the registrar covering Majors, he was simply assigned to a different section of A&E, but Ali didn't want to go over her registrar's head and wake up the consultant at three in the morning.

Harry nodded. 'Who's the reg?'

'Dr De Russo,' said Ali, adding, 'the locum.'

Harry remembered him. It was an irony that the staffing crisis which had allowed him to walk into a staff grade job in A&E was now the bane of his life. They were meant to have twelve doctors tonight but had only eight, four of whom were locums. He had reported the rota gap to the managers, who had told him that the trust's cost-saving policy stated that no more than four locums were ever to be hired on any one evening, so he would have to do the job of two registrars, grit his teeth and bear it. It was Harry's responsibility to show the locums around the department before their shifts, which meant starting an hour early, and he often got called to help them find some equipment or log in to one of the computer systems. He'd shown De Russo around six hours ago, and now remembered him, a thin, gaunt man a good few years older than Harry.

They arrived in Majors and Ali nodded to one of the cubicles, and Harry asked if anyone was inside before pulling back the curtain. The patient, Charlotte, was lying on the trolley in obvious distress, a slender young woman in pink pyjamas, one hand over her abdomen, a saline drip going into her right elbow. Ali passed Harry her chart. She'd been prescribed nothing but paracetamol for the pain and metaclopramide for nausea. A smartly dressed woman Harry assumed was her mother was sitting on the chair by her side.

'Good morning, Charlotte,' said Harry. 'I'm Harry Kent, one of the doctors. How are you feeling?'

'It hurts,' was about all that she could manage, and the words were quiet and raspy. He glanced down at the chart. Her pulse rate when she had arrived in the department had been a quite reasonable seventy-five. It was now over a hundred.

'Get a nurse,' he said to Ali. 'I want her on a monitor.'

Ali darted out of the cubicle and Harry went over to the side of the bed, taking Charlotte by the hand. She was cold and sweaty, and by now the itch at the back of Harry's mind about this one had grown into action. This girl was sick and getting sicker, and his SHO had done exactly the right thing fetching him rather than letting her patient languish in a surgical assessment ward until the morning ward round. Harry washed his hands and took a quick feel of Charlotte's abdomen, which was now tender all over, the muscles tensing involuntarily. He whispered *shit* under his breath.

'Charlotte, have you had any vaginal bleeding?'

'No,' she grimaced. 'Well, this morning.'

'It's her time of the month,' her mother interjected.

'Was it heavier than usual?' said Harry. He realised it sounded demanding, but at this point he didn't care. He already knew what the diagnosis was, and her embarrassed nodding just confirmed it. He darted out of the cubicle, where Ali was returning with a nurse and a portable monitor.

'Hook her up and get me a BP,' he said to the nurse, then turning to Ali: 'Get me the ultrasound machine, right now.'

Harry left the room and grabbed Charlotte's chart and started flicking through it for her lab results. The one test they should have done wasn't on the list. With his other hand he picked up the nearest phone, called the switchboard and asked them to fast-bleep the on-call gynae registrar to Majors. Just as he was realising what a disaster it was, a voice piped up from behind him.

'Can I help you? This is my patient.'

Harry turned. It was Dr De Russo, the locum registrar, in his cobalt-blue scrubs, the insignia of the agency who employed him across the breast. De Russo would be earning at least twice Harry's hourly pay for the same work.

'Tell me you did a pregnancy test!' Harry demanded.

De Russo shook his head.

'She is not pregnant,' he said. 'She said she is always careful and not recently with a man.'

'A sexually active woman comes in with tachycardia and abdo pain and you didn't do a pregnancy test?'

Harry realised he'd said it loud and a couple of nurses at the nearby station turned to eavesdrop. Dr Ali came back, wheeling the ultrasound machine, and Harry grabbed her arm before she headed into the cubicle.

'She said is no possible.'

'Take bloods for Group and Save, crossmatch four units, and send off another FBC and a Beta-HCG. Get a urine Beta-HCG if you can as well, although I expect she's drier than the fucking Sahara.'

Ali nodded and ran at full pace to the stores to gather blood-taking equipment. Harry glanced over his shoulder, checking that the nurse, Charlotte Osugu, was taking the required observations. De Russo stood, arms folded, watching him, an angry scowl on his face.

'You got a problem?' said Harry.

'I have a problem when you interfere with my patient. I have made diagnosis, we have organised plan, and you interfere.'

Harry stormed past him and back into the cubicle. Osugu had a blood pressure cuff on and was finishing the first reading. The blood pressure was low, and Harry swore again. He turned to the mother and said, 'I'm sorry, but I need to examine your daughter internally. Would you step outside, please?'

It was a variation of the trick he'd used on Michelle Roberts, and it worked. Awkwardly, the mother got up, squeezed her daughter's hand, and shuffled outside the cordon. Harry headed straight to Charlotte's side, took her hand and squatted down.

'Don't worry,' he said. 'I don't need to examine you. But I wanted to speak to you by yourself.'

'What's going on?' asked Charlotte, terrified.

Harry squeezed her hand and said, 'I need to know if there's any chance at all you might be pregnant.'

She cried and nodded. 'I thought I'd been careful . . . My last period was really light, and I missed the one before that, but when

299

I started bleeding yesterday I thought it was normal. I . . . I don't want Mum to know. She doesn't even know I have a boyfriend.'

'It's ok,' Harry said. 'You're going to be just fine. I'll be back in a second, and my colleague here needs to take some blood. I'll let your mum back in.'

'Ectopic,' said Ali, shaking her head. 'Should have spotted it.'

'Yes, you should,' said Harry. 'But everyone misses them. Did he specifically tell you not to dip the urine?'

'He said she wasn't pregnant,' said Ali.

'Go get the bloods.'

By now, the gynae reg had arrived. When Harry explained that a pregnancy test had not been done in a young woman with abdominal pain, she was just as appalled as he had been. Harry apologised even though it wasn't his fault. As the gynae reg grabbed the ultrasound and darted in to see Charlotte, swapping places with Ali, who came out with fresh blood samples, De Russo, who had been watching from the nurses' station, coffee in hand, rolled his eyes. Harry went up to him, got in his face, hissed the words so the poor young woman and her distraught mother didn't hear him.

'Appendicitis, eh?' he said. 'What the hell were you thinking?'

'This is very disrespectful,' De Russo said. 'She look like she have appendicitis, I make appropriate referral.'

'You didn't do a pregnancy test!'

Despite Harry's attempts to keep his voice down, De Russo spoke at full volume.

'She say she is no pregnant.'

'Because she's eighteen and her mum was in the fucking room! Christ, were you born yesterday?'

De Russo squared up to Harry, his eyebrows narrowing.

'I have seen this before,' he said. 'You think because I am locum doctor, because I am foreign doctor, I am stupid.'

'No,' said Harry. 'I think you're stupid because you can't spot a blind-fucking-obvious medical emergency and your SHO has to come and bail you out by fetching me.'

De Russo seemed on the verge of pushing forward, and they were only interrupted by the gynae registrar sticking her head out of the cubicle.

'She's got free fluid in the pelvis,' she said. 'And a mass in the right adnexa. Ectopic until proven otherwise. We need to cross-match blood and get her to theatre right away. Can you fast-bleep the anaesthetist?'

'Will do,' said Harry. 'You'll sort theatres, yeah?'

The gynae reg flashed him a thumbs-up and disappeared behind the curtain again, and Harry picked up the phone and bleeped the duty anaesthetist. De Russo was still there, his face burning red, his eyes fixed on Harry.

Before he knew what was happening to him, or what he was saying, Harry had dropped the phone so it swung from its cord, and was in the other doctor's face, screaming.

'Get out of here!'

'I'm sorry?'

'You heard,' said Harry. 'Go home, you fucking useless piece of shit.'

'You cannot speak to me like this!' De Russo said. He took a step forward and Harry snapped, charging in, bringing up a fist, and it was only when a nearby paramedic grabbed his arm that his own voice begin to echo in his head. *You're losing it, Harry. You're out of fucking control.*

The chest pains had started at maybe two in the morning, maybe three, he wasn't sure. After De Russo had departed, Harry had been left covering both Majors and Resus. He was writing up notes for an African man who'd come in unconscious, maybe with malaria, maybe with HIV, maybe with meningitis, and had fallen asleep on the desk, in the brightly lit Resus department. A nurse had shaken him awake and he'd slunk back to the staff room, embarrassed, whilst he took a pill. The pains had started about an hour later and had grown gradually worse, but he'd ignored them of course, as he had a department to clear and five ambulances queueing outside. None of the patients were actually ill, and all of them could have been seen in the morning by a GP, but he didn't want to leave them for the day team or there'd be hell to pay.

After he handed over, he made his way to the changing room, doused in sweat, and as the stress of the shift began to ease he became aware of the tightness in his chest. It was not a stitch, nor the aching howl behind the sternum that came with guilt, but more of a pressure, an ever-shortening band around his ribcage. He had never had a heart attack, but he had seen hundreds of patients who had, and it always sounded a little bit like this.

He was going to ignore it, cycle home, maybe take an aspirin or two, when the pain started shooting down his left arm. So he went into the corridor, found an ECG machine and wheeled it into an empty examination room, locking and bolting the door, before using the mirror to stick the dots to his chest, untangling the leads, and clipping them on. He tried his best to keep still as the machine took its reading, but his hands were shaking, almost uncontrollably. He knew it was because he was worrying about it, that it wasn't so bad when his mind was occupied, or he would have been a useless wreck on the shop floor overnight. So he tried to occupy his mind – to think about Elyas Mohamed, sweating in a police cell, or Charlotte, who had been rushed to theatre, where about a litre of blood had been found in her pelvic cavity. She had lost a fallopian tube but ought to pull through.

The printout finished and Harry held it up to the light. His heart rate was a hundred and twenty-nine beats per minute, almost exactly double his resting average. The bright lights of the examination room surrounded the paper like a halo, invading his retinas, turning the sharp lines of the ECG into a mad kaleidoscope of edges and lights. He managed to close his eyes and force away those shapes, and examine the trace. Aside from its pace, it was normal. He wasn't having a heart attack.

Briefly, Harry saw himself on the end of the bed, from the perspective of the ceiling perhaps, shirtless on the end of a hospital trolley in a brightly lit, bolted room, wires attached to dots adhered to his sweaty, rancid skin, his eyes bloodshot, his face stubbled and unclean, his mouth forlorn, his hands resting pathetically on his knees, his gaze out to some distant place in which he could not find what he was looking for.

NINE

Friday, 29 August
Morning

It took two of the Ruskin's biggest security guards to break down the door, and that was saying something, given that the staff could probably hold their own against most of the country's best rugby teams. The nurse on the morning round had noticed that the examination room in Majors 2 was bolted, and had assumed that someone was using it. Only when this had been reported to her twice in the following hours did she become concerned and call hospital security. Repeated pounding and knocking on the door, and even ringing of the phone inside the room had failed to garner a response. As the security staff set about drilling out the bolt, the nurse had started to get worried. A patient could have slunk off in the early hours the morning, locked themselves in the room and taken an overdose of God-knows-what. Or worse, hanged themselves from the light fitting or cut their throat. The hangers were always the worst. If they were lucky it would just be one of the regulars who'd pirated a bottle of alcohol hand-scrub and had the time of their lives.

In the back of her mind, of course, was the possibility that it could be a staff member. No-one was absent from the day shift as far as she knew, but the night shift disappeared quicker than sugar in tea, and if someone went astray they wouldn't necessarily be missed. At her last hospital, one of the doctors, going through a nasty divorce and on a seemingly endless rota of night shifts, had done just that. Signed out some fentanyl for his last patient, ensured all the drug charts were in order, gone into the toilets and slammed the whole lot into a vein.

So though her heart sank when the door was forced open to reveal a man in scrub bottoms, lying sprawled on the trolley, attached up to an ECG machine – strange way to do it – she wasn't entirely surprised.

'Bollocks!' she said. 'Crash call!'

She ran to the man, and was instantly reassured that he was warm to touch, his chest heaving a little. He stank of sweat and fatigue, but he was breathing. Her eyes were drawn to an ID badge

305

on the floor, and she stooped to pick it up, at once recognising the name and designation written on it.

'Oh, shit,' she said.

'Are you sure it's not even worth an extension, sir?'

Noble had only been awake two hours but it felt like much, much longer. She'd gone home this time rather than sleeping in the office, though it had been in an Uber rather than driving herself – she was that knackered. The night had been spent eating up the twenty-four hours they could legally hold Elyas Mohamed. If she was asking her team to work until three or four, the least she could do was to lead by example. The poor sods in Forensics had been earning their overtime, too, in the hope that they could find something which placed Mohamed inside Bayliss's flat. But there was nothing. No DNA, no prints, nothing. Other detectives had trawled CCTV of all conceivable routes between Sevenoaks and Myatt's Fields, looking for his BMW, as well as cameras on the 27th, looking for him travelling on foot between the O2, where his car had been parked, and Wellington Terrace, where Roberts was attacked. But they had fuck-all.

This hadn't stopped Grenaghan and Noble calling in the CPS though. But like amateur poker players overbetting their hands, they were drawing dead. No crown prosecutor in their right mind would take a well-connected surgeon with the means to hire the best defence QC in London, to court for a murder with only circumstantial evidence. With a less high-profile case, perhaps, but this type of investigation could end careers if handled badly. Christ, she thought, it had already put the brakes on hers.

'He'd appeal it straightaway. And then what? You know what the magistrate will ask me for, don't you?'

Noble prayed that Grenaghan was being rhetorical.

'What'll he ask me for?'

'What new evidence we're likely to get in the next twenty-four hours that we couldn't get previously,' Noble said.

'Exactly.'

'We're in no hurry,' said Grenaghan, 'And Mohamed, he's no flight risk. Not with two kids, a wife, and a career to protect. We'll bail him to appear in two weeks and see what we have then. In the meantime, we have to consider the fact we may be up the wrong tree here.'

'Sir . . .' she began.

'Come on now, Frances.' He always used her full name, just like her father. 'I could tell you of hundreds of killers who've spent longer on the prowl than they should have done, due to tunnel vision. I'll not have ours be one of them.'

Frustratingly, she knew he was right. Already, further work was being carried out to investigate the personal histories of the fifty or so staff members of the cardiac unit at the Belgrave, starting with those who'd worked most closely with Bayliss and Mohamed, looking for both the obvious signs – convictions, disciplinaries at work, violent crimes – but also the softer signs. Someone was working on a matrix of names mentioned in the earlier interviews as those who had abrasive personalities, tended to clash with colleagues or take things personally. They were searching for other clues too – threatening letters or emails to Bayliss or Roberts, posts on internet forums, that kind of thing. So far they had nothing.

Support was also growing for the theory that they were looking at a former patient, or a parent of a patient whom Mohamed had saved, and who idolised him, and was unwilling to accept the accusations against the man who'd given their child life. It was a bold theory, and certainly possible. But it meant widening the net to an almost unmanageable degree. With a police officer lying in hospital, they could get any resources they wanted. Grenaghan wasn't yet convinced, though.

In the Uber, Noble had woken Sue Everscott up, not for the first time. They'd agreed the day was probably a good-going eight, and that whilst Grenaghan taking over the investigation was a positive thing, she still needed an exit strategy. She was too exhausted for the cross-trainer, so tired she wanted nothing more than her bed and a vodka bottle and blissful oblivion. If Harry Kent was involved in that oblivion too, then more the better, but that looked like a vanishingly small probability. She hadn't really thought about what she wanted in that respect, whether she'd really thought he would come charging back into her life and save her from her self-pity, or perhaps replace it with his own.

'You're in the belly of the beast,' Everscott had said. 'Just get through it, and then we'll take a weekend away. A walk out on the Downs or something. Look forward to that.'

Noble tried to, as she moved through the Incident Room and headed downstairs towards the custody suite, the eyes of her team burning into the back of her neck. She had the unshakable feeling that she had failed. Here was a man whose life the victims had planned to destroy completely, without an alibi for either crime, and his numberplate captured on CCTV, walking distance from the Roberts property, and they were opening up the cell door and letting him walk free.

Unshaven, wearing jeans and a grey Uniqlo sweater, Mohamed still stood proud, upstanding, as Noble read the bail notice out. Ordinarily this would have been delegated to a junior detective, but Noble didn't want to seem as if she were chickening out. She was taking responsibility of this failure herself.

'Mr Elyas Mohamed, you are hereby bailed to return to this police station on Monday, 15 September, 2014. In the meantime you are to have no contact with Michelle Roberts or any members of her family, and you are not to travel outside Great Britain. Failure to present yourself at that date or to comply with those conditions is a criminal offence and may result in a large fine or a custodial sentence. Is that clear?'

'Yes,' said Mohamed, looking straight at her with his soapstone eyes.

She signed the notice and passed it over to him, as the custody sergeant returned his possessions.

'So that's it?' he said. 'I'm free to go?'

A smirk passed across his face.

'Fuck you,' she said.

Harry sat in Dr Kinirons' office, feeling stupid. All of last night was a blur. He could hardly remember a single patient, but he recalled a pain in his chest, swinging at one of the locums, and falling asleep in the examination room. Waking up to see the two security guards breaking down the door was definitely reality, but where wakefulness had ended and the hallucinations of his half-asleep state had begun was anyone's guess. He was fairly sure he was awake now, that this was real. They'd let him sort himself out, shower and change, after checking he was physically ok. Now he sat with his head in his hands, trying not to think about how quickly the gossip would be spreading around the department.

'So,' Kinirons said, matriarchal but concerned. 'Are you alright?'

'I guess not,' said Harry.

'Would you like to tell me what happened?'

'I'm not really sure.'

'Well, I was planning to speak to you anyway. Constance called me last night to say you'd sent home one of the locum registrars. Which, I need not say, is not within your jurisdiction. Not even close.'

'I didn't send him home. I told him to go home. It was a turn of phrase.'

'Well, from what I heard you also had handbags with him in the middle of Majors, for all to see. And you had to be restrained from attacking him physically. So no matter what you said, that's grossly unacceptable. Who the hell do you think you are?'

So that part had been real, not a product of his addled cortex. Harry looked at the furrows of the carpet and wished they might swallow him.

'If I didn't know you so well, I would be thoroughly disappointed,' she went on. 'But I have to say, the conclusion I'm reaching is that you were not acting entirely of your own volition. Especially given the events of this morning.'

'I don't follow.'

'You're found, asleep, dripping in sweat, hooked up to an ECG machine. Do you remember that?'

'Not really. I think I had some chest pains and I wanted to check myself over.'

'And you didn't want to seek help from a colleague?'

'They were busy,' Harry muttered.

'Don't try that with me,' said Kinirons. 'What facts did you know that you didn't want to share with anyone else?'

'I'm sorry?'

He was getting tired of pretending he didn't know where she was going. All he wanted was sleep. Sleep, perhaps eternal. But already he was getting the headache, the tightness in his chest, the twitches of withdrawal. Worse now than ever before. Fuck it, he thought.

'I am a drug addict,' he said.

Kinirons blew out air and leant backwards.

'Oh, Harry,' she said. 'What is it?'

'Amphetamines.'

'Self-prescribed?'

'Internet.'

'Dosage?'

'Seventy or eighty mg a day.'

'Jesus wept!'

'I have a plan,' said Harry. 'My girlfriend knows. She's got this place out in Norfolk, she's going to drive me there, she's going to manage my withdrawal. And then I'm going to present to the Practitioner Health Programme.'

'GMC?' said Kinirons.

'I'm at your mercy,' said Harry.

He wanted to avoid that if at all possible. Too often with the doctors' regulator, justice had to be seen to be done more than it had to actually be done. They criminalised simple fallibility whilst having a unique tolerance for incompetence. Harry clung desperately to a belief that his life could still be rescued, but that chance might disappear if the GMC got involved.

'I'm signing you off for a month. On sick leave,' she said. 'I'll sort it with management. You give me weekly phone calls. You abstain totally following withdrawal. You never work under the influence of anything stronger than a double espresso ever again, or I will throw you to the wolves. Is that clear?'

'Very clear,' said Harry, through tears.

'What's more, you work Christmas and New Year this year. And you bring in cakes every day.'

'Ok.'

'You should have come to me earlier. If I didn't know what you'd been through, I wouldn't be doing this. Remember that.'

'Ok.'

'Right. Now go and sort yourself out.'

'Thank you.'

★   ★   ★

As he stood in splendid Indian summer sunshine, overnight bag at his feet, Harry felt he should probably be considering the chain of events that had led him to this point. But there didn't seem to be anything to gain by that now. Maybe later, in the inevitable counselling sessions. Now all he wanted to do was sleep and get it over with.

Kinirons had put him in a taxi, from which he'd called Beth, who'd managed to swap her shift at the last minute and was on her way over, ready for a long drive. Then he called Kingston, where he was told Tammas was asleep. He seemed to be on the mend though, and the antibiotics were working. On the phone, Beth had insisted on knowing what happened, but he had said it didn't matter, that he knew he needed to get better, and she was well within her rights to leave him to rot, even though he knew she couldn't. He'd rarely felt so pitiful as when she drove her spluttering Hyundai around the corner.

'Get in, you bastard.'

He did so, throwing his bag before him. Though it was midday and the sun was bright, he had no trouble sleeping, lying fishlike across the back seats, restrained only by the seatbelts. Twice he half-woke, shaking in a cold sweat, begging her for water – she stopped at a garage to pick up a six-pack, and threw the bottles behind her. Three or four times they had to pull over and open the door to let him vomit onto the hard shoulder.

They were just outside Stansted Airport when his phone rang.

'Who is it?' said Harry.

Beth looked down.

'Doesn't say.'

'Give it here,' said Harry.

'Come on, whoever it is, does it matter?'

'It might be someone from Kingston,' Harry murmured, sounding drunk. 'About Peter.'

Wordlessly, she threw the phone back. He caught it. It buzzed in his hands. He sat up. The world span.

'Hello?'

'Harry Kent, *ja*?'

An accent Harry recognised but couldn't immediately place.

'Who is this?'

'Dr Utting from University College. You came to visit me the other day.'

He'd almost managed to forget that had happened. Not just the visit, but the whole investigation. His memory of the last few months was vacant, like he'd had some kind of stroke.

'Yes?'

'I have the results of the toxicology tests on those samples. Emmanuel Abediji was clear. But Olivia Roberts had nortryptiline in her serum. That's the active metabolite of amitryptiline.'

'Amitryptiline?'

They were in the middle lane of the M11, though it felt like they were on a fishing trawler during a winter storm. Amitryptiline was a tricyclic antidepressant, an old drug. It was old because it was particularly easy to overdose on. It caused cardiac arrythmias. It was also used for migraines and chronic pain.

Pain of the kind you might get from having rheumatoid arthritis.

'Was that it?' said Harry.

'Well, not entirely. There was amiodarone, atropine. But those are the drugs they gave her in A&E, so that's not unusual. I cannot explain the nortryptiline however.'

Olivia Roberts had died at the age of four. Antidepressants were hardly ever dished out to prepubescent children, and Harry had read almost all of her medical notes and seen no mention of migraines. There was no natural reason for her to have an antidepressant in her bloodstream.

'And Emmanuel was clear?'

Beth called back, 'Harry, what the hell are you talking about?'

The periphery of the world was grey, and Harry's chest hurt again. Now he was fully awake, he yearned for his pills more than he ever had before. His stomach felt torn in half.

'Pull over, I need to throw up!'

'I beg your pardon?' said Utting.

'Sorry, I'm in the car. Was Emmanuel clear?'

'Yes.'

'You're sure?'

'Again, we ran it twice. I am sure.'

'How much amitryptiline did you find? Enough to have killed her?'

'We only ran a qualitative analysis,' Utting said. 'A quantitative protocol would take a while longer. It is possible, and I will do one, but I thought I would give you a heads up.'

'What's the likelihood this is a false positive?' Harry said.

'Virtually impossible,' said Utting. 'I supervised the mass spec myself. We ran it twice, and we're running it a third time as we speak. I've had two independent technicians interpret the signal. It's definite.'

'Harry, what's going on?' Beth cried.

'Thank you,' said Harry, and hung up. The pain was shooting down his left arm again. Jesus Christ, this was torture. He was never going to be able to do this. In hospital, patients in with-drawal syndrome were given high doses of benzodiazepenes to quell their tremors. That's what he needed. Either that or the pills Beth was guarding in the glove compartment.

'Can we pull over?' he said.

'Who was that?'

'It doesn't matter. When's the next junction? Can we come off?'

'It's in a mile. What the hell's going on, Harry?'

'Just come off.'

'There's a services here.'

'Come off then, for fuck's sake!'

'Harry!'

'I'm sorry,' he said, as she welled up in the front. 'I'm so sorry, I'm sorry.' He kept talking as she indicated into the nearside lane, and he searched his contacts for Noble's number. 'Beth, I'm really sorry, but I've got to do this. I wouldn't unless I had to, unless I really, really had to.'

'Fuck you, Harry.'

At the services, they parked up and Harry ran to a bin and vomited into it, ignoring the sickly stench of rotting rubbish and the wasps circling the exterior. Nearby families on their way to and from camping holidays sat around McDonald's bags and KFC buckets, parents telling their bored or excited kids not to go near the strange man at the bin with sweat running off him and eyes as wide as ping-pong balls.

'Get me a pill. Just one,' he said.

'No!'

'I need to put my thoughts together. That was a pathologist at UCL. He ran some toxicology on Olivia Roberts. She had amitryptiline in her blood. That's significant. It means . . . I think I know what it means, and it's a big deal, and I need to be able to think and I can't fucking think to save my life, so can I just have a pill please.'

'And then what?'

'And then I'll call Frankie and I'll explain it all and we'll go to Norfolk and I'll get better.'

'You'll have to stop taking them eventually,' she said, grabbing his hands. 'You're just delaying the inevitable.'

'I know, but I've got to be able to think,' he said. He was trying to drag amitryptiline out of the scrapbook of medical information stuck in his head. He had treated amitryptiline overdoses before, and with a dose high enough the heart could stop. How had Olivia Roberts died? How many pills would be needed to kill a four-year-old child? He did the maths. Three or four would do the trick. That couldn't be an accident.

'Come on, you were doing so well.'

'Because I was asleep!'

'So go back to sleep, then!'

'I can't, Beth! I've got this information, and I've got to pass it on. It's important! It's a murder investigation!'

'So pass it on and then go back to sleep.'

'I can't just pass it on. Because when I call Frankie and tell her, she'll ask me what it means, and I haven't worked that out yet. So just give me a pill. Just one, please!'

'Harry, please. Don't let Frankie do this to you. You don't owe her anything. You've got to do this for yourself.'

'Shut up! I'm not doing it for anyone.' It was a lie, because he was doing it for Susan Bayliss, and Moses Wilson and now, it seemed, Olivia Roberts, who was a murder victim too.

'Don't tell me to shut up!'

A headache, like a thunderclap, starting right on the top of his head and down into his temples like he was a lightning conductor, and spreading down into his spine. That was called something, wasn't it, that feeling?

'Please, don't make me beg you. Give me that, at least.'

'This is going to hurt, you know that, don't you?' she said. 'You know coming off isn't going to be easy.'

'I didn't want the bastard to call now, ok?' said Harry. 'I'm sorry. Just give me the pills!'

'You promise to take one, just one. You call her and then we go to the cottage.'

'Yes, I bloody promise!'

Of course, he would have given up a kidney or the keys to his flat or his own mother, were she alive, to get a single white caplet, a mixture of ten milligrams of the right-handed isomer of amphetamine and good old pharmaceutical sugar powder onto his tongue. The longer he kept it in his mouth before swallowing, the faster and more intense the hit. The quicker he felt alive again. The hit began as he saw Beth, eyes wet, face red, run to the glove compartment, cup her hands, and walk over to him.

'The last one, ok?'

'The last. Just give it here!'

She did, crying, and he took it, and the world was right again. He felt sick but had to keep it down lest he lose the hit.

'Water,' he said.

'You owe me so many dinners for this. A holiday, even.'

'Ok.'

'That safari.'

'Whatever you want,' he said as he drank a whole half-litre in one gulp. 'Now let me make this phone call.'

Noble answered on the seventh ring.

'Can you talk?' he said.

'Yes. What is it?'

'I think I know who did it. And I don't think it was Elyas Mohamed.'

'You better not be talking out of your arse, Harry.'

'I'm not. Dr Utting called. The pathologist. He's got the initial results back from the toxicology. It found—'

'Hang on, hang on,' Noble said. He could hear footsteps, voices talking. Harry had decided to stroll over to a free verge of grass and sit down, where he'd watched the traffic on the motorway for a while. He'd started with three or four ideas, and then out of nowhere they had all pulled together into a single coherent strand. And then he knew. Just like that, like the final punch that ends the round, it was over. Or so it seemed.

'I'm putting you on speaker,' Noble said. 'Just in my office, with Shona, Dave and Superintendent Grenaghan. You still there, Harry?'

'Yeah.'

'Go on.'

'Like I said, Dr Utting called me with the toxicology results—'

'Why didn't they come straight to us?' asked Grenaghan.

'Shut up!' Noble snapped, followed by, 'Erm, sorry, sir, I meant . . .'

Grenaghan snorted. 'Carry on, Dr Kent.'

'There were metabolites of a compound called amitryptiline in Olivia Roberts's blood. Only hers, nothing in Emmanuel's. It's a relatively common drug, an antidepressant, it's used for migraines as well. Fell out of favour, because it's easy to overdose on. Just ten or twenty pills can kill you, and that's in an adult. In a child, three or four could do it. And it would fit entirely with what we know about how Olivia died. It would fit with a sudden collapse. And it's not something that the resuscitation team would ever have thought to look for.'

'So someone gave her the wrong drug?' McGovern said. 'Like, the hospital prescribed the wrong thing?'

'I don't think so,' said Harry. 'Well, I don't think it was an accident. I think Olivia Roberts was murdered by the same person who killed Susan Bayliss.'

'Who?'

He took a deep breath. Thought of the woman he had comforted in her hospital bed.

'Her mother.'

Silence on the end of the phone. The row of the motorway, either outside or inside his own head, Harry wasn't sure. Beth leant on the bonnet of her car, watching him from a distance.

'She's prescribed amitryptiline. I saw it on her drug chart when I documented her wounds at the Ruskin.'

Noble spoke first.

'You're saying that Michelle Roberts killed her own daughter, killed Susan Bayliss, almost killed a police officer, stabbed herself fourteen times and nearly gouged out her own eye?'

'I think so. Yes.'

'You better start making some sense, Harry, because you're starting to make me worried.'

'Ok,' he said. 'I'll try explaining.'

He drained the remnants of a bottle of water. It was swelteringly hot, and his T-shirt stuck to his chest hair like sap.

'Nobody ever found a cause for Olivia Roberts's repeated infections, did they? Her mother took her to seven different hospitals, she constantly wanted new referrals, but every test they did came up negative. Michelle had a blog about the trials of having a sick daughter, and she was quick to join up with the other families when Olivia ended up needing heart surgery. Michelle has rheumatoid arthritis. One of her other medications is called methotrexate. It suppresses the immune system. I think Michelle may have been poisoning Olivia with her own medication. It would cause all of the repeated infections.'

'Why would anyone do that to their own child?' said McGovern.

'There's a psychiatric syndrome,' said Harry, 'called Munchausen's by proxy. Parents make their children sick deliberately, because they crave the attention and the sympathy. It's rare, but it exists. I think Michelle Roberts may have it.'

'And what evidence do you have for that?'

'A few things,' said Harry. 'She's initiated everything. She approached us, to point us towards the Belgrave and Elyas Mohamed in particular. And I didn't spot it at the time, I should have done, but her injury pattern's not quite right. The bathroom door at her house, for instance. Mo's a big guy – there's no way that someone capable of overpowering him wouldn't be able to take down that door, or the front door for that matter. And there's the improbability that she suffered wounds to her face, shoulders, back, buttocks, but not a single injury to her chest, neck or vital areas. And she had a wound to her buttock, but she's not that tall, is she? And all the holes in the door were in the top half . . . So how did she get that wound?'

'Unless she inflicted it herself,' Noble finished his sentence. 'Jesus Christ . . .'

'Why kill Bayliss?' said Grenaghan.

'Of course,' said Harry. 'Why kill Bayliss? I think Michelle had Bayliss under her thumb. Maybe now Olivia was dead and her sympathy was running out, if that was her motive, she had to keep it going somehow, and she chose Mohamed for that, because they slept together. Frankie, do you remember the solicitor, whatever his name was, coming up to us after we met the families that night?'

'Skelton,' said Noble. 'Yeah, I do. He said . . . Oh, Jesus fucking Christ.'

'What did he say?' demanded Grenaghan.

Harry took over.

'He said the last he heard from Bayliss, she asked him if he knew any private companies who could run a toxicology test.'

'Fucking hell!' said Grenaghan. 'She'd worked it out!'

'Bayliss knew,' Harry said. Everyone in the conversation had seen it, but he had to verbalise it, to get those thoughts out and make them real. 'She knew Michelle was a killer.'

Silence again. The sun brighter, the motorway louder.

'Harry, how quickly can you get to the station?' Noble said.

He looked across and saw Beth, now pacing in front of the car, arms folded.

'About that . . .' he said.

There had been a lot of crying. He had apologised, a lot, and begged her just to let him go, drive him back. Or drop him off at a station and he'd get a train, and then he would come out Saturday morning like they'd originally planned. But no, he was just choosing Frankie over her like he always had. She'd got in her car and started the engine, his pills in the glove compartment, and he had stood in front of the car and then reached over and thrown open the passenger door and opened up the compartment whilst she tried to pull his arm away, and he'd told her to get off him, and she'd told him to get off her, and get out of her car, and how the hell could he do this to her. He'd apologised again as he pulled the pill-bottle free, and he'd screamed sorry at the car as it pulled away towards the motorway.

Then he'd got a taxi to Bishop's Stortford and the first train into London. On the way, he'd called Noble again, who had sent officers to Lewisham to access Olivia Roberts's medical records, and called in the forensics team who'd done the Wellington Terrace crime scene. Then he rang a fellow FME, a psychiatrist in his day job, to find out if he knew much about Munchausen's by proxy.

'Don't call it that.'

'What?' said Harry.

'It's not called that anymore. And it's bloody controversial. Get senior advice quickly, mate, before this one goes south.'

'From who?'

He told Harry that if he wanted an expert on medical child abuse, he needed to contact Dr Sreena Gathani, a consultant community paediatrician based in Lambeth. A minute later, he had a number.

When he got into Liverpool Street, a police car was waiting for him. The journey flew by – phone calls to Gathani, who was on her way to Peckham, to Kingston, who said Peter was awake but tired and not in the mood for talking, but doing well, and fleetingly to Beth, who didn't pick up, about which Harry was secretly glad.

At the station, the buzz was palpable, like the tunnel before the big game. Noble greeted him professionally, but failed to disguise the excitement and pride in her smile, and Harry couldn't help but smile too. He was due a win, and though the implications of his deductions were abhorrent, it was impossible not to drink in the feeling. Maybe the fact his skin was glowing from the chemicals helped a bit, too. In the Incident Room, a man Harry recognised as Oscar, the borough forensic manager, was standing before a computer screen, comparing side-by-side images of the bathroom door from Michelle Roberts's house and the injury photographs Harry had taken at the hospital.

'You were right about the injuries, man,' he said. 'Roberts is five-seven. She'd have to stand on a four-inch block for her buttock to line up with the lowest hole in the door.'

'Will that hold up in court?' said Noble.

'Hundred per cent.'

'I should have spotted it sooner,' said Harry.

'Fucking hell, we should have spotted it. Full stop,' Noble said.

He didn't want to sound falsely modest, but it did frustrate him.

He had been the first person to properly assess Michelle Roberts's injuries who'd also been at the scene on Wellington Terrace. He was sure if his mind had been clearer, he would have noticed the mismatch earlier. The bloody pills, and his bloody lack of self-control.

'So is that where we're going with this?' asked McGovern. 'That Michelle put a screwdriver into her own face, just to keep us distracted?'

'It worked,' Noble said. 'The moment she was attacked we completely discounted her as a suspect. Even when we found out about the liaison with Mohamed.'

'But is she really capable of this?'

Harry thought about that. He'd been close to utterly sure of his theory when he called Noble – the amitryptiline in Olivia's blood had opened the floodgates to a wave of suspicion, of things that had subconsciously bothered him about Michelle Roberts ever since she'd followed him from the hospital. Oscar confirming the forensics didn't add up vindicated him somewhat, but it also meant that they had all grossly underestimated her, physically and mentally. She had been strong enough to single-handedly hold down Susan Bayliss whilst she bled to death, and smart enough to outwit an entire murder investigation for a good few days. And whatever delusion drove her, it was sufficiently powerful to keep her hand steady as she thrust a screwdriver into herself fourteen times.

'If our theory's true, she's capable of an awful lot,' Harry said. 'Where is she now?'

'Under police protection,' Noble said. 'At a hotel, up in Euston. Don't worry, we're not going to be lifting it anytime soon. I've informed the FLO that we're looking into Roberts, and not to let her out of her sight.'

Nods from around the room.

'Dr Gathani's here!' someone called.

As they headed downstairs, Noble making it very clear that Harry was welcome to stay, and Harry making it very clear that he intended to, he took her aside.

'Did you tell the liaison officer not to allow Michelle to be alone with her son?'

'Not explicitly,' said Noble.

'If she's already killed one of her children . . .'

'Shit,' said Noble, reaching for her phone.

Dr Gathani had got to the station within twenty minutes, and sat with a cup of green tea she'd picked up on the way steaming on the table in front of her. Harry was on the sofa opposite, with Noble and McGovern on the one closest to the paediatrician, who seemed entirely at ease in this environment. They'd searched her on Google and ResearchGate while waiting. Gathani was the designated paediatrician for child welfare issues for the whole borough, and a leading expert in child protection, with special interests in what she termed 'medical child abuse'. They'd been strictly told, at the start of conversation, that the label 'Munchausen's by proxy' was not helpful.

'Now, I'm not saying that this condition doesn't exist,' Gathani said. 'In fact, a lot of my research sets about proving that it does. I've seen three cases personally, which were independently confirmed, that's about as sure as anyone can be in this profession, and a handful more which I've suspected. But it's not a disease by itself. The best way to explain it is as a pattern of behaviour which may be exhibited by individuals with any number of psychopathological disorders.'

'So what do you call it now?' Harry said.

'The correct terminology is factitious or induced illness by proxy. FIIP.' Gathani leant forward and sipped her tea. 'The motivation of the caregiver varies. Most of the patients have a background of a long-term psychiatric condition, usually a personality disorder or a long-standing mood disorder. Many of them are also sufferers of factitious or induced disorder themselves, what we used to call Munchausen's. That means they either fake symptoms of disease or induce disease in themselves, as well as in their children.'

She coughed.

'You think you may have a case?'

Harry leant back into the sofa, looking at Noble, who said, 'We have circumstantial physical evidence that a four-year-old child died following amitryptiline poisoning. We believe the girl's mother may be responsible.'

'Tell me the story,' Gathani said.

Noble looked across: 'You do it, Harry.'

Harry reached over to the table, picked up a glass of water, and drank the lot. His heart was hammering again, another of the palpitations, but that didn't bother him much anymore. Compared to what he'd seen of the lows, the effects of the high were a walk in the park. They had a copy of Olivia Roberts's medical notes, a summary anyway, in front of them. Harry remembered most of the detail, but referred to the pages occasionally.

'The, erm, suspected victim is a four-year-old girl,' Harry said, stuttering, forehead sweaty. 'She had a history of recurrent infections for approximately two years, with frequent attendance at A&E and primary care services. Sometimes UTIs, sometimes unknown cause. She was extensively investigated – immune screenings, radiology, you name it – presented to seven different hospitals in London over the two years, and was an outpatient under three separate clinics. She had repeated low blood counts, particularly white blood cells, but no-one could find a medical cause for her recurrent infections, and they diagnosed her with a 'cryptogenic immune deficiency.'

'Cryptogenic?' Noble said. 'In English?'

'Bollocks medical speak for "we don't know what causes it",' said Harry. 'She's had three inpatient admissions, too, culminating in an episode of infective endocarditis in January, when she underwent surgery at Belgrave.'

'Surgery?' said Gathani.

'Ross procedure – aortic valve replacement. She had aortic valve problems after the endocarditis,' said Harry. 'Postoperatively she did well. No further healthcare attendances other than follow-up. In April, she suffered a cardiac arrest at her nursery and died.'

'And they found amitryptiline in her blood?'

'Not at the time,' said Noble. 'We had samples tested recently, following some other investigations.'

She looked at Harry, that half-grin again. Gathani sipped her tea, now sitting bolt upright.

'Is this linked to the dead doctor?' she said. 'And the police officer who was stabbed?'

'Yes,' said Noble. Harry looked across at her, surprised that she'd let that go so easily, but he could follow her thoughts. At this stage, they wanted something that fitted with their preconceptions.

'Who's your suspect?'

'The girl's mother,' said Harry. 'She was also injured in the attack on Wednesday. We have evidence that suggests her injuries were self-inflicted, and the entire attack was staged.'

'What other evidence do you have?'

'The mother has rheumatoid arthritis,' he said. 'And she's prescribed amitryptiline. And methotrexate.'

Gathani nodded, thinking out loud.

'You found amitryptiline in the daughter's blood,' she said. 'And the methotrexate could explain the infections. That would fit. Mothers are the abusers in ninety per cent of reported cases. Age? Occupation? Socioeconomic group?'

'Late thirties. Housewife. Well off.'

'The husband,' said Gathani, 'is he distant? Away from the family unit a lot? Doesn't appear interested in her or the children?'

Noble looked across at Harry, mouth open in shock. Even she was unable to hide her obvious awe at Gathani's description of Euan Roberts, a man she had never met. This apparent super-power of some truly expert doctors, of course a function only of statistics and a knack for pattern-recognition, always made Harry's hair stand on end.

'I'll take that as a yes, then. Second question. Is she knowledge-able about medicine? Does she like to discuss the treatments with the doctors and nurses, or even suggest them? Does she try and ingratiate herself into the medical team, or socialise with the doctors?'

'Jesus . . .' said McGovern.

Gathani looked between them, so Harry explained.

'Yes, on both counts. She was working very closely with Susan Bayliss, one of the registrars. They were trying to pursue a legal case against the hospital . . . She also had sex with her daughter's consultant surgeon, on the night her daughter was in ICU.'

Harry thought of Elyas Mohamed, his protestations that

Roberts had initiated their encounter, that she had seduced him, not the other way round. At the time he had dismissed it as arrogance, misogyny, but now it had the ring of truth about it.

'Wow . . .' Gathani said. 'I'm asking you leading questions. But I've seen it before, a mother with a chronic health condition inducing illness by poisoning the child with their own medication. Usually it's a diabetic mother injecting their child with insulin. I've never heard it happen with methotrexate, but it would make sense, wouldn't it?'

'Sorry,' said Noble. 'Forgive my ignorance, but how would it make sense?'

'Methotrexate weakens the immune system,' explained Harry. 'That's why it's useful in autoimmune diseases like rheumatoid. But its major side effect is a propensity for the kind of infections Olivia Roberts suffered with her whole life.'

'Shit,' said Noble.

'I know some of this is difficult to hear,' Gathani said. 'And I should be quite clear. I'm not saying that this is a case of FIIP. I'm saying it's a possibility.'

'But the story fits?' said Noble.

Gathani drummed her fingers on the table.

'Elements of it certainly fit. The suspect's demographic profile, intimate relationships with the medical staff, presence of a chronic illness in the mother, public appearances, internet blogs. And certainly, injuring oneself to avoid suspicion or to garner sympathy would fit, very much so. Previous cases have feigned medical emergencies themselves or in their children when questioned . . .' she tailed off. 'The amitryptiline is unusual . . . Did the daughter ever have any cardiac problems previous to the endocarditis?'

'Not that I know of,' said Harry.

'And the mother, was she ever challenged about the infections, ever accused of causing them?'

'Again, not that we know of,' said Noble.

And Harry was back in the cafe by Southwark Cathedral, listening to an outraged, charismatic Michelle Roberts recount her daughter's story of pain and suffering. She'd sold him a story and he'd bought every inch of it.

'Well, not maliciously,' said Harry. 'She said that at times the nurses had suggested she was somehow failing to care for her daughter when she was going to the toilet. That that might be the cause of the infections. She took that to mean they were accusing her of being a bad mother.'

'Most cases of FIIP have a single method of abuse,' said Gathani. 'A modus operandi, for want of a better term. Smothering, poisoning with salt, or something that causes a large amount of medical intervention and investigation and hence attention for the perpetrator. It's unusual for the perpetrator to switch methods of abuse. So I don't see, if this woman has been poisoning her child for years with methotrexate, why she would suddenly switch to antidepressants.'

'What if that's not why she switched to it?' said Harry.

'I'm sorry?'

'Olivia Roberts was prescribed antibiotics for six months after she was discharged,' he said. 'To stop her new valve getting infected. That might have prevented the infections.'

Harry's brain was moving quickly now, and he realised that, if he was right, the connection between Roberts and the rest of the cases was becoming obvious.

'Three weeks before Olivia died, another child suffered a cardiac arrest. A boy whose parents had been in the support group Michelle Roberts ran. If you're saying that this is all about attention, could that be what prompted her to do something more drastic?'

Gathani was drumming her fingers again, evidently sitting on the fence. In Harry's head, it all made sense, and whilst some of the police officers were still getting their heads around it all, he could tell Noble bought it, too. Slowly, he watched Gathani's face change.

'Does this woman have any other children?' she said.

'Yes, a son,' said Noble. 'They're under police guard.'

'Good,' said Gathani. 'It sounds like you might have a particularly dangerous individual here. If this is all true, she's not only driven by a powerful psychopathological need – one which overrides even her most basic desires as a mother – but she is also organised and determined enough to cover her tracks. I've never encountered such an individual before.'

Harry could agree with that summary. Roberts's greatest asset had been how non-threatening she seemed to the world. Perhaps that had been Wilson's downfall. He was unlucky enough to be first on the scene and he'd opened the door to see a damsel in distress, covered in blood, and dropped his guard. Not seeing the screwdriver in her hand until it was plunged into his own body.

'How do we catch her?' said Noble.

'Bloody carefully,' said Gathani. 'I'll tell you right now that if you charge this woman, you can forget about using a diagnosis of FIIP against her in court. It's so controversial, the lawyers won't even mention it. In fact, the defence might attack you for even talking about it during the investigation.'

'Why?' asked Noble.

'Because it's not proven that this entity exists yet,' said Gathani. 'And moreover, there was a series of cases in the 2000s where innocent women whose children had died of SIDS – sudden infant death syndrome – were sent to prison purely based on a trumped-up diagnosis of Munchausen's by proxy. All were later exonerated, but like I said, it's a toxic word. The lawyers won't go anywhere near it.'

'Point taken,' said Noble. Harry had always loved her impatience. Gathani raised a hand.

'What I mean by that is, if you make an arrest you have to have solid evidence that will stand up in court irrespective of what I've said or any psychiatric evidence. Or you'll never make it stick.'

'How do we catch her, then?' said Noble.

Gathani thought for a while. Harry was thinking, too. It would be a difficult one if it ever came to court. There was no way to prove that the amitryptiline in Olivia Roberts's blood had been put there by her mother, and whilst it seemed obvious to them that Michelle Roberts had staged the entire attack on her, a jury would likely take more convincing. Could they get evidence that Roberts had killed Bayliss? Probably not. The two had been friends, Roberts had visited the flat before. That could explain any DNA evidence they might find.

'I'd start with her past,' said Gathani. 'If she's managed to build up to murder to cover up her abuse, I'd bet there's something previous, which can be used in court as long as you avoid giving her a label. A series of unexplained injuries or illnesses in children under her care, younger siblings, kids she's babysat for. Maybe even the death of a previous child – in twenty-five per cent of cases, an older child is already dead by the time the abuse is recognised.'

Harry thought about that. Already, Olivia Roberts was a statistic.

'Or a history of factitious or induced illness in herself,' Gathani continued. 'The classic would be school or university friends believing she had cancer or some other life-threatening disease, which is totally fictitious.'

'Ok,' said Noble. 'You've been incredibly helpful. Thank you so much.'

She got up to leave, McGovern following her. Harry went to do the same, before something else occurred to him.

'Sorry, just one more thing.'

'Yes?'

'If we do end up making an arrest, how is she likely to react?'

Gathani looked down at her tea and nodded slowly.

'Good question. The only thing these individuals really have in common is that they're unpredictable. The husbands and family usually defend them to the hilt. Some women break down and confess the moment they're confronted. That would be one end of the spectrum . . .'

'And the other?' said Noble.

Gathani looked up, now completely serious.

'I've known of one case where the woman concerned found out about the hospital's suspicions. She killed herself and her child.'

Noble looked up at Harry, her face hard. He got her message. That would not be happening on her watch, and in that silent moment Harry vowed that he would do everything in his power to ensure it.

'I'm not saying that'll happen,' Gathani said. 'I mean it's obviously a worst-case scenario . . .'

Her words, of course, were lost.

'Right!' Noble said, standing on a chair in a corner of the Incident Room. 'We have a clear prime suspect. We have a child at risk. This is it, ladies and gentlemen. I need your very best work over the next few hours. We cannot fuck this one up. Is that clear?'

'Yes, guv!' came the chorus. They had no idea how much she was shitting herself. The words sunk in more when she was tub-thumping like this. Grenaghan was setting up a task force with the sole purpose of arresting and charging Michelle Roberts: he was liaising with the Crown Prosecution Service, the Coroner's Office, the Child Protection Unit and everyone else he could think of. In the meantime he had put Noble in charge of finding out as much about this woman as they possibly could. Whether that was a show of faith or hanging her out to dry she wasn't sure, and didn't care. The task force would meet at six o'clock, and Grenaghan wanted as much information as possible by that time.

She delegated roles quickly. They were fortunate enough to still have access to the Roberts home as a crime scene, and thus didn't need a warrant to search it. Oscar's team from Forensics were on their way over now to strip the floorboards, prowl through the rubbish and deconstruct Michelle Roberts's physical life. Others were set with ripping apart the rest of this woman's existence – credit card bills, purchases, university records – had she attended? nobody knew – friends, relatives, childhood experiences, medical records. Anything that could be useful, that could give them something. Others still went for more conventional work – reviewing CCTV of the streets, bus stops and train stations near the Bayliss flat on the night of her murder, looking for Roberts or someone who could be Roberts. Of course, if they could find the phone or the SIM card she'd used to lure Mohamed to North Greenwich, they'd have a slam dunk.

Harry meanwhile had demanded full copies of Olivia Roberts's medical records for her entire four years of life, not just her heart operations, and Noble had accordingly sent officers to Lewisham General, the Belgrave and the Evelina with express orders not to come back empty-handed, no matter who tried to bullshit them away. Noble had asked for Michelle's records, too. They needed the paper-trail to prove that she was on amitryptiline at the time of Olivia's murder, and she knew first-hand how bloody-minded doctors were about handing out their patients' records. She was also dispatching detectives to track down all of Olivia Roberts's previous doctors on the off-chance they remembered anything suspicious – not an easy task, seeing how frequently she had changed hospitals.

They also had to prove that Harry was right, that Olivia had been poisoned by methotrexate. Calls to Forensics and a professor of toxicology had revealed that, like most drugs, the longest it would hang around would be in hair, and their window for that was ninety days. Given that hair tended to degrade slowly after death, Oscar thought that they might be lucky if they dug her up soon, but that itself was a catch-22. To get permission to exhume a child would need a decent amount of evidence, which they could acquire only by doing it.

At the back of the room, whilst she threw out these tasks, Harry was leaning against the wall, arms folded, deep in thought. Something about him wasn't right, hadn't been right this past week, and yet still, within all that bullshit and madness, was the angle from which he had seen things connect. Nobody else had done that.

'Come on, then,' Noble exhorted the detectives as they moved to their assigned stations. 'I want to be in the pub by the end of the week, buying all of you bastards a drink!'

And having a lime and tonic all to myself, she thought.

Late in the afternoon some of the initial excitement had worn off, and Harry found himself in the trough after the peak. Noble had let him stay in her office, whilst she alternated between smoking outside with the phone in her hand and taking queries from her team. He had lowered the blinds to give himself some shade and sat down cross-legged on the floor. Until anything else medically related came up he was something of a spare part. He could leave now, head held high, the man of the hour, reconvene with Beth and head off to Norfolk, in the unlikely event she would give him a fourth, perhaps a fifth chance. Or clear out his savings account and check into one of those celebrity rehab clinics.

Then Olivia Roberts's full records arrived from Lewisham and the Evelina. He took a pill and read in the half-dark, looking either for minor clues or things he'd missed the first time he'd looked at them. If they were right, and he had little doubt they were, then once the dust settled there would inevitably be an inquiry into how five separate NHS trusts had missed a gross case of child abuse over three years, culminating in the murder of two people. But that could wait. Like Noble had said, there was a child at risk, and a dangerous woman who needed to be in either a prison or a hospital that felt like one.

And he felt some need to see it through, to the end. Not that it mattered, really. Maybe it was a want, not a need. Just like the pills. He tried not to think about his cowardice, not sticking it out with Beth. If he'd just called, if he hadn't returned to explain it, then maybe they wouldn't have focussed so quickly on Roberts. Whether that changed anything, whether it had been worth wrecking his best chance in months at meaningful recovery . . .

He read and read and saw just what he'd seen before. Blood test after blood test showing a low white cell count, anaemia. Bone marrow tests and MRI scans and biopsies to rule out leukaemia, lymphoma, aplastic anaemia, those life-threatening diseases.

It all fitted their theory about methotrexate, but there was nothing to prove it.

He read some more, got up and went to the toilet and vomited until his throat was raw. Took his pulse, reassured himself it was less than one-twenty, and wished – the irony plain and apparent – that the pill pot labelled aspirin actually contained some, to ease the pain in his chest.

He went back to the room, feeling the leaden weight of sleep dragging at the corners of his mind.

Took a pill.

A knock on the door brought him out of rumination.

'Hey,' said Noble. 'Are you meditating or something?'

Harry shook his head.

'D'you want tea? Coffee? Diet Coke?'

'I'm fine,' he said.

'Michelle Roberts's GP isn't budging on her records.'

'She takes them both,' Harry said. 'I saw it on her chart at the Ruskin.'

'I believe you,' said Noble. 'We're working on it.'

She left him be and he kept reading – all the notes from the Evelina, all the stumped doctors, then back to the ones from Lewisham, more results, more tests, more investigations. He finished with the pink paper of the A&E notes from the 8th April describing Olivia Roberts's last few minutes of life, and he was reminded again of the similar efforts to save Emmanuel. If some genius had thought about amitryptiline then, could they have saved her? Probably not, Harry thought.

He found what he needed right at the end of the page. It wasn't what he was looking for but it was a break, perhaps the first bit of luck they'd had in a while.

He reread it and stood up and opened the door and shouted, 'Frankie!'

She came quickly.

'What is it?'

'Look,' said Harry, and pointed to the last entry in the A&E notes for Olivia Roberts.

Bereavement Liaison Team – SN Mukherjee

Called to Paediatric Resus by ED doctor. Met with mother (Michelle) – informed father out of the country with work. Explained resuscitation and escorted mother to witness resuscitation and decision to cease resuscitative efforts.

Withdrew Mrs Roberts to Relatives Room and comforted with chaplain Fr. Simon.

Once ED had prepared body escorted Mrs Roberts to viewing room. Created Memories Box (photo, hand and footprints, lock of hair) which Mrs Roberts took with her. Agreed to stay with Mrs Roberts until husband could be found. Friend arrived shortly afterwards.

Counselled re services available for follow-up as per Child Bereavement Protocol.

Noble had spotted it too.

'A lock of hair? In a Memories Box.'

'They do it for children who've died,' Harry said. 'The bereavement nurses come around and do hand and footprints of the child, take a lock of hair. Assuming she hasn't got rid of it, that means a sample of Olivia's hair we can test.'

'Without digging her up,' said Noble. 'Fucking brilliant.'

'It might be nothing,' said Harry. 'She might not have given her any methotrexate in the last few months.'

'Yeah, but if she has, we've got her fucking nailed.'

Noble got on the phone and called the DC who was leading the search of the Roberts house, telling him about the Memories Box and the lock of hair, to make finding it a priority. Harry got out of his chair and stumbled over, his peripheries greying again, his heart trying to break free of its ribcage prison walls.

'Jesus, are you alright?'

'Fine. Just dehydrated.'

'You know, you can go home if you want, Harry. You've done a top job on this one, we genuinely couldn't have done it without you. I'll make sure you invoice for all your hours and the rest, and we'll speak to the AC about getting you a civilian commendation or something.'

'I'm fine, Frankie!'

'Ok,' she said, lowering her voice. Speaking to him as if he were crazy. 'You don't smell too good. There's a shower down on the ground floor, in the uniform's changing room. No-one'll mind.'

She slipped her key-card into his hand. He felt the touch of her skin, cold and pure against his. Was it the first time he'd touched her since they'd been working together? Wasn't that sad?

'The briefing's at six,' she said. 'Take a break, freshen up, get something to drink, something to eat.'

He said nothing, just nodded like a child.

'And if you change your mind and you wanna go home, just go, ok? I'm not having you keeling over on me, alright? I've got enough friends in hospital already.'

Harry smiled, but felt like crying. The trajectories of the last week had reached their destinations, and their roles were now fully and totally reversed. He the addict, blinded to the fact that the chemicals with which he was intoxicated were obliterating any ability to do his job properly, she the caring partner, torn between her loyalty to say nothing – because of course she knew, how couldn't she? – and her inability to simply watch him fall apart and say nothing.

'See you then,' he said.

First he walked to Marks & Spencer and bought a fresh shirt, a can of deodorant and a sandwich, although he could manage only a few bites. Then he went and took a long, cold shower. He felt a little better as he filed into the Incident Room a few minutes before six o'clock. One of the detectives had an expensive digital watch that could measure the temperature, and had earlier informed the crowd that despite the air-con and the opening of every available window, it was a balmy thirty-one degrees.

It felt like he'd been at the police station for days, as if the morning – in Kinirons's office, in the car with Beth, leaving her at the motorway services – was a mere hallucination, a different reality.

When he arrived, the Incident Room had a buzz to it, a group of detectives crowding around a single desk, looking excited. He spotted Noble amongst them and went over.

'What is it?' he mouthed.

Noble left the huddle and came to him, her voice low.

'DC Bhalla's on the phone to some sergeant from Police Scotland.'

'Scotland?' said Harry.

'We traced Roberts through passport and census records,' said McGovern. 'She was born Michelle Knox in Perth, and grew up in a small village called –' she looked at a printout – 'Bridge of Earn. We've tracked down the neighbourhood officer, a Sergeant Bannerman.'

Harry looked over at Noble, confused, and she nodded, the telepathy complete. Roberts had not sounded Scottish in the slightest.

'You are sure you've got the right person?' said Noble.

'Yeah. Marriage certificate lists Knox as her maiden name, place of birth in her passport is Perth, Scotland.'

'Look,' said Bhalla, obviously excited, 'just hear what the man has to say, alright?'

Everyone shut up. Bhalla removed his hand.

'Sergeant, I'm putting you on speakerphone. My Chief Inspector's listening. Would you mind repeating everything you've told me?'

'Aye, for sure,' Bannerman said, sounding like an extra on *Monarch of the Glen*. 'I was wondering when someone would call about Michelle Knox, truth be told. I'm no' surprised it's London.'

At that titbit, eyes met across the room. It was obvious that Bannerman was relishing this moment, and wanted to tell the story his way, frustrating as it was. Harry pictured him in some rural cottage police station, rolling hills in the background, although he knew in reality he was probably in a centralised concrete block by a motorway somewhere. Noble looked on the verge of starting an interrogation when Bannerman resumed talking.

'Knox family never did fit in around here. They were from Edinburgh, big land developers. The father bought up land for golf courses. They lived out in their own place, didn't mix much with the locals, sent Michelle to a private school down in the Borders where they all get English accents.'

Harry presumed that Bhalla had uncovered more than just an unhappy childhood. He listened intently.

'From that kind of upbringing we were all surprised when the lass married so young, nineteen or so, and a local boy, too, one of the MacKenzies. Big farming family. Her folks were furious. I don't believe they even attended the wedding, but the newlyweds seemed happy enough. Had a little place on the edge of the village. Still feel so sorry for what happened to them.'

Harry had a terrifying feeling of where this was going, and had to steady himself on the edge of a desk. Bannerman was enjoying his moment too much, and Noble cut in.

'What happened?'

'They had a wee lad. I forget his name. Angus, I think. The boy died.'

Harry's stomach twisted. Everyone crowded round. Bhalla played with the phone to up the volume.

'Someone get the super,' Noble barked.

'How?'

'He'd been sickly for a while. They were always up at the hospital, and there were ambulances at the house a good few times. Kept getting these infections, if I remember rightly. I remember hearing they were taking him to Glasgow for appointments, to try and find out what was going on. And then one morning they woke up and Angus was dead, had died in his sleep. Absolute tragedy. Doctors said it was septicaemia.'

'God damn her,' someone said. Harry shook his head. If Michelle had killed her first child, too, it put her total number of victims at three. Four if Moses Wilson was counted. It was horrifying.

334

'After that, poor Michelle was destroyed. She walked out on her husband a few months later, said she was going off to some retreat in California. No-one ever heard from her again. Parents moved away pretty shortly, too. God's truth, I always thought she wasn't long for this world. I always thought I'd get a call like this, to tell me she'd been found somewhere, that she'd taken her own life. Poor wee lass.'

'Was there an investigation?' Noble demanded. 'Into the death?'

'Oh, no,' said Bannerman. 'I mean, I visited them, the doctor went around the house and all that, one of our Child Protection girls from Stirling came down, but there was nothing suspicious at all. No signs of shaking, neither of them had ever had any previous trouble. Doctors were all happy, too. Said the poor lad's blood was full of bugs. I wasn't going to start pulling their lives apart, not in that situation.'

Noble wore a look of anger which mirrored a few of her colleagues'. They might never tell if a full investigation would have uncovered signs of abuse. Hindsight was a wonderful thing.

'What about a post-mortem?' said Harry.

'Aye, there was. I had to drive the poor thing down to Glasgow for that. Septicaemia, like I said.'

Silence in the room, unless you counted the sounds of blinds flapping in the winds of the twelve or so fans valiantly trying to cool the air. Twenty or so individuals realising the magnitude of what they had uncovered. Harry thought back to that heavy Sunday morning, bag over his shoulder, heading into the Bayliss flat to certify her death. He had not in his worst nightmares imagined it leading here. In that instant he regretted everything – allowing Noble to go into his flat or answering her calls, allowing himself to be dragged into this world of horror. Pretending it was one he did not already inhabit.

'Anyway,' Bannerman said. 'Why the interest?'

The sergeant sounded like this phone call was the highlight of his year. Noble shook her head and started back towards her office.

'One of you tell him,' she said.

★   ★   ★

Noble's office.

Harry leant back against the wall. Grenaghan sat in the swivel chair, fingers in a V about his angular jaw, Noble perched on the desk, as many buttons undone on her blouse as decorum would allow. Dr Gathani was in there as well, on another chair.

'I've spoken to the CPS,' said Grenaghan. 'I tried, I really did, but even with the stuff about this other child in Scotland, they'll not budge.'

'How long will the forensics take on the hair sample?' said Noble.

She had let Harry know as soon as the search team had recovered the Memories Box from a drawer of teddies in Olivia's still-preserved room at the Roberts house. Harry, in turn, had called Utting and Dr Wynn-Jones, who had told him not to get his hopes up, something that Oscar the forensics manager had then confirmed.

'A week or so even on a priority,' he said. 'Maybe more if the sample's degraded or the results are uncertain.'

'Bloody forensics,' said Grenaghan. 'And we've got bugger-all from CCTV.'

The thumping of the air-conditioning filled the silence, each rotation a fresh headache for Harry. No-one spoke, so he thought he might as well.

'As far as I'm concerned, this is beyond a criminal case,' said Harry. 'This is a child protection issue. We've got a boy currently living with a woman who, as far as we know, has killed two of her three children. We need to get him into protective care.'

'It's a good point,' said Gathani. 'And I agree entirely. Social services should certainly be involved by now – we need to have a case conference about Preston based on these concerns about Olivia.'

'With respect, doctors,' Grenaghan said. 'This is a murder investigation, and that takes primacy.'

'What if she hurts him?' Noble said.

Grenaghan yawned and covered his mouth with a hand.

'How likely is that to happen?' he said.

'If she's abused and killed both her other children, I'd say it's inevitable,' said Gathani. 'Not necessarily soon, and if it's methotrexate, it could be months, years even, before Preston begins to feel the effects.'

'So there's no acute danger,' said Grenaghan.

'Of course there's an acute danger,' said Harry. 'She's a mentally unstable woman and she's under a lot of stress. Even if she doesn't suspect that we're onto her, she's going to be grossly paranoid.'

'If we arrest her now without sufficient evidence we'll have to let her go after forty-eight hours, and then she'll know we're onto her,' said Grenaghan. 'I agree, Preston would be safer if we arrest her right this evening, but if we do that, we blow our best shot at a conviction.'

'I've got an idea, sir . . .'

It was Noble, who had appeared deep in thought whilst Harry and Gathani bickered with the superintendent. She had a knowing look in her eyes which Harry recognised.

'We move the Roberts family to another location. Another hotel room, tell them it's a standard security measure. We bring in covert surveillance, microphones and cameras, the full shebang, give her a laptop on which we monitor the keystrokes. Leave her alone for most of the time, have at least four officers on stand-by, a senior officer on-call. If we can catch her in the act, giving Preston her medication, then we've got her. Gives us time to wait on the toxicology or anything else, and also means that we can keep Preston safe.'

'I like it,' said Grenaghan. 'One of these methotrexate pills won't kill him, will it?'

'Not one,' said Harry. 'But you do realise that this approach is effectively using him as bait, don't you?'

'We'll have them under 24/7 surveillance,' said Noble. 'With an arrest team ready to go. The moment we get any evidence we can use against her, we'll nick her.'

Harry stood, again furious that he hadn't made the connection earlier between Michelle's methotrexate prescription and her daughter's recurrent infections. Neither, it seemed, had any of the other doctors who'd seen or treated Olivia Roberts over the four years of her life. Assuming they broke it, this case would surely spark one of the biggest serious case reviews in recent memory. Heads would roll, scapegoats would be found, and very little would change.

He realised they were looking at him, seeking his assent to the surveillance. Even if he objected, it wouldn't really mean anything.

He shrugged.

'Ok.'

Noble could not fail to be impressed by the speed at which everything had been set up. Maybe it was the spectre of one of their colleagues in hospital, or the high-profile nature of the investigation, but the oft-lethargic Metropolitan Police apparatus had swung into a gear she had never seen before. Two nondescript vans had arrived at a block of holiday apartments on Southwark Bridge Road where the Met had hired out a two-bedroom mezzanine in which to safeguard the Roberts family. It took the surveillance team, working in almost absolute silence, about forty-five minutes to install cameras in the living room, kitchen, master bedroom and child's bedroom, into which they had moved a box of Preston's favourite toys and blankets from the house in Greenwich. That latter point had been Harry's idea, another way of trying to minimise the chances of Roberts suspecting that they suspected her.

The command room in which they now sat was across the road in a Premier Inn, a ground-floor business suite fitted out with four different camera screens and outputs from the ten microphones secreted in the apartment. They could also listen in to any phone conversations, watch in real-time whatever was displayed on the screen of the apartment's computer, and, through a device placed on the apartment's Wi-Fi modem, read anything that Roberts accessed over the internet on her phone.

Noble made a point of thanking the surveillance unit as they left, and watched on CCTV as Michelle Roberts unloaded a Waitrose delivery into the fridge. For the first time since the attack on Wednesday, she had been left in peace. There were two police officers outside the seventh-floor apartment, and another four in plain-clothes in the lobby outside, working shifts, but inside she was alone.

Noble watched as Euan Roberts emerged from Preston's bedroom, wheeling a carry-on bag behind him, his pilot's uniform folded in a suit-bag over one shoulder.

'Do you *have* to go to Heathrow tonight?' said Michelle, her voice tinny over the speakers in the control room.

'Wheels up at six-thirty,' he said, 'need to be there half-four. If I get a taxi, that means I'm up at three. And I need the sleep.'

He kissed her coolly on the cheek and headed for the door.

'Maybe you and Preston should come out to Dubai for a week or two. The company's been very supportive, they'd put you up in a suite in one of the resorts. Get away from this shit.'

'When this comes out, it's gonna hit him like a ton of bricks,' said Harry Kent's voice behind her.

Noble turned.

'Maybe,' she said. 'But then again, maybe it won't. He hasn't given a shit about the family for four years, why would he start now?'

Harry shook his head.

'His wife's murdered his child. And kept a previous marriage from him, so we assume,' he said. 'I can't imagine that'll be easy.'

Noble looked at him, dressed in a shirt on which she could still see the creases from the box. Where had he been going earlier, when he had interrupted his morning to call and tell her what the pathologist had found in Olivia Roberts's blood? For a while now, he hadn't seemed right. If he had been any other of her colleagues perhaps she would have taken him aside and sat him down, maybe had a quiet drink with him, found out whether there was anything amiss. But instead, she had exploited Harry. Because she enjoyed having him around, or because he was useful. He had broken their case and delivered them a triple murderer. Without him a colleague and friend would be dead.

'Why are you here?' she said. While they had set up the operation, he had gone with Dr Gathani to open a child protection review case for Preston with social services.

'I wanted to stick around,' said Harry. 'It's not every day you get to watch an operation like this one.'

'Fair enough,' said Noble.

'Anyway, I'm leaving now,' said Harry. 'Just wanted to say good luck, and call me if you need me, or if anything happens.'

'I'll see you out,' said Noble.

She left the room, giving instructions to the detective in charge of the control room – they were doing six-hour shifts in groups of

four – to call her if anything unusual happened. Most of the officers had been drafted in, and she was not familiar with them.
Ordinarily she would have delegated it to McGovern, but she had
gone up to Scotland to begin the investigation into Angus
MacKenzie's death.

'Are you alright, Harry?'

He looked at her with worn-out eyes, and she remembered
coming into her office and seeing him cross-legged on the floor,
Olivia Roberts's notes laid out in front of him, exhaustion personified. It could be drink, she thought. In the time they'd spent
together, he had often had a glass of Jameson's to send him to
sleep. In fact, she thought that their relationship had probably
made him cut down a little. Maybe now she wasn't around to
serve as a breathing reminder of the hell of addiction, his defences
had broken down.

'I've been better,' he said. 'This has all been a bit much.'

Noble nodded as they descended carpeted stairs.

'You go and sort yourself out, then,' she said. 'We couldn't have
done this without you, but we have it under wraps now.'

'No. I want to see this through till the end.'

He looked at her, his voice cracking.

'I think you're probably the only person who understands why
that's important to me.'

'Ok,' Noble said, feeling as if she'd swallowed acid. God, how
many people's lives had she trashed? 'I'll keep you in the loop.'

'Thanks, Frankie. I'll see you around.'

Harry wandered back to his flat, stopping now and then, staring
at office-block windows or drain covers or the neon lights in
newsagents' windows.

Looking at a streetlamp on the corner of Great Suffolk Street,
he thought back to the conversation with Kinirons. In a single day,
he had managed to pretty much lose his job and, given that Beth
had not responded to a single one of his pathetic apology texts, his
relationship, too. He stared at his phone. Tammas, delirious and
insensate, could not console him tonight. Briefly, he considered
calling the hospital and asking for Tennyson Ward, and for the
phone to be placed to Zara's ear so he could recount his troubles

to her, knowing that in her truncated consciousness she would not judge him. Then he laughed at that proposal.

Reaching into the pocket of his jeans, he fingered the pills which had consumed him like a cancer. He thought again of the emphysematous young man in A&E, fighting for each and every breath but unable to stop himself lifting a cigarette to his lips the moment he was discharged.

Young and old people passed him by, on buses and on bikes, in taxis and holding hands, swigging beer in the August sunshine between pubs, on their way to bars.

He was just another man sobbing on a London street on a Friday night.

He hailed a taxi, took it back home. Stood in the lift up to his apartment, head heavy, asleep standing up, awoken by the ping announcing his arrival. Came through his door, leaving in his key, not bothering to lock it behind him. Fell asleep face-down on his bed, fully dressed.

When he woke he felt better, although he had no comprehension of how much time had really passed. He became slowly aware of a figure at the end of the bed. It was his old friend, James Lahiri.

'Long time no speak,' Harry said.

'Yeah. How have you been?'

'Better,' said Harry.

'How's the boss?'

'Not too good. Got a UTI, they're thinking about taking him to hospital. But he doesn't want to go.'

'Of course he doesn't. They'd have to drag him kicking and screaming. Well, not much kicking.'

Harry laughed. Lahiri always had been humorous about the boss's predicament.

'Why did you leave me?' Lahiri asked.

'I didn't. I came back for you.'

'But it was too late. Just like you were too late with the boss.'

'It wouldn't have made a difference,' Harry said. It was true, but it still felt like a lie that he was telling himself.

'Who can say, what makes a difference and what doesn't?' Lahiri said, gesturing around him at the city, now the walls of his apartment had collapsed. Harry looked across the whole of London, the lights potent as they had been from Susan Bayliss's balcony.

Figures hung in the darkness, suspended from wires that disappeared up into the black sky.

Victor Proud, being resuscitated, seizing. Moses Wilson with his chest open. Michelle Roberts cowering in fear, covered in wood splinters, blood dripping from her lips. Charlotte writhing on the trolley. Elyas Mohamed on a video screen. Susan Bayliss, arms akimbo in a black pool of blood. Frankie Noble, tights around her ankles, hand on his back, pulling him deeper inside her. The question was pertinent. How did he know which of these lives his interventions had changed, where his wind had caught the sails? He couldn't know.

'You left me,' James said.

'I didn't.'

'You did. Once for Alice, and again on the boat. After all I did for you.'

'I paid it back. I found the men who did it. I made sure they got justice.'

'What, three weeks in agony or twenty years in Belmarsh?'

'They paid for what they did.'

'Will you?'

Harry looked James in the eyes.

'Will I what?'

TEN

Saturday, 30 August
Morning

He woke in pain. A throbbing, physical pain in his head, and the fear of full-blown withdrawal, heart pounding in his chest, the taste of acid and metal in his mouth, his clothes drenched with sweat. He staggered to the kitchen, drank two pints of water. Staggered to the bathroom, took two pills and one paracetamol. Pulled off his clothes and sat down in the shower, letting water drift over him.

He remembered the dream or the hallucination, or whatever it had been. Again, time disappeared. He could have been in the shower ten minutes or an hour. The water ran hot then cold but he didn't really notice. He was deep in thought, remembering Noble's words.

We couldn't have done this without you.

He had helped catch a dangerous woman, potentially saved the life of a vulnerable child.

He'd expected elation, a feeling of release, but had no such comfort. This coping strategy, using other people's suffering as a crutch, had failed completely. He could no longer hide behind others' needs, because they had no need for it anymore. Some damage was irretrievable. Beth was lost to him, perhaps his job too . . .

He got out of the shower and looked out at the city, then opened up his computer and found the number of the helpline Beth had recommended: the Practitioner Health Programme. Holding his phone in his hand, he stared at the computer screen.

Could he really do this? Go through it all? The agony of withdrawal, of feeling like he was dying, of scratching at his skin until he bled? He no longer believed he could get clean by himself – not with Beth out of the picture. He'd blown it. It would require an inpatient admission in some ill-funded psychiatric ward somewhere. He'd done it before, after Afghanistan, and it had been hell. He was not sure it was a hell which he could tolerate repeating – of course, the alternative was non-existent, but still . . . Then the inevitable GMC referral which would follow, years of hearings, having to beg for his vocation to three fuckers who'd either never done a day's real work in their lives or were medics so far removed from the coalface they barely remembered what it was like.

345

What was the alternative, though? Carry on like this, waking in his own sweat. Talking to his dead friends every night. Taking pills until his body gave out before his mind and he died, a heart attack at thirty-four, a coroner's case. A cautionary tale.

He stared at the computer screen and slowly dialled the number, one digit at a time.

Halfway through, his phone rang in his hand.

'Hello?'

'Harry, it's me,' said Noble. 'I might need to take you up on that offer of helping us out.'

His hand trembled as he held the coffee. In the control room behind them, the detectives were changing shifts, and came and went, exchanging small-talk. Noble looked well rested and determined, far better than he reckoned he did. He had dressed and then cycled over, locking his bike up at the back entrance to the hotel.

'Talk me through it again,' Harry said.

He understood the main reasons for what Noble was proposing. At ten o'clock that morning, Michelle Roberts had booked a first-class flight from London Heathrow to Dubai, which had been free thanks to her husband's work and left on Monday. Michelle had seemed reluctant when Euan had suggested the trip last night. She had evidently changed her mind, and whilst she was yet to discuss it with the police, simply planning to flee the country was not the evidence they needed.

'Do you think it means she's onto you?' Harry had asked when Noble called him.

'Not necessarily,' Noble had replied. 'We can't assume that she thinks she's got away with it, though. Bayliss figured it out, so she might think we will, too.'

And they faced the conundrum that they couldn't stop her leaving without arresting her, but couldn't suggest that she didn't leave without raising her suspicions. So a plan had been drawn up to change the state of play.

'You go in and ask her sensitively if she takes amitryptiline,' said Noble. 'You explain that, because of the allegations against Mr Mohamed, they ran a more extensive panel of tests on Olivia's blood samples, and found the drug. You're just making sure that it wasn't a tragic mix-up. Make sure she thinks that you think the hospital might be covering up some kind of drug error.'

'Ok,' said Harry. 'Should I mention the hair?'

'You might as well. Ask her, though, if she wouldn't mind. Say it'll only be two or three strands.'

In reality, the hair had been recovered and couriered overnight to a specialist laboratory in Oxford. But of course Michelle Roberts didn't know that.

'And your intention is to put her on edge and force her into covering her tracks? Or making a mistake?'

'Well, if she lies to you about the amitryptiline, we've got something. Or if she doesn't, then she'll realise we've rumbled her and freak out. Call somebody, incriminate herself maybe.'

'What if she just runs?' said Harry. 'Books a flight tonight or something?'

Noble shook her head, and Harry briefly regretted pushing it. No plan was perfect, and evidently circumstances had forced their hand. He had washed another pill down with the coffee upon arrival, and the doldrums of last night felt a mile away. He could postpone his decisions as long as there were people who needed him, depended on him. There was a missed call on his phone from DS Cameron, too, who might have some news.

'We cross that bridge when we come to it.'

'Ok.'

'We're good then?'

Noble moved towards the door.

'Just one more thing . . .'

She turned.

'Why me?' said Harry.

'She has a rapport with you,' Noble said. 'I think she trusts you more than she trusts us. If the approach comes from a police officer, she's more likely to suspect we're watching her, to go to ground. The big risk is that she smells a rat and refuses to talk without a lawyer, and then we're fucked. I think she's less likely to do that to you. If you're not comfortable with it, you don't have to do this. Not at all. I only asked because . . .'

'No,' said Harry. 'I'll do it. I trust your judgement.'

It was true. He had considered the conflict of interest quite carefully when she first proposed it. At one time, indeed twice, Michelle Roberts had been his patient. His job, particularly in the context of an FME, was to advocate for his patient. But suspected child abuse was one of the clear-cut situations in which that sacrosanct doctor-patient relationship was voided, and Harry would lose no sleep over betraying Michelle's trust if it meant securing her son's safety. Not that he had much to lose.

'Let's go, then.'

He had needed another tablet to perk himself up, and he rubbed his palms together in the lift up to Roberts's apartment, black balls of dead skin sloughing off. In the lobby, a Canadian family, evidently renting out one of the other apartments for a holiday, had argued about the best way to get to South Kensington. One of the plain-clothes police officers had stepped in to help.

He took a deep breath and nodded to the two protection officers outside the door, sharing sections of the weekend *Telegraph*.

He pressed the intercom.

'Hello?'

'Michelle, it's Dr Kent. Can I come in?'

She buzzed him in. He opened the door and came right into the living room, the apartment not unlike his own, spartan furnishings, floor-to-ceiling glass. It had a view of the river, though, brown and splendid in the August sun.

Michelle Roberts strolled smiling out of the open-plan kitchen and Harry smiled back. He smiled despite the memories that came to him, the images vividly projected onto the glass windows. Susan Bayliss's rigid body in the wicker chair. He pictured her thrashing about, this woman – not much of her – pinning Bayliss down, one hand over her mouth, an arm across her chest. Wiping down the chair-handles and the floorboards with make-up removers. Emptying the pill-bottle into her throat. That, perhaps, a subconscious connection to the way she had killed her own children, one pill at a time until they slowly succumbed.

All for what? The sympathies of people like him? Harry thought about the whole process, about his failings, and those of the team. Had they underestimated Michelle Roberts simply because she was the wrong demographic for a villain – rich, female, white, and helpless? A damsel in distress? She'd got away with abuse and murder her whole life because people had been blinded by their pity. Again, he cursed his own distractedness.

'Aren't you going to say hello?'

'You look much better,' said Harry. He stepped forwards. It hadn't been a lie. The swelling underneath her eye was healing well already, and the bruises she had inflicted on herself were well covered, no doubt by make-up.

Fucking hell, this woman was crazy.

'Thanks,' she said. 'Do you want tea?'

'I'm fine, thanks. How are you holding up?'

'Ok,' she said. 'This place is much nicer than that hotel.'

'I guess there are worse places to be holed up.'

'Sit down!' said Roberts, sliding herself onto an L-shaped sofa next to a coffee table with a bowl of fruit. 'Help yourself.'

Harry sat down too. He could hear the faint sound of cartoons coming from the bedroom.

'How's Preston?' he said.

'Alright. I can tell he doesn't want to be here, though. Wants to be at home.'

'Have they said how long they'll be keeping you here?'

'Too long,' said Michelle. She lowered her voice. 'I haven't told them yet, but . . . I can trust you, can't I?'

Harry nodded. She was still speaking in a whisper, perhaps to avoid being overheard by the policemen outside the door. He had no doubt the microphones would pick it up.

'I've booked a flight to Dubai, for Monday,' she said. 'Euan's on the Dubai-Hong Kong route all week so we'll spend it out there, I'll get to see him more. It will be good for Preston, too. Get away from all this crap. They can't stop me going, can they?'

'I don't think they can, no,' said Harry. The lies were getting easy now. He had lied, through omission, to Beth for their entire relationship. And to Frankie, for theirs. This was no different.

'Good,' said Michelle. 'Do you know if they've got anything else on Mohamed?'

He wondered, if he had an earpiece with Noble's voice in it, what she would say. Imagined her in the control room, watching and listening. Decided that Michelle believing the police were still after Mohamed, with full force, couldn't be a bad thing. He had not planned to think so intensely today, and his brain ached.

'I think so,' he said. 'They found some threatening emails he sent to Susan. And they're waiting on some DNA tests. If they can put him in her flat then he's toast – he denied ever having been there.'

'Bastard.'

'They'll get him,' said Harry, looking straight into Roberts's eyes and not breaking his resolve. 'It's just a matter of time.'

He made a point of trying to say 'they' instead of 'we'. Make sure she thought he was on her side, not the police's.

Roberts nodded, and sipped at a glass of sparkling water, and eventually spoke.

'So, is this just a social visit?'

Her body language was not right at all. She was resting against the back of the sofa, legs crossed at the top so her dress rode up a little. She made no attempt whatsoever to hide the three inches of thigh on which she rested her left hand, her fingernails painted a slightly darker blue than her dress. Harry wondered if this was what Elyas Mohamed had been unable to resist.

Harry leant backwards.

'Not entirely,' he said. 'I'm sorry.'

'Oh . . .'

He shuffled, interlinked his fingers. Adopted the tone of voice he used for relatives of the dead, or those in the nether lands of life.

'In fact, I've got some news which you might find a bit difficult to hear.'

'What is it?'

She uncrossed her legs, leant forward, her eyes holding something that might have been panic.

'Because of the questions raised about Mr Mohamed, we decided to run some more extensive tests on the samples of Olivia's blood and tissue that were kept after her post-mortem,' Harry began. 'I think the police would have told you this at the time, but this was the afternoon you were attacked, so they thought they'd wait until things had settled a bit . . .'

Roberts nodded, her face still stricken with worry. She asked no questions, just waited for Harry to play his cards before disclosing her own.

'The tests found the presence of a drug called amitryptiline in Olivia's blood.'

Michelle Roberts's face didn't move an inch. He wondered how many times that reaction would be replayed – in the control room, in court, in the inevitable budget-channel documentaries that people would make about this woman.

'Did that kill her?' she said.

'They don't know,' said Harry. 'They're still waiting for the tests to show how much there was. But we know it was there. And it could cause the kind of problems that she died of.'

'What, so she was poisoned? How could that have happened?'

Shift the focus away from her, Harry reminded himself. Make sure she thinks she's clear.

'They don't think it was deliberate,' he said. 'They think it might have been a mistake with the pharmacy, or her prescriptions. And maybe that's what the hospital was trying to cover up all this time . . .'

'Oh my God . . .' said Roberts.

'I know it's a lot to take in,' said Harry. 'I wanted to be the one who told you, you know, in case you had any questions, about the drug or anything.'

'Thanks,' she said, leaning over, squeezing his wrist. He felt again the stiffness that he had felt the very first time he'd shaken her hand. Rheumatoid arthritis. Methotrexate. A child with recurrent infections. Why the fuck hadn't he spotted it earlier?

'I'd much rather have heard it from you than those bloody family liaison officers. All they do is make tea, don't answer any questions. I'm glad they've pissed off.'

Harry nodded.

'There's something else, isn't there?' said Roberts.

'Yes,' said Harry. 'I've got a few things I need to ask you.'

'Go on, then.'

'First, you've never heard of amitryptiline, have you? There's no way either you or Euan are taking it, and Olivia could have swallowed a tablet by mistake, or something?'

Roberts gulped her water.

'No,' she said. 'I've never heard of it.'

Harry's heart swelled. He pictured the detectives in the control

351

room jumping and slapping each other's backs with excitement as she denied ever having heard of the drug Harry had seen written on her chart.

'I thought that'd be the case,' said Harry. 'The other question's a little more, erm, delicate.'

'Just get it over with.'

'Ok. The blood tests for drugs aren't that sensitive. They only pick up things that have been in the system in the last hours or few days, depending on the drug.'

'I see.'

'Because of what they found, the police want to run some more tests to back up their theory – that the hospital or the pharmacy or someone got her drugs wrong. But they need to go further back than the time-period allowed by the bloods.'

'Ok . . . You're not going to dig my baby up, are you? Please, God, no . . .'

She dabbed at her uninjured eye and Harry reached across, touching her knee. Playing her game, he told himself. You put Olivia in the ground, don't you cry for her.

'They don't want to do that. The best test would be a sample of Olivia's hair.'

He let that roll around the room for a while. She was nodding and looking at him.

'Do you know where we could find one?' he said. 'Did you keep a hairbrush or anything like that?'

Roberts shook her head.

'This is horrible.'

'I know, I'm so sorry.'

'I didn't keep anything like that, I don't think. Sorry, Harry, I can't really think straight. This is all . . . too much . . .'

She cried and cried, and he said, 'That's ok, don't worry,' and kept his hand on her knee and she slid across the sofa and sobbed on his shoulder. He imagined the pain of a screwdriver going into his body, heard again Wilson's desperate calls for help over the radio, the screeching tone of the panic button. At least Olivia and Angus had never known that their mother was hurting them, had been too young to know the fear of encroaching death. There was some mercy in that.

'It's ok,' Harry said. He looked around the room, unsure of where the cameras were. Prayed they could see him.

Harry left the apartment at a pace, heading into the stairwell where he collapsed into the wall, his breath short, all of the contempt he had suppressed in that conversation exploding out of him. He took his own pulse – well over a hundred and twenty.

Fucking hell, that was hard. If she had suspected his deception, she hadn't let on. But then again, the one hard lesson he'd learnt over the past twenty-four hours was that this was a woman with a great capability of hiding her true intent.

He took the stairs down, and crossed the road to the control room, flashing his ID at the door on the ground floor to be allowed into the suite. Already the atmosphere was transformed, the tired formality of a day-long stakeout replaced with an anxious temerity, like a football team before a penalty shoot-out. Noble had her back to him, surrounded by a group of detectives, but turned the moment he walked in the door.

'Bloody hell!' said Noble. 'Just to let you know, if you ever fuck up the whole medicine thing, you'd walk into a job in covert policing!'

Don't joke, Harry thought but didn't say.

'Ma'am, you'll wanna see this!' said an officer with long, greasy hair and an AC/DC T-shirt, whom Harry assumed to be one of the surveillance team.

Noble headed over to her desk, and Harry followed. The officer had a computer screen in front of him showing a list of webpage URLs, the majority starting with www.google.co.uk/

'These are all the websites the target is accessing through the apartment Wi-Fi,' the surveillance officer said. 'She's doing Google searches. I think the terms might be interesting.'

'Tell me,' said Noble.

'She just searched "how long does methotrexate stay in your system".'

Silence in the room, until someone said, 'We've got her!'

'She's browsing pages,' the surveillance officer continued, giving a running commentary. 'The Wikipedia page . . . something from a university in Colorado . . .'

They watched as Michelle went through the search results,

before entering other queries – 'Can methotrexate be detected in hair' and 'Methotrexate side effects'. Every time, the surveillance officer announced it, the pitch of his voice rising with his excitement. All of this would be recorded and documented, ready for use in the inevitable court case.

Noble spoke quietly, almost a whisper in Harry's ear.

'This is brilliant, Harry,' she said. 'This is absolutely fucking brilliant.'

'It was your idea,' he said.

'Maybe, but you came through when I really needed you. I never doubted you.'

Harry felt a pang of guilt. He had managed to come through for Frankie when he had failed so many others. What did that say about him?

'Is it enough to make an arrest?' he asked.

'Should be. She lied about the amitryptiline, and we can prove that. And her Google searches of the methotrexate. You never mentioned it by name, you only talked about analysing Olivia's hair. We never put it to her. The only explanation for her to look that up is that she's guilty and she's checking if her tracks are covered.'

'Do you mind if I stick around?'

He didn't want to be anywhere else.

'You be my guest,' said Noble. 'You've bloody earned it.'

She headed for the door.

'I'm gonna call the super,' she announced. 'Get him to give this to the CPS, and get their go-ahead for an arrest.' She turned to one of their other detectives: 'Simon, can you call Child Protection and get some officers up here to look after Preston once we nick her. And call the custody suite at Peckham, let them know we've got a major investigation suspect coming in.'

Whoever Simon was nodded, and Noble turned to Harry and said, 'You stay here. Like I said, after that performance you deserve to see the cuffs get slapped on.'

She headed out of the room, and though she was gone the surveillance officer continued his commentary.

'She's moved on now. She's googling flights to Dubai this evening.'

'Someone tell the boss!' said a cop, turning around in a chair.

'She's on the phone.'

'Forget it,' said someone else, a more senior detective whom Harry recognised. 'We're going in ASAP anyway, let her talk to the super.'

Harry turned his eyes to the video monitors. Roberts's demeanour had changed completely from the collected, vulnerable-looking woman with a glint of sex in her eye who had greeted him at the door. Through the grainy eyes of the surveillance cameras, he watched as she paced around the apartment, pulling at her hair, tapping furiously on her phone, stamping on the ground. It was all unravelling now.

He wondered what the plan would have been from Dubai? Stay there, and hope that she got away with it? Or doing as she'd done in 2006, dumping Preston with his father and moving somewhere else, Canada or Australia perhaps? Finding another husband and having another child to poison. He thought of Euan, cruising at thirty-eight thousand feet somewhere, how his life was about to be unimaginably altered.

He realised he hadn't eaten and wandered to the hotel lobby. Bought a sandwich and a muffin from the cafe there and sat down at a table.

The world seemed to spin around him.

It was all done. He could not run anymore, not from Beth, not from his addiction. The weeks and months ahead, of withdrawal, shame and self-pity would be horrific, worse even than his previous psychological breakdowns, but that fear and apprehension was a mere undercurrent of the wave of emotion that was gripping him.

The feeling, Harry realised after a while, was elation. From the moment he had stepped into Susan Bayliss's apartment and felt that anger at the death of one of his medical fraternity, he had wanted to bring about this moment. At so many times he could, indeed, should have stepped aside and let the police do their job, but he had persisted. And he was bloody glad of it. Because despite the fact that it had taken all of his restraint to walk into the apartment with Michelle Roberts and not just screech 'Why?' at the top of his voice, they'd done it. He'd done it. Whichever prison or psychiatric hospital Roberts ended up in would not be kind to her once the media got wind of a serial child-killer.

After eating, Harry headed back to the control room. He had no intention of missing the dénouement.

Nobody stopped or challenged him, even though he wasn't wearing his ID. A medical school tutor had once told him that sleeves rolled up and a determined look will get you almost anywhere.

Noble re-entered the room almost at the same time as him.

'Well?' said Harry.

Everyone listened.

'Grenaghan wants to run it by someone senior at the CPS, but he said let's get ready to go. Shouldn't be more than half an hour. What's she doing?'

Harry turned and looked at the computer screens, scanning the monitors, seeing different angles of the living room, empty, the kitchen, empty, the bedroom, empty – a half-packed suitcase on the bed, clothes strewn everywhere.

'Where is she?' he demanded.

'In the bathroom,' said one of the surveillance officers. 'She ran a bath.'

'Has she got Preston?'

'Yeah . . .'

Harry looked at Noble, his face saying everything it needed to.

'We've got no camera in there,' said Noble. 'Do we have audio?'

'Fuck that, get in there!' Harry yelled.

'What?'

'We've just told her we know she murdered her daughter!'

All he could hear was Dr Gathani's voice, a broken record in his head. *I've heard of one case where the woman found out about the hospital's suspicions. She killed herself and her child.*

Evidently Noble was hearing it too, because she started running, grabbing a radio and putting it up to her mouth.

'All officers, this is DI Noble. Make entry and secure all targets! Go! Go! Go!'

Harry had no difficulty keeping up as they stormed out of the hotel entrance, stopping the traffic, moving at a sprint towards the apartment block. He watched the team of protection officers downstairs get into the lift and head up, the doors closing just as he and Noble made it into the foyer. That was not a problem. They took the stairs, two at a time.

Harry listened as Noble's radio crackled into life.

'Control, we need an ambulance! Shit, she's got a sharp!'

'TASER TASER TASER!'

'Get some fucking backup in here!'

The walls seemed to come in around Harry, the stairs like Escher's, leading nowhere. Floor numbers shot past. More noise on the radio.

'Subject secured!'

Onto the seventh floor and into the corridor, one door opened, a plain-clothes officer running back down the other way, gone to get a first aid kit probably.

Harry turned into the apartment doorway. Saw blinding light coming in through the windows. Michelle Roberts, naked, face-down on the living room carpet, four officers surrounding her, bloodied hands cuffed behind her back. One officer still aiming his Taser. A trail of blood leading back to the bathroom.

'Get off me!' she screamed. 'Get off me, you bastards!'

Harry looked at her and for perhaps the first time in his life felt pure, unadulterated hatred.

'In here, guv!'

Noble went first, Harry behind. No longer running. Taking small, paralysed steps.

'You fucking perverts! If you've done anything to hurt Preston, I'll fucking kill you!'

There were three officers in the bathroom, Noble as well. The bath was a third full, the water tinged pink. Preston Roberts lay supine on a bathmat, as grey as a December sky, not a scratch on his pristine body.

'He's not breathing!' one of the officers said.

Noble picked him up and passed him to Harry, who moved on autopilot. Carried him in his arms to the kitchen, and laid him on the breakfast bar. Leant down and sealed his mouth over the child's mouth. Blew five times, watching each time as his chest swelled like a balloon. She must have got into the bath, held him under until he passed out, and then slashed herself.

They'd gone in in time to save her, but perhaps not her son.

After the fifth breath the boy was grey and still, like a stone cherub.

Harry linked his hands around Preston's chest and pushed with his thumbs, feeling his own heart tear as the ribs snapped. He had no idea if anyone else was around him. None of that mattered.

Behind him, he heard Noble speak.

'Michelle Roberts, I am arresting you on suspicion of the murders of Susan Bayliss, Olivia Roberts and Angus MacKenzie, and the attempted murders of Moses Wilson and Preston Roberts. You do not have to say anything, but—'

Harry counted the compressions in his head. *Thirteen, Fourteen, Fifteen.*

Leant down again and blew. The boy's lips were blue but his skin was warm. Maybe that was the water, though.

'It may harm your defence if you do not mention when questioned something you later rely on in court.'

He heard them pull Roberts to her feet as he blew into Preston's mouth again.

'My baby! My baby!'

'Shut up, bitch!' someone shouted.

'Get a dressing gown and cover her up!' snapped Noble, 'Then get her out of here!'

He went back to compressions, pushing harder this time. Bloodstained bathwater gargled out of Preston's mouth with each thrust, and after fifteen Harry turned him on his side and slapped his back, pretending he was in the simulation lab, in a mock-up in one of his exams. Anywhere but here, resuscitating the boy he had seen running playfully around his home just a few days ago.

More water flooded from Preston's mouth. Harry tipped his head back to clear the rest.

Leant down and blew into his airway once more, pulled up to inhale.

Heard a guttural cough, which morphed into a retch, and spun the boy around so that the watery vomit didn't go back down and aspirate.

Then silence. Then another cough, and another.

It was the most beautiful sound Harry had ever heard.

The team from Professional Standards set themselves up on the ground floor of the hotel opposite the apartment block, which had now been taken over completely. Forensics officers had moved in to secure the apartment, with precise instructions not to touch a single piece of the surveillance equipment. Southwark Bridge

Road had been cordoned off for a good quarter-mile. There must have been upwards of a hundred officers there now, Noble thought. As soon as Professional Standards had arrived, headed up by the inimitable Detective Superintendent Marcus Fairweather, they had each been isolated in a separate room. Noble, the surveillance unit commander, Harry, the protection commander. They were offered cigarettes and cups of tea by uniformed colleagues before the PSD detectives arrived to take their statements.

Frances Noble felt numb. Acting DCI – not for much longer, surely. She was yet to see Grenaghan turn up at the scene, even though this had ostensibly been his investigation. Too busy licking the arses of the CPS while a woman drowned her child.

The DC who took her statement looked about twelve, with glasses half an inch thick. Noble didn't bother with the bullshit.

'Did you explicitly instruct the surveillance officer to inform you if at any time Michelle Roberts was out of sight?'

'I informed them that I wished to be aware of any suspicious behaviour from the target.'

She should probably be being questioned by a more senior officer, she should probably have her federation rep, but she didn't give a shit.

'Did you define what you meant by suspicious behaviour?'

'What do you think suspicious behaviour is?'

'Please answer the question, Inspector.'

'*Detective* Inspector. In fact, it should be ma'am to you.'

'My apologies. Please answer the question, ma'am.'

Noble said nothing. In the madness between getting Roberts in the back of a police van and the PSD lot turning up, she had placed a single phone call to Susan Everscott, who was making her way to Southwark as she spoke. She had hoped that the duty FME could come and examine Roberts, and clear her for custody, but he was tied up at a mental health job down in Croydon, and Harry was in no state to do anything vital. So the police had taken her, with armed escort, to A&E at St Thomas's – the very same hospital where Preston Roberts was battling for his life. The last she had heard, he was unconscious and on a ventilator.

'Were you aware that Mrs Roberts had access to shaving razors, ma'am?'

'Oh, for God's sake! How fucking covert would that have been, removing all the sharp objects? Kitchen without any cutlery. Anyway, she didn't use a razor on him, did she? She used a bath! Should we have removed the running water as well? Jesus Christ, what a fucking stupid question . . .'

'This conversation is being recorded, ma'am.'

'Did I fucking stutter?' said Noble, standing up. 'I've had enough of this. I'd like my federation rep, please, and acknowledgement of my right to be questioned by an officer who's been a detective for more than ten minutes.'

The detective shook his head, looking at Noble, then stood up and left the room. Noble pulled out a cigarette and lit it, almost hoping the fire alarm would go off and Professional Standards could throw a hissy fit. It didn't. She knew her anger at them was based on the fact that they were right. She'd fucked it up. She could go round in circles about the what-ifs, the lines of divergence. It didn't matter if the inquiry began today or in a month or in a year. The simple fact was, they could have raised suspicions about Roberts earlier, days earlier. Treated her as a suspect rather than a witness, and they could have arrested her before all of this, maybe even before Wilson.

Another fuckup. She'd promised him – a genuine act – to get the fucker who'd put him in hospital.

Now she had, but she couldn't be proud of it. Not for one second.

There had been no victory today.

'You can't smoke in here, Detective Inspector.'

Noble looked up. In the doorway, the diminutive frame of Marcus Fairweather, waistcoat over starched shirt, bald shiny head. Noble took a long puff and looked straight at him.

'You really are a shining example of everything that's wrong with the Metropolitan Police Service, aren't you,' he said. 'A proven track record of failure, an alcoholic, and still you're allowed to run a major investigation. Why? Connections? A surname that means something sentimental to a few people in high places. And where does that lead us? Here. I spoke to my colleague at St Thomas's. The doctors think Preston will have severe brain damage for the rest of his life. *If* he survives. How does that play on your conscience, eh?'

She'd hit this man once before, and the temptation to do it again was almost unbearable. Instead she just inhaled and exhaled, hot smoke filling her lungs, pure anger filling his face.

'You're finished, Frankie. There's no get out of jail free card this time. No redemption. Do you hear me? Finished. I will make absolutely sure you go no further in this service.'

Had she done her best? Not by a long shot. Fairweather was right. She'd had her chance. People had depended on her, and she'd let them down. Perhaps she'd been distracted, by Harry, by all of the shit that was involved. They would come after her for that, surely, letting a civilian work that closely with a police investigation. But then again, if they hadn't had Harry, maybe Michelle Roberts would have killed her son anyway – it was just a matter of time. All things rotted eventually. All rivers flowed to the sea.

They let her go after what felt like hours, and she headed out into the hotel lobby, blue lights reflected in glass and the amber sun of a Friday summer's evening. She did not want them to see her cry. On balance, they didn't have enough to dismiss her, but they could make bloody sure she was only ever an Acting DCI, and that she stopped acting pretty bloody soon.

'Franks.'

Susan Everscott was waiting, arms folded, her leather jacket reflecting the sun. She was just outside the hotel entrance, past the outer cordon. How she'd got through wasn't hard to guess. Statistics said that one of the officers working the cordon had had his own battle with the eternal demon, and if he had, he'd know Everscott's face.

'Come here,' Everscott said. They embraced.

'I really want a drink, Sue.'

'But you're here. And you called me instead of running to the pub. Because you're a fighter, Franks. Can we get out of here?'

'Shortly. I need to wait for someone.'

Harry didn't know how much time had passed, or even if any had passed at all.

The detective who was debriefing him was from Professional Standards, one of Fairweather's minions. She had taken him through all the events. He spoke like a robot, his mind full of pictures. Michelle wrestled naked to the floor. Preston ashen faced on the kitchen-top. Bayliss, dead. The graveyard in his mind's eye was growing at quite a pace, it had to be said. She asked him bullshit questions about Noble and her decisions, and Harry supported every single one of them, but didn't rise to the detective's baiting. He couldn't bear to think about the consequences of this day. He had already decided he might not be around to see them.

He felt sick at the memory of himself, just a few hours earlier, patting himself on the back for the job he'd done. Poking Michelle Roberts, allowing a child to be used as bait, encouraging it even. He had put the victory first because he wanted it, because he needed it.

And, as always, others had suffered. Preston Roberts might not walk or talk again, but at least Harry would have his sense of closure to stave off the other fuckups of his life for a few days.

Until the next one.

Until the next life he ruined.

'You said those exact words, did you? *It's just a matter of time.* With the intention of leading Mrs Roberts to believe that the police would soon get full toxicology reports on her children.'

'You've got the transcripts. It was all recorded.'

'And Mrs Roberts was not under caution at any point? As far as she knew, she was speaking in confidence to you?'

Not his fucking problem. He knew that Michelle Roberts was guilty. Of three murders, probably four after today, despite his best efforts. Mo in hospital. Elyas Mohamed's life and reputation in ruins, though he only had himself to blame for that. Susan Bayliss would finally bring down her man, albeit for the wrong reasons and utterly under the shadow of what had happened today.

Plenty more lives in shreds. The other families, who would get nothing but renewed pain from this. Noble. Himself – although that was entirely self-inflicted, too.

They let him go after one-word answers to a few more questions. He wandered through the hotel lobby, imagining he was on holiday, or perhaps at a conference somewhere. His thoughts ran to his life and his experiences. Nights spent on bunk beds in a forward operation base. On a country estate in Sussex with his now-dead friend. Upright in a chair next to Tammas. Exhausted on the sofa in the doctors' mess. He got to the entrance, was checked out of the cordon, and looked left and right. The road had been closed off totally, the traffic backing up either side of the blockade.

'Harry.'

It was Noble, standing with a woman in a leather jacket he didn't recognise. He stared right into her eyes. Their shared experiences, the things they had seen together, had given them a connection that would never die. As he embraced her, he felt more like he was holding a fellow soldier than an ex-girlfriend.

'Bye, Frankie,' he said.

She said nothing. He walked away without looking back, turned towards Waterloo, and crossed over where the road was open. Hailed a cab and told the driver to head south, towards his flat, and the controlled drugs pack kept in a safe in his bedroom. Then he changed his mind and asked to go to the Ruskin instead. He said nothing and thought about little in the drive over. The cabbie had the radio on. Magic 105.4. Cyndi Lauper singing 'Time After Time'. Mellow Magic in the evening giving way to news headlines.

'Police have confirmed that a 27-year-old woman has been arrested in connection with a number of offences, including the murder last weekend of NHS whistleblower Susan Bayliss. Police are yet to release—'

'Can you turn that off please, mate?'

'Suit yourself.'

He travelled to the sounds of a London evening: motorbikes and horns and music and laughter and sirens. Harry set out his plan in his head. He had fortuitously bumped into Frankie. Beth was still not answering his calls, and was in all likelihood cooped up with her parents, taking their boat out or eating fish and chips. Cursing his name. He had treated her unforgivably, and it was probably best if he just let it be. Others, though, he could not ignore.

'Marigold House.'

'Can you put me through to Room Nine, please?'

'Harry?'

'Yeah.' He almost smiled.

'Peter's not too well today, I think he's asleep. Doctor's been round, he's on the mend, but he just needs his rest. I'd rather not wake him. Can I take a message?'

'Sure, just tell him I called.'

'Will do. Anything else?'
'Yeah. Tell him I'm sorry.'

He was in tears as he walked through the Ruskin. Though it had almost killed him on a few occasions, the place had been the scene of many happy memories. Here he had arrived, fresh faced and twenty years old, for his first taste of clinical medical training. He had returned as an SHO, and later a registrar. He recalled patients, young and old, sickle crises, cancers, dementia, heart attacks, abscesses. Old homeless men passing away on a bed with only him and a student nurse for company, teenagers off their tits on tabs vividly recounting their hilarious hallucinations. Trauma victims on the brink of death, that camaraderie, everyone pitching in. Nothing beat it. He would miss it dearly, but so it goes.

He briefly thought of heading to the pharmacy with another fake prescription, doing calculations in his head. He had thirty milligrams in the safe in his bedroom. It should be enough, but more would make sure. He had no intention of surviving in a hypoxic coma. Thirty would have to do – the risk of someone catching him at the pharmacy, asking for a controlled drug like that, was too great. He could just put a tourniquet on, inject it, and then loosen the tourniquet so the whole dose got delivered at once.

The lift dumped him on the seventh floor. It was a Saturday evening. A&E would be manic, but Tennyson Ward had its usual serene calm. It was lucky that the nurses and healthcare assistants on duty knew his face, otherwise the man who approached them with bloodshot eyes and a bloodied shirt would surely have been turned away.

He stepped over the floral tributes at the foot of Zara's room, many of which were now starting to wilt, and entered. She was just as peaceful as she always had been.

'Hey,' he said.

Her eyes opened and looked at him, flicking right and left. He thought she recognised him, as did Niebaum and the other nurses. Harry did not believe in fate or any higher power, because he could not fathom the possibility that an omnipotent being would decide that the woman should suffer like this – meaning behind her eyes, yet without any capacity to understand or communicate it. He felt the tears come and he held her hand and kissed it, his heart straining and aching, his hands shaking. He was withdrawing, had been for the last few hours, but it didn't matter, because it would all be over soon.

'I'm sorry,' he said. This was why he'd had to come. He had to be sure enough to leave her.

'Don't go,' she said. He had never heard her voice before. He had expected an accent, something Eastern European, but her voice was clear as arctic ice. It was the most beautiful voice he had ever heard.

'I have to,' said Harry, sobbing, a smile on his face. 'I can't go on any longer.'

'Don't leave me,' said Zara. 'You promised me you'd carry on. For me.'

'I know. And I've let you down. Just like I let Frankie down, I let James down, I let the boss down, I let Beth down. I can't do it anymore. I can't just carry on fucking up the lives of the people I care about.'

'What about me?'

He stroked her pink hair and wept some more.

'Someone else will come along,' he said. 'Maybe Cameron, maybe another detective, maybe someone like me. Are you suffering? Are you in pain?'

'No.'

'Good,' Harry said. 'Good . . . I'm sorry, I really am. I'm so sorry.'

He barely heard the door open and close behind him. The first thing he knew of someone else in the room was the hand on his shoulder.

'Hey, man. What's up?'

He turned slowly. It was Nathan Klein, whose uncle occupied the room opposite, *The Times* folded underneath his arm.

'Don't mind me,' said Harry.

'What's going on? You're in floods of tears. What's the matter?'

'It's nothing. I'm just saying my goodbyes.'

'Your goodbyes? Are you leaving?'

Harry said nothing. Perhaps that was a good way to think about it.

'It's alright. She's ok, she doesn't mind. She told me.'

Klein looked at Harry, then down at Zara, whose eyes flickered a little, maybe afraid.

'She told you?' said Klein.

'Yeah.'

'Can you hear her? Her voice?'

'Of course I can,' said Harry, getting up to leave. 'I'd better go.'

'No, no,' said Klein, patting him on the shoulder. 'You stay, have your moment. I'll leave you be.'

He left the room, and Harry went back to Zara, though he could not hear her anymore. He sobbed some more, thoughts and memories from the day which he had tried his best to expunge. Images he couldn't remove from his head. He looked up at Zara, her face pale and pure. He longed to hear her voice again. It had been so perfect.

Klein came back, after how much time Harry did not know. This time, there were others with him, one of the ward nurses, and two women wearing cardigans and NHS lanyards. He recognised both of them from A&E. Liaison psychiatry.

'Hi, Dr Kent,' the younger one said. 'You remember me? I'm Sarah, one of the doctors.'

He looked between them, still crying.

'Nathan here called us, he said he was worried about you. Do you fancy coming with us? We can have a bit of a chat, a cup of tea maybe? Find out what's been going on?'

He shouldn't have done this, goddammit. Shouldn't have been so self-indulgent as to say goodbye to someone who had probably never even been conscious of his existence. Should have just gone home and got on with it.

He stood up.

'It's ok, Harry, we're here to help.'

He cried and doubled over, and before he knew it he was on his knees, howling at the floor, Klein's hand on his shoulder, rolling over onto his back, screaming. Words and phrases entwined. 'Make it stop. Make it stop. Make it stop.'

A hand stilled him. Presented him with tablets and a cup of water.

So it begins, he thought.

'Don't worry, Harry, you're safe now, ok? You're safe now.'

ELEVEN

Monday, 1 September
Morning

Thick raindrops fell like gobs of spit on the shoulders of the four men who stood in silence at the foot of the grave in the shadow of Dunbardey Parish Church. At the side of the cemetery, blue strobes fell on granite headstones: two patrol cars parked to keep the paparazzi away from this moment.

Two men sent by the county.council rested on tall shovels, shaking their heads as they looked down. George Bannerman had called them on Saturday evening. The other man was a forensic archaeologist who had come up from Dundee, the Centre for Human Identification, or something like that. Not that there would be much need for identification in this particular case, thought Bannerman as he looked at the headstone.

Angus MacKenzie
Came Down from Heaven 8th November 2004
Flew Home to the Angels 11th January 2006.

'We're digging him up just in case he has hair, aye?' one of the men said.

'Aye.'

'He's in one of those marble coffins,' said the archaeologist. 'He's more likely to be preserved.'

'Seems a bit extreme, dun'it. I mean, she'll be in prison for her whole life won't she?'

'Boxes have to be ticked,' said Bannerman.

The gravedigger shrugged his shoulders and hefted the shovel above him.

They all winced when its blade first hit the earth.

Author's Note

The Belgrave Hospital for Children was opened in 1886 in Pimlico, London, moved to new premises in Kennington in 1903, and was closed in 1985, becoming a Grade II listed building. During the following decades it became a popular location for squatters and was left derelict. Following the common death pathway for all historical buildings in London, it has now been converted into luxury flats.

It should bear no resemblance to any specific currently operating children's hospital, and any such resemblance is a pure coincidence.

The events of this book, at least as far as scandals in heart surgery are concerned, are partly based on the tragic deaths of scores of children at the Bristol Royal Infirmary during the 1990s, which were exposed by whistleblower Dr Stephen Bolsin, who was duly forced out of the country and now practises in Australia. Despite cover-ups by a number of public bodies (including the hospital trust, the Royal College of Surgeons, and elements of the Department of Health), an inquiry eventually led to two surgeons being struck off for gross misconduct and a third suspended. The inquiry also led to the mandatory reporting of outcomes by hospital and individual surgeons for all paediatric cardiac surgical procedures, which continues today.

The concept of factitious or induced illness by proxy (FIIP), formerly known as Munchausen's syndrome by proxy, was first described by a paediatrician called Sir Roy Meadow in the 1970s. In the early 2000s, Meadow testified in a number of controversial court cases in which mothers stood accused of murdering infant children who had ostensibly died of sudden infant death syndrome (SIDS). He diagnosed them with Munchausen's by proxy and presented flawed statistical evidence which formed the majority of the case against them. Almost all of these convictions were over-turned at appeal, and Meadow was struck off by the GMC for wilfully misleading the jury, though this was reduced to suspension following an appeal.

Debate continues amongst the psychiatric, paediatric and forensic medical community as to the existence and nature of FIIP.

TELL THE WORLD THIS BOOK WAS

GOOD	BAD	SO-SO

Acknowledgements

This book would be much the poorer without the support and guidance of a number of people. Firstly, the great team at Hodder and Mulholland for their hard work, constant patience and persistence in getting me to reply to things – thanks in particular to Ruth, Becca and Cicely for putting up with me. Likewise, to my indomitable agent Jane and all of her team: Stephanie, Irene, Claire, Mary, Sara and Terry – thank you so much for your continued support. I'm indebted to the other residents of Fish Eagles who provided some timely and useful criticism, and all the friends who have continued to support me. Special gratitude to Maddy for keeping me creative and sane and never letting an opinion to go unchallenged. I owe a great deal of thanks to my wonderful parents, in particular to Mum for her eagle eyes and tolerance of my profanity, and Dad for buying me a copy of *Echo Park* all those years ago. And lastly – my wonderful girlfriend, for her encyclopaedic knowledge of London's food scene, her ability to sleep through the sound of nocturnal typing, and for patiently listening to every idea I've ever come up with.